THE ULTIMATE

THE ULTIMATE

SUPER-VILLAINS ™

STAN LEE

Editor

BYRON PREISS MULTIMEDIA COMPANY, INC.

NEW YORK

BOULEVARD BOOKS, NEW YORK

THE ULTIMATE SUPER-VILLAINS

A Boulevard Book
A Byron Preiss Multimedia Company, Inc. Book

Special thanks to Ginjer Buchanan, Lara Stein, Stacy Gittelman,
the gang at Marvel Creative Services, GraceAnne A. DeCandido, and
especially Steve Roman and Keith R.A. DeCandido.

PRINTING HISTORY
Boulevard edition / August 1996

The Putnam Berkley World Wide Web site address is
http://www.berkley.com

Check out the Byron Preiss Multimedia Company World Wide Web site address:
http:///www.byronpreiss.com

ISBN 1-57297-113-4

CONTENTS

INTRODUCTION

STAN LEE

Illustration by Mike Zeck

SEVENTEEN STORIES ABOUT BAD GUYS! Truly, the mind doth boggle!

But, after pondering a moment, you might ask, "Why feature the savage and sinister super-villains? Why not chronicle the exciting exploits of our proud and praiseworthy heroes?"

Since we never want a loyal Marvelite to wallow in a sea of doubt and uncertainty, permit me to address that cogent query in a valiant attempt to set your mind at ease.

First of all, in presenting stories featuring villains, there is one eternal, inflexible rule: the villain must have someone to battle. Okay, who inevitably fights the villains? The heroes! Therefore, most sagas featuring super-villains will certainly feature super heroes as well! So you need not worry about the good guys being staunchly represented.

But why do we stress the importance of villains? Here's why. . . .

The viler the villain, the more heroic the hero!

Think about it. Would David have seemed so heroic battling Goliath if Goliath had been a five-foot-tall accountant? Would legend have paid homage to the battle between Ulysses and Cyclops if Cyclops had merely been a mild-mannered optician? Would you have thrilled to the exploits of Robin Hood quite as much if the Sheriff of Nottingham had been a charitable official famed for his kindness and charity?

Now let's take some examples that are closer to home. . . .

Would loyal readers have followed the exploits of the Fantastic Four all these years if their arch-enemy, Dr. Victor Von Doom, was a beloved Bavarian pediatrician? And what about Spider-Man? How exciting would his adventures have been if Carnage was a gentle, fun-loving philanthropist whose greatest pleasure was helping those who were less fortunate than he? Take the mighty Thor. Imagine how excited you'd be about his battles with Loki if Loki was a sensitive and caring brother who spent his time writing poetry and wrapping bandages for the Asgardian branch of the Red Cross!

Now then, since mighty Marvel has always had the most evil villains of all in its ever-expanding universe, then as surely as night doth follow day, so it must verily follow that ours are the most heroic heroes of all! And you, O lucky reader, are about to savor the thrills and excitement when our heroes and villains clash—as clash they surely will!

Y'know, many times at comic book conventions, bookstores, and the various exotic places where super hero fans gather—whoops, let me clarify that for a moment: by "super hero fans" I mean fans of the super hero genre, not fans who *are* super heroes (although one can probably find more super heroes among comic book fans than in any other group of erudite literature lovers). At any rate, often when I visit with a gregarious gaggle of fans, I'm asked how super-villains are created. How difficult is it to dream up the wild, way-out do-badders who continually proliferate on our pandemonious pages?

Now, for the first time ever in print, let me answer that awesome question.

It's real tough!

Here's why it's so tough. There are many important qualities a super-villain must possess. First and foremost, he or she must have some sort of awesome super power. Without such *super* power, all we have is an ordinary, everyday, catchpenny type of villain, acceptable in other publications perhaps, but hardly suitable for the supremely critical, highly demanding Marvel reader! However, as you undoubtedly know, virtually all the super powers have long ago been taken. After all, there are countless super-villains already in existence. We presently have baddies who can fly, who are possessed of super strength, who can control the elements, who can travel through time and dimensions, who have magical powers, mental powers, magnetic powers, hypnotic powers, space-traveling powers, body-changing powers, and virtually anything else you can think of. So what super powers are left? Hey, even if I knew the answer, I wouldn't mention it here; you know how our competitors always read our books. No way I'll tip them off!

Another important quality any super-villain must have is the "interest factor." That is, we have to find a way to make you, the reader, genuinely *interested* in our dastardly baddie. It's okay to have a super-villain, for instance, who is strong enough to knock over the Empire State Building. But why should we care about him? We know that one of the good guys will defeat him sooner or later. So why should we want to avidly follow the story? That's where the writer must be clever and even tricky. The writer must find a way to breathe life into the super-villain in such a way that you'll care about him and be interested in him—not only in whether he'll win or lose, but in the how of it and the why of it and the suspense of it and the dramatic impact of it and the entire gestalt of it. The reader must feel he or she knows what motivates our super-villains, what they're trying to accomplish and what made them the way they are. Otherwise, they're just hollow, two-dimensional characters—and you know we'd never subject you to that.

So, as you can see, there's more to super-villain creating than dreaming up a catchy name and costume.

Oh, and speaking of costumes, that's another element that requires a lot of thought. Just think of all the super-villains running around the comic book cosmos right now. No two of them look alike, right? Well then, imagine all the hours of thinking, agonizing, head-scratching, and soul-searching that an artist goes through in an effort to come up with an original costume, an unusual image, and an exciting look for the new super-villain who is about to be unleashed upon a helpless and unsuspecting world!

Even the selection of a new, villainous name becomes an almost insurmountable obstacle. At first blush, it seems that all the good names have already been taken. But we cannot let that stop us. We cannot fail you, O frantic one, you whose passion for super-villains grows ever more insatiable with each passing month.

But when all is said and done, you mustn't let the problems that face us dampen your ardor or curb your enthusiasm. We'll get by somehow. Promise not to worry about us. No matter how difficult the task, we'll find a way to continue bringing you the most murderously morbid and maniacal super-villains of all. And to prove that we speaketh not mere hollow words, just turn the page and start thrilling to the titanic tales of Marvel's best and baddest—*The Ultimate Super-Villains*!

Oh, how I envy the enjoyment that awaits you!

Excelsior!

Stan

Stan Lee

Kang The Conqueror

TO THE VICTOR

RICHARD LEE BYERS

Illustration by Chuck Wojtkiewicz

KANG THE CONQUEROR surveyed the lush green field, the flourishing trees, and the lofty towers rising beyond them. The balmy evening breeze stirred the folds of his magenta cloak and brought him the scent of verdure. A carriage passed in the distance, the horse's hooves clopping. Except for the crumbling length of Cleopatra's Needle, rising at his back, this Central Park, this Manhattan, was utterly unlike the shattered, barren landscapes of his own 40th century.

But the small silver globe atop the tripod, plundered from one of the forgotten armories of his own dying era, would change that. When it exploded, the vegetation would burn and the skyscrapers would fly apart. Everyone in this wonderland of a city, even Thor, the Thing, and the other superhuman champions who'd appeared over the course of the last few months, would die.

It was what Kang had come to accomplish, but now he hesitated. He'd always fought his enemies face-to-face, exulting when they fell before him. There wouldn't be any comparable thrill in eliminating them with a nuclear weapon. Indeed, the tactic seemed cowardly.

The Conqueror grimaced behind his blue metal mask. Whether the scheme was honorable or not, the sad truth of the matter was that the Avengers and the Fantastic Four had bested him in one fight after another. With the weight of numbers on their side, they always would. If he didn't set off the bomb, he might as well abandon all hope of subjugating this splendid age. He would have to concede *defeat*, and that was simply unthinkable. The servomechanisms in his armor whirring, he slid open a panel in the side of the bomb, exposing the control buttons, armed the device, and set the timer for three minutes.

Afterward, taking a final look at the city, he wondered sardonically if he'd cut the timing so close to wring at least a little excitement out of the proceedings. If so, the ploy failed, because he knew he was in no danger. As per its programming, his time ship, waiting in Limbo with his troops in tow, teleported him aboard precisely on schedule. The bomb went off a split second later.

* * *

The President of the United States was a fleshy, ruddy-faced man whose gray hair shone dully in the afternoon sunlight. Kang thought he looked like a jovial fellow, but he wasn't smiling now. As he bent to sign the surrender document, he seemed less resentful than bewildered.

Most of the world leaders summoned here to the Rose Garden to pay homage before the crowd and the television cameras had that same dazed expression. Kang didn't blame them. It must seem incredible that an army of ten thousand had subjugated a population of five billion. But 20th-century arms couldn't stand up to power rifles, plasma cannons, anti-grav fighters, or the even more potent weaponry wielded by the Conqueror himself.

Even so, he suspected that his new subjects might have kept fighting longer if he hadn't dangled the threat of further nuclear holocausts over their heads. He'd made sure they understood that his ability to flit through space-time gave him the power to detonate a second bomb anywhere.

What they didn't know was that he hadn't *had* a second bomb. He'd only ever found the one.

The final chief of state, a diminutive, raven-haired woman in a sari, set down the pen. Kang's soldiers cheered. He rather wished that some of his new vassals had done the same—it might have sparked the elation that was strangely absent inside himself—but none did. Some looked frightened or mournful, and a few, the boldest or least prudent, scowled.

Their new monarch assured himself that he'd win their affection soon enough. Pomp and spectacle would do the trick, just as they had in the 40th century and ancient Egypt too.

A metallic crash sounded at the edge of the lawn. Power rifles whined, filling the air with the smell of ozone, and people screamed. His pulse quickening, Kang activated his armor's combat systems, snatched his pistol from its holster, and soared above the crowd to see what was going on.

Two men and a monster had torn down a section of the wrought-iron fence and were making their way across the grass. A bearded, burly, middle-aged man wrapped in a high-collared olive cloak strode confidently in the lead. Behind him glided a lean, crouched fellow whose impossibly sinuous movements suggested a cobra as much as his hooded, scaly costume. And the creature, a hairless green ogre with pointed ears, lumbered in the rear, his two-toed feet indenting the earth. Spectators scrambled frantically to get out of the trio's way. The broken bodies of the sentries who'd tried to stop them littered the ground behind them.

Surmising that the newcomers were would-be regicides, Kang pointed his gun at the bearded man, who surprised him by bowing deeply. "Good morning, Your Majesty," the stranger said. "May we introduce ourselves?"

Puzzled, Kang inclined his head.

"I'm Baron Mordo," the bearded man said. "Accompanying me are Mr. Voorhees and Mr. Blonsky, better known as the Cobra and the Abomination. I regret the harm to your servants, but they shouldn't have tried to keep us away from you. We've come to offer you our services."

"And why would I want them?" asked Kang. Deciding that the hostilities were over, at least for the moment, he floated to the ground, but kept the pistol in his hand.

Mordo's mouth tightened and his dark eyes narrowed, affording Kang a glimpse of the arrogance lurking behind his unctuous manner. "You haven't heard of me, then. I thought that even in your age, tales of my deeds—But no matter. I'm a scholar of the mystic arts. A sorcerer. My companions possess paranormal talents of their own. In exchange for appropriate recompense— may I suggest territorial governorships?—we'll put our abilities at your disposal. The offer may seem a bit presumptuous, but even the mightiest warlord needs able lieutenants, and you are most assuredly going to need us."

Kang looked at the sly avidity in Mordo and the Cobra's faces, and the savagery writ plainly in the Abomination's hideous countenance, and decided that he wanted no part of them. "Frankly, Baron, I doubt that."

"Don't," Mordo replied. "This rabble—" he waved a contemptuous hand at Kang's dead and unconscious soldiers "—may be able to vanquish ordinary humans, but they're no match for beings like ourselves."

"Scarcely a problem," said Kang, "since the other superhumans died in New York."

"Forgive me for contradicting you," the sorcerer answered, "but that isn't so. By and large, only the self-righteous, crusading ones like the Avengers made their homes there. Scores, perhaps hundreds, remain, and many will challenge your rule. More than even you can handle alone." He smiled smugly. "Indeed, my etheric senses inform me that an insurrection is commencing even now."

The comlink in Kang's armor chimed, advising him of an incoming call. He switched the system on, listened to a panicky officer's report, and then glowered back at Mordo's smirk.

"I just received a message from one of my men," the Conqueror admitted. "Soldiers with blue skin, and dozens of huge animals, are rising from the Potomac to attack the city. An immensely strong man with wings on his feet is leading the assault."

"That would be Prince Namor of Atlantis," Mordo said. "He too wants to rule the world." His smile widened. "So many of us demigods do. *Now* what do you say, Your Majesty? May we fight beside you?"

Kang hesitated. He had the unpleasant feeling that he was losing control of events, and there was still something about Mordo and his confederates that made his skin crawl. But if the aquatic monsters were as formidable as his subordinate claimed, he doubted that he could defeat them and their master by himself, any more than he'd ever managed to vanquish all the Avengers.

"All right," he growled. "Help me now and we'll discuss the terms of your service later."

"Thank you, Your Majesty," said Mordo. "With your permission, I'll transport us to the battlefield." He moved his hands in an intricate pattern, leaving trails of crimson light. Abruptly the throng of onlookers vanished, and the colonnaded façade of the Lincoln Memorial popped into view in its place. Roaring, yellow foam spraying from its sharklike jaws, a tentacled, slate-gray, fishy-smelling monstrosity reared up behind the monument. The Abomination charged to meet it.

His handsome face a mask of rage, berserk as the wildest of Kang's barbarian soldiers, Namor hurtled at the Conqueror, hovering three hundred feet above the river, trying again to ram through his force field. The feathery white pinions on the merman's ankles beat so rapidly that they became invisible.

Kang waited until Namor was within five yards of him, then dodged to the side. As the muscular Atlantean hurtled by, the time traveler irradiated him with his anti-graviton beamer, one of several devices built into his gauntlets.

When Namor tried to wheel, he tumbled helplessly, out of control. The bombardment had rendered him temporarily weightless and now none of his aerial maneuvers would work as they had before. Until he learned to compensate, he'd only be able to fly clumsily, a handicap which ought to make him a sitting duck.

It did. Kang blasted him with one concussion ray after another, smashing him across the sky, until finally even the headstrong prince realized the futility of prolonging the battle. He snarled, turned, and flew down toward the surface of the Potomac, somehow managing at least a measure of his former speed.

Kang let him go. Too many of his weapon and defensive systems had exhausted themselves to make pursuit a prudent option. Instead he peered down, surveying the battlefield.

All the sea monsters lay dead or stunned. The surviving invaders in their water-filled helmets were fleeing for the river with his own troops harrying their backs.

Grinning, he flew down into the blood, smoke, and ozone stink of war, to Mordo, the Abomination, and the Cobra. They'd fought well, though the performance of the latter two had been less than impeccable. The ogre had hurled cars and chunks of demolished building at Atlanteans in close combat with Kang's soldiers, killing foe and friend alike, while the human serpent had sometimes balked in the face of danger, hanging back and awaiting a chance to strike from behind.

Still, at that moment, exultant with triumph, Kang didn't feel as much distaste for the trio as he had before. When all was said and done, they *had* fought for him, and he couldn't have won without them.

"What territories did you have in mind?" he asked.

The Abomination grinned, exposing stained and jagged tusks. "Russia," he said.

"I have a list," said Mordo, clasping a bloody gash in his shoulder. His hand glowed amber and the wound healed. "Tibet, Egypt, Transylvania, Cornwall, Easter Island—"

"I was thinking more along the lines of a city-state apiece," Kang said dryly. His comlink chimed. "A report's coming in." He adjusted the system so his companions could hear it too.

"Kang here. Have we chased them all back into the river yet? Take the anti-grav ships that can fight underwater and keep after them—"

"Excuse me, sire, but I'm not calling about that," said the officer on the other end of the link, his voice high and breathless with excitement. "We have an alert in Europe. An army of robots is marching on a city called Berlin."

Kang felt a pang of dismay. Though he often regarded war as a kind of game, he wouldn't enjoy playing when he was already bruised and weary, with many of his armor's resources depleted.

"If it's robots," said Mordo, "I suspect we're dealing with Dr. Doom, particularly since I didn't see him at the surrender ceremony. You'd best get used to this, Your Majesty. Over the next few weeks, most of your rivals will launch an attack somewhere, trying to destroy you before you can consolidate your rule." He raised his hands. "Shall I transport us to Berlin?"

Kang sighed. "Yes."

One by one, the components of the parade set off down Pennsylvania Avenue. Kang's legions in anti-grav vehicles. Columns of human and humanoid prisoners, Atlanteans, pasty, squinting Subterraneans, and emerald-skinned Skrulls among them, trudging in chains. Gigantic monsters from beneath the sea and the cavern world hidden in the Earth's crust. One of the latter, a scarlet lizard seemingly made of slabs of stone, suddenly lunged at Kang's open hovercar. The creature's handler brandished his control rod. The hexagonal studs embedded in the monster's hide released a crackling burst of electricity, dropping it in its tracks. The handler then employed milder jolts, applied to only one side of its body, to goad it in the right direction.

Kang smiled. The campaign against Doom had proved arduous in the extreme. The Latverian monarch had nearly usurped control of all Europe before the Conqueror managed to destroy his army of robots and drive him into hiding. Moreover, as Mordo had predicted, Namor and Doom's offensives had merely been the opening salvos in a wave of attacks initiated by superhuman rebels around the globe. But the hostilities had finally halted, at least for the time being, leaving Kang victorious. And surely now, witnessing the martial pageantry of the parade, the people of the 20th century would begin to warm to him. After all, he'd been defending them as much as his own suzerainty. Namor and the squat little gnome called the Mole Man didn't just want to rule the "surface dwellers" but to wreak a terrible revenge on them. And the xenophobic Skrulls would have enslaved and exploited Earthmen as callously as humans bred, caged, and slaughtered domestic animals.

Still, as Kang awaited his turn to start down the street, a certain edginess began to undermine his contentment. Finally he realized what was wrong. Turning to Mordo, lounging on the plush leather seat beside him, he said, "I don't hear any cheering."

The mystic shrugged. "Nor do I, Your Majesty. Perhaps the people are saving their acclamation for when you yourself come into view."

Kang's driver started down the parade route. Within half a block, the time traveler knew that Mordo had been mistaken. The spectators looked frightened or sullen, as if they wouldn't even have turned out if soldiers hadn't herded them onto the street.

"What's *wrong* with them?" Kang muttered, and then he spotted the graffiti some malcontent had spray-painted high on a brick wall. The outline of a mushroom cloud with the word "BUTCHER" underneath. The emblems of the Avengers and the Fantastic Four.

Kang felt a pang of shame, which quickly transformed itself into a surge of fury. "You ungrateful scum," he growled.

Mordo raised his hand. Black sparks danced on his fingertips. "Allow me. I'll bring that wall crashing down on their miserable heads."

The magician's cruelty was like a dash of cold water, partially quelling Kang's own anger. "No. You don't even know that the culprit is still here standing beneath his handiwork."

"What difference does it make?" Mordo replied. "It will still teach the mob a lesson."

"No. Let it go. This is a day of celebration. Besides—" he hesitated, not quite certain what he truly meant to say "—I don't deal out justice so haphazardly."

Mordo inclined his head. "As you wish." Kang saw the hint of a sneer at the corners of his mouth, and realized that his squeamishness had cost him a measure of the other man's respect.

Grimacing, the Conqueror settled back in his seat. His good

mood had been thoroughly quashed, but with the whole world watching on television, there was nothing for it but to finish the parade. As the hovercar floated down the street, he spotted more graffiti, all of it expressing hatred of the new master of the world.

Kang told himself that the people of this era had only seen him wage war. They didn't truly know him yet. When he took up the reins of government, when his subjects discovered that he was a wise and benevolent ruler, their loathing would give way to acceptance, respect, and ultimately even affection.

His armor felt stifling hot. He adjusted the temperature control, but it didn't help as much as he would have liked.

The camera panned along the rows of corpses, wasted, skeletal things with bloated bellies. Many of them were children.

Kang's mask lay on his desk. He resisted an impulse to grab it and throw it across the Oval Office at the television. "I said I wanted those people fed," he growled.

The Cobra, whose responsibilities included the administration of Africa, shrugged. "I gave the order. The food was flown in. The tribal leaders didn't distribute it. They're using the famine to kill their rivals."

"Then you should have sent soldiers to depose them."

"I did, but the country's in chaos, and your men aren't exactly expert politicians."

Kang glumly conceded the point. His warriors had been utter savages in another time and place, slaughtering one another with the relics of a forgotten science until Kang found them and gave them a purpose.

"They couldn't tell who was on our side and who wasn't," the Cobra continued. "You wouldn't have wanted them to kill everybody, would you?'

Kang sighed. "No, of course not."

"And anyway, after a few days," said the Cobra, still intent on proving that the fiasco wasn't his fault, "you pulled all the troops out of my lands to keep the Arabs and Israelis from fighting."

"And to put down the riot in Los Angeles, deal with the Kree raid, and foil that latest scheme of Zemo's," added Mordo, lounging on the sofa. The sorcerer sounded bored, as if he'd rather be overseeing the new religion, a sort of modern mystery cult he'd founded, or inspecting one of the archaeological digs he'd established, than attending a Cabinet meeting.

"I remember," said Kang. He looked back at the Cobra. "All right, Klaus, perhaps it isn't your fault. But I wish you'd told me the effort failed. I don't like learning about it from the evening news."

"We should abolish the news media," said Mordo, waving his hand. The crystal cognac decanter rose from the sideboard, floated across the room, unstoppered and upended itself, and refilled his snifter. "They only make the rabble discontent."

Kang grimaced. He wanted to improve 20th century civilization, not dismantle its achievements. "That's not what we're discussing."

The Abomination stood near the door, swinging a huge barbell up and down. The floorboards squeaked beneath his misshapen feet. "Do you *really* want us to come running to you every time an operation hits a snag?"

"I suppose not," Kang said grudgingly. He obviously couldn't oversee every detail of the planetary government personally.

Mordo raised his drink, inhaled its aroma, and sipped. "With all due respect, Your Majesty, aren't you fretting needlessly? As long as we're firmly in control, what do we care if the masses suffer or abuse one another? Actually, ethnic hatred serves a purpose. Better that, say, the Serbs and Bosnians should strive to exterminate one another than that they should unite against us."

"Perhaps, but when the people wage war on one another, they destroy *my* property. You know, our problem is that we don't really *have* a government. Ten thousand barbarians with advanced weapons can wring a formal surrender out of a population of five billion, but they can't police it or direct its activities. If only the officials of the old regimes would work *with* us, instead of subverting our plans whenever they think they can get away with it!"

"If I may speak frankly," Mordo said, "the wretches balk because they still despise you. If they considered you a hero, an Iron Man or a Captain America, things would be very different."

Kang smiled crookedly. "Scarcely a week goes by when I don't take the field against the Red Skull, Diablo, or some other madman."

"But you're fighting enemies who covet your throne, and your subjects know it. Suppose you slew a dragon which is no threat to you personally, but which terrifies every common man in the world." The sorcerer nodded toward the TV. "What a coincidence. There's the very beast I had in mind."

Kang turned. The picture on the screen was jerky and out of focus, as if the cameraman had been scurrying backward, but clear enough to reveal a green-skinned giant in tattered trousers, caving in a building with a single swipe of his arm. The brute's every move and flicker of expression conveyed a fury that put even Namor's battle-rage to shame. Despite his manlike form, he seemed more akin to one of the Mole Man's mindless behemoths than to anything human.

The Conqueror nodded thoughtfully. Perhaps he *could* win his subjects' admiration by eliminating this menace. And at the very least the hunt would be an adventure, a temporary escape from the frustrations of his awkward, faltering kingship.

"The creature," Mordo said, "is called the Hulk."

The open-air market was a shambles, the stalls shattered, serapes, straw sombreros, toy guitars, piñatas, and matador dolls littering the ground. From one of the narrow side streets came the crash of something else being smashed to rubble.

As Kang stalked toward the noise, he noticed that Tijuana, like every other city in the world, had its share of seditious graffiti, mushroom clouds with "ASESINO" and "TIRANO" scrawled around them, and K's inside circles bisected by diagonal bars.

He pushed his irritation aside to focus on the task at hand. His mouth dry and his heart thumping, he wondered when he'd see his quarry. He could have found the Hulk easily by flying in over the rooftops, but then the creature might have seen him coming, and fled with one prodigious leap.

Besides, slinking through the dusty lanes with their patches of sunlight and shadow, knowing that the next turn might bring him face to face with the enemy, was more exciting. Kang needed something exciting.

The sounds of demolition grew louder. Rounding a final corner, Kang spied the Hulk in the center of a flagstone plaza, ripping apart a dry fountain. A number of people, some American tourists, some Mexican nationals, cowered in the far corner of the square, probably afraid that, if they ran, they'd attract the monster's attention.

Kang and his lieutenants had planned to enter the area at different points, converge on the Hulk, and surround him. The Conqueror switched on his comlink. "I found him. Home in on this signal and come running."

To his surprise, no one replied.

The Hulk bellowed and rounded on the spectators. If he intended to kill them, he could do it in a heartbeat; Kang couldn't wait for reinforcements. He switched his pistol to full autofire, aimed, and emptied the magazine.

The barrage of micromissiles exploded against the Hulk's back. The giant roared, lurched around, and charged.

Now, Kang decided, he'd better take to the air. He tried to levitate and a red icon, projected into one of his mask's protective lenses, blinked at the corner of his vision. His anti-grav systems had shut down.

He couldn't understand it. He'd run a check on his armor just before leaving the White House. But there was no time to ponder the mystery now. He dropped his pistol, extended both arms, and fired his concussion rays.

Azure light flared from his gauntlets into the Hulk's chest, staggering him. But only for a moment. Then the ray projectors shut down. The brute recovered his balance and lumbered forward, shaking the earth with every stride.

Kang attempted to activate his vibration ray and his force field. Neither worked. The Hulk's onrushing form now filling his view, he tried to seal his armor and release its supply of nerve gas.

His mask clicked shut, his oxygen started flowing, and after a moment's hesitation, his left gauntlet sprayed sickly yellow vapor. The Hulk plunged through the center of the cloud. But instead of passing out, he punched Kang in the chest.

The blow flung the Conqueror thirty feet to crash through a stone wall. Despite his armor, his body throbbed with pain. The world grew dim, slipping away.

He struggled to hold onto consciousness. After a moment, his head cleared; he heard a rapid pounding and felt the ground vibrate. Raising his eyes, he saw the Hulk charging. He scrambled up and assumed a fighting stance.

After the first exchange of blows, he realized he had no chance battling hand-to-hand. Though his armor augmented his strength, he was nowhere near as powerful as the Hulk, nor was he any faster. And despite his apparent mindlessness, the giant fought not only ferociously but well, as a shark or tiger would.

As the Conqueror narrowly ducked another punch, one of the tourists shouted, "My god! That's *Kang*! Kill him, Hulk! Kill the butcher!" A number of onlookers took up the cry, cheering on the brute who'd been menacing them only moments before.

Kang lunged inside the Hulk's superior reach and struck at his throat. The giant blocked the blow, then grabbed his opponent, swung him over his head, and slammed him to the ground.

Kang's head rang and he couldn't catch his breath. The Hulk raised both fists to batter him. The Conqueror tried to lift his own arms to fend off the attack, only to discover that he couldn't move.

But then the Hulk swayed and his eyes rolled up in his head. Groaning, he collapsed on top of Kang. The nerve gas had finally done its work.

The Conqueror tried to move again, and this time found it possible. As he dragged himself from beneath the unconscious monster, green icons blinked at the edges of his sight. His systems were coming back online. After a moment the Hulk began to change, shrinking from a giant to a skinny, brown-haired man.

Panting, Kang stood up and looked around. The people he'd rescued, the wretches who'd then cried for his blood, had disappeared. Mordo, the Cobra, and the Abomination dashed into the plaza.

"Are you all right?" Mordo cried.

"No," Kang replied. "I have some cracked ribs at the very least. Where were you people? Why didn't you answer when I called?"

"I didn't hear you," said the magician. He looked at his fellow lieutenants. "Did either of you?" The Cobra and the Abomination shook their heads.

For an instant, glaring at Mordo's concerned, puzzled expression, Kang was almost certain that the sorcerer had sabotaged his armor with magic and set him up to face the Hulk alone. He opened his mouth to accuse him, then hesitated.

He didn't *know* that Mordo had betrayed him. Perhaps one of his rivals had found a way to interfere with his weaponry, or maybe it had been a freak mechanical problem. And even if the magician was to blame, it wasn't clear whether the other governors had been in on the plot. Conceivably they really hadn't heard Kang's call. Maybe his comlink had malfunctioned along with everything else.

And if any of the trio was innocent, Kang couldn't afford to accuse him falsely. He'd been king for over two years, but he needed them as much as ever. Best to keep silent for now and watch his back.

"Well," he grunted, "don't worry about it. I managed without you."

"Let me do the honors," said the Abomination, advancing on the still-unconscious prisoner. "Banner and I have a score to settle."

Kang pictured the green ogre ripping the helpless man apart, the way the Hulk had nearly mauled him, and felt a spasm of revulsion. "Wait. We're here to rehabilitate my image, and I'm not sure that killing him now would create the proper impression."

Mordo arched an eyebrow. "I respectfully disagree. Your subjects hate the Hulk. They'll rejoice to hear of his death."

Yes, Kang thought bitterly, *just as they'd dance in the streets at news of my own demise. To hell with what they want.* "Perhaps, but I choose to spare him. We'll put him in the Pentagon cryo-prison. He'll be harmless enough in hibernation."

Mordo inclined his head. "As Your Majesty wishes, of course."

Sprawled on his back, Kang looked up the snow-covered slope at the alien bestriding the mountaintop, a titan clad in an ornate purple helmet. An immense spherical spaceship floated in the sky behind him. Familiar as he was with superhumans, nothing in the Conqueror's experience had prepared him for the godlike might of this titan called Galactus. Aided by the silvery herald on the flying surfboard, the colossus was striking down his attackers as easily as a human crushing ants, while a second giant, with a toga, spindly limbs, and a grotesquely large bald head, looked on impassively.

For a moment Kang was tempted to flee the battlefield, as, apparently, Mordo and the Cobra had already. Perhaps he could reach his time ship before Galactus finished constructing the machine that would enable him to consume the Earth. Flee into the past.

Then he scowled, disgusted with his own cowardice. No, damn it, he wouldn't turn tail. Not while there was any chance at all. Not when he had allies—the berserk Abomination, battered, exhausted Namor, and the super-powered strangers who called themselves Inhumans—still standing their ground. He soared into the air and fired his concussion rays at Galactus's face.

The azure beams had no effect. The herald, his metal skin gleaming in the Alpine sunlight, thrust out his hand and fired a dazzling ray. The energy blew Namor's body apart. Meanwhile Galactus blasted the Inhuman with the hooves and super-strong legs into a crumpled heap.

Then came a pop of displaced air. Frowning, Galactus peered at something on the ground. Kang turned and looked in the same direction.

The oversized bulldog with the shining antenna and its honey-blond adolescent mistress had teleported back onto the mountain. Her delicate jaw set and her blue eyes narrowed, the girl pointed an odd, stubby handgun at Galactus.

Kang felt a swell of jubilation. Shortly after Mordo and the Cobra disappeared, the strange, bald-headed giant in the toga, who called himself the Watcher, had whispered to him that Galactus's ship contained a weapon powerful enough to destroy even the devourer of worlds. While everyone else fought a diversionary action, the youthful Inhuman and her pet had gone to find it. And evidently they had!

A hush fell over the battlefield; for a second, no one moved. Then Mordo and the Cobra appeared out of nowhere just behind the Inhuman girl. Both governors gazed avidly at the gun.

If they coveted the device for themselves, if they tried to snatch it away from her, they might give Galactus a chance to regain the upper hand. "No!" shouted Kang. He dived at them, gauntlets extended. Startled, the two governors scrambled backward.

"You have no idea," rumbled Galactus after a time, "what the Nullifier truly is. If you pull the trigger, you'll destroy this entire solar system."

"If our world is going to die in any case," Kang replied, "what difference does it make? At least that way we'll take you with us."

Galactus turned toward the Watcher. "This is your doing, Uatu. So much for your oath of non-interference."

Uatu hung his head.

Galactus returned his gaze to the blond Inhuman. "I concede defeat. Return the Nullifier and I'll leave you in peace." He extended his purple-gloved hand. The girl nervously shook her head. "You may not keep the weapon, daughter of Attilan. I'd rather face it now than never know when some champion will bear it against me. And you shouldn't want to retain such a perilous thing."

"You must think we're idiots," Mordo sneered.

Kang essentially agreed with him. His every instinct rebelled at the thought of handing over their only effective means of attack, bought with the lives of their fallen comrades. But they had to resolve the standoff somehow. He looked at Uatu, who hesitated, then nodded.

"Give it to him," said Kang. "He'll keep his word."

"Your Majesty!" Mordo exploded. The blond Inhuman hesitantly laid the gun on Galactus's palm. The bulldog whined.

Kang held his breath until Galactus, the herald, and the half-assembled doomsday machine rose into the air and flew toward the spaceship, which opened a hatch to receive them. As soon as they were aboard, the vessel shot upward. In seconds it was gone.

Uatu gave the battlefield a last look, then disappeared. The surviving Inhumans began to collect their dead.

From their somber demeanor, Kang gathered that they meant to depart at once. And judging from the way they'd fought Galactus, fearlessly but without the hysteria of bloodlust, they were cut from very different cloth than his own self-serving lieutenants. He had to find out who they were and enlist them in his service!

He hurried over to their leader, a mute clad in a black costume with a glowing antenna almost like the bulldog's affixed to the cowl. The Inhuman held the corpse of the small karate master in white and green cradled against his chest. "Please, don't rush off!" said Kang. "Come back to Washington with us. My personal physicians will tend your wounds."

The mute scowled and turned away.

"What's the matter?" asked the Conqueror. "I'm telling you I want to be your friend."

"Black Bolt spurns the friendship of murderers and tyrants," said another Inhuman, a tall woman whose red, ankle-length tresses writhed and coiled like tentacles. "Like Namor, we never would have made common cause with you except to preserve the Earth itself, and we hope never to see you again. Don't look for us unless you want a war."

The Inhumans clustered around the bulldog. The creature's antenna sparkled and crackled, and the group vanished.

"Insolent swine," said Mordo. "You don't need their kind at court."

Kang sighed. "No, of course not. Not as long as I have you."

The guard ushered Banner into Kang's Pentagon office, then departed when his master dismissed him with a wave. The prisoner looked pale but resolute, a man struggling to control his fear. His copper-colored metal collar and the attached filaments hugging the back and sides of his head gleamed in the fluorescent light.

Kang had removed his mask and gauntlets for the meeting. He smiled, rose from behind his paper-littered desk, and held out his hand. Banner ignored the gesture.

"Please sit down," the Conqueror said.

Banner swallowed. "I'd rather stand."

Kang shrugged. "As you like." He dropped back into his swivel chair. "I hope your new headgear isn't uncomfortable."

Banner hesitated, then said, "I'd like to know what it is."

"Part of it is a monitor, which will shock you unconscious if you try to remove it, escape, or behave seditiously. But the important part is a neural regulator. No matter how angry you become, the seizure that triggers your transformation simply can't happen. In other words, I've rid you of the Hulk."

"And of my freedom. Do you expect me to be grateful?"

Kang grimaced. "I've given up expecting anyone to be grateful for anything."

"And who should be? The citizens of New York? Your sneak attack killed *millions* of innocent people. The Resistance circulates a book of photos of the bodies of your victims. You should look at it some time. And while you're at it, look at the incidence of cancer and birth defects throughout North America."

Kang shifted uncomfortably in his seat. "Sadly, people suffer during a war."

"That's no excuse for the man who started it."

The Conqueror scowled. "This isn't what I want to discuss."

"All right. Lord knows, I'm wasting my breath trying to induce an attack of conscience in a thug like you. What *do* you want?"

"For starters, to say that I didn't come here to hurt your people. I came because your age fascinated me. I admired its accomplishments."

"Like democracy?"

Kang ignored the gibe. "I thought I could rule you well. I managed all right in ancient Egypt and the 40th century. But those were small, primitive societies, where my subjects virtually worshipped me as a god. My experiences there didn't prepare me to govern a huge, sophisticated world like this." He waved a hand at the documents heaped before him. "Look at these. Reports of racial strife. Plague. Pollution. Famine. Poverty. Crime. Drugs. All of it steadily getting worse."

"If you *know* you're an incompetent king, abdicate."

Kang's mouth tightened. "I never surrender, no matter what the fight. I do, however, recruit assistants."

Banner blinked. "What are you talking about?"

"I'm told you're a genius and a decent man. As a native, you understand your time in a way I never can. And we've both been hated and misunderstood. Perhaps we have enough in common—"

The prisoner sneered. "I promise you, we have *nothing* in common."

Kang sighed. "If you say so. In any case, how would you like to be my advisor?"

"That's ridiculous. I'm no politician and I'm certainly not a quisling."

Kang discovered that Banner's impudence had nearly exhausted his patience. "Fine. *Don't* help, if you're too noble to collaborate with a fiend like me. Live out your days in idleness, like a pet cat, knowing that the world is falling apart, and you refused to lift a finger to stop the decay."

Banner hesitated, then grumbled, "All right. I don't know what you expect of me, but maybe there's something I can do."

* * *

Banner pounced as soon as Kang trudged into the Oval Office. "Mordo's church is conducting human sacrifices!" the advisor cried.

Kang winced. "Do you know that for certain?"

"Well, no," Banner admitted, "but that's the rumor. Supposedly he has *thousands* of bodies buried in the Carpathians."

Kang dropped his mask, gauntlets, and gun belt on the leather sofa, then slumped down beside them. "I'll look into it," he said. He fully intended to investigate the alleged malfeasance of all three of his governors. Just as soon as he found the time.

"Your programs will never get anywhere as long as you're depending on psychopaths like that to carry them out. If you had any sense—"

"I said I'll look into it!" the Conqueror snarled.

Banner grimaced. "Fine. I assume you want your briefing. The Brazilians are clearing rain forest again. I guess they never heard of satellite surveillance. The PLO blew up a bus in Gaza."

Kang rubbed his aching eyes. "I thought they agreed to a cease-fire."

"This was a dissident faction of the PLO."

The Conqueror raised his hand. "I'm sorry. I'm too tired for this. We'll tackle it tomorrow."

Banner looked down at him. For once his expression betrayed a hint of sympathy. "Was it a particularly rough fight this time?"

Kang shrugged. "The Mandarin was the Mandarin. I don't suppose he was really much more formidable today than he was four years ago. The difference is that the battles have stopped being fun. I guess it's more enjoyable to be the aggressor than the defender, particularly over the long haul. The aggressor is the one who picks the time and place, and the defender is the one with something to lose."

The time traveler shook his head. "It's strange, the blind spots people have. When I was a boy, I yearned to be an adventurer, and the conquerors of antiquity—Genghis Khan, Cortes, and the rest—were my models. But I only imagined their moments of triumph. I never wondered what their lives were like afterward.

"On the flight back from Peking, I had an urge to jump in my time ship and abandon this place. I couldn't return to either of the futures I've known—by transforming your age, I've erased them from this continuum—but there are countless other eras to explore."

Banner snorted. "By all means, go. Nobody here will shed any tears."

Kang smiled wearily. "And if I did leave, who'd protect the people from the Mandarin, Attuma, and the rest of the scum? When I killed the Avengers, I condemned myself to take their place."

Banner's eyes widened. "I never thought I'd live to hear this. You *do* feel guilty for nuking New York."

"I thought your degree was in physics, not psychiatry. I do *not* feel guilty about anything." The Conqueror sighed. "But somewhere along the line, I do seem to have developed a sense of duty." He waved his hand. "Go away. I want to rest."

"Suits me," Banner said. "Maybe Betty's still awake." He paused in the doorway. "For what it's worth, as mass murderers go, you could be worse. Some of your schemes have done some good. Just don't expect anyone to love you for it." He disappeared down the hall.

Kang strove to empty his mind. Gradually his eyelids drooped, his head lolled, and the room melted into darkness. Some time after that, the screech of a siren jolted him awake.

The scaly yellow horror furled its batlike wings and dove. Streaking through Kang's force screen as if the barrier didn't exist, it slashed at the human with three-inch iron talons, ripping his shirt, his already-damaged armor, and the flesh beneath.

Kang blasted the creature with concussion rays. For a moment the weapon had no more effect than a flashlight. Then it knocked the monster away from him. Stunned, the thing plummeted through the smoky air toward the white dome of the Capitol.

Grimly Kang surveyed the burning city. Everywhere his surviving troops were falling back in disarray. They were having problems with their equipment, too.

Kang didn't claim to understand the supernatural, but after years with Mordo, he knew it when he saw it. The horde of invaders who'd suddenly materialized out of nowhere, the humanoid with the flaming head and his ghastly minions, were some kind of demon, whose magical nature accounted for their resistance to technological armaments.

Kang switched on his comlink. "Mordo! Come in! I need you!"

"I'm in the Pentagon," the sorcerer's voice replied. "Meet me in your office."

When Kang rushed in, he found all three of his lieutenants. None looked disheveled; evidently they had yet to take part in the battle raging outside. An intricate pentagram, composed of lines and arcs of scarlet phosphorescence, smoldered on the floor. The air reeked of bitter incense.

Kang looked at Mordo. "This attack falls in your area of expertise. Can you handle it?"

"I can now," said the sorcerer, nodding at the magical circle. "I just completed the proper ritual and I'm ready to join the fray."

"Good," said Kang, pivoting back toward the door. "Then let's get out there—"

Something slammed into his back. Red icons flamed at the corners of his vision. His knees buckled, dumping him on the floor.

He was spastic with pain, and his armor's servomechanisms had shut down with the rest of his systems, but somehow he managed to flop over onto his back. His fellow superhumans leered down at him. "I'm afraid," said Mordo, his hands glowing, "that your reign has come to an end."

Kang crawled backward like a crab. "Are you insane? You can't turn on me now! It'll take all of us to defeat this new monster!"

"Please," said Mordo, "speak respectfully of your worthy successor and our new patron, the dread Dormammu."

Kang kept edging away. The Cobra and the Abomination stalked after him, slowly, drawing out the moment. "Klaus," pleaded the Conqueror, "Emil, *think*! You aren't improving your position. If Mordo's demon takes over, you'll still have a king above you. At least I'm a human being!"

The Cobra flexed his long, pliant strangler's fingers. "But the baron says Dormammu will let us run things the way we want to."

The Abomination nodded. "And we're sick of you, Kang. We've been sick of you for a long time."

Mordo spread his hands. "You might as well give up, my friend. You're beaten. When you slaughtered Strange and the other heroes, when you actually managed to conquer the world, I was impressed. I thought I'd be wise to ally with you, at least until I took your measure. But in retrospect it's clear that you were never any match for me."

Kang's shoulders bumped the wall. He groped along its base. "Surrender *now*," he said. "This instant. Or die."

Mordo chuckled. "Nice bluff. But I'm quite certain that I disabled your armor completely this time."

"And you're right," said Kang. He pressed one of the sixty buttons hidden throughout the office.

Sections of wall dropped. Four hundred power guns blazed, over and over again, drenching the room with the smell of ozone, blowing Mordo, the Cobra, and the Abomination to bits before they even had a chance to react. Kang huddled on the floor. The targeting computer was supposed to recognize him and direct its fire elsewhere, but he saw no point in tempting fate.

"You should have realized I suspected you," he told Mordo's shattered corpse. "You should have expected me to take precautions. But you never could credit that anyone else could be as clever as you."

After a few seconds the barrage ceased. Shaking with pain and weakness, Kang dragged himself to his feet. Bits of his armor broke away and fell tinkling to the floor. So did spatters of his blood. Amber icons flickered before him as some of his systems struggled back online. He stumbled to a monitor, switched it on, and cried out in anguish.

The capital he'd defended against Namor, Doom, and so many others was virtually gone, the buildings and alabaster monuments burning or ripped apart, the populace lying butchered in the streets. Grown tall as a skyscraper, flinging colossal fireballs apparently just for the joy of it, Dormammu marched toward the Pentagon with his troops behind him.

All his toil and struggles, Kang realized dully, had come to this. This devil with the crown of flame was going to ravage his world. He couldn't possibly prevent it.

Then a realization struck him.

No, *he* couldn't defeat Dormammu, but perhaps the Avengers or some of their super-powered allies could have. Indeed, in another reality, they *must* have. Otherwise the stagnant but placid future of Kang's birth could never have come to be.

And that meant there was one chance left.

Kang materialized in a starlit field. A mild breeze toyed with the tattered remains of his cape. A horse's hooves clopped somewhere in the gloom.

He lurched around, seeking his bearings, saw the pale shaft of Cleopatra's Needle, and felt a jolt of dismay. Another Kang, his armor intact, stood before the obelisk. He was just lifting his hand away from a small silver orb on a tripod.

Kang had intended to reach Central Park *before* his younger self, to give himself as much time to deal with him as possible. But the time-ship controls interfaced with his armor, and perhaps as a result of the damage the suit had sustained, he'd arrived afterward. His twin had already set the timer.

"Don't do it!" the Conqueror cried.

His double pivoted, whipping out his pistol, then faltered. "What's the meaning of this?" he demanded.

"You're making a mistake! Shut down the device!"

After a moment's hesitation, the younger man said, "No." He positioned himself in front of the bomb, shielding it. "I've made my decision. This is the only way to win."

Kang yanked off his mask. "Don't you understand? I'm *you*, come back to warn you that it's all going to go wrong!"

"Are you indeed," said his double, his voice now cold and steady.

Kang gaped at him. "How can you doubt it?"

"You may be some enemy in disguise. Or a doppelgänger from an alternate continuum. The *real* Kang might jump back in time to help his younger self win a war, but never to tell him to forfeit one. And no matter what hardships befell him, he could never look as panicky, as beaten and pathetic, as you."

"You arrogant fool," said Kang. He simultaneously beamed a signal to his time ship and fired a concussion ray.

The azure beam glanced harmlessly off his twin's iridescent force field. The younger man discharged his pistol. The barrage of micromissiles exploded against Kang's energy shield, which proved too weak to cushion the blow completely. The blast hurled him backward and slammed him to the ground. His mask flew from his hand.

Kang's head rang. His face was raw, his nose flattened. Shaking off the shock of injury, he tried to take to the air, but his anti-grav was gone. He scrambled up and fired another ray.

He'd known going in that a duel like this was hopeless. Wounded and with damaged gear, he couldn't defeat his younger self. But, fearing that his twin would prove intransigent, he'd conceived a plan, which provided for the appearance of something that might.

But it was beginning to look as if it wasn't *going* to appear. Perhaps his battered armor hadn't transmitted a clear signal. Or maybe the time ship had teleported its remaining passenger to the wrong moment, just as it had Kang. With the bomb less than two minutes from detonation, there was little margin for error.

Kang's double knocked him down with a vibro-ray. The fall gave his spine an agonizing wrench. Gasping, he wondered if he'd be able to get up again. He wondered if it mattered.

"You've lost," the younger man said, an unaccustomed note of pity in his voice. "Teleport out if you can. No need for you to die in the explosion."

"You forget," croaked Kang, forcing himself to his knees, "Kang the Conqueror *never* surrenders." And then, when he'd all but given up hope, a patch of air shimmered, and Banner stumbled from Limbo onto the grass.

After all these years the scrawny physicist looked odd without his collar and cap of wires. He was shuddering and drenched in sweat from the massive dose of amphetamines Kang had given him.

But he wasn't changing shape. Perhaps the neural regulator had done its job too well. Maybe the Hulk was gone beyond recall.

The young Kang peered at Banner. "Another meddler?" he asked contemptuously. "You're even more of a joke than my shadow here." He casually pointed his gauntlet at the scientist.

Terrified that his counterpart would kill Banner, Kang frantically thrust out his own arm and shot first, with a low-intensity beam. With luck it would merely sting Banner and knock him down.

The beam blasted Banner off his feet. Kang's double pivoted back toward him. "I don't understand," the younger man said. "Are you on my side now?"

"Hardly," said Kang, lurching up and firing a ray at him. They traded shots until something growled.

Startled, Kang's double whirled, just as a green-skinned giant lumbered out of the darkness. Ignoring the younger warlord, the monster advanced on the man who'd hurt him.

"No!" Kang cried. "The *bomb*, Hulk! Remember the *bomb*!"

For a moment it seemed that the enraged behemoth *didn't* remember, that he didn't have even a trace of Banner left inside him. But then he snarled, pivoted, and launched himself at Kang's counterpart, punching furiously. The younger Conqueror reeled backward, his overtaxed force field rippling with rainbows.

Staggering, Kang ran to the tripod. According to the readout on the control panel, he had six seconds.

Clumsy with haste and pain, he fumbled with the tiny buttons, finally halting the countdown with two seconds left. He checked to be sure his armor still had super-strength, then hefted the orb and threw it high and far enough to reach the ocean.

Kang's double screamed in outrage, then vanished, his time ship snatching him away as instructed.

The Hulk goggled at the empty space his opponent had occupied, then jerked around and charged the remaining Kang. But on his third stride he faded away as well.

A sensation of lightness and numbness washed away the Conqueror's myriad pains. Peering down, he saw his gauntleted hands become translucent.

Of course, he thought. By preventing the events that had brought them to this pass from ever occurring in the first place, Banner and he had created a logical paradox. Reality, stressed beyond tolerance, was resolving it by expunging them from existence, though doppelgängers would live on in the timeline they'd restored.

Kang found that he didn't fear dissolution. He was tired of his life. And at least he'd done one thing right before the end, even if it was only to remedy one of his own mistakes.

He just wished he'd understood himself better, back when it all began. Grasped that he didn't really want a throne, only adventure. It could all have been different. He could have wandered time as a kind of knight errant, fighting the Dooms and Mordos for the fun of it. He could have been loved instead of hated.

Perhaps, he thought, smiling wryly as he faded away, he could even have joined the Avengers.

Magneto

CONNECT THE DOTS

ADAM-TROY CASTRO

Illustration by Roger Cruz

SUNSET FALLS WAS a city in pain.

It should have been a rustic paradise. Nestled in an isolated valley in upstate New York, a comfortable half-hour's drive from the Interstate, it was a community that had always been defined by family, tradition, and hard work. It was a town with one diner, one general store, and three intersections, a town where most people with cars usually kept them parked; a town where a fair percentage of the citizenry had always been content without ever, even once, setting foot outside the county.

Today, it was inhabited by people who were no longer what they had once been; people who lurched from place with mismatched steps, and whose features seemed to blur with every breath they took. Every single one of them—man, woman, and child—stopped at least once each day to gaze at the white clapboard house at the end of Metcalf Street with expressions of mingled fear and loathing.

Joshua, who lived in that house, sat on the porch playing connect the dots.

He liked connect the dots. It was a fun game. It was the only game he knew, the only game that made sense to him. All the other games were about too much—they had too many rules, and too many things he had to remember, and they hurt his head to think about. Once, when he had both Daddy and Mommy, he'd run screaming from a Little League baseball game. There had been two different teams, and crowds of people watching, and some other people taking pictures, and they'd all been doing different things. Like pieces of one big body, ripped apart and scattered across the field. It had scared him. He'd screamed and cried and made his daddy take him home.

That was okay, now.

Nobody played baseball in Sunset Falls anymore.

He sat on his porch, rocking slowly, playing connect the dots. Staring at the puzzle book page, making the little black circles of ink slide across the page until they became one. The pages looked better that way. Cleaner. Nicer to look at. And they didn't hurt his head so much.

He hummed happily, wondering what to connect next.

* * *

High above the skies of Westchester County, in New York State, one of the most powerful and most feared figures of all time flew above the clouds. He wore a regal suit of red steel mesh dreaded by armies and law-enforcement agencies all over the world, a suit marked by the distinctive horned helmet and the flowing purple cape that flapped behind him as magnetic currents pulled him north at the speed of sound. The helmet came down over his forehead and across his cheeks to cover most of his face, leaving only an oval cutout around his eyes and a narrow slit exposing his nose and mouth. The horns were meant to mock the demon that so many people thought he was.

But he was not a demon, and he was not a villain.

He was Magneto, master of magnetism. And it was his most cherished dream to conquer the world, not out of any personal lust for power, but to make it a safe place for the race of super-powered people that had begun to make its existence known in this, the closing half of the twentieth century: mutants, people born with extraordinary powers and/or abilities that set them apart from "mainstream" humanity. He'd committed any number of atrocities in pursuit of that goal—he'd killed, and waged war, and ravished countries, and destroyed cities. It gave him no pleasure, but it was necessary. *Homo sapiens* had proven it could not be trusted. *Homo superior* had to fight for survival. Nothing else mattered. Not family, not friendship, not happiness, not even his own soul. Nothing.

And as he flew toward his rendezvous in Sunset Falls, where his instruments had informed him he might find an ally powerful enough to make a difference in this war, he looked down upon the farmland below—the rolling hills, the grain silos, the patchwork quilts of cultivated fields, the herds of grazing cattle, and, from place to place, the scattered collections of buildings that represented towns—and his lips curled. It was a beautiful view, one he wished he had the leisure to savor more fully. He loved the countryside. He'd been born and raised in such a countryside, a world away from here: a fallow, foolish, utterly normal youth with no ambitions beyond the little village he'd called his home. He hadn't dreamed of adventure, or travel, or glory. He'd just wanted to work on the family farm, with his brothers and sisters and the new generations yet to come. He'd always won-

dered what life would have been like, if it had been allowed to
go on that way . . .

. . . if the army hadn't come.

. . . if he hadn't lost everybody he'd ever known.

. . . if he hadn't learned that *homo sapiens* would always be
ruled by hate.

His momentary smile became a grimace. He was Magneto. He
was a law unto himself. He had no place for memories. He just
had his mission.

Especially today.

Today, business was bringing him within a hundred miles of
his most dangerous enemies, the X-Men. They headquartered at
the Xavier Institute, in Salem Center, New York. To be sure, his
latest intelligence placed them out of the country—their wheel-
chair-bound leader, Charles Xavier, being the only one still at
home—but they could return at any time, and if they did, their
mutant detection device, Cerebro, would certainly pick up the
signs of the tremendously powerful, previously undiscovered mutant emerging so close to their own backyard. Magneto was determined to recruit that potential soldier before they did. . . . or
before a true monster like Apocalypse did.

As he flew in closer, he realized that there was something
mightily disturbing about Sunset Falls itself. Magneto had re-
searched the area thoroughly, as he always did before exposing
himself to a potential new battlefield. And while his most up-to-
date census, only six months old, described a thriving town of
about four hundred and twenty people, his satellite instruments
only picked up a population of about half that size. Magneto did
not have a good feeling about that, at all . . .

. . . but he was Magneto.

The mutant race was counting on him.

Hesitation was a luxury he could not afford.

He skimmed low over the mountains, spotted the cluster of
modest houses and narrow streets that could only be the village
of Sunset Falls, quickly scanned the area for signs of super heroes
or government forces lying in wait, then, satisfied, came to a
landing on the median of the sole road leading into town. As his
feet touched pavement, he mentally rearranged the metallic fi-
bres in his clothing, transforming it to a reasonable facsimile of
a conservative gray suit. He checked his new image to make sure

it was nothing too memorable, then ran a hand over his shock of distinguished white hair, straightened his tasteful red tie, and marched into town with the self-confidence of a man who knew he could flatten every building in sight with but an errant thought.

He had chosen stealth only because it suited his current purposes. He could just hurtle down from the sky, make short work of its pathetic defenders, and carry away the new mutant in a cage of re-arranged plumbing. Certainly he'd done it before. But sometimes there were advantages in not tipping one's hand too early. Especially in Xavier's neighborhood.

No: today he would be a stranded motorist in search of a tow truck.

And while in town, he would simply knock on the mutant's door and present his case.

He would call himself a messenger, here to bestow a birthright. That was good. It was even literally true. If the mutant in question turned out to be young enough to still be in the care of its parents, he'd then impress upon them the need to surrender guardianship. That wasn't difficult, most of the time. Young mutants being what they were, their parents were often relieved to be rid of them.

And then, once he spoke to the mutant directly, Magneto would use one of his three basic approaches. One began with: You have been given a great gift. Another began with: You are superior to those around you. The third began with: You must learn to fight the world before it fights you. He tailored the presentation to the individual, secure in the knowledge that they all said essentially the same thing. In this life, being born different or superior was always an invitation to a life spent at war.

He'd discovered that at the bottom of the mass grave, beneath the bodies of everybody he'd ever known, beneath the lime they'd poured on the corpses, beneath the agony of the bullet that had wounded but not killed him, as his own developing powers kept him alive long enough to claw his way upward . . .

His eyes narrowed as he regarded the blandly curious faces of the people of Sunset Falls, as they peered at him from their storefronts and front porches. They considered themselves safe. They considered themselves immune. They thought that what they had would be theirs forever. They were sheep, and they were the enemy.

He was halfway to the wood frame house at the end of Metcalf Avenue before he began to realize that there was also something terribly wrong with them.

Take that big burly workman, busily repairing the wall outside the video store. The man had the barrel chest of a veteran laborer, but the skinny little toothpick arms of a sedentary accountant. He moved slowly and tentatively, like a man not at home in his own body.

Or that little boy bouncing the ball against the side wall of the corner grocery. He seemed like a normal child, until he glanced up to face the silver-haired stranger in town: then he revealed a face lined with wrinkles, that would have been more appropriate on a seventy-year-old.

Or that old person, rocking on the porch swing: at first he seemed to be a man, but when he tilted his head a certain way, the lines of his face seemed to shift, becoming instead the features of an old woman. And the two women arguing on the corner: Magneto caught a fragment of their conversation as he passed by, and he got the distinct impression of four separate voices . . .

Everybody he saw looked normal at first, until he looked closer and spotted the young faces on withered bodies, the adult faces on the bodies of children, the creatures that were not immediately identifiable as either men or women, and those that lurched along with arms and legs that all seemed determined to work independently of one another.

By the time Magneto spotted the big white house at the end of Metcalf Avenue, which he knew to be his mutant's home, he'd caught the pattern. Whatever was responsible for this merged people both physically and mentally. It took two people and made them one: four people and made them two. It robbed them of their individuality, and turned them into parody compromised versions of themselves, like figures of clay melded together in a mad sculptor's fist.

Tracks left by the mutant in Sunset Falls? Or something else?

A lesser man would have fled and returned with an army. But lesser men were not Magneto: and dangerous mutants were what he needed. Utterly unafraid, he pushed open the arched gate in the picket fence that surrounded the home of the mutant he'd come here to see, and strode right up the front walk, with an unhurried calm that utterly belied his willingness to do battle at any moment.

He was just vain enough to ring the bell magnetically, without actually touching the button with his fingers.

The thing that opened the door took his breath away.

It was a man. It was a woman. It was both red-headed and blonde. It was overweight in some places and trim in others. Its eyes were simultaneously brown and hazel. Its face was a crazy-quilt combination of features, all of which managed to be in the proper places and still avoid linking together in any sensible way.

The thing said, "Can I help you?" In four separate voices.

Magneto detected a teenaged girl, a gravelly-voiced middle-aged man, a sweet-voiced middle-aged woman, and an old lady . . . all speaking in unison, from one mouth. For one of the few times in a life of speechmaking, shock almost rendered him mute. Then, with an effort, he gathered up his composure and said: "Uh . . . yes. My name's . . ."

He did not get a chance to finish that sentence . . .

. . . for at that moment, something else entered the foyer: a skinny teenage boy, with sandy blond hair and a slack-jawed expression punctuated by a chocolate milk moustache of not-very-recent vintage. The dogeared copy of *101 Connect the Dots* in his right hand flapped open as he shuffled over to the door, displaying pages reduced to slashing whirls of random crayon. "Maaaaa," he said.

"Joshua," said the crazy-quilt who'd answered the door. "We have a guest."

The boy peered at Magneto with eyes devoid of comprehension. There was nothing behind those eyes except an empty black void—and then something flared in there, lighting up his face, and twisting his lips into an offended little O.

Joshua screamed: "*You're not connected to anything!*"

Magneto felt the boy's power reaching out for him, and instantly, instinctively, surrounded himself with a wall of magnetic force. It was a shield that had repelled bullets, shells, and the fists of beings with enough strength to level mountains.

Joshua's power engulfed him anyway. Magneto felt his soul shudder, as if the moorings that connected it to his body were being ripped loose. He screamed, and with a tremendous effort of will, launched himself away from the white clapboard house. He managed to get about two hundred feet straight up before the agony overcame him, then tumbled head-over-heels to the ground, in a jerky series of free falls that he only barely managed to control. His conservative business suit turned pink, then scarlet, transforming itself into the familiar red costume . . . then back into a business suit, the two outfits strobing uncontrollably. The crash onto the pavement was just violent enough to knock the breath out of him. He stood painfully, and staggered into the street, just in time to come within inches of getting walloped by the nondescript green van that chose that moment to turn onto Metcalf Avenue.

The driver braked in time, staring at Magneto with shock and recognition.

Magneto stared too. It was his closest friend and most dangerous enemy.

In the instant before Joshua's power swallowed them both, Magneto whispered, "Xavier . . . !"

The bald man in the wheelchair-equipped van did not say, *Magneto.*

He said, "Magnus . . . !"

Tel Aviv, many years ago. It was a world still healing from the wounds of its greatest war, a world that still hoped for a better future, a world that did not yet know the multiplying crises that would come to dominate the closing years of the twentieth century.

Two young men sat in a sidewalk café, lost in one of the heated debates that had come to define their relationship. It was a rare day off for both of them; they'd both come to Israel to weigh the directions their lives were to take, they'd both ended up volunteering at the same kibbutz, and they'd both spent the past week digging drainage ditches under the hot Mediterranean sun.

The silver-haired man called himself Magnus, still several years away from the reign of terror that would earn him the feared name Magneto. The bald man was Charles Xavier, himself several years away from the accident that would cost him the use of his legs.

They had more in common than even they guessed.

Their friendship came naturally. So did their arguments.

On this particular day, Magnus said, "So. Let us suppose you are correct. Let us suppose that humanity has reached the next evolutionary step, and that a new race of super-powered people is coming into existence. This is your theory, correct?"

"It's more than a theory," said Charles Xavier. "It's a clearly documented fact. I myself have seen several examples of—"

"As have I. I just never put it together as concisely as you." He tipped his coffee cup in mock salute. "But to continue: if we accept the existence of this super race—*homo superior*, if you will—then won't ordinary, powerless *homo sapiens* hate and fear it? Indeed, even take steps to destroy it? Aren't we saying that sooner or later we'll be seeing yet another attempt at extermination on a global scale?"

Xavier's eyes lowered. "Not necessarily," he said. "The fossil record clearly shows that the first Cro-Magnons existed side by side with Neanderthals for many tens of thousands of years. There's no reason to believe they never got along, or that there was ever any unusual degree of conflict between them."

"Except that there don't seem to be any Neanderthals seated at any of the other tables, do there? Unless—" Magnus said puckishly, indicating a bearded man ravenously decorating his lap with scrambled eggs, "—you count that fellow over there."

Xavier resisted the temptation to look. "They probably crossbred. Only, there were more Cro-Magnons, so they eventually absorbed the entire Neanderthal population. The same thing happened—"

"Charles," said Magneto, paternally. "Look at us. We are living in a country ruled by a people the world recently tried to exterminate, which is surrounded on all sides by enemies who consider it their holy duty to finish the job. A country where everybody knows that their only options are to fight or die. How can you presume to know that anything will ever be different?"

"Because I have faith. And because I firmly believe that both sides will someday be led by people who value compromise over blood."

Magnus stared—not in the manner of a man who also believed, but as one to whom the words could only be nonsense, spoken in a language that he did not know. "There are no such people,

Charles. I know that. There are only the strong, the weak . . . and those who know they must kill to survive."

Xavier's eyes betrayed a chill. "Listen to yourself, Magnus. Listen to what you're saying. You . . . sound like Hitler talking."

It was maybe the only thing anybody could have said that was capable of bringing out the rage that forever burned in Magnus's heart. For a moment, as the blood pounded in his ears, Magnus came very close to stopping Xavier's heart with a thought. But the moment passed. Magnus stood, took out his wallet, and with a single contemptuous flip tossed payment in full upon the table. And he said: "You are a friend, so I will refrain from punishing you for that. But don't you . . . ever . . . say anything like that to me again. Ever."

They would remain friends, for some time after that. They would not become enemies for more than a decade. But from that moment on, a new element had been added to their relationship: something of which they'd never speak, that would remain a silent secret between them.

Recognition.

Joshua tasted the shared memory without understanding it. The words meant nothing to him. They never meant anything to him. He didn't have much use for words; they were just sounds in the air and marks on the page, as beyond him as the maddeningly separate dots that glowed in the nighttime sky.

The only thing Joshua had ever understood was connections.

Connections were simple. Mother was connected to father, uncle connected to aunt, sister connected to brother, friend connected to friend, enemy connected to enemy. Joshua had always been able to see those connections in his mind—to him, they resembled glowing silver cords that bound one person to another even when they were worlds away—and their intangibility had always been a source of great pain to him; why be connected to anything at all, when you were still so far apart?

It made no sense to him. If his brain craved anything at all, it was unity.

He hadn't known that he was able to do anything about it until that day last summer when he'd been sitting upstairs in his room, ragged old puzzle book in one hand, black crayon in the other, obsessively redrawing the same lines he'd used to connect the dot-drawings yesterday, and the day before, and the day before that. And he heard some yipping noises from outside and he looked out the window and he saw the neighbor's brand new golden retriever puppies batting a ball back and forth across the backyard. There were four of the creatures, and they were connected by invisible silver cords that looped back and forth as they wrestled and gnawed at each other, but they were separate too, and their separateness hurt Joshua's head, so much he couldn't play with the puzzle-book anymore, and he put down the book and he put down the crayons and he concentrated on more tightly connecting the puppies so they weren't separate dogs anymore.

And the dogs started yipping more loudly, not in play but in terror, and the silver cords binding them grew taut, and then everything was all right, because now there weren't four separate puppies anymore. There was just one big dog, whining in the afternoon sun.

Joshua had felt so good about this that he promptly went downstairs and connected Mom, Dad, Grandma, and his older sister.

And over the days that followed, he connected everybody in town.

The white-haired man had almost ruined everything. He wasn't connected to anybody. Oh, he had several invisible silver cords trailing off into the sky, but even if there was anybody on the other end, the cords themselves were weak and tenuous things, that all had the sick feel of connections long broken. At first, Joshua had been afraid that he wouldn't be able to fix things at all. But things have a way of turning out for the best, and as it happened the white-haired man and the man driving down the street were already as tightly bound as anybody Joshua had ever known.

Which was definitely a relief.

Of course, there was still no excuse for them to still be two separate people.

But that was easy to fix.

Joshua closed his eyes and concentrated . . .

For Magneto, it was like that moment when he awoke at the bottom of the mass grave, with the lime burning his arms and legs and back, and he had to claw his way upward, through the bodies of his friends and family. It was like those terrible months as a weak, starving prisoner, being poked and prodded by white-suited doctors determined to find the secret of his paranormal abilities; and like that other moment, decades later, when a hated fellow mutant regressed him to infancy: gave him the squalling, helpless body of a babe, while leaving a distant, horrified part of him cursed with the awareness of the adult.

It was like those, and a hundred other torments from his past. Except worse.

Much worse. Because this time he had to relive those moments knowing that Charles Xavier was also reliving them . . . experiencing the darkest secrets of his life, while he in turn experienced Xavier's.

They were both courageous, strong-willed men, with long histories of withstanding the worst life could throw at them; they'd both known far more than their share of horror, and they both owed their lives to their ability to keep thinking and planning even when their souls were at the breaking point. But their sudden shared memories came close to breaking them.

Xavier saw what it had been like for Magneto, to crawl half-dead from the mass grave which contained the people of his village, only to be starved and beaten at the hands of the invading soldiers . . . all for the sin of being different.

Magneto saw what it had been like for Xavier, to grow up in the home of a stepbrother who hated him, who bullied him, who would have done anything to destroy him—who, in the end, became just another enemy, in a life all too filled with enemies.

Xavier saw what it had been like for Magneto, to emerge from the final years of World War Two alone and filled with hate. To have that hate turned to love at the hands of a beautiful woman named Magda, who took the shattered pieces of the man he'd been and put them back together again. To then see her run from him in terror when he was forced to use his powers to protect her.

Magneto saw what it had been like for Xavier, to dedicate his entire life to a dream of peaceful co-existence, to see that dream shattered time and time again, by people sworn to destroy him and everything he stood for . . . all for the sin of being different.

Both Magneto and Xavier saw each other through each other's eyes: in each case, the friend they most respected, the ally they most wanted, the one person they'd fought and tried to reach for most of their adult lives.

Magneto found himself sinking to his knees as his strong, athletic legs were suddenly twisted with unbearable pain. He had a ghostly memory of even more horrendous pain, as a great stone reduced them to splintered kindling . . . then felt his personality subsumed, as a new gestalt personality was born..

The silver glow faded. A new figure sat, shivering, in the center of Metcalf Avenue, blocking a van that had been idling, but which was now as dead as both the individuals Magneto and Charles Xavier.

As for Joshua, he thought that was much better. Even better than he'd thought it would be. Because right now he felt stronger and more powerful than ever before.

He was not capable of understanding why. Analytical thought was beyond him. He did not know what the law of conservation of energy had to say about suddenly halving two of the most powerful mutants on the planet. And he most certainly did not know the word "vampirism." He just knew that connecting the two men had filled him with energy. Enough to do anything.

He concentrated, and sent forth his mind, to encompass all of Sunset Falls at once . . .

Magneto and Xavier might have been shattered . . . were it not for one thing.

Each man had just, in a very real sense, become his own worst enemy. Each man remembered a lifetime of conflict with the other: a never-ending war that had only been rendered more bitter for all the respect between them.

The divisions between them allowed them each to retain a small portion of their individuality, within the greater gestalt personality that had been formed.

And neither was capable of showing weakness before the other.

In that instant, each knew why the other had come. Magneto saw that Xavier had detected the nascent mutant's presence on the instrument he called Cerebro, and had come by himself when unable to contact the X-Men. Even this close to home, it was a tremendously risky act, given the mutant's unknown intentions and capabilities, and Xavier's physical limitations. Magneto couldn't help but feel an unwanted wave of admiration.

So, what do we call ourselves now, Charles? Professor Magneto? The Magnetic Brain? The Bipolar Man?

A million years passed before Xavier's own mind answered: *For now? Allies.*

Agreed.

And together, they stood.

They were now a tall, thin man, wearing a brown suit which bore an unusual metallic sheen. They had distinguished silvery hair on the sides of their head and complete baldness on top. Their eyes were penetrating green circles bearing an expression that could have been either anger or compassion; their legs were wobbly, pain-wracked things, just barely steady enough to permit walking. As they took their first steps, they winced with shared pain and almost tumbled back to the ground, but their shared will refused to accept such an ignoble defeat and they succeeded in lurching forward, toward the wooden clapboard house on Metcalf Avenue.

The boy named Joshua still sat on the porch, watching them approach. But there was no longer anything dull about his expression; if anything, he was ecstatic. Worried, Magneto/Xavier probed him—

—caught a quick mental image of the streets of Sunset Falls as seen from Joshua's eyes: a complex mesh of glowing silver cords—

—being pulled suddenly under his direction—

—and all over town, the already merged people of Sunset Falls falling to their knees in pain, as Joshua's newly empowered mind swallowed them whole.

Magneto/Xavier shouted in two separate voices.

Joshua's psychic energy converged like a glowing sun in the center of Metcalf Avenue, turning all the world blinding white. Magneto/Xavier staggered from the sheer force of it. The Magneto half of them gestured, and a lime-green van bearing the legend "EMPIRE EXTERMINATORS" and an ornate painting of a humanoid cockroach being strapped into an electric chair buckled, twisted . . . and compressed into a disk-shaped shield that immediately flew between them and the forces at play before them. The Xavier half sensed Joshua reaching out for them, to meld them with the creature being put together from all the people of Sunset Falls . . . and threw up a mental shield that came close to being shattered into pieces by Joshua's will.

Damn you, Charles, you've got to protect us better than that! If he merges us with the others, we're lost!

Don't worry about me, Xavier responded. *Just keep him occupied. I'll—*

And then they both froze.

Because, just up ahead, something inhuman was screaming in four hundred separate voices.

It was one of the worst sounds Magneto/Xavier had ever heard.

Magneto/Xavier acted instinctively. They hurled the remnants of the van away from them with all the magnetic force at their command. Unfortunately, that was not much, since Joshua had drained them so badly. Magneto at the peak of his powers could have stood on the ground and nonchalantly hurled a city bus three miles straight up. Magneto/Xavier merely managed to propel the hulk of twisted metal away from them at roughly the force of a runaway truck. Still, that would have been more than enough to mash Joshua flat and reduce his house to a collection of toothpicks . . .

. . . if something hadn't caught it.

In its hands.

And hurled it to one side with a bellow of rage.

For one confused heartbeat, Magneto/Xavier looked out upon the monster and wondered how the hell the Hulk had gotten involved in all this. But then the last of Joshua's glow faded, and took their confusion with it. This creature didn't look anything like the Hulk. It wasn't green, for one thing. Or gray. Or any combination thereof.

It was also quite a bit larger than the Hulk had ever been.

It stood thirteen feet tall, almost that wide, possessed of arms larger than most domestic makes of car . . . and was covered with hundreds of faces. Ranging from infants to old men and women, all screaming, they lined its gnarled limbs like obscene tattoos . . . some of them sinking beneath the skin even as others rose to the surface to join the tormented choir. About all the faces had in common was the madness of ordinary people trapped in a nightmare beyond their understanding . . . and the need to lash out at the world that had done this to them.

The world that, right now, stood symbolized by the wobbly-legged man who had just hurled the wreckage at them.

The creature that had been the entire population of Sunset Falls stumbled toward them.

It moved with terrifying speed, but it moved clumsily—more like a toddler plunging forward than a creature learning how to walk. The hundreds of separate wills that controlled it had yet to learn the cooperation needed to properly guide its body. All it could manage was a painful, lurching shuffle, which may have had enough power behind it to make the ground quake, but was not yet swift enough to catch a being who only had to reconcile two wills.

Magneto/Xavier rose wobbily into the sky, just barely evading the creature's deadly grip. They flew in short, punctuated jerks, their twisted legs twitching weakly beneath them, their face contorting with the shared pain of four hundred townspeople warring within one cage of flesh.

Th-their thoughts . . . I can't. . . .

Block them out, Xavier—that's what you're good for!

Xavier tried. And were he wholly Xavier, he might have succeeded.

But he wasn't wholly Xavier.

Not now, when for once Magneto needed him to be Xavier.

And that's when the children trapped within the creature all started screaming.

Mommy Daddy where are we we're scared it hurts in this place Mommy help us somebody help us somebody.

The psychic intensity of it hit Magneto/Xavier with all the force of a freight train. They emitted an anguished gasp, and stiffened, their eyes rolling back in their sockets. Magneto's powers of flight abandoned them, and they fell ten full feet, toward the creature's arms.

It drew back its massive arm and swung at their falling body, with a strength that would have killed Magneto/Xavier instantly.

In the last heartbeat before the blow landed, Magneto/Xavier recovered enough to broadcast a silent, telepathic *"No!!!"* The creature pulled its punch, striking them only with enough strength to crumple a bank safe like tinfoil. The magnetic barrier they managed to erect at the last second absorbed most of the remaining impact, enough to keep Magneto/Xavier from being killed instantly but not enough to keep their shared form from being thrown three blocks. Their hurtling body, shielded by a magnetic force-bubble, passed through four separate houses before slowing down. All four collapsed in a row, like consecutive balloons burst by a shot from a rifle. Mushroom clouds of dust and debris rose into the blue appalachian sky. Magneto/Xavier skipped along the pavement, rolled, and then lay very still, darkness gathering all around them . . .

For Magnus, it had all seemed very simple.

Here he was, one of the most feared figures on the face of the planet, the champion of the mutant underclass, the reviled villain whose crusade to conquer the world for the new race of humanity had made him a hated and hunted figure all over the world. Back when he first declared war on *homo sapiens*, he had fully expected to win his battle within a matter of years. Why not? Not only was his cause just, and his side growing more powerful and numerous with every day, but he himself was plugged into one of the inherent binding forces of the universe. There would be no denying him.

Except that there was.

An army of super-powered champions had risen out of nowhere to oppose him. Few were even remotely as powerful as he . . . certainly, none of Xavier's students were, in the early days . . . but they had this nasty habit of winning. Even Captain America had thwarted his will once. And he was just a man. Not a specimen of *homo superior* at all. Just a man, empowered by courage and his own faith in right and wrong.

When Magneto found himself attempting deadly force against a fourteen-year-old X-Man named Kitty Pryde, he saw himself reflected in her eyes . . . and for the first time in decades saw himself as others saw him.

Had he become the kind of monster he sought to fight?

He withdrew his forces and went off alone, searching the places of his past for the critical moment when everything had begun to go wrong.

And he found it.

Magda had secretly been with child when she fled. She had given birth to twins. A beautiful girl, the image of her mother . . . a strong and healthy boy, the image of his father. And—life being a terrible and miraculous thing—they were not strangers to him, but people he already knew, people who he'd bullied and harassed and terrorized for years. They were the only family he'd had since the soldiers came . . . and they were lined up on the side of his enemies.

It was true. His whole life had been a lie.

But it didn't have to stay that way. No. He could turn his life around. He could atone for the omissions of the past. He could reach out to his son and daughter, make peace with them, and build a new future for all of them.

It all seemed so simple, to him. So cleancut. So easy a path to redemption

But they thought it was an attack. They fought him . . . And when he explained why he had come . . . they rejected him.

They told him his crimes were beyond all redemption.

They told him they wanted nothing to do with him.

They told him he'd always be their enemy.

They told him to leave.

The thundering footsteps of the approaching composite creature brought Magneto/Xavier back to consciousness. When they stumbled from the crater they'd gouged in the pavement, their eyes were filled with tears: tears that Magneto had always denied himself, that he had not been able to weep for decades.

They were wrong, Magnus. They should have forgiven you.

No, I was wrong. I can't afford family. Maybe once . . . but not anymore. Too much time has passed. Too much blood . . .

Maybe it was too late for them to accept you as a father . . . but it's never too late to offer compassion. Or redemption. Or even a second chance at trust.

It's too late for me.

No it's not! Remember when I left Earth to help Lilandra and invited you to run my school in my absence? Remember how you accepted, despite everything that had ever passed between us?

You were a fool.

I was a friend. *And I still am.*

Had Magneto possessed a voice of his own, he would have been speechless.

But voice or not, they'd run out of time. The composite creature built from the hapless people of Sunset Falls was almost upon them. All the faces that made up its skin were screaming.

Magneto/Xavier tried to shield themselves from the sheer heat of the psychic energy that preceded the thing like a blast wave, but couldn't block out the terror of all the people who suddenly knew the deepest and most shameful secrets of four hundred others all at once. A tidal wave of confusing images drove Magneto/Xavier to the ground: dirty little secrets, shameful little lies, grudges nursed but never revealed, love felt but never declared, the thousand and one thoughts that all human beings harbor in the most hidden parts of themselves—all mixed up in one cauldron and fed to the very people who had spent their entire lives keeping them hidden.

• *You loved me all those years* • *I didn't want you to know* • *I stole that money you were blamed for* • *I spy on you while you're sleeping* • *Remember what you did to me last year* • *My Daddy hits my Mommy* • *I need a drink* • *You're a liar* • *I hate mutants* • *I want to die* • *Leave me alone all of you get out of my head* •

The pavement shattered. A pipe snaked up out of the street, like a cobra preparing to strike, and blasted the creature with a faceful of cold water. It fell back, not from the water pressure, but from surprise. For an instant the psychic tidal wave relented.

Charles, we waste our time fighting that thing! That boy's our true enemy. If we have any hope at all, it's taking this battle back to him.

Agreed. Go!

Magneto/Xavier rose into the sky again, not wobbling at all this time, but rising straight up, with the steady grace of a rocket. They faltered once, fifty feet up, but they righted themselves almost immediately, and began to accelerate.

Not so fast, Magnus—it has to follow us. We have to lead it back to Joshua, so he can reverse what he's done.

I don't think following us is going to present that thing much difficulty, Charles . . .

The composite planted its gigantic feet against the ground and with a mighty thoom, launched itself into the air after the flying figure. Magneto/Xavier braced for impact. But controlled as it was by the minds of so many different people, most of whom were lost in the anguish of seeing their greatest secrets spread out before everybody they ever known, it wasn't exactly the most coordinated foe the two mutants had ever fought. Flailing wildly, it missed Magneto/Xavier by a good fifty feet and plunged earthward again, caving in the roof of the local video emporium. Four hundred shrieks of anger emerged from the hole. The building started shaking. The front window exploded in a shower of razor-sharp glass. The building imploded in a cloud of dust. The composite creature staggered from the smoke, looking pale, some of its faces still and unmoving.

Magneto/Xavier set down two blocks away in the front yard of the house on Metcalf Avenue. Joshua was still sitting on the front porch, puzzle-book in hand, tranquilly connecting the dots—mentally imposing his will on the printed page, not using a pencil. He blinked several times before he registered that the flying man was back. "Hello," said Joshua.

Magneto/Xavier hesitated. They were both used to enemies who knew they were enemies: people who spit bile and made speeches, declaring their eternal opposition to everything they stood for. They'd even fulfilled this function in each other's lives. Now, joined together, they faced a boy who didn't even know he was an enemy, a boy who in his own limited way of looking at things had only been trying to make things better. It didn't seem right to fight him. It wasn't the way to defeat him . . .

"You weren't connected to anything," Joshua explained. "You have to be connected to something."

"We were connected to a lot of things," they said, uncomfortably aware of the ominous thumping drumbeat that meant the composite creature was approaching. "Our beliefs, our causes, our pasts. We don't need you to do this to us."

Joshua remained tranquil. "I like to connect things."

The composite creature came around the corner, two blocks behind them. Magneto/Xavier heard its scream, and whirled to fight, but then they saw that it was dragging one leg, and having trouble remaining upright. It was still powerful, still dangerous. But it was failing. Dying fast. The strain of just being alive, in such a grotesque form, was proving too much for it.

Still, it would live more than long enough to kill Magneto/Xavier . . . if they let it. They concentrated, and a lamp-pole uprooted itself, twisted into a U-shape, and hurled itself at the creature. Four hundred faces contorted in agony as the pole encircled them, tying itself into a knot around their collective back. It grabbed for the pole and began to peel it back, but before it was even close to free another pair of lamp poles had come alive and encircled its legs. The creature stumbled, fell . . .

then sank massive fingers into the pavement and began to pull itself forward.

Magneto/Xavier would have summoned all the metal in town to cage it, but then Joshua attacked again, on the psychic plane. This time they weren't prepared at all. The energy surrounded them, infused them, became part of them. They felt their shared soul shrivelling, their shared body in flame; they staggered, fell to their knees, and for half a heartbeat saw a tenuous silver cord materializing between the composite and themselves.

"You've been fighting," said Joshua. "That means you know each other. That means I can connect you to them."

The silver cord drew taut. For an instant Magneto/Xavier felt themselves waver in and out as existence, as everything they were, was pulled toward the composite.

If they became part of that thing, they'd never be able to fight their way free.

With a massive effort of will, Magneto/Xavier stood, and gestured at the street between them and the inexorably approaching composite. Xavier's customized van crumpled into a mass of twisted metal, then lifted off the ground and hurled itself, not at the composite . . . but at the placidly concentrating boy on the porch of the house at the end of Metcalf Avenue. Joshua watched the oncoming missile without alarm, blinking not at all as it grew larger in the sky above him, his dull cowlike eyes showing no comprehension as it hurtled toward him with enough force to reduce the land where he sat to a smoking crater.

Magneto, stop, you'll kill him!

You underestimate me, Charles.

The van levelled off just before striking the boy, clearing the top of his head by mere inches, plowing into the front of the house instead. It hit with enough force to collapse the entire structure like a popped balloon. The roof buckled like a living thing, and shingles exploded outward and upward like confetti. A concussion wave lifted Joshua right off his seat and hurled him into the air. As he screamed, his arms and legs flailing, the glow linking Magneto/Xavier and the composite creature blinked out like a candle blown out by a strong wind.

Just getting the boy's attention.

Joshua stopped falling mere inches from the ground. For a heartbeat he dangled above the lawn like an object hanging from

an invisible string, then he up-ended and began to spin at dizzying speed.

*See? If I can keep him off-balance, I can keep him from using his
powers on us.*

*It's only a temporary solution, Magnus. You can't keep it up forever.
We're weakening as it is. And even if we weren't, it won't cure the people
of Sunset Falls . . . or us.*

I'm open to suggestions, Charles.

Just up the street, the composite creature rose to its feet,
having peeled off the last of the bonds that had imprisoned it.
The faces that covered its skin looked pale, almost diseased; most
of them were sweaty and still, their eyes closed, their expressions
slack. The few that remained conscious and alert were askew to
the point of insanity. When they spotted Magneto/Xavier, limp-
ing in circles by the house at the end of Metcalf Avenue, they all
contorted in rage. There was the enemy. There was the dirty
mutant freak who had done this to them. They would destroy
that enemy first, and then they would destroy the boy. It was the
only way to free them from the pain. Screeching hatred in a
multitude of voices, they stumbled forward.

Charles? If you do have an idea, you better hurry.

*I need your memory, Magnus! The one I sensed before! The mass grave!
Concentrate on it!*

Startled, Magneto complied.

He brought it all back as vividly as he could—more vividly than
he'd ever dared remember it before. He remembered a place of
darkness, a place of pain, a place where the faces and forms of
all the people he'd ever known had been reduced to just another
vast crushing weight, intent on stamping him down to nothingness. He remembered the love he'd felt for all those people
turned into hate, into revulsion, into the uncontrolled animal
need to claw himself free. He remembered being too paralyzed
by pain and fear and grief to fight, until the burning lime began
dribbling down through the corpses and the little boy he'd been
caught the first glimpse of the vengeance-driven monster he
would someday become.

And most of all he remembered the inner strength he'd never
known was his, that sprung out of nowhere to drive him upward
toward the light.

The vows to himself, burning like fire at the base of his spine.

I will not die.
I will not be buried here.
I will not be faceless in this pit.
I will claw myself free. I will live.

Exactly what the people of Sunset Falls needed to feel.

Xavier took those memories and focused every ounce of his considerable will on projecting them into each and every one of the four hundred minds trapped inside the composite. It stiffened at once, overcome with the memory . . . and every single unconscious face on its massive form suddenly narrowed its eyes, with a fresh resolve that was terrifying in its simple purity.

Escape.

Escape on the mind of Horace Wilson, the town dentist, who had fought in two wars and raised eight kids; escape on the mind of Jackie Frazier, the elementary school teacher, who painted in her spare time and worried constantly about her weight; escape in the mind of Joshua's mother, who lived day to day with the knowledge of what she had brought into the world. Escape on the mind of every citizen of Sunset Falls, who wanted to live as an individual, who needed to be human again. All fighting for freedom. All fighting Joshua.

And this time it was Joshua's mind that exploded with pain and anguish.

Nooooo! They're connected! They must stay connected!

A sphere of glowing green energy coalesced around the composite creature, sent by Joshua in a desperate attempt to force it to stay together against its will. The composite creature sank to its knees and roared, clutching its head with hammy fists. Magneto/Xavier's mind blared over the collected force of four hundred others: *Can't you see what you've done, Joshua? You've put all these people in hell!*

"I put them together! I connected them!"

You can't drive people together against their will! It's not right! You've got to understand, Joshua: it's our individuality that makes our connections so precious! You've turned that into an obscenity . . . and you have to be stopped!

"No!" Joshua screamed, his voice cracking. "*They must be connected!*"

And a louder voice, erupting from four hundred minds: "*No! We must be free!*"

The peaceful valley that cradled Sunset Falls erupted with blinding green light . . . which pulsed . . . flared . . . and was gone.

When Charles Xavier awoke, sprawled in the middle of the street, the sun was much lower in the sky. The overwhelming impression was quiet: not just the familiar, discomfiting silence that rules all battlegrounds, once the armies have all gone home, but the silence that came from once again being alone in his own mind, without Magneto's thoughts threading in and out of his own. He scanned the surrounding area, as he always did upon waking, and found it uncomfortably quiet too. The people of Sunset Falls were present, but they were all unconscious, and lost in the oblivion of dreamless sleep. He craned his neck, and saw that they were all around him: crumpled on the shattered pavement just like he was, like dolls dropped from a height.

The only mind he sensed was Magneto's. And, as always, he couldn't read that mind at all—he could only sense the tremendous rage and tremendous sadness that had always marked the man's presence. A mixture that Xavier now understood for the very first time in all the years they'd known each other.

Something shiny circled high overhead, lost in the glare of the sun. An airplane? One of Magneto's allies? A new menace?

Xavier squinted, and recognized it. Of course. So obvious . . . now.

A wheelchair.

It descended quickly, landing with a soft pat right beside Xavier. It was not the same wheelchair Xavier had been using earlier, which must have been destroyed with the van, but another one, apparently freshly liberated from some local drug store or hospital. A gift, for him. Xavier winced, not entirely out of physical pain alone, as invisible hands gently levitated him off the ground, and lowered him to a seated position on the canvas seat.

"Thank you," said Xavier.

Magneto alighted a second later, once again clad in the familiar red armor. "The least I can do," he said, averting his eyes. "When we were . . . together . . . I had a small taste of what it feels like, for you. I always imagined they were insensate . . . as they would be if you were merely paralyzed. But it's more than just paralysis, isn't it? They're crushed. They hurt all the time."

Xavier saw no reason to lie about it. "Yes."

"So we have more in common than I ever thought."

"I never doubted it," said Xavier. "We both come from shattered families. We're both driven by our separate visions of what's best for the future of our people. We both pay the price for our lonely uphill battle every single day of our lives. But I think we both understand that a little bit more, today. It may make things more difficult, the next time we have to fight each other . . . which is probably all for the best."

"And Joshua?"

Xavier looked around, and found the one crumpled form among hundreds, lying unconscious by the house at the end of Metcalf Avenue. "He is still alive. But the psychic feedback of all those people fighting him at the same time utterly erased his mind—destroying everything that he was. It's possible that I might be able to reach him some day, to give him another chance at life, but for now he's a total vegetable. His threat is over."

"Not something I'll mourn. He was . . . monstrous."

"Was he? Think about it. Think about what he could have done with his power had he only possessed enough of a mind to understand it. He could make people see their worst enemies from the inside. He could force them to see and experience the ties that bind us all. He could make peace where before there was only war. He could have been the end to all the battles that humanity has ever fought. And he could have been the end to all the meaningless battles between you and I."

Xavier gestured at the unconscious citizens of Sunset Falls. "Within hours, all these people will be waking up, with the worst headaches of their lives. The trauma was worse for them, and it will almost certainly prevent them from remembering much of what happened here. They will only know that they lived through a nightmare, and that the nightmare is done; they won't be able to use any of what they learned about their neighbors and themselves, to grow, or change, or live better lives. But we remember what we lived through, Magnus. We remember what we learned about each other, and how for a few precious minutes we rebuilt the trust that was shattered so long ago. Are we just going to forget it ever happened? Or are we going to just go on fighting each other, year after year, in an endless, pointless war that can only end with one of us being forced to kill the other?"

Magneto shook his head with exasperation. "You're an annoying man, Xavier."

"You've made your own share of long-winded speeches, in your time. But don't change the subject. Will we find common ground, or not?"

The silence stretched between them, amplifying the distance between the two men who'd spent so many years proving it possible to be friends, and strangers, and mortal enemies, and brothers—all at the same time.

And then Magneto slumped, all at once, and heaved the kind of sigh reserved for men who have seen far too much wasted blood. "I'm sorry," he said. "I can't. Too much time has passed, too many battles have been fought. And the one time you persuaded me to give your way a chance—when you handed me your school—it fell to pieces in my hands. We will have to be enemies again, the next time we meet."

"If so," Xavier said grimly, "I don't suppose either one of us has ever regretted it more."

Under normal circumstances, Magneto would have said something else: he'd never been the kind of man capable of letting others have the last word. But what Xavier had spoken had been in his own heart as well: and continuing this meaningless discussion would only distract him from the world conquest that he saw as the only hope of saving his people. And so, he nodded, and turned away, and rose into the sky above Sunset Falls, without looking back.

Loki

FIRETRAP

MICHAEL JAN FRIEDMAN

Illustration by Ron Frenz & Patrick Olliffe

S OFTLY, SILENTLY, HE floated through the frigid, twisting sheets of snow and hail—a horn-helmed wraith, thin to the point of emaciation, wrapped tight in a cloak the color of Envy.

At least, it was the color *mortals* painted Envy, given their pitifully limited range of experience. In truth, he knew, Envy wasn't green at all. It was more of a purplish thing, with deep networks of black, throbbing veins running through it—but then, it would take a god to know that, and not just any god.

Only him. Only Loki.

He gazed from beneath the horns of his snow-crusted helm on the blizzard-bound city called New York. All in all, he reflected, it was not so different from Jotunheim, the icebound kingdom of his birth. Like Jotunheim, it had its share of brutality, of swift and random violence. Like Jotunheim, it had its share of blind, unfeeling cruelty.

Except tonight. Tonight, there was no one on the streets. It was too cold, too icy, too dangerous to be plying one's vehicle through thoroughfares choked with wild, drifting snow.

Instead, the mortals who lived here had abandoned their— (What were they called again? Autocars or some such thing?)— their auto*mobiles* all along the sidewalks, parked at odd angles wherever they could be squeezed in. As these desperate beings were fond of saying, it was not a fit night out for man nor beast.

But a god . . . well, that was a different story. Especially the god whom superstitious Earthers had called Mischief-Worker and Joy-Slayer and Peace-Breaker. Someone like him was undaunted by such trivialities as weather. After all, he had business to take care of in this most dreary of the Nine Worlds.

And rather urgent business, at that.

A ghost of frozen spindrift sidled up to him, then whirled away. Loki laughed—an ugly sound, he knew, but one he'd grown used to. Even a ghost knew better than to keep company with the shifty-eyed snake in Odin's Eden.

That rather amusing image had only just occurred to him when he saw a glow of red in the distance, half-obscured by the billowing snow. It resembled an angry ember, he thought. Or a bloody wound. He was, after all, fond of such self-styled poetry.

In fact, it was neither of these things. As he drifted closer to the glow, his cloak flapping viciously in the wind, he saw that it was a fire in one of the city's older and less cared-for buildings.

A *tenement*, he reflected, in the words of the mortals themselves. In times past, the word had meant only that someone lived there. Now, in this place and age, it suggested minimum standards of sanitation, safety, and comfort.

In short, a place inhabited by the poor, who had no power to withstand the whims of their lords. Loki grinned at the concept. After all, fire was the surest recipe for misery.

The closer he wafted, the easier it was to see the serpent-tongued flames and the roiling, black smoke—and the wide-eyed scarecrow figures inadequately dressed for such weather, who'd rushed out into the night rather than be char-broiled within.

Such drama, he mused. *Such pathos.*

Even separated from them by curtain after curtain of driven sleet, he could taste their fear and anger and hopelessness. He could revel in their unmitigated terror as they watched their home burn savagely, out of control.

In the greater distance, he could see a pack of firefighters careening toward the scene in their blood-red trucks, exhibiting courage that well exceeded the mortal norm. Even their sirens sounded brave, though they were muffled by the howling of the storm.

Still, with conditions being what they were, it was clear to Loki these men would never arrive in time to accomplish anything. That was unfortunate for the mortals below him—not that the mischief-god cared in the least.

Mortals were insects. They deserved whatever horrors came their way.

As an example, he chose the several people still trapped in the blazing tenement house. Floating closer to a top-floor window, he caught a glimpse of three of them, quivering before their fate like a clutch of startled birds.

If events followed their natural course, these denizens of Earth would breathe their last this night. They would die a hideous and—for him, at least—delicious death.

They had but one hope. One chance at what passed for survival in this bleak and wretched land.

As Loki watched, the skin of his face stretched taut under the onslaught of the elements, that hope manifested itself . . . in a streak of red and a flash of blue that made the god's jaw clench in black-biled hatred.

These were the colors of the mighty Thor, God of Thunder—Loki's stepbrother and rival for Odin's throne in Asgard—and most importantly, his sworn enemy.

Every age in the history of Time had rung with the sound of their battles. Loki had always played the conniver, the subtle puppet-master, the spinner of great plots. In short, the villain.

And Thor, who was Odin's natural son, always played the fair-haired hero. The one who triumphed by dint of strength, devotion to duty and—let it be said openly—his incredible, odds-defying luck.

Loki felt his lip curling at the thought of it. If there were any justice in the Nine Worlds, he'd have been the only sun in Odin's firmament by now.

But somehow, frustration of frustrations, Thor always managed to survive. To prosper. To be everything Loki was not.

Then again, he sneered, there was a first time for everything.

As the mischief-maker hovered, Thor approached the tenement like a bolt of lightning, dragged along behind the mystical hammer the dwarves had fashioned for him. Without a thought for his own well-being, he crashed through a soot-blackened window and was instantly obscured from sight by the snapping flames.

The mischief-god shook his head in gleeful derision. Such a creature of habit, his stepbrother. So predictable.

In a tumultuous storm like this one, Thor was sure to be lending help wherever it was needed. Even an idiot would know that. And certainly, his help was needed *here*.

Loki smiled. It was Thor's predictability that would be his downfall. Everyone knew he had a soft spot for these mortals.

So, for the sake of argument, he remarked inwardly, *if one were to . . . oh, set a trap for the thunder god . . . this tenement fire would be a serviceable lure, would it not? A* more *than serviceable lure.*

His smile widened considerably, until it wrapped halfway around his head and erased any illusion that he was like other beings. There was only one Loki—and of all creatures, only he saw all the possibilities.

Still grinning, he followed Thor into the building—not

through the broken window, as someone else might have, but by melting through the hot, brick wall beside it.

To be sure, the Norn sisters' magicks had their uses. Hardly a day went by that he wasn't grateful for having studied their ways as a child.

His thoughts were wending in the wrong direction when he pulled them back on course. *No distractions,* Loki told himself. Not tonight, when he would need his wits about him.

Hovering in the flames unscathed, he looked on as Thor encircled the three trapped people in his cloak and, hurling his hammer, followed it out through the broken window. A moment later, Loki saw through the wall—another gift of his studies under the Norns—that the thunder-god had landed thigh-deep in a drift of snow and set the mortals on safe ground.

Then, hearing the screams of other mortals over the roar of the flames, Thor whirled his hammer again and hurtled back toward the window. Watching from behind a wall of flames, Loki saw Thor re-enter the place and slide to a halt in the smoke-filled room.

For a moment, there were no screams at all, and the thunder god seemed at a loss. Holding his hand up to shield him from the blaze, he peered this way and that, searching. Then the chorus of panicked shrieks started up again and he knew which way to go.

Twirling his hammer before him like a mighty fan to keep the flames at bay, Thor made his way into the heart of the fiery structure. The heat there was incredible, the firelight and the smoke enough to blind any mere man. Despite it all, he plunged ahead like a big, mangy dog, too stupid to come out of the rain.

Typical, thought Loki. His stepbrother was always blundering forward, fixated on doing good without any appreciation for the bigger picture.

And *this* was Odin's favorite son!

Finally, Thor reached the core of the conflagration. Again, he looked around, his ice-blue eyes seeking someone to rescue.

But there was no one there to deliver, no one clamoring for a big, blond-haired savior. Not anymore. Only a ring of flame that surrounded him on every side.

Loki snorted. *Surprise, surprise.*

Then the rest of the scene unfolded, as a single, misshapen

form separated itself from the flames—and burned even brighter on its own. So bright, in fact, that it was hard for even the mischief-maker to keep an eye on it.

Even before this being could identify himself, Loki chanted his name silently, in the confines of his own skull. The lumbering newcomer was Hrok—prince and heir to Surtur, lord of the fire-giants in Muspelheim.

Loki had seen the shambling, molten-skinned warrior before, in the course of his travels—just as he'd seen the ill-formed, volcanic forces that swirled about Hrok, hungry for a thunder god's soul.

"Who are you?" Thor bellowed. "What is your purpose here?"

Always the direct approach. Loki sighed. Apparently, you really *can't* teach a god new tricks.

The fire-giant laughed—a sound like the crackling of logs in a blazing hearth. His eyes, imperfect orbs that glowed red like coals, narrowed with unholy glee.

"I am Hrok," he rasped, "eldest of the Surtursons. And you are the bumbling fool who pranced so willingly into my trap."

By then, Loki mused, Thor had to have realized what was happening to him. By the Norn-Queen's wicked smile, even a *stone* would have figured it out.

"There were no screaming mortals in *this* room," Hrok boasted. "It was only an illusion, designed to bring you to me." With an awkward gesture, he indicated the fiery forces roiling behind him. "And now, I have succeeded."

"Succeeded at what?" Thor thundered.

"Of your own volition," the Surturson cackled, "you've crossed over the line between worlds—onto the very threshold of Muspelheim."

Looking down at his feet, Thor saw that it was true. The expression on his face was absolutely priceless, Loki mused.

"And once I've drawn you in the rest of the way," Hrok went on, "you'll twist over infernal fires for the remainder of your immortal days."

Loki found the image rather appealing. But then, he was fond of most anything that involved Thor's agony.

"More importantly," Hrok added, "I will be feared throughout the Nine Worlds. I will be known as the most powerful of magicians, for how else could I have made the thunder god my eternal prisoner?''

In other words, Loki remarked inwardly, *the youngling's reputation will have been made. And all in one fell swoop. Or more accurately, one fallen swain.*

"By Odin's beard," Thor cried, "I am no one's entertainment. I am a prince of Asgard—and if need be, I'll die like one!"

Hrok smiled a crooked smile. "That would be the next best thing," he said, "to be known as the mage who destroyed the mighty Thor."

Abruptly, it became apparent that the time for words was over. The battle was about to be joined.

With a grasping gesture, not unlike that of a mortal orchestra conductor demanding a crescendo, the Surturson called forth a firestorm of immense power and magnitude—and brought it down on his enemy's head.

Loki didn't think his stepbrother could withstand that kind of onslaught. He was only half right.

Whirling his hammer as before, Thor managed to create a tiny pocket of protection for himself. It wasn't much against all of Hrok's power. It didn't keep the room from filling with the smell of burnt hair and burnt flesh. But it was enough to keep the thunder god alive.

Then Hrok redoubled his efforts. The firestorm blossomed into something even greater, something even more deadly—a vast, blistering, molten vision of apocalypse. There hadn't been anything like it in the Nine Worlds since life took hold in Midgard's primordial seas.

Thor was a god, but he was still made of flesh and blood, and no match for such an inferno. Ever so gradually, though his heart refused to yield, his flesh betrayed him. He was driven to one knee by the sheer malevolence of Hrok's attack.

Dehydrated and deprived of oxygen by the explosive heat, the thunder god began to falter. To lose consciousness. And finally, to sprawl forward on what remained of the floor.

Loki grunted in admiration for the Surturson. *Not bad for a beginner,* he mused. *Not bad at all.*

But he had no intention of letting this confrontation progress to the conclusion Hrok had in mind.

"Pardon me," said the mischief-maker, drifting forward

through the wall of flame assailing his stepbrother. "I hate to spoil your fun, but . . ."

Gathering his mystical resources, Loki sent a prodigious blast of frigid, snow-laden air howling at the Surturson. It caused Hrok to desist for a moment, to stop short of turning Thor into a blackened husk.

The fire-giant seemed annoyed as he turned to face Loki. His molten face twisted with anger.

"I know you, second son of Odin. What is your business here?" he crackled.

Loki shrugged his narrow shoulders. "In case you hadn't heard, Thor is *my* adversary—and my kinsman as well. I don't think Odin would be very pleased with me if I let him fall to one of *your* kind."

Hrok took a lumbering step forward. "You would fight me for him—when I'm carrying out *your* purpose as well as mine?"

"My purpose is to *win*," the mischief-maker told him. "Not to watch someone else do it. In other words, you can't have my stepbrother—no matter what it would mean to your reputation."

The Surturson raised his huge fist and shook it at Loki. "I warn you, Trickster. I was tutored by the same Norn witch-women who instructed you in the darkest of magics."

Loki harrumphed. "The Norns only gave me my start," he corrected. "Experience has made me what I am today—astute enough, for instance, to sense your magical snare all the way from Asgard."

The fire-giant bellowed his rage, unable to control himself. After all, he was so close to fulfilling his ambition. Unwilling to give up on it now, Hrok brought back his arm and let it fly forward, propelling a multitude of heat daggers at his adversary. But Loki was ready for them.

Filling his lungs, he exhaled with all his might—and dissolved the oncoming heat daggers with a blast of arctic air. Before the fire-giant could recover, Loki wove a spindly-fingered gesture of his own in the air before him—and suddenly, Hrok was encased in a thick sheathe of impenetrable ice.

Sweeping aside his cloak with a flourish, the trickster revealed the enchanted sword that dangled from his belt. Even within the encasing ice, the fire-giant must have seen what he intended—though, of course, he could do nothing about it.

Advancing on Hrok, Loki turned the sword over in his hand. "Give my regards to your father," he told the Surturson. "And be sure to tell him how much pain I caused you."

Then he lifted his blade above his head and brought it down square in the center of Hrok's forehead. As sparks flew helter-skelter from the impact, the ice—and Hrok himself—cracked right down the middle.

There was a long, low whimper of agony, as the fire-giant collapsed in a pool of his own molten, steaming blood. But he didn't remain that way for long.

As Loki looked on, Hrok's body and the icy shards that clung to it slithered away over the fiery threshold of Muspelheim, where—after much care and anguish—the Surturson would no doubt be made whole again. But it would be a long time before Hrok presumed to attack Thor or any other Asgardian.

Satisfied with the outcome, Loki turned to his stepbrother, who was still endangered by the fire consuming the tenement. Enveloping him in his own personal squall, the Trickster not only shielded him from the flames, but roused him to consciousness.

Then he hid behind a wall that was still relatively intact and waited. It took a while before the thunder god groaned and rolled over, and a few seconds more for him to open his eyes. They seemed even bluer in a face streaked black with soot.

Little by little, Thor seemed to remember where he was and what had transpired. Slowly, he got to his feet and looked around.

Still concealed behind the wall, Loki could easily imagine the questions Thor was asking himself. What happened to Hrok? Why did the fire-giant fail to kill him when he had the chance? Indeed, why go to all this trouble just to leave the thunder god where he found him—still alive, still whole?

The mischief-maker didn't feel the need to stay any longer. Melting backward through the outer wall of the building, he wrapped his cloak about himself and spiralled upward into the blizzard-bound dome of heaven.

But before the city below him was lost to sight, he looked down and saw a figure streak through its skies, pulled by a dark, grey hammer. Loki grinned. Odin's lapdog was at it again.

Someday, he vowed, the thunder god would fall—and fall hard. But when that day came, it would be by Loki's hand and no one else's.

Softly, silently, he vanished into the storm.

The Ringmaster

IF WISHES WERE HORSES

TONY ISABELLA AND
BOB INGERSOLL

Illustration by Paul Ryan

THEY HAD TAKEN to playing the smaller venues to avoid larger problems. When they played Madison Square Garden, it seemed like every masked nuisance from the Avengers to Zorro would line up to take them down. But the small towns were different. Spider-Man was a New Yorker. He wouldn't follow them to Columbia, Missouri. Daredevil didn't know from Duluth. And, for all his prodigious leaping about, the Hulk had never been seen in Provo.

Which was precisely why the "MacFadden Brothers Circus" had come to Peoria, Illinois. It was perfect for their needs, large enough to have good crowds, small enough to be ignored.

All around the fairgrounds, the roustabouts and hired hands labored to put up the big top and midway for the evening's show. The grunt of straining muscles merged with the smell of liniment as the massive, brightly colored tent was raised high above their heads. There had been unforeseen delays on the road coming here and so they struggled to make up the lost time, working against both the clock and their own fatigue.

In his wagon, the Ringmaster of this circus faced a struggle of his own as he inhaled deeply and tugged at a morning coat that seemed to get tighter each year. So much was a struggle of late.

"Hey, Maynard," a voice called from outside his wagon, "Are you decent?"

The Ringmaster tapped a button on the side of his dressing table. Silent hydraulics opened the door to his wagon suddenly, so that he could simply appear in it bowing from the waist. He was ever the showman looking for an entrance.

"My dear Zelda, am I ever otherwise? But, please, you know I prefer to be called the Ringmaster. Maynard Tiboldt may, indeed, be my given name, but not, I assure you, the one I would have given myself. Now then, what can I do for you?"

As he looked at Zelda DuBois, the circus's snake charmer who performed under the name Princess Python, the Ringmaster was glad of two things: that she was wearing her very attractive, and very tight, costume, and that her infernal pet snake was not with her. He hated how the nasty beast would literally get underfoot at the most inconvenient times.

Then the Ringmaster saw the check Zelda was holding and he became glad of a third thing.

"Just wanted to tell you Mrs. Huddleston stopped by with her check," she said, smiling sweetly as she displayed the bank draft at eye-level with her abundant bosom. And when he took the check from her, she let out a breathy sigh.

Showmanship, he thought to himself. She had always been one of his best students.

"I do so love it when a charity buys out the house as a fund-raiser. It seems to be the only time we sell out lately. I have thanked you for arranging this booking while I was indisposed, have I not?"

"Not nearly enough," the princess cooed. "But I expect that some new costumes for our drab little band would settle accounts. You would look quite handsome in the red coat and black pants."

The Ringmaster glanced down at his bright green morning coat with its embroidered black stars and startling purple pants beneath it and he smiled self-consciously.

"This was the color scheme my father favored when he was the owner and ringmaster of this circus, my princess, long before you joined our little troupe. I wear it in memory of those marvelous times. A family tradition, if you will."

The Ringmaster had not spoken, nor scarcely thought, for that matter, of his father in years. But, as soon as he mentioned the late Fritz Tiboldt, he found himself thinking back to those days, those glorious days, when the wonder of the circus was the center of his existence.

Around him, Austria was rebuilding from the damage, physical and psychological, inflicted on it by the Second World War. But, as the country was only Maynard's homeland and not his true home, the young man paid little heed.

Beyond Austria, Europe was likewise digging itself out from under the rubble. London was healing from the destruction caused by the V2 rockets that had dropped on her like the hard rain of a hurricane, but the other great cities weren't as lucky.

Berlin lived as a city divided. Dresden was battered beyond recognition. Throughout Europe, even a decade after the war, one could see the twisted, charred remains of it, buildings that looked like nothing so much as gnarled, knobbed, skeletal fingers reaching up from the grave.

But that was Europe and Europe was not Maynard's world. His world reached to the distant corners of central Europe, bringing with it a hope that other world so desperately needed.

It was the circus his family owned and operated. The animals and their trainers. Acrobats. Clowns. Beautiful riders on great horses. The strongman, the fire-eater, and all the rest. His world was no more vast than the perimeter of the colorful tent that held it and a world that knew no borders.

To be young and living in the circus; there was, Maynard had decided, no better way to grow up. To have sawdust in his blood, cotton candy in his heart. To know that no matter how many times he saw the big top, he always saw it with the same awe as the first time. For a ten-year-old boy, it was a magical time of life, a time to love every moment. Every sight. Every sound. Every smell, even the ones coming from the elephant pen.

And the very best part of it was that his world didn't exist just for him. It existed for the people in that sad and battered other world. His world's purpose—its very reason for being—was nothing more, nor less, than to bring joy and wonder and magic to the rest of the world. To make the other world a better place by sharing the smiles of his world.

Maynard wanted nothing more than to be a part of that magic, to continue his family's proud tradition. But he had not decided how he would fit into the circus. He was ten, long past the time to begin his training, to prepare himself for the one special act he would perform, and he had yet to determine what that act would be. His indecision was a weight on his young shoulders. What if he would never find his passion?

"You worry too much, Maynard," his father told him when once he found the courage to give voice to his fear. "You can't force the calling. You must wait for it to come to you.

"And come it will. You will not know when or why. But, one day, you will see something and you will know that it is the most important, the most beautiful thing there is, that it is what you want to do, above all else. I envy you the moment, my son, it is a wonderful, magical moment in a performer's life."

His father's words were comforting to Maynard, but they grew less so as the weeks passed without him hearing the calling. And then one day, when some trifling dispute with the authorities had temporarily closed their own circus, his father took him to see a performance of the Royal Lippizan Stallions.

From the first moment Maynard saw those magnificent steeds—their shimmering white coats and their milky manes blowing in the wind—he was mesmerized. Yes, he had seen the horses in American cowboy movies perform their tricks, Tom Mix's wonder pony and Roy Rogers's Trigger. But these stallions were so much more elegant and stately. They were the most beautiful things Maynard had ever seen. At that moment, he knew what he wanted to do. And he hoped and prayed and wished—how he wished—that someday he would ride such horses in his family's circus.

Soon, there was nothing else in Maynard's life. He rode the Tiboldt Family Circus horses and trained. Chores, studies, play, these were of no concern.

At first, the elder Tiboldt allowed his son some leeway, for he did not want to deny Maynard his magical moment. But, after a time, he stepped in to remind the boy that, even from those who'd found their calling, there were other things, important things to be attended to as well. Maynard agreed reluctantly. But, though he no longer neglected chores and studies, he rushed through them so that he could return to his horses that much sooner.

For months, Maynard rode the horses, training and preparing, living in the magic of the moment and never once thinking that it would end.

Until, of course, it did.

He was performing a particularly difficult standing transfer between horses when Maynard's own mount reared unexpectedly. He fell, landing beneath the hooves of the horse he was transferring to. It came down on the boy's leg with its full weight, snapping the fibia. It barely missed his head. Through the pain, Maynard could see every detail of the hooves dancing inches away from his face. It was an image he would never forget.

The other riders told him that, if you fall from your horse, you must brush yourself off and get right back on. But Maynard's injury prevented him from doing that.

In the torpid weeks that followed, while he healed so damned slowly, Maynard could think of nothing but what happened. How he had never anticipated the horse's sudden shift. How he had never suspected it would throw him. How, for all his arrogant belief that he had mastered the horse, he had not. He was, and always would be, at the mercy of the beast.

When Maynard did return to his horses, he was more conscious of the fact that he could be thrown in the twinkling of an eye, could be hurt again, could even die. He could still ride, but never with the same abandon he had once enjoyed. He was hesitant and tentative, no longer confident of his ability to perform the tricks he had so recently mastered. Uncertain that he could ever control the beast.

In his heart, Maynard knew he would never be able to ride in the circus. He had held that moment his father had promised him, but it had slipped through his hands like the reins of the horse. The magic was fading.

"Ringmaster, are you all right?"

The Ringmaster shook his head and looked at Princess Python, strangely moved by the look of concern on her face.

"Forgive me, Princess. I was simply lost, for a moment, in memories of days long past."

"They must have been some pretty good ones for you to blank out that way."

"They were, for the most part, pleasant, yes."

Ringmaster walked to the safe in his wagon, spun the dial to unlock it, and set Mrs. Huddleston's check within. He closed the door, spun the dial once more, and turned back to Python.

"Are the others ready for tonight?" he asked.

"Yes."

"Everyone?"

"*Yes*, Maynard."

"Very well. Just so everyone knows, I want them at top form tonight. Whatever else we may be, we are a circus. I don't want any replays of that last unfortunate incident."

The Ringmaster frowned as he thought back to that last show. Despite his many warnings that the troupe had to keep its mind on the performance, Luigi Gambonno—that oaf—was thinking well past the acrobatic act he and his brother put on; thinking of when the Ringmaster would take center stage to commence the evening's real festivities. Thinking so hard of it, in fact, that he missed his take-off on a back handspring to a twisting back flip combination and landed quite spectacularly on his back. It was nothing short of humiliating for the standing of the circus, and the Ringmaster had had to make certain no one in the audience would remember the incident. He had nearly done far worse to Luigi.

"I spoke with Luigi this morning," Princess Python reassured the Ringmaster. "I informed him that any repeat of that incident might prompt me to send my pet after him. And you know how Luigi feels about snakes."

The Ringmaster smiled beneath his waxed moustache. The idea of Luigi with the Princess's pet might be worth the embarrassment of another gaffe. But, no, the professional stature of the circus must remain intact.

"Thank you, Zelda. You have blossomed into a most efficient second-in-command. My mother, for all her devotion to him, could never have been that for my father. If he'd had someone like you to assist him with our circus, things might have gone differently for us back then."

The crowds had stopped coming. After the war, the people of Europe had needed a diversion and they came to the circus looking for, yearning for, magic. But, as their scarred memories scabbed over, they turned their gaze and resources to other pursuits: new buildings, refurbished shops, restored factories. They looked to a wizardry more practical than that to be found in the tents of a small travelling circus.

After far too many months of dwindling crowds, Fritz Tiboldt took circus and family to America, where, he hoped, that nation's post-war boom would offer them new and eager audiences. But that very prosperity worked against them in their new land.

In every city, suburbs grew with relatively affordable tract housing that would allow returning GI's to co-own their slice of the American Dream. But, to live in their new homes, they needed cars to take them to work. Mortgage payments and car loans; they paid dearly for their dreams.

In virtually every one of those dream houses, as Fritz would learn, there was a television set; entertainment that came to the Americans, so that they did not have to go out for it. And, when they did go out, it was to movies—grand spectaculars in the new, wide-screen formats to showcase what movies offered that even the upstart television could not.

A new music—rock and roll—sounded across the nation. It, too, stole the audience and their dollars from the Tiboldt Family Circus as it screamed from radios and record players.

And, if all this weren't enough, out in California there was— what was it called?—Disneyland. Acres of flamboyant rides and attractions, all to commemorate—the madness—some cartoon mouse. But everyone wanted to go to Disneyland, saving and scrimping for months so that they could afford to fly or take the train all the way to the west coast.

It was a lean time for the circuses. They were the old joy, hardly television or rock and roll or Disneyland. They were what one's parents did and they held little appeal to a new generation trying to assert itself, establish its own identity.

Many of the smaller shows failed. Even the biggest had been forced to consolidate rather than compete with each other for the remains of their audience.

The Tiboldt Family Circus somehow managed to survive. Those years in post-war Europe had taught it to be a lean operation, so it survived. Barely, and it did not thrive, but it survived. It travelled the back roads and rutted fields of America looking for new audiences, new venues.

And, while the father searched desperately for some brighter tomorrow, his son again looked for an act.

The old trunk was battered from countless years of travel in a bumpy circus wagon. Its hinges were more rust than metal. Its color, whatever it had been, was now the nondescript shade of the overcast sky. It squatted in the farthest corner of their wagon, back in the shadows. Certainly not the place where Maynard might expect to find an idea for his act. But he felt the need to look inside the trunk nonetheless.

He could not have said why this was so. Perhaps because the trunk was so aged and weathered. Perhaps because he'd never seen it before, as if his father did not want him to find it. Perhaps because it, of all the trunks and storage areas in the wagon, had a lock on it. But, when Maynard saw it, he knew he had to see in it as well.

Picking the lock was easily done. Though he lacked the fine

dexterity necessary for performance, the skills he'd gleaned from their long-since-retired magician served Maynard well.

The contents of the trunk initially disappointed him. Old photo albums and older clothes almost jumped out at him, bursting forth from years of being squeezed into the overstuffed trunk and straining constantly against the sides and the lock.

Maynard knew he would not be able to replace the contents as they had been. Then he realized that no one had opened the trunk for years and would likely not open it again for as long. He had only to get everything back into the trunk and lock it again. No one would know he had been inside.

The teen went through the trunk as a prospector sifting sand through his pan, expecting to find nothing but watching carefully so that he would not overlook anything either.

Which is how he found the journal.

It was inside a folded shirt, carefully secreted between the layers of linen. It was a small journal in his father's own hand.

Maynard flipped through the pages, reading a random passage but finding nothing of particular interest in his father's simple reflections from those early days when he was learning how to run a circus. Nothing of interest, that is, until the several sheets of folded paper, placed toward the rear of the journal, fell into Maynard's lap.

They were plans, detailed schematic drawings for a fantastic device called a Nullatron. Maynard did not understand everything in the drawings, but what he could glean indicated this Nullatron was a hypnosis device the German war effort had developed for the Red Skull.

The Red Skull? Wasn't he that Nazi agent who had fought the legendary Captain America during the war? Yes, that was the name he had heard mentioned, or, more accurately, whispered, as people spoke of those bleak days. The Red Skull. But why, he wondered, would his father, a simple and humble circus operator, have plans for a device commissioned by that war criminal?

Maynard no longer skimmed the journal. He found the section covering the war years and read it carefully, determined to learn what connected his father to the Red Skull.

He did not have to read far.

It was in 1941, shortly before America entered World War II. Fritz Tiboldt took his travelling circus to America on the direct orders of Berlin, using the magic and the merriment of the circus as a cover for covert operations designed to eliminate persons important to the American war effort.

Maynard's eyes opened wide in horror as he read the journal, the way they had widened when, as a child in Austria, he had seen, and later read, *Frankenstein*. But this was no imagined horror from the mind of a nineteenth-century woman or inspired Hollywood director, no fiction crafted to induce chills in its readers. This was the true story of how his father had killed—murdered—in the name of an unspeakable evil.

This was the story of, not just how his father had murdered, but how he had used their family circus and its singular magic in that foul task, despoiling, violating, perverting the magic until he was, at last, stopped by Captain America.

Awaiting execution for his murders, the elder Tiboldt's life was spared when a fortunate, albeit mysterious, prisoner exchange returned him to Germany. He had never questioned his mission; he would likewise never question his deliverance.

"I had hoped you would never find that."

Maynard turned to see his father standing in the wagon. He had been so absorbed in the journal that he had failed to realize Fritz Tiboldt had entered the wagon until he heard the sad voice, familiar, and yet somehow that of a stranger, calling to him from a world that would never, could never, be the same.

Maynard retreated into the shadows at the rear of the wagon, stared at his father uncertainly, wondering fearfully what such a man, a man who could use his circus to kill, might be capable of even now.

Fritz Tiboldt smiled weakly and held out his open hand in a gesture that demanded the book while, he hoped, allaying the fear he saw in his son's eyes. As he took it from Maynard's trembling hand, he spoke as softly as he could.

"I should have destroyed this years ago."

Maynard could only look up at his father with ill-disguised fury, but when he tried to put words to his rage, it came out as nothing more than a child's timorous question.

"Why?"

"I was an Austrian. Austria was part of Germany and Germany was at war. It was my duty. Can you see that? Can you see that duty can make a man do things he would not do otherwise?"

Maynard stared deeply into his father's eyes as they started to mist over. He delighted in the old man's pain, but found that he could not bring himself to add to it.

"Yes, Papa," he lied.

"Good. Then let us say nothing more about this. Maybe it's a good thing, your finding this. Now maybe I'll have the courage to do what I should have done so many years ago."

Fritz Tiboldt dropped the journal into a waste basket. Then he threw his arms around Maynard, embracing him. Maynard allowed himself to be hugged, but did not, could not, return the embrace. He stiffened involuntarily at the touch. His father stepped back as if he had been shot. The too-long silence that followed ended with a sad smile and a weak wave.

"Run along now, Maynard. You have chores and I have . . . a bit of cleaning up to do."

They would never talk of these things again.

Maynard ran down the nearly-deserted midway, heading nowhere in particular, just away from his father. When he leaned against Madame Leah's wagon, gasping for breath, his hand brushed against the carefully folded papers he had placed in his coat just before his entire world changed.

The Nullatron plans.

Maynard chuckled bitterly as he realized what his circus act would be. It was all so perfect. He would study this Nullatron, use it to become the greatest hypnotist the world would ever see. He would use its secrets to return to the circus a portion of the magic his father had taken from it.

Yes, he knew what his act would be. But it was not with the same wonder that he had felt years earlier, when he saw the Royal Lippizans. That magic was gone, and once gone, it could never be recaptured. Only echoed imperfectly.

"Boy, you should see all the limousines pullin' up outside," the Clown snickered, his actual smile broad and visible under the fake smile applied to his face with grease paint. "Didn't figure there'd be so many fat cats in a hick berg like this. This ain't gonna be like takin' candy from babies, it'll be like pullin' the silver spoons right outta their mouths."

The Ringmaster glanced past the Clown at the winding line of sleek, black, chauffeur-driven automobiles pulling up to the main tent. Yes, it would be a good show, a profitable show.

Looking back at the Clown, the Ringmaster's brow wrinkled in mild annoyance. As always, the jester rode his unicycle, rocking it back and forth in place while juggling his ever-present rubber balls. It was a nervous habit, and the Ringmaster considered all such habits to be . . . unprofessional. He had the same reactions to the Gambonnos' humming, the Human Cannonball's fingernail biting, and even Zelda's stroking of her pets.

"Must you do that, Eliot? You know how it grates on me."

"Hey, boss, I gotta keep in practice. Gotta keep my fingers limber and ready for liftin' wallets, don't I? Don't want anyone should feel anythin' when I ride by."

"Eliot, by the time you ride by, the people wouldn't feel an earthquake registering eight-point-two on the Richter scale."

The Clown giggled, performed a particularly complicated high throw and suspended drop maneuver with his rubber balls, and then bowed to the spiral-shaped disk in the middle of the Ringmaster's top hat.

"Brother, ain't that the truth!" he chortled. "The luckiest thing that ever happened to us was when you found that Nullatron. Turned this whole operation around."

Not found it, the Ringmaster thought with a slight frown on his lips. *When I first decided to use it.*

The more time passed, the more difficult things became for the Tiboldt Family Circus. Fritz Tiboldt was forced to dismiss many of his employees and performers. Good people he had known for years, friends, almost family, let go simply because he could not afford them any longer. It all wore on him. Each time he had to release a friend, each time his circus played to crowds minuscule and unenthusiastic, each time his beloved show suffered some new indignity heaped upon it by a country that simply had no use for him, it took a little more of his spirit. And when Lola, his wife, the only source of strength that remained to him, died, Fritz simply ceased. He died quietly and all alone in his sleep, a flint that had been worn down to its nub by the uncaring years, a flint without a spark.

When he learned of his father's passage, Maynard Tiboldt was doing what he had been doing for the last several years—studying the works of Mesmer, Freud, and Jung, learning how the human mind functioned and how it could be controlled, laboring tirelessly to perfect the Nullatron. He thanked the messenger and put his work aside. After all, he no longer needed an act. He had the circus itself to master. Now, he was the Ringmaster.

One look at the ledger books his father had left behind told Tiboldt that, barring a dramatic change in fortunes, he would not have a circus much longer. How could a troupe as small as theirs run up so many past-due invoices?

Tiboldt tried to run the circus as frugally as he could. If an act left, it was not replaced. When an act failed to bring in customers, he cast it adrift. And still, the customers would not come to his no-longer-magical world.

The bills, of course, did come. They came and they came and they came, until, finally, the day that Tiboldt always knew would come likewise came.

"Don't you understand anything I've said to you?" Tiboldt half-screamed at the granite-faced man in his wagon. "If you seize my animals, I won't be able to operate this circus. And, then, I'll never be able to pay you."

The granite-faced man was clearly unconcerned. He puffed on the thick and foul-smelling cigar crammed between his fat lips as if only it was worthy of his regard. Tiboldt would have loved to ask, no, demand, that the man remove the offensive weed, but knew he could not. He didn't dare risk anything that would antagonize this bloated and cruel caricature of a human being.

"Like I should give a spit about you and this Bozo the Clown operation. You owe me. You owe me big! You ain't got the money to pay me, fine. But you do got animals an' the court order says I can take them an' sell them. To other circuses an' to zoos an' even to dog food companies. I may not get everything you owe me, but I ain't gonna get stiffed, neither."

"And what of the people who work for me, the people who come to see me? What of them?"

"Hey, for all I care, you and Jo-Jo the Dog-Faced Boy can go retire to the country an' raise little puppy-faced kids. Because what happens to you ain't my concern. You know that old bit about how the show must go on? Well, here's a news flash for you. Tonight, *yours* ain't."

Then, as if to drive home his point, the unspeakable monster blew a cloud of chalky smoke directly into the Ringmaster's face. Tiboldt coughed spasmodically, uncontrollably, so much that tears began to form in his eyes.

Tiboldt reached into a desk drawer for a tissue and, through blurred vision, saw Mesmer's text lying there. He had not looked at it in months, but, now, it inspired him.

"My good man, if I can but persuade you to hold off for just a short time, I guarantee you things will be turning around quite dramatically for the Tiboldt Family Circus. You see, we're about to introduce a new act, an act that will revolutionize the entire institution of the circus and draw crowds of unimaginable numbers to our own show."

"Yeah, right, an' my mother-in-law is gonna turn into Raquel Welch an' start runnin' around wit' dinosaurs."

"No, seriously. I guarantee this act will change your mind. You must allow me to demonstrate."

Tiboldt had not misjudged his tormentor. The wry smile that flashed across the dolt's face spoke volumes. *Maybe,* he imagined the fool thinking, *Circus Boy has something here. Something else I can take from him.*

From another desk drawer, Tiboldt took a prototype Nullatron that he had been working on, a small circle with a spiral pattern painted on it and mounted on a motor. Praying that its batteries had not run dry in the months since last he had experimented with it, Tiboldt threw the switch on its back. Immediately the circle spun and the spiral whirled.

"What the hell is that?" the granite-faced man demanded, but his eyes were immediately drawn to the spiral, as it rotated. He found himself unable to look away from it. He stared at it, just stared, forgetting everything else. His cigar dangled ominously from his unmoving lips, its tip cooling to a dying ash.

"Shh. Do not speak. Listen. Hear nothing but the sound of my voice. Look. Look only at the spiral. See how it moves ever inward? How it forms a tunnel, a tunnel that moves into infinity itself? Look into that tunnel, travel down it. Let it carry you to infinity.

"Now study infinity, learn its grandeur, know its mysteries. And know also that a man who has contemplated the infinite has no need for something as mundane as money. Have you?

"There is no need to answer, no need to speak. You can show

me what you have learned. When you return from the infinite, you will be unconcerned with money, particularly the money I owe you. Indeed, you will forgive that debt entirely. And, after you have done that, you will remember none of this. All you will remember is that, as far as you are concerned, now and forever, my debt to you has been paid in full."

Tiboldt turned off the Nullatron. His former tormentor, whose face now resembled the softest clay, took a pen from a frayed coat pocket, and wrote "PAID IN FULL" on each of the invoices Tiboldt handed him. Then, as if Tiboldt were not even present, the mesmerized man strolled silently from the wagon and onto the midway. The ash toppled from his cigar, bounced off his sleeve, and mixed with the dust of the fairgrounds.

Now Tiboldt began to understand what his father had asked him to accept so many years ago, how duty, his duty to the circus people who had again become his family, could make even him do something he would never have considered otherwise.

Tiboldt did not see this as perverting the circus, at least, not in the way his father had. After all, what he did, he did to preserve their circus, so that its unique magic could survive the cruelty of that other world. But, just as his father had learned so long ago, performing one's duty exacted a price most dear. He would never again view the circus with the wide-eyed innocence of that ten-year-old boy in Austria.

The next time Tiboldt had to employ the Nullatron to sustain the circus was easier. Another indignant bill collector came and went with his invoices now marked "PAID IN FULL," never to bother Tiboldt again. Then another. And yet another. Until the master of the circus realized the constant stream of bill collectors was a distraction that kept him from managing the circus efficiently. Wouldn't it be better, he determined, to pay the invoices before they were past due, so that these cretins would no longer pester him with their endless phone calls and annoying visits?

It would. And so he acted. A little bit here, a little bit there. Hypnotize someone and pick his pocket for small invoices. Entrance a crowd for the larger ones, but always taking only what was needed. It was an easy thing and it served to keep the other world from distracting him.

In time, Tiboldt began to consider whether merely paying the circus's invoices was sufficient. What of his own desires? More importantly, what of his acts? They had been loyal to him for so long. Didn't they deserve to live in conditions that were better than subsistence at the poverty level? Tiboldt decided that they—and he—did. And so, "only what was needed" grew.

And grew.

And grew.

Until Tiboldt realized what his circus had become. Realized that each time an act left his circus, he replaced its performers with individuals who had had brushes with the law, who would have few qualms about picking the occasional pocket or lifting the odd purse. Realized that the once-proud Tiboldt Family Circus was no more than a front for their crimes.

Realized that he himself was no longer the ringmaster of his little troupe, but their ringleader.

"Always play to your audience."

The Ringmaster followed the advice his father had once given him. He spoke to them in a practiced voice, one he had developed over the long years of searching for just the right timbre, using inflections that demanded they listen to him. And when they did, he activated the disk built into his purple top hat.

At first, he projected only quick bursts from the Nullatron, bursts designed to make the audience receptive. Then, gradually, he would increase the power, insuring that they would hang on his every word. A little more and they could not help but keep their widening eyes on him at all times. Until, finally, having raised their anticipation to a crest, he would let loose the full effect of his Nullatron.

Its spiral, combined with the Ringmaster's calm and constant voice, mesmerized the audience, plunging them into a deep trance, transforming them from customers to unknowing victims.

The performers would surge into the helpless crowd, stealing jewelry and wallets while their leader left behind false memories of a night at the circus. The memory that the circus was a touch more expensive than the guest had anticipated, or that they must not have brought as much money to the circus as they thought they had, or, that they didn't really recall the last time they'd seen their Rolex, their ring, but that surely they would not have worn them to the circus. Anything to divert suspicion from the circus and its denizens.

It was no longer the Tiboldt Family Circus. It was, for two years, the Circus Romeo, a play on words that only the Ringmaster himself appreciated. (Tybalt, as he once explained to Zelda, was the nephew of Lady Capulet in *Romeo and Juliet*. She didn't quite see the humor, which disappointed him far more than he would have thought possible.) For a time, they became the Ringmaster Circus and the MacFadden Brothers Circus. Later still, as a result of a headline writer's pursuit of the sensational, they achieved their greatest "fame" as the Ringmaster's Circus of Crime.

Naturally, the Ringmaster and his troupe never used the name themselves. They might think of the paying customers as "rubes," but they certainly didn't believe those customers were so witless as to attend something called "The Circus of Crime." Perhaps out in California, where people were making that infernal memorial to an animated mouse such a success that they actually built a second one in Florida, there were cretins who might willingly come to a "Circus of Crime," but that garish name would never play in Poughkeepsie.

Still, the Ringmaster and his performers had only themselves to blame for the notoriety attached to their circus. First, they got too confident. Then, they got careless. And, finally, worst of all, they got greedy.

They wanted to make bigger killings with bigger audiences in New York City. It brought them to the attention of such costumed interlopers as Spider-Man and Daredevil and, seemingly, any idiot who could squeeze into a pair of tights. Before long, they found they had traded the glorious freedom of their world for the cold, unyielding prison walls of that other world. Again and again and again.

Eventually, the Ringmaster learned from his mistakes. While he languished in prison, he ordered the MacFadden Brothers Circus to refrain from playing big cities, venues where their activities might draw the unwanted attention of so-called super heroes. The small towns might not yield rewards as substantial as those to be plucked from the cities, but of what use were rewards of any size if one was not free to spend them?

The Ringmaster's circus came and went from one small town to the next, unnoticed by anyone, remaining only long enough to loot the audience, and then slipping away before anyone recalled the inexplicably missing watch or wallet or family heirloom that they last saw just before their rather uneventful night at the circus. It was a plan that worked to perfection, a plan which had brought them to Peoria and the line of limousines dropping off passengers to be plucked at their leisure.

The Ringmaster glanced out the tent again and, for the first time, noticed the limousines were not discharging rich patrons in their gowns and tuxedos. No, most of the vehicles appeared to be carrying simple families, with each family including at least one young child in a wheelchair.

He turned to Zelda and asked quietly, "Perhaps I should have inquired earlier, Princess, but exactly what is the nature of the charity that has engaged us for the evening?"

"The Wishing Star Foundation," she answered.

"The Wishing Star Foundation," he repeated.

As if on cue, the ebullient form of Mrs. Huddleston appeared, virtually materialized, before them. She was wheeling a balding, fragile child with eyes as wide as the infinite.

"Mr. Maynard, I just wanted to personally thank you for your cooperation. This event has turned out to be the most successful fund raiser our Peoria chapter of the Wishing Star Foundation has ever had. Not just because of the monies raised, but because all of these little ones are getting to see a real circus.

"What with skyrocketing medical costs and all, most of their families can't afford much in the way of entertainment. A circus is something they never thought they would see. Your performance tonight will truly be a dream come true for them."

The Ringmaster looked down at the face of the small child in the wheelchair, who smiled up at him. It was a weak smile, to be sure, one savaged by the debilitating combination of leukemia and chemotherapy, but a smile nonetheless.

"You do our circus a great honor, dear lady," the Ringmaster said, bowing to kiss the hand of the small child before him, much as the royalty of his native Austria had done so long ago.

Turning to Mrs. Huddleston, Tiboldt gestured at the entrance to the main tent with a flourish.

"I promise you a most spectacular show, Mrs. Huddleston, one unequalled in the history of the Tiboldt Family Circus."

"But I thought this was the MacFadden Circus."

"I am afraid there has been a misunderstanding. Although we recently acquired the MacFadden operation, this circus has always been the Tiboldt Family Circus. It was founded by my father, the legendary Fritz Tiboldt. I am Maynard Tiboldt, at your most kind and gracious service.''

Showmanship, he thought to himself, and smiled.

''There are some minor matters to which I must now attend, my friends. We will talk again after the show.''

As the society matron wheeled her young charge into the main tent, a perplexed Princess Python looked at the Ringmaster. Even the Clown had stopped rocking back and forth.

''I don't get it,'' she asked, ''why did you tell her your real name? Are you running some outside game?''

''Nothing so devious, Princess. You see, for tonight, I will once again *be* Maynard Tiboldt, and this, this will *be* the Tiboldt Family Circus, just as it was, just as it always should have been when my poor father first brought it to these shores.

''And that means that, for tonight, we will not take from our most welcome patrons.''

Both Princess Python and the Clown started in disbelief, but he silenced them with a wave of his hand.

''For these children, this could well be the only circus they will ever attend. For them, the dream and its magic still lives, lives as it once did for us. I cannot allow our usual activities to pervert their dreams. For tonight, the circus will perform as it was meant to, will present, in fact, the finest performance of its history. It will remain pure . . . for them.''

The Ringmaster activated the Nullatron. He would not debate the matter with either of them.

''No, my friends, no protests. No words. Not from you. You will hear only my words. You will look into my hat. See how its tunnel seems to reach into infinity. Look at it, contemplate it, contemplate the infinite. And remember, the infinite has no need of such mundane things as money.

''But even the infinite has need of magic, our kind of magic. Tonight we will be a circus. Only a circus. And we will provide that magic while giving the finest performances of our lives. Is that understood?''

Maynard Tiboldt barely heard their responses, before he sent Princess Python and the Clown off to prepare their acts. So many others had to be told, made to understand. The Gambonnos and the Human Cannonball. Live Wire and Strongman. Carneys, performers, roustabouts. Because it would take each and every one of them to make the magic.

Adjusting his coat, he walked off into the night to look for them, practicing his most convincing voice as he went.

The show was everything the Ringmaster had promised it would be, a spectacular. Perhaps not "the greatest show on earth," but as close as his troupe was capable.

It was a night of magic and wishes.

And, when it was over, when the magic had left the worn main tent to take up residence in the hearts and souls of those it was made for, the master of the big top had his performers line up to speak to each of the children, to crouch by their wheelchairs and touch them one last time, to receive their thanks and thank them, in turn, for coming.

As the last of the sleek, black, chauffeur-driven cars pulled away from the fairgrounds, the Ringmaster looked longingly at its receding taillights. The others returned to their wagons to fall into a deep sleep that would wash away all memories of this magic night. Except, he thought, for their memories of bright smiles on tired young faces. He owed them that much.

Tonight, they had been a circus, a real circus.

Tomorrow, they would be the Circus of Crime once more. They would go from small town to small town, robbing their patrons and fleeing into the night. Until they were recognized by some keen-eyed sheriff or would-be super hero and they were put behind iron bars and stone walls once more.

That was his life now, the life, not of Maynard Tiboldt, but of the Ringmaster. For him, the memories were all that were left of a ten-year-old boy in Austria. The magic of the past was just that, past. The wishes were dead and buried. He was what he was and nothing could change that.

He held fast his morning coat against the chill of the night and walked slowly back to his wagon.

DOOM²

JOEY CAVALIERI

Illustration by John Romita Sr.

I T WASN'T THE first time an experiment had blown up in Victor Von Doom's face.

This time, though, the loss of face was strictly embarrassment, not a physical disfiguring.

Like all of Doom's robot doubles, this one was programmed to duplicate Victor Von Doom's actions, reflexes, defenses, and patterns of thought and speech. It mirrored the emerald-cloaked monarch in every way but one. Doom had trepanned it, to increase its intelligence a hundredfold. Tangles of cables and wires extruded from its skull, spiraling tightly to the ceiling like so much ramen. It sat on a high-backed wooden chair, grasping the armrests like a ham actor in *Henry V*. Its expression was every bit as dour as its maker's.

The cables held the robot on a short tether. Doom paced the dank, stone floor, if only to demonstrate the difference between himself and his creation. There were, after all, a mind and muscles behind the metal, not just chips and servo-motors.

His eyes focused on the table's game board. The robot was clearly far ahead. There's a theological conundrum that runs: Can God make a boulder that's so big even He can't lift it? Had Doom created a robot that surpassed his own intellect?

Ego had superseded pride in his achievement. Doom had to beat his robot at this game.

It was a Latverian game called Parcek, a cross between the Japanese Go and the American Battleship. Its object required the quick and sudden arrangement of tiles in a particular aesthetic order, divining your opponent's pattern before it is complete, to replace it with one of your own.

"Mine should be easy for you to discern," the robot said, its voice an eerie simulacrum of Doom's. "It is only fair to warn you that I am about to win. Why haven't you figured my plan out yet? It should be particularly easy for you," it taunted. "Can it be that Doom is outwitted by a machine?"

A chilly wind blew through Castle Doom. The draft fluttered the medieval tapestries against the bricks in the wall. The noise broke Doom's concentration.

It seemed to distract the robot, too. Whether a defense mechanism, a momentary glitch, or a stark imitation of his master,

Doom was unsure. The wind had died down, yet the robot kept looking to the tapestry.

Worked into the fabric's warp and woof were embroidered stars, a constellation that hung in the night sky above Latveria.

Doom watched the machine's eyes dart from the gameboard to the banner and discerned, *The robot is using the tapestry for reference. Yes! I see it now! The pattern it's making is the constellation!*

Doom quickly moved his tokens to halt the robot's advance. He won. The robot reacted just as Doom would to defeat. It pounded its fist against the table and knocked the board over.

Doom yanked the cables from the android's skull. It shorted out and slumped in the chair. Victory was short-lived. He seemed almost sad that he had beaten his robot.

This was the closest I've had to an intellectual sparring partner. It was built to be more than Doom . . . but it was still no match. Nothing is left to keep me sharp. He ascended the stairs.

The robot, bereft of its artificial life, reminded Doom somehow of Reed Richards. But it's been said that an autumn leaf wafting across a Latverian lawn, the gentle tapping of rain against the stained glass windows of Castle Doom, or the tuning of gypsy violins would bring his mind back to his longtime foe as easily. No one likes the people in our lives who teach us lessons the hard way, but no one forgets them, either. *Richards is ranked by the world at large as being my intellectual equal, if not my superior. Yet, if this robot could be restored to my liking, I would respect its reasoning far above Richards.* He sneered at his foe's name. *Richards tends far too often to let issues of ethics and morality cloud his thinking. Factors that have no bearing on the scientific method. A thing true is simply true, never mind if it is fair or not.*

Doom rose to the turret he used as his observation deck. *Morality is for the meek. Ethics are rules for people who cannot face the verities of life on this planet. They cannot deal with its inherently predatory nature, so they whine about ethics and fairness. A "level playing ground," they want.* Through a telescope, he trained his eye on the neighboring country of Sylvania. *Ah! Here is a playing ground I shall level myself.*

Mystifying! Amazing! Perplexing!
Appearing for the first time in
LATVERIA

Don't miss this once-in-a-lifetime opportunity
to see
The Great
THEO
Sorcerer Extraordinaire
Escape Artiste
Super Genius
Theo Ausbrecker has performed in the royal court of every
nation in Europe, after learning his mystical craft amid the
untraversed mountains of Asia Minor.
He will THRILL you. He will ASTOUND you.
He makes the MIND REEL!

These posters were wheatpasted everywhere in the village square, despite the fact that defacing any Latverian civil structure was punishable by death.

Strangers were as common in Doom's Latveria as skyscrapers, that is to say, they did not exist—at least not for long. The nation's borders were jealously guarded to keep its population within and untroubled by the problems of the world at large. Yet, Doom's beneficent policy for keeping his people from the chaos beyond his country's borders also meant that conversely, no one from outside could contaminate his pacified population. So Theodore Ausbrecker was not only an escape artist, he seemed capable of breaking *in* as well.

For no other reason, he drew a crowd.

"Ladies and gentlemen," said Theo the Great from the makeshift stage he and Rysa, his assistant, had set up in the small park on the outskirts of Doomstadt, "you have all heard of the Iron Maiden, the dreaded device used to extract confessions during the reign of the tyrant Torquemada. Today, for your diversion and delight, I will attempt an escape from a fate far worse. I give to you . . . the Iron Madman!"

A rope was tugged, and the dropcloth was pulled from the device. It resembled an open mummy case. As Theo stepped inside, the murmuring audience could see him silhouetted by a series of metal spikes. While an Iron Maiden's spikes were meant to puncture its victim, these spikes were meant to hold its prisoner ever tighter within. Theo was bound in chains from head to foot, an eyeless helmet placed over his head. The audience had been invited to examine the case's spikes, its hinges, its pad-locks. They were solid, they were heavy, they were real.

At a signal, Theo's assistant slammed the door shut. The re-sounding thud made all the pigeons in the park flutter off in fright. She spoke as she fastened the great padlocks to their hinges. "In sixty seconds, there will be no more oxygen inside the Iron Madman. If he cannot escape, there will be no point in freeing him: the case will serve as his coffin!" She gestured to a timer, which had only a red second hand.

The seconds ticked off.

The hand made a complete circuit about the face of the clock.

The minute was up, and silence reigned inside and outside the Iron Madman.

The crowd fidgeted nervously. Years of living under a totali-tarian regime made them nervous about taking any sudden ac-tion.

The clock was reset. Another minute passed.

And then another.

Now, the crowd could not contain themselves. Some began to shout. Others began to shake their fist at the woman alone on stage. "You've killed him!"

The spectators knit closer. Worry crossed the assistant's face. One man used the treads of his boot soles to gain a foothold on the stage. He stalked the assistant.

With a whir, the Iron Madman began to rise and turn. The sudden noise, like a motor, scared the interloper off the plat-form.

Slowly, the Iron Madman did a complete turn. Now everyone in the village square, and the rubberneckers craning for a view from the hills beyond, could see what had been painted on its back.

The sculpted figure on the case held a portrait of Doom.

As soon as their leader's frightening features were registered and recognized by the crowd, then and only then, the hinges flew open.

In theatre, there is meaning beyond the surface. Here, the metaphor was too clear to deny.

Escape from Doom. I did it.

So can you.

* * *

The Iron Madman was an illusion that had its origins with Houdini. The hinges were tricked up. The pins that held them together could be removed, but only once the door was shut. While the door remained open, they seemed as solid as the hinges on any door in Castle Doom.

Theo's reveling in his trickery was cut short by a voice in the small jack that lay hidden in his ear. "You're celebrating too quickly! You're not out of danger, yet. Doom should have set his guards on you. They should have confiscated the Iron Madman and hauled the two of you off to some rat-infested dungeon underneath that pile of mildew he calls a castle."

"And you're underestimating my talents as a showman," Theo replied. "By the time I was locked inside the Iron Madman, the guards were so taken with us they'd forgotten their purpose there!"

The next thing he heard over his headset was Phoebus' laugh.

He had heard it before. But he never got tired of it. The booming, satisfied, infectious laugh of a proud uncle who's rewarding his nephew with an ice cream factory for getting a gold star at school. Phoebus was Sylvania's leader. Where Doom dominated, Phoebus ingratiated. His warm and engaging manner came through even over their encrypted radio broadcasts.

When Phoebus was done laughing, he said, "The tighter he holds Latveria, the looser his grip! And why should he be permitted to have it, if he's going to rule it by pacing back and forth in that gloomy castle? Why, the only thing you can get in Castle Doom is a cold. The things of this fleeting earth were meant to be enjoyed while they're presented to us. If Doom cannot see the worth in the art, the treasure, the resources of Latveria, then it falls to me to take it all from him, and to show him how to use it."

"What do we do next?"

"Follow the plan. Take the battle to him."

"Enter Castle Doom? Are you sure that's wise?"

Theo's fears were answered with the resounding laugh. "When he finds out how you managed to infiltrate the Latverian border, he'll fold up and die, if I know him. Oh, I'd like to see his face when he makes that discovery!"

"Then you don't know him. And by all accounts, we're better off not seeing his face."

"Like a magician, he is all façade, Theo! Have you stopped to consider that all his bluster and displays of force are expended on holding a country the size of Manhattan, whose ideas of high culture are yodeling, lederhosen, and oompah bands? No, trust me, we'll be introducing a little decadence to Latveria yet!"

Theo felt it was easy for Phoebus to laugh. He was back in the opulent Sylvanian palace, while Theo and Rysa must figure an entrance into Castle Doom, their enemy's stronghold. "We're being toyed with," he said later on, as night descended.

"What makes you so sure?"

"Think, Rysa. Our mere presence in Latveria is an insult, in the same way a germ can be said to be an insult to a body's system. So where are the antibodies? Where are his guards?"

"The Castle's defenses must be mechanized. Surely that must be more efficient than a contingent of stony-faced guards like Buckingham Palace."

Castle Doom was utterly black. Not a light shone anywhere within. It was as if someone had put up a thick velvet curtain against the night.

Before the castle's spiked gate, they came across a clock tower.

"I don't remember this from the briefing." Theo pulled one of his own flyers from his pocket, and ran a small pen-like stylus over the words Mystifying! Amazing! Perplexing! A blueprint of the castle's perimeter appeared. Sure enough, this clock tower was conspicuous by its absence.

Each of the four faces of the clock read DOOM. None of them displayed the correct time. Especially the last face, the dial of which was cracked. It was missing its minute hand.

An inscription ran below the clock's front face.

AECIX OLSTA KORZY RCIHD BNKGA

"Latverian?" said Rysa hesitantly. She could speak the local language, but had no facility with the written version.

"No. If this clock wasn't here previously, it was put here as a message to outsiders, to us. Therefore, it's in a language an outsider can understand."

"Then why isn't it in English or Russian or German?"

"I told you, we're being toyed with."

He wasted no time in copying the words down in their correct order.

AECIX
BNKGA
RCIHD
OLSTA
KORZY

He then read the letters downward, beginning in the first column.

ABROK ENCLO CKISR IGHTZ XADAY

Then it came to him. "Of course! I would have pieced this together sooner, but I misread the numeral 3 as the letter Z."

A BROKEN CLOCK IS RIGHT 3X A DAY

"The expression is '*two* times a day,' isn't it?" asked Rysa.

"My guess is that the inscription refers not only to the broken side of the clock tower, but its three remaining faces." He looked thoughtful. "There is a numeral planted in the inscription, so a numeral must somehow fit into the solution."

"The solution to what?"

"The inscription is fractured English, so a knowledge of English must also figure in the solution."

"The solution to *what*?" Rysa repeated.

Theo wrote. Like a child's code, the letters on the clock dial correspond to their numerical place in the English alphabet.

DOOM
4-15-15-13

Rysa's mind made the connection. The numbers referred to times on the clock! 4:15. 1:51. 3:00. She set the hands on the three unbroken faces.

"Wait! Rysa! There's another solution!"

But it was too late. A red light winked on from somewhere within the clock tower's spired roof. The red light grew and became a concentrated beam of light. It shone on Rysa's peasant blouse, tagging her. Without a sound, the red beam pierced her.

The smell of singed and smoky flesh filled Theo's nostrils. It made him gag. Rysa had fallen dead.

It was a lesson in overconfidence to Theo, who quickly reset the hands of the clock. "3X a day," he said to no one, now. "3X. Doom told us that solution was wrong."

The hands were now set at 4:00, 1:51 and 5:13.

The spiked gate opened to its combination.

Theo slowly walked the path to Castle Doom.

A door was open for him.

Inside, outside, it made no difference. Both were equally as black.

Theo felt his way forward in the dark. He reached a room that to his touch seemingly had brick walls.

Light finally permeated the room. All four walls were brick. There was no sign of an entrance. How did he get in? More important, how would he get out?

You're an escape artist, Theo. Slowly. Don't panic. Think.

He ran his hands against the texture of the walls. They were brick but, oddly, not cemented. He pushed against them. There was some give, but the bricks were locked together tightly in place.

This alone gave Theo the clue. Puzzles like this are more often made of wood. They're made of blocks that interlock, and the object is to take them apart. The Japanese call them *kumiki*.

There's often a principle behind them. One very special piece must be turned a certain way, perhaps clockwise, to free the rest of them. His hands searched along the walls for a brick that had more give than the rest.

It turned. The structure came apart as he thought it would.

What he hadn't taken into account was that this was no mere child's game of blocks. The bricks were heavy, and as they fell, deadly. They began to collapse in a mound of red dust, but not before the heaviest stones at the top came crashing down . . . on Theo's legs.

He crawled from the chalky red rocks. His trousers were torn, his legs meat-red.

Then, he heard footfalls.

No ordinary footsteps these. Their heavy tread led Theo to

understand that the man approaching had had his weight augmented . . . with armor.

Theo looked up at his armored captor and for the first time understood why he more often went by simply "Doom" rather than the more proper "Von Doom."

"Escape artist," Doom snorted. "There is no escape, not anywhere on this planet. It's been said about our brief existences that they are all similar in one respect: no one ever gets out alive."

From the folds of his jade cloak, Doom produced an ornate set of manacles. They caught the light. Were they glass? Diamond? Adamantium? Their shine split the light into little spectrums that darted around the room.

Doom fastened the manacles to his prisoner's wrists. "One last challenge. Indulge me."

"Why should I?"

"You can't resist. You've made a spectacle of yourself, or rather a target, since you entered Latveria. It's a hallmark of foolish, bright youth. The show-off syndrome. You can't wait to brag and demonstrate to everyone how much you know. Believe me, I encountered it in my own youth."

Theo noticed that Doom did not claim to suffer that affliction himself.

From his glove, Doom produced three lockpicks. One shaped like a cross. One shaped like a star. One shaped like a helix.

"Here, this will increase your chances of escape," Doom said.

Theo took one up in his fingers and set to work, trying to poke it into the crystalline lock.

"I see you favor the helical lockpick. I knew you'd appreciate its symbolic value. For you see, I know how you managed to enter Latveria. Your leader, Phoebus, he changed your DNA structure, did he not? Your designer DNA matches my own configuration now. May I ask how he procured a sample from me?"

Theo remained silent, working away at the lock.

"Not in the mood to brag anymore?"

Theo stabbed at the lock.

"My perimeter defenses are keyed to recognizing my DNA pattern. Since you and your formerly pretty assistant waltzed by said defenses, I can assume you have been changed to share my DNA pattern, correct?"

Theo made a face. Sweat made the lockpick slippery in his hands. It fell and he had to pick it up again.

"Doom is not accustomed to repeating himself," the monarch said in a dangerously quiet voice.

"That really worries you, doesn't it?" the young man finally said. "There are more where we came from. A younger generation, as smart as you, as capable as you, as ruthless as you. We can infiltrate your backward country at will, and assume positions of leadership throughout it." The lockpick slipped again. "You'll see. That will be your undoing. Who can beat Doom? Doom plural. Better yet, *young* Doom. We will outlive you, and our progeny will wipe the name off your headstone. Does that get to you the way it was intended to?" There was an audible click. The manacles snapped open at last. "You see? There is no challenge you can throw down that we cannot rise above!" He rattled the open cuffs to Doom's face. A hinge on them popped and fell to the floor. The diamond-like manacles shattered.

From them, a liquid oozed, wafting a steady stream of smoke toward their former prisoner.

Theo was suddenly overcome. Unable to walk away, the pungent smoke reached him full in the face. When the steam cleared, boils and blisters began to pop on his exposed skin.

"It is a shame you share my DNA," said Doom. "I have a genetic predisposition toward that particular virus. And it would affect me far more than any other man, but for my armor's filtration unit. However, I see you are not as well-equipped."

Purple blotches spread all over Theo's face and arms. The skin split and separated like scabs. With no resilience left, his skin simply broke apart, flaking and turning to dust.

Theo's remains were collected and sent in an urn to the Sylvanian palace.

The urn bore a cryptogrammatic inscription. Phoebus' staff spent three days decoding it.

It read, "Age and treachery will always survive over youth and skill."

In anger, Phoebus threw the urn to the floor.

A liquid ooze poured out from the shattered ceramic, wafting a steady stream of smoke throughout Phoebus's castle.

Mephisto

CHILD'S PLAY

ROBERT L. WASHINGTON III

Illustration by John Paul Leon

THE STRANGER WITH the burning face erupted out of the night riding a wall of smoke and flame that ended in a motorcycle, all hot chrome and cracked leather rocket aimed at the circle of cloaked and hooded figures, trailing a sound like the growling of some demonic beast chained inside its engine. The stranger's black jeans wrapped around the frame of the cycle that looked like a metal demon curled up on its haunches, his black leather jacket smoking from the infernal heat sheathed inside. The smokeless flames flickered and warped back and forth in the wind around the naked skull that was his head.

The circle refused to yield, even now forging the image of their dread master in the smoke rising from the bonfire at the center of the circle. Instead, the group locked hands and redoubled the intensity and speed of their chanting. The image of smoke and vapor seemed to respond by assuming a human-like form, all of smoke, with writhing shoulder-length hair, a cape, and eyes formed from the embers of the bonfire. Those eyes seemed to dance with the tale of a thousand corrupt promises as they turned to regard the eternally-grinning stranger with flesh of fire, and rumbled with a voice of ash and crackling coals as an arm of vapor pointed a smoky finger at the stranger.

"Do not dare to disrupt my doings, Ghost Rider. Your predecessor suffered untold misery for defying me. Do you think you will fare better?"

The stranger offered no reply save his silent, bony grin. The fire pouring around his visible skull curled back into a flaming ponytail as his motorcycle hauled back on its rear wheel like the beast had reared to pounce. A gout of flame from the stranger's hands arced in front of the wheel and over the circle of figures, and the stranger was aloft, riding the arc of fire like a ramp over their heads.

The image in the smoke roiled in fury as the stranger landed in the circle, fishtailing the howling motorcycle to a stop near the sacrificial altar. Its flaming wheels scorched the earth beneath it as it skidded, then lurched foward again as the stranger moved the motorcycle in toward the altar and the bound figure that lay upon it.

But the demon shivered in fury and suddenly began to shake off large portions of itself in its rage. The resulting curls of smoke, rather than drifting away, coiled themselves into nightmare shapes and moved to intercept the stranger.

The stranger reached up his right hand, and hurled a fist-sized fireball at the nearest of the oncoming smoke figures as the larger figure reconstituted itself from the smoke of the bonfire.

"An *amusing* way of attempting to stop a vexation of smoke and fire," chuckled the demon. Indeed, the smoke demon ignored the fireball that passed harmlessly through it and moved to intercept the stranger, blocking the vision of the stranger's eyeless sockets and forcing him to stop the motorcycle.

The stranger tried waving the demon off to no avail, its tendrils closing in around him instead as he clutched at its gaseous entrails fruitlessly. The demon laughed as the stranger finally clasped at the chains adorning his black leather jacket, the other smoke demons closing in.

But the demon's laughter and its servants' dry, husky chitterings of victory were cut short as the stranger began whirling the chains around his head fiercely with a strength belying his skeletal countenence. The frenzied whipping of the chains and the wind they stirred began to shred the vaporous minions apart; their cries of dissolution sounded like the hissing of water upon hot coals.

The stranger guided his motorcycle with a lurch towards the altar, pulling up alongside it. He brushed past the leader of the hooded ritualists. The impact pushed back the intricately embroidered robes of the cultist to reveal the skinny, unimposing teenager underneath them. The stranger regarded the ritualist, prepared for a struggle.

But Randy Conners, who had only been *so* interested in, like, actually *sacrificing* his science teacher and stuff and had never expected this to work anyway, was more than willing to concede the futility of any further struggles and stepped back, dropping the old book he had led the rite from as he went.

The stranger turned to the figure on the makeshift altar, reaching for the bonds that held it. His fiery touch instantly unraveled the ropes with fire as the victim freed himself and hopped down.

The demon howled in rage. "Fool! Any of my other minions will gladly take their place on the altar in his stead! Should I choose to use them *all*, the power gained would be unreal! Return my offering to me, or—"

"Or nothing," the stranger replied, with a voice that echoed hollowly despite the open space in which they stood. "None of the others can offer themselves without breaking the circle, which would break your ritual anyway. And without this—" he picked up the tome the boy had dropped, its pages turning into black butterflies from the fire in his hands as he held it aloft "—your followers won't be trying this again. Your scheme is over, Mephisto." The stranger turned his back on the figure and helped the sacrificial victim onto the motorcycle.

The enormous, forboding figure of smoke roiled along, the whole of its outline in fury. "It is over when *I* say so, and not before! Beware, Ghost Rider—I will not suffer your insolence lightly! We shall meet again, and you will pay for your interference!"

The figure exploded into a mushroom cloud, then dispersed itself as the stranger shrugged and started up his engine. "As you wish."

The stranger glided his motorcycle through the now-broken ranks of the demon's would-be minions, oblivious to the glances admiring his imposingly rebellious image from a few of the confused teenagers as he sped off into the night.

A timeless time later, in a placeless place, a flock of formless forms shifted and writhed in their attempts to avoid facing their Lord. When Mephisto was irritated, nations fell; when he was angry, planets trembled.

Right now, Mephisto was furious.

"How dare he! *Years* of whispering sweet corruptions in the ears of those youths, of carefully urging them to the brink. *Months* of moving that book through the hands of tiresome occultists, debunkers, and scholars, souls too weak to be of value or too tainted to have any worth. Are all my aspirations to be undone so easily?" he howled at a Petty Grudge, which slithered away from his wrath, quivering.

"Am I not Mephisto, Master of Malice and Lord of Lies? Am I not Mephisto, Securer of the Seven Sins, the Whisperer in Darkness, the Foul Pact Maker, the Dread Persuader? Am I to be undone by the cowardice of *children*?" he inquired of a Judgment-Impairing Rage, even its natural fury shamed by its master's irritation. The Grudge, grateful for the distraction, shuddered away into darkness, pelted by the infernal thunderclouds that represented Mephisto's rancor and lashed at the whole of the realm.

Mephisto allowed his angry consciousness to melt into liquidity and move through the spaceless space, pondering as he shifted along. He raged against the inevitable, he knew. Weakness at inopportune moments was a natural consequence of the kind of people most susceptible to his influence. He mulled over the problem as a flock of Nagging Doubts flapped off in search of prey. With such minions as were easily swayed by these, it was a wonder he had progressed as far as he had in the hierarchy of darkness.

That was what was so damnably frustrating about this latest setback. (For, despite the loss of the Book of Summonings, who would dare to label any of his works a failure?) He had been so careful in his selection of supplicants this time, trying to offset their natural tendency to waver with the brash impetuousness of youth.

And the power their corrupted innocence would release. *That* was to have been the additional touch that would insure his success this time. The greater the step from innocence to corruption, the greater the power, and the faster it would be unleashed.

But the Ghost Rider had undone it all in a few seconds. And winning the vengeance he had promised the skull-faced parody of a demon would be more difficult than he had let on. A human fueled by that level of demonic power might go for years without succumbing to his most intricate temptations, and the power required for a direct assault would be enormous. Hundreds, perhaps thousands of corrupt souls' worth of power, at the rate he collected it from the average victim.

But as he looked up and chanced to witness the spawning of a swollen Compulsive Need as it pulsed and erupted into a flock of butterfly-winged children, a Devious Inspiration (which had indeed been kept close by for just such an occasion) worked up the nerve to shamble over to him and whisper in his psyche.

Mephisto, caught unawares by the Inspiration, resisted his initial urge to chastise it and allowed the thought it had left to flower, then crystallize in his mind.

"Yes, the corruption of a single soul close enough to true in-nocence *could* easily yield enough power, and more. And the rash impulsiveness of youth does indeed loom large in children as well. An adolescent is very open to my call, but the inherent difficulty in successfully tempting a *child* to act as my agent might well offer enough deviant energy to . . . yesss . . ."

Mephisto spread his lips in a smile, a smile with a certain gleam to it, a mixture of satisfaction and anticipation. Denizens through-out his realm could feel it. The scowl-red and iron-black thunder-heads ceased their weeping and broke open, revealing the foggy, inconsistent flickering that was the sunless sun. From the Unthink-ing Cruelties to the Neurotic Self-Destructive Urges, the residents of the realm dared to look up and hope for some small abatement of their misery (that faint hope being the whole of their relief).

Mephisto had a scheme again, and all was well with his world.

It was almost as soon as he had outlined his plan to himself that Mephisto allowed his consciousness to swell and diffuse its way into the mortal world. Lesser beings might have described the sensation as akin to the feeling of rising while spinning gid-dily, accompanied by the feeling of being pulled into a thousand pieces at once. In this way, Mephisto was able to make perhaps the most impressive use of his gifts as Lord of Temptation, be-coming one with every corrupting thought on Earth and sifting through their thinkers for his prey.

He wandered lonely, as a cloud of despair in the mind of an ad-dict, passed through obsessive lusts as they chased senators. Too large by half to be attached to a subject suitable for his purpose. Mephisto (or rather, his consciousness) pulsed and divided itself, and moved to intercept some of the smaller thoughts.

Mephisto pushed his way through minor rages and insecure needs, hyperbolic reactions and hidden jealousies. He paused briefly to chuckle over certain barely repressed urges in the mind of a well-known celebrity, having just slipped through an *enormous* cloud of unwarranted suspicion about the celebrity speculating on the exact opposite indulgence.

But in another space he found himself as a cyclone of childish fearful rage, in the same egospace with a small squad of crushed hopes and one or two envious resentments, and he stopped, fo-cusing more of himself there. The size of the fear of death almost made him move on, but there was something so very genuine about the cyclone . . . he withdrew himself to look into the section of the real world corresponding to this egospace.

It was a boy. About nine. Running through a section of Brooklyn, New York quite plentiful in the kinds of thoughts useful to him.

Mephisto's consciousness smiled, and allowed itself to meld with the child's. . . .

It was them boys. They was after me again.

They don't have nothing better to do with themselves but act like they a gang, you know, they walk up and down the street all bad and like that, and that's supposed to be them "rolling," like the real gangstas aren't riding up and down the block in big jeeps with the music going, *really* rolling, right there in the street in front of them, making them look all stupid. They're twelve and thirteen—big enough to be in a gang, but they not, not a *real* gang. It ain't but four or five of 'em *anyway*.

I think they look stupid. But I don't say nothing. So why do they all come after me? Everybody comin' from school has to walk through here. If it's supposed to be they turf or something, they could go fight with anybody for crossing through they homeground and stuff.

Why me? They make me so *mad*. See, they just some punks. If my brother were here, they'd *all* run.

Instead of *me* runnin'.

But I'm runnin'.

I get to the street and the light says "Don't Walk" but it's flashing, so I stop and look both ways and cross anyway. It's a big street, so I *mad* rush, and it's only one I'm holding up when the light turns green, and he waits.

But no way can those guys get through all that traffic. I'm straight, but I keep going and make a left through a alley. I stop and go back to laugh at them, but I see them coming tryin' to rush the traffic, so I just yell once and keep going.

"*Hey y'all! Just hop in yo' ride and drive on past 'em!*" I yell, and take off.

But see, even if they had a ride, my big brother is old enough to drive, and *he'd* have a ride to pick me up from school in.

If he could drive still.

I gotta walk past some junkies to come out of the alley. One of them asks me for some change. I shake my head and keep walking. I don't say anything. Grownups who need to get money from kids are just sad, Momma says. I think maybe one day one of the super heroes will come down here and help all the good people and beat up all the bad people and slap all the fools upside the head. Momma says all the heroes are too busy fighting each other and fancying around (that's how she says it, "fancying around") on other planets and stuff to be bothered with our neighborhood, but she don't believe in Daredevil either, and one of my homeboys said he *saw* Daredevil once. He said it was phat.

I stop in the party store across from my house and get some candy, the soft kind with the fruit flavors. The man behind me in line looks at me mean until I'm done. I can see he has a twenty-dollar bill in his hand. He puts it in the change place in the bulletproof window in front of the counter, and picks up a little bitty baggie the man behind the counter shoves through.

I know what's going on. But the store has the good candy, the kind my brother and I can share. He can't eat the hard candy no more.

He can't do a lot of things no more.

I cross the street and go into my house, moving past the people on the stoop. They kind of just hang around a lot, but they're okay. They don't bother no kids or nothing.

Momma's napping on the couch when I come in. She works nights at the all-night store so she can be with my brother during the day. I have to make my own breakfast mostly, but it's okay. I know how things are. Things are tight since Daddy died.

But I wish she was around for me more sometimes. I wish she didn't have to work so hard.

I go to the back, to my brother's room. I'm not supposed to, 'cause Momma thinks I'll knock something over if I'm in there by myself. My brother told her it's okay, but I'm still supposed to wait.

I go in anyway. I'm big. I know what to be careful about.

I come and move past the big machines near the door and the ones closer to the bed. He's there, in the big bed. He's always there. He was sleeping, but his eyes opened when I came in. He smiled.

"Invasion of da dwarfs. Whassup, James? How's my punk kid brother?"

He tried to sit up, but I told him to lay back, 'cause I could see from the face he made when he tried he wasn't feeling too good. Besides, if he moves around too much, the tubes will get all messed up, and Momma will know he been doing something, and know I been in here.

But we watched TV anyway and had some candy. The TV is in his room. Sometimes I wish we could get another, 'cause we can only watch it when he's up and feeling good. But I know how it is. The medicine for my brother is expensive, and the machines too. Most of our money goes to that, even though he's still sick and he's still going to—

But Momma says don't think like that, so I don't.

He falls asleep pretty soon—he's tired a lot—and I'm watching TV by myself. I was going to turn off the TV and go, 'cause I know Momma doesn't like it when I'm there by myself. I know not to knock out any of my brother's tubes or anything, but she still worries.

But somehow, I got mad instead. Mad about having to sneak watch cartoons because we only have one TV and it's in my brother's room when dumb kids and mean kids have stuff I don't, mad because stupid kids chase me because I'm small and my big brother is sick, mad about all the people doing bad stuff in our neighborhood and getting away with it in front of little kids and stuff.

So I sat there, just because I wanted to watch cartoons and everything wasn't fair, no matter what Momma said, and *I* wanted something for once. It didn't feel *right*, but it made me feel *better*, somehow. So I sat there.

And I didn't *want* to, but I started thinking about all the things I wished I had. I wished we had more food and stuff, that I was bad enough to stand up by myself, that my brother was better. Mostly I wished for that; if he wasn't sick and going to . . . you know, we would have more money and he could help me and Momma wouldn't be tired from working and taking care of him too. It made me so *mad,* all the kids who were running around breaking up things and picking on people and acting like a fool when my brother couldn't even get out of bed. I found myself crying, like a little kid, looking like a fool crying over the cartoons on TV or something.

And then I wished I was big enough and could take care of all that stuff myself, big enough to do something, to do anything. If I was big enough to be a doctor, *I* could make my brother well, I bet. I'd be smart, and be careful with all my doctor money so I could take care of him and Momma. I knew it was stupid when I thought it, like when I thought I could grow up and be a super hero, like there's a school for it or something, but I didn't care. I really *could* take care of things, if I had a chance.

Then I got mad for wasting my time thinking things like that. I was just a dumb kid. Even if somebody gave me a chance to do something to help, I would probably mess it up. I wasn't anybody special. Even if I could do something, I probably wouldn't do *anything* I had to, not really, not if it was something scary or something. I didn't care about him *that* much.

Then I got madder at myself. That wasn't true! I *wouldn't* goof it up! That was dumb and stupid, thinking I wouldn't do any-thing if I had the chance! I would so do anything to make my brother better, *really* anything! I almost felt like two people, a mean one, telling me I wouldn't do nothing, and the real me, saying I would.

But it wasn't fair. Nothing I said or did would make any dif-ference. No one was going to let some dumb little kid do any-thing like that, even though I wished they would, even if I really could. And I really wished both.

That's when I heard the voice in the corner.

It sounded like the voice I have in my head sometimes, like the one I was just arguing with.

"What would you do to make him better?"

I jumped. I almost knocked over one of the machines. I stepped back and looked at my brother.

Still sacked out.

I looked around, then moved for the door. I mean the bed-room door; I wasn't letting no freakazoid kidnap me or my brother. I opened my mouth.

"Don't call for your Momma. She's trying to sleep. You know me. Come over here, if you think you can really do something."

I stopped. How did they know what I was about to do?

"Come on now, you attracted my attention, don't you want my help?"

I looked around, then moved toward the corner, careful.

I was gonna turn on the light switch—the only light in the

room was from the TV and it was gettin' dark out—but the voice said, "Don't turn on the light."

I couldn't see anything in the corner at first. Then as I stared at the dark, there was almost a figure, and a head with long hair and kind of scary eyes.

And a cape.

But it was all shadowy and stuff, just shapes that could almost be shadows from all the toys and clothes and records and stuff piled up in the room, except they seemed too much like a person in the shadows.

"Are—are you a super hero?" I said.

"I have powers, yes. I use them to help people who deserve it get what they want. That's what I do. Once they've helped me, showed me they're deserving, I use my powers to give them what they need."

"Can you heal people and stuff? What's your name?"

"I can do all sorts of things. And I'd prefer to keep my name a secret for now. My enemies are everywhere. Just saying you're my friend can get you in a lot of trouble with some people."

"Like Spider-Man?" I said. I thought I was beginning to understand.

"Yes. Exactly. Like Spider-Man." I thought I saw him smile, but it was a shadowy smile.

"But how did you find me? Momma says—"

"Momma says a lot of things that aren't quite correct. You know that. Everyone's mother does."

"Don't be talkin' about my Moms!" I wasn't too sure I liked this guy anymore.

"I didn't mean anything. But you know it's true. She says you're too little to help out, doesn't she? But maybe you are. Maybe she's right."

"No I'm not! I could so help! I'm big enough to know what's going on!"

"Perhaps you are. Perhaps you can help me and I can help you."

"Really? Could you help my brother?"

"I could. If I felt you had done enough for me to deserve it."

"L-like what?" Now he was starting to sound like maybe he *was* some kind of freakazoid.

"Well, if it was just something like some money or a new bike or something like that, I might ask you to go help old ladies cross the street for a year, or something like that.''

''You have people do stuff like *that?*''

''I told you—I help people get what they deserve. Doesn't that sound right to you?''

''I—I guess. You make it sound like you're Santa Claus or something.''

''Well, I give people things they want, and only ask for a little in return. Perhaps I *am* like Santa Claus, a little. Except I'm real.''

''But how—''

''It's how I choose to use my powers. Do you want me to answer a bunch of questions, or do you want me to help your brother?'' He seemed upset enough to leave.

''*No!* I mean help my brother. I mean, what do you want me to do?''

''Do you know that thing they call the Ghost Rider?''

''Yeah. He's scary-looking.'' I had seen pictures of the Ghost Rider, in a magazine about super people that has gory pictures Momma don't want me seeing. ''He has like a skull head and is all fiery.''

''*That's* the one. He acts real tough, but all he does mostly is ride around on a big tough-looking motorcycle and scare people a lot. Some friends of mine were trying to help me and he hurt them. Just to show he was tough.''

I didn't know much about Ghost Rider, except that a lot of people thought he was scary and he had been seen around a lot of scary things that happened. He sounded pretty mean. ''That's not fair. You should do something about him.''

''Maybe. Or maybe *you* should.''

I looked at him crazy. ''I'm just a kid! I can't fight no super guy!''

The shadowy smile came back. ''Well, then, I guess I'd just have to make you a 'super guy' first, then.''

I pulled my head back. ''You can't do that!'' Then I pulled it back in. ''*Can* you do that?''

''If you're going to stop a super-villain for me, you'll have to be a super hero, right? Besides, if you stop someone as evil as Ghost Rider, you'll *deserve* to be a hero.''

''And have my brother better?''

''Well, if you're a super hero, the power to heal your brother won't be all that much. But you can't fail—you'll have to be sure Ghost Rider can't bother me or my friends anymore.''

"I won't goof up! Make me a hero, and give me the power to heal my brother, and I'll—I'll wipe Ghost Rider off the face of the Earth!''

Then the face seemed to come out of the corner, a dark, mean face, with a horrible smile that seemed to get bigger and bigger as it came close to my face, bigger than my head, bigger than its head, bigger than the whole wall, and I could hear the voice in my head and in my ears, as loud as a plane overhead, and there was thunder and a funny green fire all around.

"It's a deal.''

And then there was nothing, and the shadows really *were* shadows, and I had this feeling, like I had to go someplace, but I mean just *had* to go someplace. I stumbled out and downstairs and outside. I felt like I was going to throw up, so I stumbled into the alley.

And then I exploded.

I felt sick and cold, like ice was forming inside me. Or that's what it felt like. There was more of that green fire like before. I fell over, feeling dizzy and stiff.

I think it was the funny scraping sounds when I hit the ground and got up that first told me something was different. I looked around, but the noise was close by me and I couldn't see anything. At first I thought the voice was back, but then I looked down, and realized the scraping was me.

My icy blue claws scraping against the ground.

I jumped back and stared at my arms. They were longer, and looked like blue snow or ice, all ragged and sharp. My whole body was like that. I wasn't a lot bigger, but I *was* bigger.

And I was powerful. I could feel it, the cold flowing through me, like the opposite of a fever. I curled up my hand, and a ball of blue icy fire was in it. I threw it at the wall, watched it hit and spread out, leaving a patch of frost and icicles there. I looked at myself in a window facing the alley—I was all blue and icy and ragged all over, almost half again as tall as I was before. Even my face looked different—like a boogey monster, an ogre, or a gremlin, made of ice.

I was a super hero.

An ice hero. The opposite of fire. To destroy fire.

I felt the same thing that made me go outside, a feeling like hunger, pulling me somewhere.

It was pretty cool to be a hero, I mean *really* phat, but somehow, it didn't feel all correct. I didn't have time to stop, though. The feeling wanted me to go someplace, fast.

I tried to walk, but almost ended up slipping. I looked down. The ground had frozen under my feet. It kept freezing wherever I set them down. At first, I thought I would trip all over the place, but then I figured out a kind of skating-around move. Once I got the hang of it, I could skate around pretty fast.

I started moving in the direction I felt I had to go.

As I skated along, I started to feel more and more better about what was going on. Ghost Rider was mean and scary; by helping to stop him, I could help my brother *and* make things better for other people. It didn't matter that he hadn't done anything to *me*, I knew from the other guy he was bad.

I was just starting to think over what I knew about the guy who gave me the powers when I saw him. I mean Ghost Rider. He looked just as scary as in the picture, with a skull for a head, in a leather jacket and black jeans, fire coming from off the skull like hair. He was standing over this woman and some guys was running from him.

He was turned away from me and looking at the lady. I knew it wasn't fair, but then I thought he might hurt her, so I made a freezeball and threw it at his back. It made a hissy noise and melted almost as soon as it hit, but he stood up and grabbed at his back. I could see it hurt.

"Halt your evilness, demon . . . thing! You'll menace nobody else today!" I tried to talk like a hero. They say things different, all impressive and stuff, you know. I thought it sounded pretty good, plus my voice was different, all screechy and creaky-sounding, like a cold wind.

He stood up, looked at me, and made a sort-of fist. Suddenly he had a fireball in his hand. He threw it at me while he talked to me, in a voice a *lot* spookier than mine.

"You have a great deal of gall, insulting *my* supposed demonic nature. Or do you believe I cannot smell the source of your power?"

I ducked out of the way of the fireball. I moved almost as fast as I had thought to move. I really *was* a super hero! "I fight you with the power of goodness, and I'll fight you until you are gone, never to return!''

It felt just like in the comic books.

Mephisto watched the events from his realm gleefully, edging his consciousness ever so slowly back into the boy's mind to assert his control as the battle progressed. He stoked the boy's childish pride in his new abilities, provoking a devastating assault on the Ghost Rider from the boy's desire to show off and win attention. Ghost Rider's blistering response allowed him to twist the boy's anger at being bullied into firming the child's resolve. The next round was extensive and wearing on both of the combatants.

But that was more than acceptable to the promoter of the match.

However, Mephisto was suddenly finding it difficult to maintain the boy's focus. Swarms of moral imperatives kept battering at the small fortress Mephisto had constructed in the boy's ego. Mephisto moved closer to the boy's center of consciousness to better reassert himself. . . .

It didn't feel like in the comic books anymore. Not at all.

Comic books don't show anywhere near as many people running and screaming and stuff, nobody seems to get really hurt at all, and there's hardly any stuff broken. It seemed like people was coming out of they houses just to yell and run around us, and every time we turned around, there was something in the way getting broken or smashed up—cars and vans and fruit stands and trash cans and mailboxes and streetlights and telephone poles and fences and bushes and all kinds of things, sometimes people. I didn't mean to break up anything or knock into anybody, they was just *there.*

And it *hurt.* I was stronger than I was, a *lot* stronger, and I couldn't get hurt as *much,* but it still hurt. He knocked me into things, like a car or a pole, and they'd crunch up, and I'd get back up, but it still hurt pretty bad.

But he was hurting too. I could see that. I had learnt to use my ice power fast. It wasn't real ice at all, but a kind of blue fire, like the opposite of real fire, that froze things, and it hurt him bad when I hit him with it. That part was kinda phat. The fire made ice when I wanted it to, instead of just being cold—whenever *I* wanted, just like that!—and I made ice shields and ice swords and ice darts and ice bombs and things. He couldn't hard-

ly stand to be around something I had hit, even, it was so cold.
I wasn't sure if he was as bad off as me, but I could see I was
getting to him. At first I was scaredy-cat to hit him back hard,
but then he hit me in the stomach once good and I got mad,
and I started hitting *him* hard.

And I was starting to think maybe this wasn't such a good idea.
People was getting hurt, and I was busting up stuff. Plus, Ghost
Rider was a good fighter but not a dirty fighter. He didn't hit
me until I got up, and he didn't throw things at me or nothing.
It didn't seem right somehow. I started to feel like maybe he was
mad 'cause I hit him first.

But I couldn't stop. Not if I wanted my brother helped. Besides, maybe he was just tricking me. Mean guys do that, trick
people all the time.

I didn't usually think like that, but before I thought about it
more, I heard somebody yelling for help.

I looked around. So did Ghost Rider.

It was this big heavyset lady. She was stuck under one of the
poles we had knocked down. She was struggling and yelling, but
she couldn't move it off her. There was some people near, but
they looked at us—me and Ghost Rider, I mean—and ran,
scared.

I didn't feel so proud of my powers anymore as I moved over
to her.

*An enraged Mephisto bellowed as self-sacrifice burst through the door of
his stronghold in the boy's psyche, closely followed by responsibility. He
summoned the boy's desperation and sense of powerlessness, and the twin
horrors leapt at the boy's better aspects. . . .*

The lady scrambled away as Ghost Rider and me pulled up the
pole. She said "Th-th-th-thank you," like in a cartoon, and
crawled away from us, still scared even though we saved her.

I let go of the pole, but Ghost Rider still had it, trying to move
it out of the way.

Suddenly I wanted to hit him, really hard. I knew I had to,
there wasn't any other way. If I didn't, I wouldn't be nothing, I
wouldn't get nothing, my brother would . . . my brother would
die. A deal was a deal.

But he still had his back to me, waiting till the lady was far enough away so he could set it down.

I had to know. "Why did you stop to help me help her? You're from evil and everything." I forgot to talk like a hero, but I didn't care.

"My powers come from the infernal, but I use them in the service of good. I could no more allow your attack to harm an innocent than I would allow it to harm me."

Somewhere, I wanted to belive he was lying. I could almost hear a voice saying it.

But I looked at him, and I looked at the woman crawling away, as afraid of me as she was of Ghost Rider, and somehow I just couldn't believe it anymore.

He threw away the pole and turned to me. I help up my hands. "No. Stop. I don't know what I'm gonna do now, but I don't wanna fight anymore. I didn't mean to do all this. I'm just a kid."

Mephisto, forced to flee the boy's mind, hastily shifted into the physical world with as much of himself as he could muster. The boy might not be a suitable candidate for minion anymore, but he might still win his goal. . . .

So, instead of beating him up, I told him everything. My name, how old I am, how I got to be a hero, everything. It's hard to tell what somebody's thinking if they head is just a skull, but he didn't say anything until I was finished.

"So I said if he made me a hero and saved my brother, I'd wipe you off the face of the Earth. I didn't want to hurt nobody, I just wanted to save my brother. I guess I sort of wanted to have powers too."

"And you can still have both. All you have to do is live up to the deal."

I turned around. There was the guy again, outlined in the shadows where one of the streetlights was tore up.

"No way! Ghost Rider's not mean! You lied to me!" I was mad.

"I did not lie about that. I said he had fought with some of my friends."

"All your friends are mean punks and liars, just like you!" I wasn't going to let him talk me into any more dumb stuff.

"And you are one of them. From what I can see you're going

back on our deal. You have your powers, now do as you promised.''

He had me there. A deal was a deal. I turned to Ghost Rider.

He wasn't there. He was running back to his motorcycle.

"What are you—? No! *That's not what I meant!*" yelled the shadow guy, but Ghost Rider hadn't said anything.

The shadow guy seemed to move towards Ghost Rider, but Ghost Rider was already next to his motorcycle. He was reaching for something on the gas tank.

"I do this because of James Carruthers," he said. It was kind of cool to hear him say my name like that.

And then there was a flash and some clouds. I rubbed my eyes from the flash, and when I looked again, Ghost Rider wasn't there, or his motorcycle. Just some ordinary guy and an ordinary-lookin' motorcycle. The guy got on his motorcycle and started it up.

"Congratulations, kid. You just forced the Ghost Rider off the face of the Earth," the guy said. I didn't understand.

The shadow figured howled, like a dog howl but scarier, and floated over to me. I mean yeah, floated. "Listen to me!" he said in a hissy voice. "That man is the Ghost Rider. Since his mortal form is a totally different entity, you have won your bargain.

"But I promised you the power to save your brother, and the power to be a hero, not both. To heal your brother, you need only will it, but it will take all the power I have given you, perhaps more. It may kill you as well. Destroy the Ghost Rider's mortal form, and you can have both. He is powerless now! It will require almost nothing. Do not hesitate, or all is lost!''

I thought about what he had said. He started whispering to me, other things he'd give me if I did it, money and cool gear.

I shut him out. "Take all my power back. I don't want to be this kinda hero. Take it all back. Just make my brother okay again.''

A timeless time later, in a placeless place, a flock of formless forms shifted and writhed in their attempts to avoid facing their faceless lord. When Mephisto was annoyed, cities felt his fury; when he was enraged, emperors lived in fear.

Right now, Mephisto was livid.

But as the howling rains of razors and vitriol lashed at the realm, no creature dared approach the realm's lord. Rumors sprang up about a Devious Inspiration that had tried that not very long ago, and that the new voice in the Chorus of Agony that welled up from the torture chambers of the dread one's keep belonged to said Inspiration, and that the new voice's exceptional tone and pitch was testimony to the originality and fiendish nature of the particular punishments it had earned. True or not, it would be a long, long time before anything allowed the mute parody of freedom accorded the denizens of the realm would risk it by intruding on the dread one's funks again.

But that's how I got to be a hero and fight Ghost Rider. And that's the *real* reason my brother got better, from my super powers, which I lost, but usin' 'em on my brother didn't kill me like the shadow guy said it would, neither.

Momma says it was God that made him better, but that's okay. I know how Moms are.

Quit laughin'! I know you don't believe me. Nobody do. That's okay. 'Cause I got my big brother.

The Painter of a Thousand Perils

PRIVATE EXHIBITION

PIERCE ASKEGREN

Illustration by Dick Ayers

Q: Whatever happened to the so-called Painter of a Thousand Perils?

A: Years ago, forger Wilhelm Van Vile used what he claimed were magic paints to terrorize Long Island with a series of bizarre, "impossible" crimes. The images that he created literally came to life and wreaked havoc before the Human Torch stopped him and his confederates. Van Vile was released on parole early last year and now works as a commercial illustrator; you may have seen his work in trade magazines. He shuns publicity and lives a life as quiet as his crime spree was spectacular.

(from the Daily Bugle*'s "Names in the News—*
Then and Now" column)

THEY WERE WAITING for Van Vile when he got home. He had trudged the three long blocks from the subway stop and up the four flights of stairs to the ratty Queens apartment that the parole board had found him and was fumbling with the lock when the door swung open. Van Vile got a brief glimpse of the bald man who stood framed in the doorway, just long enough to recognize him, and then a blackjack came down, hard. "Tobin," Van Vile said, and fell to the floor, unconscious.

When Van Vile awoke, he was bound securely to the tall-backed kitchen chair that he had bought for seven dollars at a local thrift store, completely immobilized with nylon cord and heavy duct tape. His head hurt and his eyes stung; when they cleared, he could see that "Scar" Tobin was still there, seated on the couch that faced Van Vile. Some blond punk stood nearby, obviously awaiting orders.

The years had not been kind to Tobin. The big man had gone soft and seemed smaller now. He still sported the shaved head and the jagged scar that he had made his trademarks, but his bushy eyebrows had gone gray and he wore thick bifocals. A cane lay across his knees. Tobin smiled when Van Vile's gaze caught his. "Hello, Willie," he said.

"Hello, Scar. How long have you been out?"

Tobin's only reply was to light a cigar and blow a long plume of blue smoke into Van Vile's still smarting eyes. When he spoke, it wasn't to his captive. "Eric," he said. "Go ahead and search this dump. Willie isn't going anywhere." In response, the blond thug who had slugged Van Vile stepped into the next room, the studio. Loud noises followed as he began ransacking the place.

Tobin stood, leaning heavily on his cane. He was careful to stay in Van Vile's field of vision as he walked around the living room. He gestured at the unframed pictures that were thumbtacked to the greasy wallpaper. "Nice work, Willie. All of these yours?"

Van Vile tried to nod in reply, but couldn't. His bonds were too constricting. "Yes," he said. "Yes, all mine, all my work. I get them back after they're published."

"Very pretty. You sell these to magazines, right?" Tobin tapped one, a drawing of a happy girl playing volleyball. Van Vile had slaved over it for many long hours before getting her features exactly right. "Very nice. Pencil and ink, and pastels, and crayons, and those funny pens."

"Markers."

"Yeah, markers. All that stuff, but I don't see any paintings."

"I don't paint anymore, Scar," Van Vile said. "One of the conditions of my parole." He sighed. "Foolish, really, since I was a con long before our little adventure. But I indulge the authorities whenever possible."

Tobin looked away from the illustration, stared at Van Vile. "Where are they, Willie?"

Van Vile knew what Tobin was talking about. He wanted the paints, the magic paints Van Vile had found years ago, the otherworldly paints that had let him reshape reality to match his will. Tobin and Van Vile had been partners in the ensuing crime campaign, with several brief, spectacular successes to their credit—until the Human Torch had brought them both down. Now Tobin was back and he wanted the paints.

"Don't be absurd, Scar. The paints are gone. The Torch burned them up, destroyed them all. You know that. You were there."

Tobin shook his head. "I don't think so," he said. "You're not stupid, Willie—careless, but not stupid. I figure you stashed some of the paints, hid them away. I know I would have." He smiled. "Then, all you'd need to do is paint a picture of more paints, and make that picture come to life. And so on, and so on, and so on."

"Good thinking, Scar. I wish I were as clever," Van Vile replied. "But I'm not." He struggled slightly against his bonds, but they were unyielding. Eric had done his work well; he was trapped in that chair until someone cut him free. "Do you think I would live in such a place, if I still had the paints?"

"Maybe you're waiting until the heat's off. Maybe you've lost your nerve or maybe you've got something planned. Or maybe you're stupid and didn't stash them at all." Tobin shrugged. "I don't believe that, but I'll find out for sure."

"You're going to kill me, aren't you?"

Tobin didn't answer. He was distracted by Eric, who had continued his search into the living room. "Look, boss," the thug said, reaching behind a bookcase. "I found something." He held up his discovery for examination.

It was another picture, small and subdued but very nearly photographic in its realism. From the taut canvas, a young man in jeans and a sports shirt gazed coolly out at the three men. Even without the distinctive costume, Tobin recognized the subject. It was Johnny Storm, but the Storm of some years ago, the teenager who had put both Scar Tobin and Wilhelm Van Vile in jail.

It was a painting of the Human Torch.

"I'm rather sorry you found that," said Van Vile. His voice was more confident now, as if he were the captor and not the captive. Tobin turned to look at him—but Eric's sudden, frightened cry made him look back at the painting again.

Storm's image was swelling, expanding, erupting from the canvas, and igniting into the flaming figure of the Torch as it did so. Eric struggled under the weight of a small canvas that was now, impossibly, too heavy for him to hold. Tobin broke into a sweat as waves of heat struck him. Storm's doppelgänger was halfway to reality now. The emerging Torch smiled tightly, reached out with flaming fingertips that Tobin knew could melt steel—

"Smash it!" Tobin yelled. "Tear the damned thing up!" Without conscious thought, he spun and lashed out at Van Vile's head with his walking stick. The blow was glancing, but hard enough to break Van Vile's concentration; the artist's eyes closed for an instant as consciousness almost fled. The Torch, nearly but not completely real, sank back into the art even as Eric destroyed it.

Tobin took a deep breath and tried to gather his wits. Eric was frantically tearing the painting into smaller and smaller shreds. Tobin ordered the frightened thug to stop, and inspected his handiwork. Johnny Storm was back on the canvas, albeit in pieces. Tobin examined one fragment and snorted derisively.

"Same old Willie," he said. "Still careless. The Torch's eyes are *blue*, you've got them *brown*. That's the kind of mistake that put both of us in the pen."

"I don't like this, boss, I don't like it at all." Eric was edgy and his voice held a note of panic. "How can pictures move like that? How does he do it?"

"Calm down," Tobin said to him. "I told you about that. Sometimes the paintings come to life, sometimes they just come true. He can turn them off, too." He paused. "Problem is, Willie makes mistakes, little flaws that snowball and screw things up. When he was a forger, he always got the details wrong. Last time around those mistakes were what got us caught. When his paintings came to life, they still had errors in them. The Torch recognized his style and came after him. Right, Willie?"

"Right enough," Van Vile said, placidly. "But you might as well leave now. I used the last of the paints to make that picture—for my own amusement. I liked being able to boss a Human Torch around. But the paints are all used up."

"I don't believe you."

"No, I didn't think you would," Van Vile said agreeably.

"Eric," Tobin said. "Tear up the rest of the pictures. I don't want any more surprises."

"But that was the only painting," Eric said, whining. "There weren't any others. I looked."

"Shut your hole and do like I say!"

Eric plucked illustrations from the wall one at a time and carefully tore each into small pieces. Van Vile watched impassively as the thug methodically shredded countless hours of work and let the debris fall to the floor. He started with a carefully rendered bouquet of roses on Bristol board, then worked his way through a series of celebrity caricatures on tracing paper and several architectural renderings as he progressed around the room. Van Vile watched silently, until Eric reached for the volleyball girl. "That really isn't necessary," he said mildly. "Those pictures are harmless. I'm harmless, without the paint."

"I've had enough of your lies," Tobin said, before Eric could respond. The gangster reached into his jacket pocket and pulled out a small leather case. He opened it, revealing a hypodermic needle and an ampoule. "Got something here that will make you tell the truth," he said. He filled the hypodermic, leaned close to the helpless Van Vile—

—and jerked back in stunned surprise as the medical instrument abruptly turned into a small white mouse.

The mouse bit him on the thumb, squirmed out of his grip, then crawled up inside his jacket sleeve. "Get it off, get it off!" Tobin yelled. Eric came to his aid, tried to dislodge the rodent. Finally, squeaking in impotent rage, the mouse fell to the floor and ran behind the bookcase that had concealed the painting. Eric headed after it, but Tobin told him not to bother; they had bigger problems.

The pictures Eric had destroyed were re-assembling themselves. Tatters of canvas and paper slid along one another, aligning their ragged edges until they matched and fused, merging back into complete units. One by one they reformed, then slithered like living things across the floor and up the walls, returning to their original placements. The last was the painting of Johnny Storm, which rolled, end over end, to go behind the bookcase. There was a squeak of protest as it thumped into place right on the hypodermic mouse.

Still bound, still helpless, Van Vile was smiling now, lips pulled back to reveal uneven teeth in a disturbing grin. "You can't be doing this," Tobin said slowly. "You can't. Your hands are tied."

Eric drew his gun, brought it close to Van Vile's head. "I've had enough," he said. "I'm gonna punch this guy's ticket—" His words became a cry of shock and pain as the gun he held grew into a blob of soft concrete that flowed around his hand, then squeezed and hardened. The heavy mass jerked his arm downward.

Tobin looked at his underling, stunned. He had seen things like this happen before. "How're you doing it, Van Vile?" he asked. "How?"

The apartment door opened. Wilhelm Van Vile walked into the room. He set down a small easel he was carrying. He held a small wooden case Tobin had seen before, years ago. It was a paint box—*the* paint box. The door closed behind him of its own accord.

Too startled to react, Tobin and Eric looked at the two versions of Van Vile, the one in the chair and the one with the easel. "Keep it down, you two," both Van Viles said, in perfect unison.

"We don't want to disturb the neighbors." Their tandem voices produced a slight echo-chamber effect.

The new Van Vile produced a palette and brush, and began to daub at his canvas. "Now, Scar," he said, "You and I go back a long way. I'm willing to forget this little incident, if you and your chum get out of here and keep your mouths shut. If you can't—well, let's just say I'll be responsible for the consequences."

The Van Vile in the chair waited for his counterpart to finish speaking. "Self-portrait," he said, then he smiled and disappeared. The ropes and tape that had held him fell in loops as he dwindled and faded, like a TV image when the set is turned off. He had gone to wherever the mouse and the concrete came from.

Eric looked up in surprise. Hurting and angry, he flung himself at the remaining Van Vile, flailing with the block of concrete that encased his hand. To Tobin's surprise, the painter didn't dodge. Eric connected and the heavy mass made a satisfying sound as it slammed against Van Vile's head. This time, the artist didn't say anything as he fell to the floor. His brush and palette fell with him, bounced on the dirty carpet and lay still.

With a cry of delight, Tobin seized the paint box. "At last, at last, I got it!" he said. He forced the box open and began trying to unscrew a jar of the magic stuff Van Vile had found years before.

"What good's that gonna do you?" Eric wanted to know. "You aren't an artist. You can't paint."

"I'll learn, dammit."

"Maybe you can do something about this?" Eric gestured at the block of concrete that enclosed his hand, streaked with Van Vile's blood. "It hurts something fierce."

"Yeah, yeah, yeah."

Eric shrugged. He looked at the canvas. It was almost blank, with only a few smears of subdued color defining an indeterminate form. "Hell, I can do better than that," he muttered. "My three-year-old nephew can do better." He looked down at Van Vile and cursed softly, then drew one foot back to kick the unconscious artist's ribs.

"I don't understand," Tobin was saying. "This thing won't open. None of them will open."

Eric swung his foot forward, fast and hard. At the very instant the tip of his loafer touched its target, Van Vile disappeared again. The unspent force of his kick threw Eric off-balance, made him stumble. Instinctively, he reached out for the easel's wooden frame to support himself, but his fingers found only air as it, too, vanished. Eric fell to the floor, cursing.

Tobin was cursing, too. He had just realized that the jar he held was just a piece of solid glass, colored to look like a container of paint. Disgusted, he dropped it, and didn't even notice it disappear.

The apartment door opened. Wilhelm Van Vile walked into the room. He set down a small easel he was carrying and smiled. "I can keep this up as long as you can," the Painter of a Thousand Perils assured his two captives.

Tobin gritted his teeth. "Is that you, Van Vile? Or another self-portrait?" Tobin asked. He paused. "Did you ever even go to jail?"

"Does it matter?" Van Vile asked with a smile.

"So, what happens now? Do you turn us into dogs or something and step on us?"

Van Vile shook his head. "Nothing so cruel," he said, and began to paint. He worked unbelievably swiftly, his brush blurring to near-invisibility as it conveyed color from palette to canvas. His tempo was only partly born of practice; the paints enabled their user to work at lightning speed. After a few seconds, Van Vile smiled and looked up. "You and your boy are going on a nice little trip, a vacation. Calcutta, I think. East India should be particularly unpleasant this time of year, and the political situation should make things interesting for you."

"Calcutta!?" Tobin and Eric shouted it in unison.

"Why are you doing this?" Tobin asked the question; Eric, still sprawled on the floor, just held his fossilized hand and whimpered. "Why do you play these games? With your kind of power, you can do anything you want."

"I need to maintain the art business and the apartment in order to qualify for parole. Your simple presence here could cost me that. I don't like jail and I don't want to go back."

"Why do you care about the parole board? With your power and my brains—"

Van Vile looked up from his work and scowled. "I have quite

enough brains of my own, thank you. I certainly intend to do and to have everything. I have another studio, Scar, and in that studio are paintings that will amaze and frighten you when they become reality. But they must be perfect." He spoke the words with great precision, shaping each syllable carefully. "Absolutely perfect."

He paused, remembering something. Then he stepped to the bookcase and pulled the portrait of the Human Torch from its hiding place. Two quick dabs with his brush, and Johnny Storm's eyes were their proper shade of blue. Van Vile grunted softly, put the painting away and returned to his easel.

"I've learned that perfection takes time," he continued, resuming his work. He painted more slowly now, obviously taking great pleasure in each brushstroke. "A great deal of time."

"So?"

"So, I don't want the Fantastic Four or Doctor Strange or any other meddlers of note dropping by before I'm ready for them. Until then, Wilhelm Van Vile will live out the quiet life the authorities have defined for him." He set his brush and palette down, stepped back from the easel and examined the finished painting. "There we go," he said, "another masterpiece. Tell me what you think of it, boys."

He smirked at Tobin and Eric, and reversed the picture. They turned pale when they saw the image. Tobin's frantic protests and Eric's whimpering were both cut off as the two men abruptly vanished.

"Enjoy yourselves," Van Vile murmured into the silence that remained behind them—but he didn't seem to mean it.

The Super-Skrull

ALL CREATURES GREAT AND SKRULL

GREG COX

Illustration by Ron Lim

THE SUPER-SKRULL hated Earth.

Ex-Commander Kl'rt, once the greatest hero of the distant Skrull Empire, cursed the wretched planet upon whose dismal surface he now walked. This seemingly insignificant mudball, he mused, had far too often played a pivotal role in interstellar affairs. Kl'rt's own standing in the Empire had been lost as a result of his past defeats at the hands of the Avengers, the Fantastic Four, and the rest of Earth's freakish defenders. He had become an exile, a Skrull without a home, and all because of this miserable, little world.

And here he was again.

The sky is too blue, he thought, and the temperature too cool for comfort. Earth's gravity, a few degrees stronger than that of Tarnax IV, his long-lost home, tugged at his feet as they tread wearily upon the concrete sidewalks of the Terran island known as Manhattan. Kl'rt looked up from where he stood. Towering skyscrapers of stone and glass largely blocked his view of the sky. The Andromeda Galaxy, sacred birthplace of the Skrull race, seemed very far away.

At the moment, he resembled an average Terran male. Not his natural form, of course; like all Skrulls, Kl'rt had the ability to disguise his shape at will. His flesh was now pink, like many of the Terrans he'd encountered, with short black hair that never fell below a pair of typically unimpressive human ears. His eyes were deceptively blue, and his black-and-purple Skrull military uniform, which he still wore proudly despite his exile status, hid behind a false façade of native attire: a rumpled brown trenchcoat, faded blue jeans, and boots. Although the city streets were full of human pedestrians, none recognized Kl'rt as possibly the most fearsome warrior the Skrull Empire had ever bred.

This was as it should be. Kl'rt had no desire to provoke a confrontation with any of Earth's volatile super-beings, at least not right away. There would be time enough later to have revenge on the likes of Mr. Fantastic and Spider-Man. Today his mission took priority over his natural desire to conquer old foes. The security of the Skrull Empire, and his own hopes of restoring his fallen honor, depended on his success here and now. Indeed, he thought, only the promise of so great a triumph could have ever lured him back to this misbegotten planet.

His target was an alien terrorist named Colonel Zyrelle Persa, a former Kree officer now associated with the renegade Kree resistance movement. The recent conquest of the loathsome Kree Empire, ancient enemy of the Skrulls, by yet another interstellar superpower, the bird-like Shi'ar, had drastically altered the balance of power throughout the known universe. An uneasy peace now existed between the Skrulls and the Shi'ar, a peace that could well be upset by the insurgency of Persa and her compatriots. Kl'rt bore no great love for the Shi'ar—in his opinion, they were a race of decadent, feathered fools—but the bitter enmity between Kree and Skrull stretched back over ten million years. Eager to regain his good name by capturing the rebel leader, he had pursued Persa across thousands of light-years to this very solar system, planet, and city. He did not know what she hoped to accomplish on Earth, but anything that aided the cause of Kree independence could not be good for the Skrulls.

Car horns blared as the lights changed at the intersection up ahead. According to metal signs posted in one of the Terrans' many barbaric tongues, Kl'rt stood near the corner of Park Avenue South and 33rd Street, facing a concrete stairway descending into the city's primitive underground transport system; the "subway" he believed it was called. Mere moments ago, soaring over the city in the form of a pigeon, he'd glimpsed Colonel Persa disappear down these very steps. He quickly consulted the colored symbols marking the subway entrance. Persa apparently intended to take the 6 train uptown. She was heading north, the Skrull concluded, but to where?

His boots smacked against the steps as he marched down into the subway terminal. The stench of the subterranean chamber, redolent of human waste and perspiration, disgusted him. Not even the prison pits of the mad Titan Thanos, whom once he had served, had exuded such an obvious sense of filth and neglect. Crude graffiti obscured the garish posters affixed to the station's walls. The defaced posters advertised all manner of vile human entertainments and consumables, none of which appealed to Kl'rt. A sense of almost unbearable homesickness swept over him as he recalled the pristine towers and temples of the Skrull throneworld. Would he never see his home again?

Kl'rt shook off his mournful musings, simultaneously strengthening his resolve to regain his rightful place in the Empire by capturing Persa before she could complete her subversive activities. *Soon*, he vowed silently, *I will once more hold a place of honor at the Empress's side, and then will all my enemies fear the power at my command.*

For good reason was he known throughout the universe as the Super-Skrull; thanks to bionic alterations made to his body many years ago, he possessed physical attributes far beyond those of ordinary Skrulls. Besides the shape-changing ability common to his race, Kl'rt had also acquired the unique super-powers of the Terran adventurers known as the Fantastic Four, making him indeed a warrior to be reckoned with. But as formidable as he already was, he reminded himself, he could yet be mightier still. His fantastic abilities were fueled by artificial power-receptors implanted within his flesh, capable of absorbing cosmic energy from a variety of sources. At present, the ambient cosmic energy of the universe was enough to maintain his power at an undeniably impressive level. It was within the Empress's power, however, to activate distant satellites that could beam cosmic energy directly into his body, amplifying his already fearsome strength until he would be virtually unstoppable. *And then*, he thought, *I will avenge all my past indignities and raise the Skrull Empire above all the civilizations within the cosmos. And Earth shall be the first to fall. . . .*

But first he had to prove his worthiness by eliminating a real and significant threat to Skrulls everywhere. He quickened his pace, only to find a horizontal metal rod barring his entrance onto the subway platform. He suspected that a fee of some sort was required, but he did not have time to bother with whatever native baubles passed for currency on this backwater planet. He glanced around him. The area around the barrier was sparsely populated at the moment. None of the humans appeared to be observing him. *Good*, he thought.

Calling upon the elastic abilities of Mr. Fantastic, he stretched his torso until it was thin enough to pass through the narrow gap between the metal bar and the gate. Once through the turnstile, he immediately reassumed normal human proportions. His momentary transformation attracted no attention from the handful of commuters milling about on the platform. Caught up in their own thoughts and affairs, the humans remained oblivious to the disguised alien in their midst.

Nor was the Skrull the only extraterrestrial lurking in this underground tunnel. Scanning the area around him, Kl'rt quickly spotted Colonel Persa at the northern end of the platform.

Like the rest of her inferior species, the Kree renegade could not change her shape, thus she looked much as she had in the datafiles Kl'rt had studied before arriving on Earth. She was pink-skinned, like a human, with short red hair and the grim expression of a hardened warrior. A thin white scar stretched across her forehead, evidence of some past battle fought in the service of her despicable cause. A slick black raincoat, cut according to local Terran fashion, helped her blend in with the unsuspecting humans around her. Aside from the telltale scar, her face was smooth and unfurrowed, her ears small and delicately rounded. Kl'rt found her remarkably unattractive.

As he stalked towards her, weaving through the clusters of humans scattered between them, Persa glanced in his direction. Her green eyes met his, and they widened in alarm. "Wraiths of the Void," he swore under his breath. Somehow the Kree agent had penetrated his disguise. Perhaps, he surmised, she had genetic scanners concealed in a pair of contact lenses; Kree military scientists had been developing technology of that nature before their empire fell to the Shi'ar. *No matter*, he thought. He had her now. There was no way she could escape.

So intent was he on his cornered prey that Kl'rt barely noticed a trio of human males until they stepped between Persa and himself, blocking his path. "Hey, dude," one of the youths said. "What's your hurry?"

The Skrull considered this unwanted distraction. Even by the low standards of the human race, these impertinent specimens seemed an unsavory group. They were clearly adolescent, about the age of the Human Torch the first time Kl'rt encountered him, and their sneering, mammalian faces were not improved by a mottling of dirt, pimples, and scraggly patches of facial fuzz. Cheap, aboriginal jewelry dangled from their measly human ears, while their bare arms bore ugly, vulgar tattoos. *And to think*, he thought, *that some consider humans a civilized species.*

"Out of my way," he barked. He tried to keep his eyes on Colonel Persa, but the striplings, jostling each other even as they crowded in front of him, kept obstructing his view. He attempted to shove his way through them.

The youth who'd spoken before shoved back, astounding Kl'rt

with his arrogance. "Whoa," he said. "Where do you think you're going?" Arms crossed atop his chest, he planted himself squarely in Kl'rt's path. "I don't think I like your attitude."

The other males laughed and egged him on: "Yeah! You tell him, Vic!" "Way to go, Vic! Who the hell he think he is?" From their behavior, Kl'rt deduced that "Vic" led this pack of feral children. All three youths rocked back and forth on their heels, full of pent-up energy and aggression. They clenched their fists, sometimes punching a closed fist against the palm of the opposite hand. *Do they actually intend to rob me,* Kl'rt wondered, *or is this merely some atavistic primate dominance ritual?* Not for the first time, he thanked the unfathomable lords of probability that his own people had descended from cool, calculating reptiles instead of a worthless tribe of braying apes.

"It's people like you," Vic continued, "that give New Yorkers a bad name." He raised his palms in front of him, ready to give Kl'rt another push if he dared to try to force his way past them again. "Stuck-up, no-good, piece of—"

"I'm from out of town," the Skrull said dryly, interrupting Vic's uninspired invective. He was tempted to use the power of the Human Torch to incinerate the whole trio, but that might attract too much attention, summoning one or more of New York's many super-powered defenders. He looked to the left and the right. The other humans on the platform, having noted the trouble brewing between him and the gang of youths, had done no more than back away to the other end of the platform. None looked inclined to get involved or, at this point, call for assistance. More importantly, he noted, Persa had not attempted to slip by him on either side; presumably she remained trapped at the northern end of the platform. *I need to dispose of these nuisances,* he concluded, *but discreetly.*

"Hey, I'm talking to you," Vic protested. He laid a fetid human paw upon Kl'rt's shoulder. *That was a mistake,* Kl'rt thought. He seized Vic's arm by the wrist, locking it in an unbreakable grip. "What the—?" Vic began. Kl'rt's eyes found Vic's and refused to let them go. The human's eyes went blank and his jaw dropped slackly, revealing cracked, scum-coated, yellow teeth. Hypnosis, as Vic had just learned, was also numbered among the Super-Skrull's abilities.

"Freeze," Kl'rt hissed. Vic's entire body stiffened. With a twist of his arm, Kl'rt sent the human's paralyzed body crashing to the platform floor where Vic laid on one side, as lifeless and immobile as a statue. Beyond Vic's fallen form, the Skrull glimpsed Persa watching the entire scene with a look of horror on her face. *Just wait,* he thought maliciously. *Your turn is coming.*

"Vic!" one of the remaining youths cried out. Rage replaced surprise on his face as he tore his gaze away from his insensate leader and stared at Kl'rt with murder in his eyes. "You stinkin' sonofabitch!" he hollered, then threw his fist at the Skrull's deceptively human face. Kl'rt blocked the blow with an invisible force field, just like those employed by the Invisible Woman of the Fantastic Four. The human yelped as his knuckles collided with an unseen obstruction. Kl'rt allowed himself a thin smile at the human's confusion and distress.

A loud rumbling noise came from somewhere behind the Skrull, accompanied by a gust of wind. The rumbling grew louder by the moment, and Kl'rt realized that a train had to be approaching the station. *Enough of this,* he resolved impatiently. He couldn't let Persa get away.

Although visibly confused by the events of the last few moments, Vic's comrades did not look ready to flee. If anything, fear had only heightened their animal fury. Both humans charged at the disguised Skrull; Kl'rt observed that a knife had appeared in the shorter youth's hand. The Skrull did not retreat from their attack. Calmly, contemptuously, he expanded the force field until it formed an invisible wall, then sent it hurling like a battering ram into the two humans. Both youths were knocked backwards by a wave of concentrated psychic energy that left them sprawled on their backs, groaning in pain. *And yet,* Kl'rt thought smugly, *not one onlooker could say they'd seen me lay my hands on either human.*

With a thought, he dissolved the force field. His would-be assailants remained strewn on the platform floor, the fight apparently knocked out of them. And just in time; accompanied by the ear-splitting screech of brakes against the subway tracks, the train pulled into the station. Kl'rt saw that the vehicle consisted of several cars linked together in a chain, each car stuffed full of human travellers.

As the train came to a stop, he stomped towards Persa—only to be halted by an unexpected tug on his ankle. Glaring downwards, he beheld one of Vic's cohorts, still lying facedown upon the concrete, clutching onto the Skrull's ankle with both hands. "You're not going anywhere, freak," the human muttered through crushed and bleeding lips. "Gonna teach you a lesson." Kl'rt was almost impressed by the human's stubborn animal defiance.

But time and Colonel Persa were slipping away. With a *whish* of released air, the doors of the 6 train slid open. Mobs of humans poured out of every car, shoving their way past the New Yorkers attempting to force their way onto the train. Peering through clashing waves of impatient humanity, Kl'rt spied Persa slipping onto the first car of the train.

"No!" the Skrull exclaimed. She was getting away. He tried to yank his leg free from the young human's grip, but the youth clung to Kl'rt's ankle with all his strength. The Skrull snarled angrily, then let the heat of his fury free. . . .

Like the Human Torch, the Super-Skrull could transform all or part of his body into a blazing inferno of flame and heat. Right now, he merely raised the temperature of his ankle high enough to sear human flesh. The unfortunate youth cried out in pain as he jerked his charred and smoking hands away from Kl'rt's super-heated leg. The Skrull had no time to enjoy the human's agony. Already the subway doors were sliding shut. Kl'rt ran across the platform towards the car Persa had disappeared into, but he was too late. Standing on the very brink of the platform, he watched the train pull out of station, taking his prey with it. Soon all he could see were the train's taillights, receding into the murky blackness of the northbound tunnel.

Not so fast, Kree, the Skrull thought. *No one escapes me that easily.* Using two of his powers simultaneously, he flamed on *and* turned invisible. One second, an ordinary-looking human appeared to be leaning out over the platform, eyeing the departing train. A heartbeat later, the disguised Skrull vanished from sight. Concealed from prying human eyes, Kl'rt's body was enveloped by flames just as invisible. Only the soft crackle of the fire betrayed his presence, but the noise of the moving train drowned that out.

Lifting off from the platform like a blazing rocket, he launched himself into the tunnel. He flew through the darkness above the subway tracks, after the retreating taillights. Transparent fire jetted out behind the Skrull, propelling him through the tunnel at top speed so that he easily caught up with Persa's train. His elastic arms reached out and caught hold of a door handle at the rear of the train. Kl'rt briefly considered using the superhuman strength of the Thing to halt the train here and now; he was certainly powerful enough to overcome the train's motorized acceleration with his bare hands. *But no*, he decided, *that would definitely be conspicuous.*

Instead he chose to board the train more traditionally. Still holding onto the door handle, he retracted his arm until he was standing on a tiny metal ledge at the end of the subway car. The wind generated by the train's headlong progress whipped past him as he extinguished his flames and restored his visibility. Once again, he resembled a completely unremarkable human being. Sliding open the subway door, he entered the rear car.

The car was packed with unsightly human cargo. The stench of too many Terrans crammed into a confined space almost made Kl'rt gag. The buzz of pointless human chatter rung in his ears. There were more passengers than seats available, so the center of the car was crowded with standing humans hanging onto shining steel posts mounted over the seated commuters' heads. Kl'rt recalled that Persa had escaped onto the train's first car, at the opposite end of the train from where he now stood. Could he make his way to the front of the train before it pulled into the next station? Kl'rt knew he would have to hurry.

He attempted to shoulder his way through the densely-populated car, but progress was maddeningly slow. The assorted passengers moved out of his way grudgingly if they moved at all. He had to squeeze and push forward, stepping carefully through an obstacle course composed of shopping bags, briefcases, and outstretched limbs. "Make way," he grunted. "Move over." The other passengers grumbled and muttered crude Terran obscenities at him. It took him at least a minute or two just to reach the entrance to the next car. Persa remained nine cars ahead. *At this rate*, Kl'rt realized, *I'm never going to catch up with her.*

Shoving his way into the next car, he considered his options. He could travel faster in the form of an insect, but, given the crowded conditions, the chances of his being swatted or stepped upon struck him as far too high. Rather, since traversing Manhattan's subway system seemed to depend on brute force and a willingness to bully your way past your fellows, Kl'rt chose to increase his width and height. With only a moment's thought, he went from a human form of unassuming proportions to one that closely resembled the incredible Hulk. His shoulders broadened, his biceps expanded. He coarsened his features as well, giving his face a more bellicose, primeval cast. *Careful,* he warned himself, *don't overdo it. The idea is to be intimidating, not unbelievable.*

Six inches taller and several pounds heavier, Kl'rt found his new appearance did in fact speed his passage through the overstuffed subway cars. Certainly, he heard fewer complaints and curses as he rushed through car after car, intent on locating the elusive Persa. Crowds parted before him, the humans stepping over each other in their eagerness to get out of his way. Occasionally, the Skrull glanced over at the windows lining both sides of the car. This train, he observed, seemed to be zooming past several available stations. Did Persa have anything to do with the train's nonstop journey, he wondered, or was this the 6 train's normal route? He quickened his pace, practically throwing unlucky humans aside in his haste to capture the Kree agent before the train reached her still-to-be-determined destination. "Out of my way!" he bellowed, abandoning all pretense of tact. From what he had seen so far, these New Yorkers would not find his behavior exceptional.

He had almost reached the front car when he thought he detected a change in the vehicle's speed. Was it just his imagination or was the train truly slowing down? *We must almost be there,* he concluded, *wherever "there" is.* He grabbed hold of the door handle marking the exit from this car. He started to pull the door open.

Then, without warning, a beefy hand descended on his shoulder. "Hold on there," a voice commanded. "What's the rush?" Kl'rt spun about to confront a large human male, only a few inches shorter than his own present form. The male had dark skin and a bushy strip of black facial hair above his upper lip. He kept one hand on Kl'rt's shoulder. With the other hand, he held up a sheath of fabric apparently stitched together from animal hides. A metallic badge was pinned to the fabric. "Transit Police," the man announced, as if the Skrull was supposed to be impressed. "What's your problem?"

"That is none of your concern, hu—" Kl'rt started to say "human" but caught himself in time. Beneath his feet he felt a change in the momentum of the floor. The train was definitely slowing down. He did not have time to waste with this irritating human. Shaking the man's hand free, he turned his back on the police officer and reached again for the door.

"Hey, I'm talking to you!" the human protested. Kl'rt swiftly erected an invisible wall between himself and the policeman. *Count yourself fortunate,* he thought, *that I can not spare precious seconds to dispose of you properly.* "What?! What's this?" the policeman shouted. "Damn!" He heard the human's fists pounding upon the force field, and his shouts of, "Stupid, freaking, mutant scum!" but the Skrull was no longer listening.

The train was pulling into a station as he jumped into the first car. His eyes searched the car for Colonel Persa, then grew wide with excitement as he spotted his target at the opposite end of the car. The Kree terrorist held open the narrow metal door separating the train's pilot from his passengers. She had a weapon pointed at the pilot's head; Kl'rt recognized it as a ZR377 Rechargeable Plasma Projector, standard issue for the Kree Imperial Forces back when they still had an empire to defend. *So,* he thought, *Persa* had *hijacked the train for her own subversive purposes.* "Kree!" he shouted in a language only she was likely to understand. "You face the Super-Skrull. Turn and surrender!"

Persa swung the muzzle of her weapon away from the subway pilot. Kl'rt guessed the human needed no further encouragement to bring the train to a halt. Through the car's windows, he saw a brightly-lit subway platform coming into view. He had to capture Persa now, he realized, before she had a chance to prolong the chase. He raised his right hand and ignited it before her eyes. His hand glowed as red as the molten core of a volcanic asteroid, threatening to throw off fiery destruction at any moment.

Persa fired first. Aiming her ZR377 straight at the Skrull, she sent a beam of incandescent green radiance hurling across the length of the car. The beam was fast, but Kl'rt was faster. His elastic body suddenly stretched sideways, out of the path of the plasma beam. The glowing emerald blast struck the roof of the train instead, slicing through the steel and into the ceiling of the tunnel beyond. Chunks of stone and cement broke free from the tunnel and crashed onto the top of the train, a rain of ash and debris falling through the razor-sharp gash in the roof of the train and into the car itself. Kl'rt blinked and shook his head amidst a dusty cloud of pulverized rubble. *Why couldn't these humans have built their tunnels out of something durable?* he thought angrily. *This is no proper arena for a battle. It might as well be made out of mud and straw.* He tried to aim his flaming fist at his enemy, but there were too many frightened humans in the way.

Persa's blast had sparked panic among the Terran commuters. Mindless screams and shouting assailed the Skrull's ears. A score of humans surged to their feet, blocking his view of Persa and getting in his way. The placid stupor of so many human cattle had become a frenzied riot, as the terrified passengers surged towards the exits, fighting and clawing each other in their desperate desire to flee the subway. Kl'rt saw a human female, grey-haired and bent with age, bite the arm of a large male who got in her way. A pair of young lovers held onto each others's hands as though their destinies depended on it, only to be torn apart by the shifting tides of the riot. The train had not fully ceased its motion, nor had the car doors opened up, but that didn't stop crazed Terrans from pounding on the doors and climbing over the people in front of them.

Through the chaos, Kl'rt spotted Persa. The Kree renegade smirked at him, clearly proud of the tumult she had created. Kl'rt grabbed for her, his elongated arm snaking its way through a maze of thrashing human bodies, his red-hot fingers poised to clutch and burn.

By the time his hand reached the far end of the car, however, Persa was no longer there, swallowed up by the noise and confusion. Then, with a lurch that almost threw Kl'rt off his feet, the train braked to a full stop. The doors slid open and the mob became a stampede, pouring out of the car. He looked for Persa, but it was no good; it was all he could do to keep from being carried away himself by the crush of humanity. Within seconds, faster than he would have thought physically possible, the car was emptied of people. Even the train's pilot fled, leaving the Skrull alone in a deserted subway car. His right hand glowed like a red-hot coal.

Kl'rt ran out of the train, through the turnstile, and up the steps to the street above. *She can't have gone far,* he thought. *I can still catch her before she completes her mission. If only I knew what that mission was. . . .*

He found himself at the corner of another busy intersection. Buses and yellow cabs dominated the traffic. More impatient honking polluted the air.

Where was Persa? Where could she have gone? Although he searched the city streets in every direction, he detected no sign of the resourceful Kree operative. *Too bad she's pink*, he thought, *like so many Terrans are. A blue Kree would be easier to spot in a crowd.*

Perhaps he could see more from above. Abandoning his human disguise, he transformed into one of the flying vermin that infested this city: a pigeon. He could also fly in his Torch form, of course, but adopting the wings of a bird expended less cosmic energy. He flapped into the sky, swiftly rising above the skyscrapers and other buildings in the vicinity. Altitude improved his view indeed; from his new vantage point, he could see for miles around. Flying west, he saw Central Park—an immense green rectangle—stretch on for several blocks to his left. He hoped Persa had not sought refuge within the Park. She could hide for hours among the Park's overgrown foliage. Veering right, he circled above the many buildings bordering the Park. He still could not see Persa anywhere. *She must be in the Park*, he thought glumly. *I'm wasting my time.*

He almost gave up. Then: there she was!

His tiny, bird-sized heart leaped as he spotted a familiar, red-headed figure emerge from the shadow of a looming stone building. Looking about anxiously, she stepped out onto the crosswalk at the corner of yet another intersection. Kl'rt could not read the street signs from this high up, but she seemed to be heading for an imposing-looking building on the street that made for the Park's eastern border. The structure, a massive stone edifice with what looked like a fully-functional launching pad on its roof, looked familiar to Kl'rt. He'd been there before, although he couldn't remember when. *I've spent far too much time on this planet,* he recalled, *fighting too many insolent Terrans all over this entire worthless globe.* How could he expect to remember one sinkhole over another?

Persa headed straight for the mansion. A set of wide marble steps led up to a pair of polished oak doors. *This is it*, he thought. He didn't know what Persa was up to, but she seemed to be making her move. Kl'rt decided he didn't want the Kree spy to reach whatever was waiting within that mansion.

The Super-Skrull shed wings and feathers to assume a more combat-ready disguise: that of Johnny Storm, the Human Torch. The pigeon dissolved into a life-sized humanoid form seemingly composed of bright red flames. Lighter than air, he hovered above the city streets, radiating heat and light. Dancing flames crackled all over his body. After his long ordeal in the cramped, reeking confines of the subway, the Super-Skrull savored this moment of airborne omnipotence, elevated above the lowly masses of Earth with all the energy of a supernova coursing through his body! Exultant, he relished the unleashed power holding him aloft, felt the pent-up fire raging within his fingertips. True, beneath the flames, he'd been obliged to assume the shape and features of a callow human youth, but that was but a minor indignity.

"Kree!" he declared, in English this time, "The chase is over! You are mine now!"

Fire trailing behind him like the tail of a comet, the Super-Skrull dived toward Persa. To her credit, Kl'rt noted, the Kree neither surrendered nor turned to flee. There on the sidewalk, only a few yards away from the door of the mansion, she drew her ZR377 and fired a chartreuse beam of destruction at the attacking Skrull.

A good try, he thought, deftly fending off the plasma ray with an invisible force field, *but not good enough.* Her precious plasma gun was no match for the firepower at his disposal. To demonstrate his superiority, he hurled a fireball at Persa. The blazing sphere of crimson fire crashed to Earth near the Kree female, scorching the pavement at her feet. *A perfect shot,* Kl'rt gloated. He didn't want to kill Persa, at least not until she divulged the nature of her mission on Earth, but she needed to learn that no Kree, pink-skinned or blue, could ever be a match for a true Skrull warrior. Another fireball coalesced in the palm of his hand.

Persa again shot a plasma beam at Kl'rt, but it was also dispersed by the Skrull's force field. To his disgust, she lowered her weapon and ran like the cowardly Kree she was for the supposed safety of the mansion. "Help!" she cried, in a passable imitation of a Terran accent. "Somebody help me!" Kl'rt cut off her retreat with a well-thrown fireball. The glowing, roiling globule of fire flew from the Skrull's hand to the marble steps below. It exploded against the steps mere inches from the fleeing Kree, stopping her in her tracks. She took a few steps backwards, perhaps driven away by the heat left behind by the fireball. Kl'rt threw an entire volley of fireballs, one after another. They surrounded her, trapping her in an ever-tightening circle of flame. The fireballs hissed and sizzled as they trapped Persa. The smell of melting blacktop reached Kl'rt's nostrils. "Help!" Persa kept shouting. "Please, won't somebody help me?"

Somebody—or something—answered her cries. To the Skrull's surprise, a figure emerged from the first floor of the brownstone. No door opened, no window gaped; the figure simply passed *through* the building's stone façade like a ghost. Defying gravity, the figure wafted upwards until it was at the same altitude as the flaming figure of Kl'rt.

Kl'rt recognized the android known as the Vision instantly. The Avenger wore a distinctive costume composed of skintight green and yellow fabric. A scarlet, diamond-shaped emblem marked his chest and a voluminous emerald cloak billowed in the wind behind him, but it was the Vision's face that most clearly betrayed his artificial origins. Sculpted from an unknown variety of malleable red plastic, his deceptively human features had a polished, reflective sheen unlike true human flesh. A translucent golden gem was embedded in the Vision's forehead; Kl'rt recalled that jewel could absorb or project solar energy.

Now, of course, the Skrull remembered why the building seemed so familiar. The edifice below was Avengers Mansion, home and headquarters of Earth's mightiest so-called heroes. *Why,* he wondered, *would Persa seek out the Avengers?* Little love was lost between the Kree and this particular team of Terran adventurers; according to all reliable reports, the Avengers had been instrumental in the Shi'ar's victory over the Kree Empire. Some even said that it was an Avenger who slew the Kree's unquestioned ruler, the Supreme Intelligence, although Kl'rt had his doubts about that rumor. In his experience, few Terrans possessed the strength and wisdom to actually kill their enemies.

Could Persa be out for revenge against the Avengers? If so, he'd almost be tempted to help her—almost.

"Johnny Storm?" the Vision asked. His voice was deep and as

cold as the depths of interstellar space. His face displayed no trace of emotion. *Perhaps*, Kl'rt thought, *I can convince him that I'm the real Human Torch.*

"Holy cow, yes!" the Skrull said, hoping he wasn't overplaying his part. "Thanks for showing up, Vizh, but I think everything's a-okay now."

The Vision looked down at Colonel Persa. The smoking remains of a dozen fireballs still smoldered around her. "It was not you I heard calling out for assistance, Johnny Storm," he observed.

"Just the usual crime-fighting gig," Kl'rt explained. "No big deal. Nothing I can't handle on my own."

"Don't listen to him!" Persa shouted from the sidewalk below. "He's a Skrull! The Super-Skrull!"

"And she's a Kree spy," Kl'rt said with only partially-feigned exasperation. "Trust me on this, Vizh, old pal. Take a look at that sci-fi peashooter she's carrying. Not exactly standard equipment for your run-of-the-mill Earth-babe."

The Vision gazed at Kl'rt speculatively. His eyes looked like tiny, glowing sparks in the shadowy caverns beneath his brows. "And yet," he observed coolly, "the Super-Skrull has been known to mimic members of the Fantastic Four. Perhaps I should take you both into custody until the matter is resolved."

"Hey, Vizh, is that really necessary?" Kl'rt didn't like the way this dialogue was heading. The last thing he wanted was to get the rest of the Avengers, and maybe the Fantastic Four, involved in his mission. "I'm a busy guy, you know. Places to go, people to see. . . ."

"Heroes to deceive!" Persa interrupted. She stared at the flying Skrull so fiercely that her eyes seemed to burn away every last vestige of his disguise. *No, wait,* Kl'rt realized, *her eyes really are burning.* A bright yellow glow blotted out the green of her eyes, then exploded into a blinding glare that, even in broad daylight, cast a powerful beam of light upon the Skrull and the Vision. Instinctively, Kl'rt summoned up another force field, yet the golden radiance seemed to contain no destructive energies to shield against. The light passed through the invisible barrier unobstructed and shone over the Skrull. The spotlight made him blink, but that was all. *Those damn Kree lenses,* he thought. *Is that the best they can do?*

Then he looked at his hands.

Dancing flames still licked his flesh, but instead of outlining the spindly human fingers of Johnny Storm, he saw instead a flame-covered version of his own powerful, black-gloved hands. Fearing the worst, he looked down at his body. Through the flames, he saw not the slender form of a human stripling but the muscular frame of the greatest of all Skrull warriors. Shouts and screams of terror rose from the city street below. Kl'rt saw that a crowd of humans had gathered to watch his confrontation with the android Avenger. Expressions of shock registered on the faces of the human mob as they stared upwards at the Super-Skrull, looking exactly as they might if the Human Torch's youthful features were suddenly replaced by the noble, reptilian face of a Skrull. "Hellhounds of the Black Nebula," he cursed out loud, realizing that his disguise was history. Somehow the Kree's cursed lenses had revealed his true form to the Vision and the world.

"The logic appears irrefutable," the Vision commented. "While the Super-Skrull can assume the guise of the Human Torch, the Human Torch cannot transform into the Super-Skrull—unless he was the Super-Skrull to begin with."

"Very well then," Kl'rt snarled. His fingers explored his features, feeling the wide, furrowed chin, stroking the points of his ears. In truth, it felt good to shed the degrading human guise he'd been forced to endure for expediency's sake. Let both Kree and Terran witness the glory of a true soldier of the Skrull Empire. "Stand aside, android," he said proudly, "or face the full power of the Super-Skrull!"

"I prefer the term synthezoid," the Vision said.

Kl'rt prepared himself for battle. Still afire, his closed fists expanded until they were size of boulders. A thick, lumpish carapace—modeled on the rock-like armor of the Thing—covered his fists and lower arms. Crimson flames raged over his hands so that each swollen, stony fist resembled a meteor burning up as it crashed through a hostile atmosphere. And like meteors, his fists flew at the Vision, the Skrull's rubbery arms stretching behind them.

The fiery cudgels blazed as they crossed the empty space dividing Kl'rt from the android, but then they kept on going, passing through the Vision's emerald form and emerging on the other side of the Avenger's floating cape. Snarling in anger, Kl'rt recalled that the Vision had the ability to turn himself intangible.

"Coward!" the Super-Skrull cursed him. "Remain immaterial if you wish. But no mere wisp of smoke will stand between me and my rightful prey." Looking away from the Vision, he saw Colonel Persa run up the steps to the front door of Avengers Mansion. The door opened before her and, as Kl'rt watched in dismay, the Kree agent disappeared into the confines of the mansion. *No*, he vowed silently, *you will find no sanctuary there. I will have you even if I must brave the very lair of my enemies.* Flames spewed behind him as he rocketed towards the building below. The Vision swooped down to block him, but the Skrull did not deviate from his flight path, fully prepared to fly through the intangible android just as his fist had done. *Never send a ghost*, he thought, *to bar a warrior's path.*

"You are mistaken," the Vision said. "I need not touch you to stop you." Glowing with an unholy radiance, thermoscopic laser beams escaped from the cavernous depths of the Vision's eyes. Unlike the harmless illumination that Persa's Kree-designed lenses had projected, these beams burned with destructive energies. Before the Skrull even thought to erect a force field, the bright solar rays struck him in the chest.

Kl'rt laughed out loud. What good were heat rays against one whose body contained the volcanic power of the Human Torch? He felt a tingling where the beams touched him, nothing more. His fists outstretched before him, he continued to dive towards the Vision and the mansion beyond. The Vision rose to meet him. Just as their trajectories intersected, Kl'rt felt a pair of solid hands grab him by the wrists. Suddenly, the wraith-like Vision felt heavy as neutronium. He plunged towards the Earth, dragging the Super-Skrull with him.

Together, they crashed into the sidewalk. The sound of their impact almost drowned out the shrieks from surrounding human spectators. Footsteps pounded on the pavement as mortal men and women fled in panic.

Using the strength of the Thing, Kl'rt tore his arms free from the Vision's grip. He staggered to his feet, his boots slipping slightly among the shattered concrete. *I should have remembered,* he thought, *that the Vision can change his density at will.* He had not expected the android to go from intangibility to super-density at the very moment they clashed. The shock of their descent had snuffed out his flame, but his elastic body had absorbed much of the impact. He rose, unharmed, from the rubble.

The Vision appeared undamaged as well; doubtless his altered density was as hard as it was heavy. They faced each other across the crater their crash landing had carved out of the cement. Kl'rt reignited the fires over his fists, but left the rest of his body flame-free.

"Do you intend to prolong this conflict?" the Vision asked in his sepulchral tones. Behind him, the front door of Avengers Mansion gaped open. Kl'rt wondered what deviltry Persa was up to inside. He took comfort from the fact that none of the other Avengers had appeared to assist the Vision. Could the android be the only hero present this afternoon? "I must warn you that you will not prevail," the Vision stated.

Kl'rt let his action deliver his reply. Swinging at the end of an elongated arm, his right fist slammed into the Vision's chin. Kl'rt was surprised by the resistance he encountered; the android's plastic face felt hard as diamond. Still, his powerful blow knocked the Vision off-balance. The android stumbled backwards, his head tipped to one side. Kl'rt kept on the offensive, rocking the Vision with blow after blow, never giving the android a chance to recover. Trailing streams of fire, his club-like hands battered the artificial Avenger, knocking his head from side to side. It was like smashing rocks with one's bare hands, but Kl'rt did not relent. With each savage punch, he felt as though he was redeeming a lifetime's worth of ignominious defeats. He would destroy this creature of Earth even as Earth had destroyed his reputation.

Yet Kl'rt underestimated his foe's computerized reflexes. Instantly, without warning, his fists met nothing at all. Although the Vision remained fixed in his sight, the synthezoid's hard exterior again became no more substantial than a mist. Unhalted by any obstacle, the force of his punch almost threw Kl'rt forward into the crater at his feet. Only by swiftly deforming his elastic body to shift his center of weight did the Skrull keep himself from tumbling into the shallow pit.

Kl'rt glared at his foe. To his disgust, the Vision looked unharmed by the pounding he had received. His shiny plastic face was neither chipped nor scorched. The android's expression remained as calmly impassive as before. "You cannot harm me," he said. "Will you surrender to my custody?"

"Never!" Kl'rt declared. "A Skrull never yields!" His green brow furrowed as he psychically constructed an impenetrable force field around the Vision, then tightened the cage in hopes of crushing the android within its invisible walls. The Skrull had destroyed countless foes with this maneuver. He looked forward to squeezing the pseudo-life out of this annoying mechanism.

It proved a waste of time. Now lighter than air, the Vision levitated off the sidewalk, passing effortlessly through the shrinking force field. Slowly, inexorably, he drifted over the cracked and broken pavement, phantom fingers reaching out for the Skrull. A geyser of flame sprayed from Kl'rt's left hand, directed at the approaching apparition, but the pyrotechnic onslaught had no effect on the Vision. He floated through the crackling wall of fire as though it wasn't there. Glowing yellow eyes locked on to the Skrull's. Fingers sheathed in golden plastic extended towards Kl'rt's exposed forehead. The fingers were only inches away. Kl'rt realized there was only one thing to do.

He disappeared. Invisible, he ducked out of the way of the Vision's outstretched hand. The Invisible Woman's ability to vanish from sight saved him just in time. He shrugged his shoulders, disappointed at having to resort to this tactic. Ideally, he would have preferred to best the Avenger in combat, but, he recalled, his mission to capture Persa took priority. *Another day, android,* he thought as he crept stealthily up the steps toward the door of the mansion.

The Vision was no fool, however. Guessing Kl'rt's objective, he flew swiftly up the steps, past the creeping Skrull, then planted himself squarely in the doorway. His eyes swept the steps with his thermoscopic vision, but the solar rays passed harmlessly through Kl'rt's fireproof and now transparent body. *No doubt he thinks he's guarding the entrance,* Kl'rt thought smugly as he considered in which form he might most easily slip past the Vision. *An insect? A snake?*

"Interesting," the android observed. "First, the Human Torch; now the Invisible Woman. Are all your advantages borrowed from human originals? Is the vaunted Super-Skrull nothing more than a pale imitation of the Fantastic Four? Have you no strength—no pride—of your own?"

How dare you! Raw fury consumed his mind, overpowering all other considerations. *How dare this* machine *slander the honor of my people?* Heart pounding, he dropped the veil of invisibility to stand defiantly before the Vision. "What do you know of pride, mechanism?" he challenged. "I need only my own strength, cosmically enhanced by advanced Skrull science, and my natural cunning to conquer the likes of you!"

Was that a smile lifting the corners of the android's mouth? "I know enough about pride, apparently, to successfully play upon yours." He launched himself off the upper steps and soared, his wide green cloak spreading out behind him, straight towards the Super-Skrull. "Now let us test a creation of human science, myself, against your Skrull bionics."

Kl'rt stood ready against the Vision's charge. The synthezoid drew back his fist, then plunged it deep into the Skrull's chest. Pain such as Kl'rt had never known erupted between his ribs. He froze, limbs convulsing, against the unparalleled shock to his system. This, he knew, was the android Avenger's deadliest trick: thrusting an intangible limb into an opponent's body, then partially resolidifying it within the other's form. The agony was almost unbearable; Kl'rt felt an alien presence within his chest, fighting with his own cells at a molecular level. Despite his pride, a scream burst past his lips. His vision dimmed. He felt close to blacking out.

Then he fought back. Using nothing but his own innate shapechanging ability, the same essential Skrull quality that had raised his people above all the other races in the cosmos, he shifted his own substance away from the invader, moving vital organs away from danger and pulling the very cells of his body out of conflict with the solid portions of the Vision's hand. The feat required enormous concentration. Perspiration broke out on his forehead, but the pain lessened slightly. "Do your worst, android!" he hissed.

In response, the Vision twisted his hand within the Skrull's torso. Kl'rt bit down on his lower lip to keep from crying out once more. The Vision varied the density of his spectral fingers, making the shock harder to compensate against, but Kl'rt persevered, defending against the Vision's attack moment by moment, cell by cell. Shapeshifter versus density-changer. Skrull versus synthezoid. "Stalemate," Kl'rt grunted through clenched fangs, even as the Vision slid his other hand into the Skrull's pain-racked body. Kl'rt refused to give up, willing to defy the android for all eternity if necessary. *The Super-Skrull never surrenders!*

Another shriek pierced the air, but this time the scream did not come from either Kl'rt or the Vision. Both combatants turned their heads towards the mansion from which the sound had emerged. The anguished cry had a feminine lilt. *Persa,* the Skrull wondered, *or someone else?* The shriek had caught the Vision's attention as well. Swiftly, silently, he withdrew his hands from the Skrull's flesh and flew away to investigate. As he floated through the open door, Kl'rt noted, the edges of the android's billowing cape passed through the brownstone walls on each side of the door. Still shaken by the awesome internal battle he had just waged, Kl'rt followed after the Vision on foot.

Only yards beyond the door, in a spacious hallway adorned with marble tile and large framed mirrors upon the walls, he came upon a dramatic tableau. Kl'rt came to a halt mere inches behind the Vision and stared over the android's shoulder at the scene before him.

Colonel Persa lay sprawled upon the floor. The Kree's face was bruised and bleeding, her nose looked broken. Standing astride the fallen terrorist, the heel of one boot dug into the base of Persa's spine, was an adolescent Shi'ar female clad in human attire. Her flesh was a rich, lustrous violet and her head was crowned by a mane of azure feathers. Scarlet tattoos marked her face, and she held in one hand Persa's plasma gun.

"Deathcry!" the Vision addressed the bird-woman. For the first time, Kl'rt thought he heard a trace of emotion in the android's voice. "Are you well?"

"I am now," the Shi'ar replied, "but this crazy woman tried to kill me." Deathcry noticed Kl'rt standing behind the Vision. "Who's the Skrull?"

"I am the Super-Skrull," Kl'rt proclaimed, "and this Kree outlaw is my prisoner!" He stomped across the floor, then knelt beside Persa's defeated form. "Tell me, Kree! What was your business here?"

Blood dripping from a broken lip, Persa spat upon the floor. She glared at Deathcry with murder in her eyes. "We had heard that a Shi'ar had attached herself to the Avengers. These humans have a bad habit of meddling in intergalactic affairs; we feared this Shi'ar's influence on the Avengers. My superiors ordered her assassination."

The Vision nodded. "Despite her youth, Deathcry is an accomplished fighter—as you seem to have learned." He turned to face Kl'rt. "My apologies, Skrull. This situation is more complicated than it first appeared."

Kl'rt rose from his crouched position. Standing, he was several inches taller than the Vision. "I want no apologies. Simply give me the Kree." In truth, part of him wished that Persa had succeeded in her mission. He too was alarmed to find a Shi'ar allied with the Avengers. Now was not the time to remedy that situation, but he would have to give the matter serious thought. *First things first*, he thought. "You are mine, Persa."

The Vision shook his head. "I am afraid that is not possible," he said. "If the Skrull Empire wishes to seek this woman's extradition, it must do so through formal channels. In the interim, I intend to turn our prisoner over to the proper Terran authorities."

"Yeah," Deathcry said. Her purple fingers gripped the hilt of Persa's weapon. "You tell him, Vision!" The young Shi'ar wore denim leggings and a cotton shirt with an illustrated representation of a rodent emblazoned on it. The shirt was the same red color as the tattoos on her face. Kl'rt found this mixture of Shi'ar and Terran culture disturbing.

"This is intolerable," he protested. "I have pursued this felon across two galaxies!" He considered the odds against him. He did not wish to take on both the android and the Shi'ar, but he would not leave empty-handed. "I must have the Kree."

"Perhaps you should have explained your mission earlier," the Vision observed, "instead of resorting to deception."

"Do not mock me, android." Waves of heat began to radiate from the Skrull's body. His muscles tensed for action.

Then a shadow fell over Kl'rt. He spun about to see several new arrivals come through the door. His green eyes grew wide as he recognized them all: Quicksilver, a human mutate gifted with extraordinary speed; Crystal, an Inhuman female whose control of the elements derived from obscene Kree experiments on her ancestors; and Hercules, the immortal strongman who claimed to be a god. "By Olympus!" the latter exclaimed. "What strange doings have transpired in mine absence? Friend Vision, dost thou require the mighty sinews of the Son of Zeus?''

''I do not believe so,'' the Vision said. His artificial eyes glowed in their sockets. ''The Super-Skrull is leaving, isn't that so?''

Kl'rt found himself surrounded by so-called super heroes. Five against one, not counting the Kree. He extinguished the flames simmering just beneath his skin and headed stiffly for the door.

The Super-Skrull hated Earth.

Venom & the Absorbing Man

THE DEVIANT ONES

GLENN GREENBERG

Illustration by Steven Butler

"I WANT TO eat your brains," said the prisoner to the Guardsman who was escorting him through the corridors of the Vault—the Colorado-based maximum security prison for super-powered criminals. The prisoner was smiling from ear to ear, and his inhuman voice rippled as if he were gargling with gravel.

The Guardsman, named Doorly, tried to suppress the chill going down his spine. Despite the fact that he was fully suited up in his state-of-the-art, high-tech protective armor, he still felt uneasy. He couldn't help it. He *always* felt that way when he had to deal with Eddie Brock, perhaps better known as the super-villain called Venom.

Maybe it was the prisoner's appearance. He was a tall, powerful figure, covered head to toe by a skin-tight mass of black, with huge white eyes and a white spider-shaped design that connected from his chest to his back. Topping it all off was an ugly, impossibly long tongue that jutted from a grotesque, wide mouth with razor-sharp fangs that seemed to perpetually have slime dripping from them.

Or maybe it was the fact that Venom was actually a human being who had *willingly* formed a physical and psychic bond with a strange, symbiotic alien creature from outer space.

Anybody who'd do a thing like that's gotta *be psycho*, Doorly thought. *And Eddie Brock was a nutcase* long *before that alien entered his life.*

Only now, Brock was a nutcase who could pummel a super hero the likes of Spider-Man right through a brick wall. And he had done so, on more than one occasion.

Maybe that was it: the fact that this alien symbiote—Brock always referred to it as his "Other"—granted its human host incredible strength and abilities. Did that make it attractive, in some perverse way?

Doorly wasn't sure of the reason. All he knew was that being around Venom definitely made him uncomfortable. To make matters worse, the prisoner seemed to be well aware of that fact, and seized every opportunity to take advantage of it.

Doorly knew that Venom was just trying to spook him. After all, it was only a rumor that Venom *actually* consumed the internal organs of his victims. But nevertheless, that crack about eating Doorly's brains, spoken in that almost demonic voice, caused the young Guardsman to shudder.

"Mmmmmmm, brains," Venom continued, licking his ebony lips with that slime-coated tongue.

Can't let him know that he makes me nervous, Doorly told himself. *Can't give him the satisfaction. Gotta show him who's in charge here.*

"Shut up, Brock," Doorly snapped, hoping he sounded authoritative enough.

"Call us Venom," the prisoner responded. "Edward Brock is but one half of what we are."

"What you are is a prisoner," Doorly shot back. "And you better do as I say. And what I say is, 'Shut up!' "

There, Doorly thought to himself. *That ought to keep him quiet!*

"You're frightened of us, aren't you?" Venom continued, in a tone that Doorly found particularly condescending. "There's no need to fear us, you know. Only those who would prey on the innocent have reason to fear us."

Oh geez, here comes the "lethal protector of the innocent" routine again, Doorly thought.

Venom actually saw himself as a do-gooder, a crusader obsessed with protecting the innocents of the world. Problem was, Venom was the *only* one who saw himself as a do-gooder. The *rest* of the world saw him as a self-righteous psychotic with delusions of grandeur. Hence his incarceration in the Vault.

Wanting to end this conversation before Venom could get started on another soliloquy about himself, Doorly sharply replied, "Well, according to your sentence, *no one* will have reason to fear you for a very long time."

The prisoner remained silent after that last exchange, which pleased Doorly to no end. But the Guardsman still kept his hand on the sonic blaster that was holstered to his thigh. Venom's symbiote was particularly vulnerable to sonics, and if he made any sudden, unexpected moves on the way to their destination, Doorly would not hesitate to blast him.

After what seemed like an eternity to Doorly, he and the prisoner finally reached their destination: the Vault's medical facility, where a major scientific procedure was about to take place.

Vault Warden Marvin Walsh was anxiously pacing in the center of the medlab, as if he were an expectant father.

Walsh was a heavy-set, balding, no-nonsense man in his mid-forties. He had been in charge of the Vault for several years, and saw himself as running the prison with a firm but fair hand. He was perpetually busy juggling one crisis after another, along with an endless stream of paperwork, but he made sure that his calendar was clear for this evening. He definitely wanted to be present for what had the potential of being an historic occasion for the Vault.

If only it would get *started,* already!

"Where the hell is Doorly with the prisoner?" Walsh bellowed to no one in particular.

As if in reply, the door to the medlab slid open, and Doorly marched in with Venom.

Walsh began walking towards the two new arrivals, and noticed the Guardsman pointing a warning finger at the prisoner.

"You'd better not try anything funny here," Walsh heard Doorly say to Venom. "There's plenty of us Guardsmen who'd love a chance to take you down."

"We'll try to keep that in mind," Venom replied as Walsh came up beside him. The warden was now joined by several stern-looking men in lab coats, along with two other Guardsmen.

"He's all yours, sirs, and you're welcome to him," Doorly said as he walked out of the lab, on his way back to his regular post.

"What was that all about, Brock?" Walsh asked

"We're sure we have no idea. And please, call us Venom."

"Whatever," Walsh replied. He then indicated the men in the lab coats. "These are the scientists who will be conducting the procedure. They'll be ready for you in a few moments. In the meantime, these Guardsmen will escort you into the waiting room. Your companion in this experiment is already there."

Venom nodded at the scientists. "Gentlemen," he said in what sounded like an attempt at courtesy, despite that gravelly, spine-chilling voice. "I look forward to working with you in this endeavor."

Then his long, hideous tongue lashed out and slowly licked his top row of fangs, dripping green slime onto the floor by the scientists' feet. He then casually walked away with the Guardsmen. One of the scientists, Dr. Parides, a tall, middle-aged man with a fairly bad toupée and a bushy mustache, walked up to the warden and said, "So that's Venom, huh? He's—Well, quite frankly, he's more repulsive that I could have possibly imagined."

Warden Walsh's eyebrow shot up, and he grimaced. Turning to Parides, he responded, "And you haven't even seen him eat."

Carl "Crusher" Creel was seated on the couch in the medical facility's waiting room, dressed in his bright orange prison jumpsuit. He had only been there for a short while, but already he was fidgeting impatiently.

When're they gonna call me in an' get started with this stupid thing? he wondered. If there was one thing that Creel hated, it was being kept waiting.

He looked down at the couch. It was upholstered with cheap, soft, yellow plastic. Creel furrowed his pronounced brow, and touched the upholstery with one finger. Instantly, his flesh transformed, taking on the physical properties of the plastic. From the tips of his toes to the top of his completely bald head, Creel now looked like cheap, beat-up, soft yellow upholstery in human form.

Then he touched the armrest of the couch, which was made of smooth, brown wood. His flesh immediately shifted, becoming hard and brown, with the same exact texture of the wood. Creel smirked.

Although absorbing the properties of a beat-up old couch was a far cry from absorbing the raw brute strength of the incredible Hulk (a feat Creel had accomplished some years ago), Creel was bored stiff waiting for this big deal procedure to begin, and had to keep himself occupied *somehow*.

It was certainly better than reflecting on how he had ended up in the Vault to begin with. Creel was a career criminal, a big, hulking, brute of a man who had spent most of his adult life in and out of prison. But several years back, through mystical means, he had gained the ability to absorb the properties of *any-thing* he touched. He became known as the Absorbing Man, one of the world's most powerful—and dangerous—super-villains. In the years since, he had faced a number of the world's most prominent super heroes, who always managed to stop his criminal plans. And it was Creel's most recent defeat that landed him here, in a prison specifically designed to contain beings such as he.

Creel's thoughts were interrupted when he suddenly heard the lock of the waiting room door being deactivated. His skin shifted back to its regular appearance as the door slid open and two Guardsmen entered, with an inmate that Creel recognized immediately.

Venom.

Oh great, Creel thought with a frown. *They're saddling me up with him.*

The Guardsmen turned to leave, after one of them told Venom to wait there until called for. They walked out of the room, and Creel could hear the door's lock being activated once again.

"Creel," Venom said in acknowledgment, with a surprisingly cheerful tone.

"Brock," the Absorbing Man replied evenly, not even bothering to look at the other inmate.

"We had no idea that *you* were our partner in this little exercise," Venom said as he began to pace in the center of the room.

"Yeah, well, I guess they wanted it to be a surprise for ya, Brock," Creel said with an edge of surliness. "Lord knows I'm thrilled to find out that I'm gonna be doin' this with you."

"Charming as always, Creel," Venom replied as he strolled over to a wall on the far side of the room, and casually began to walk up the side of it. He then continued pacing, only now he was walking on the ceiling.

"A pity that you're unable to absorb personalities," Venom continued, stopping only inches away from where Creel was sitting. "Believe us, you could use one."

They were nearly nose to nose now. Venom then broke out into a wide, toothy smile, and winked.

"Get outta my face," Creel snapped angrily.

Venom then detached his feet from the ceiling, somersaulted in mid-air, and landed gracefully back onto the floor. He took a seat on the couch right next to Creel, causing the Absorbing Man to roll his eyes in annoyance.

Nice empty chair on the other side of the room, an' he's gotta plop himself down next ta me, Creel thought disgustedly.

"Enough with the pleasantries," Creel said with a resigned sigh. "What did these bozos promise you for agreein' to be part of this experiment?"

Venom replied, "A bigger cell. And a large-screen color television, cable included."

"You asked for *that?*" Creel asked incredulously.

"We'll have access to CNN, CNBC, all the news channels," Venom explained. "Edward Brock was a top New York City newspaper reporter long before he became Venom. His love for the news, his desire to keep up with what's happening in the world, has not abated. Plus, we desire to be aware of all the injustices being visited upon the innocents, whom we should rightfully be out there protecting."

"Uh, yeah, right," Creel responded, shifting restlessly in his seat. *When are they gonna call us in, awready?* he thought desperately.

"And what are they giving you, Creel?"

"Visits with my girlfriend," Creel answered.

"Your girlfriend? You mean Titania?" Venom asked.

Creel thought longingly of Titania, the former super-villainess with whom he had been romantically linked for some time.

"That's her," Creel answered. "Why?"

"We've seen Titania come visit you many times before. What's the big deal about that?"

In response, Creel mischievously raised an eyebrow and smirked at Venom.

"Oh," Venom said, nodding in sudden understanding. "*Those* kinds of visits."

Suddenly the door slid open again, and one of the Guardsmen stood in the doorway.

"They're ready for you two," the Guardsman said.

"Too bad," Creel remarked as he got to his feet. "You've interrupted such a scintillatin' conversation."

As they were escorted into the main lab of the medical facility, Venom and Creel looked around the room, noting all the highly advanced scientific and medical devices and the rows of computer banks lining the walls.

"Impressive," Venom murmured.

"Yeah, a sci-fi fan's dream," Creel shot back.

Warden Walsh stepped up to the prisoners. "All right, you two, here's why we're all here. These scientists have developed a pair of special energy-dampening handcuffs that should neutralize the powers of whichever super-powered criminals are locked into them. We hope to incorporate these cuffs into the standard gear we use here at the Vault, to better keep the prisoners under control.''

Creel and Venom nodded.

The warden continued, ''You two are going to serve as the test subjects for the cuffs, to see how they respond. In return, you've been given perks of your own choosing. You were offered this opportunity because you've been the best-behaved prisoners here lately—believe it or not.''

Creel sneered at the warden. ''C'mon, Walsh, what's the real reason we're gettin' these 'perks'? You wouldn't be givin' us anythin' unless you felt guilted into it!''

Walsh shot Creel a cold stare. ''All right, Creel, I'll level with you. These cuffs are a prototype. They've never been tested on a live subject. We don't know for sure that they'll work as planned, or what long-term effects they may have on you. You could lose your powers permanently, for one thing. Now, from my point of view, that wouldn't be such a bad thing. . . .''

Walsh continued, ignoring the dirty glances from the two prisoners. ''The cuffs could possibly cause damage to your nervous system, if they're flawed—which, of course, we hope they're not. Basically, you're putting yourselves at risk by cooperating with us, and we feel an obligation to show our appreciation.''

Creel and Venom glanced at each other with a hint of uncertainty.

Walsh motioned to one of the scientists, an intense, medium-sized man with wavy brown hair. ''Dr. Margolin here will explain the procedure,'' the warden said.

Margolin stepped forward, and brought forth a large, bulky pair of handcuffs with dials, switches and controls along the side that were completely indecipherable to Creel. Venom studied the cuffs intently, and uttered not a word.

''The cuffs will be powered by the very same superhuman energy that they will be draining from the two of you,'' Margolin explained. ''With Venom, only the alien symbiote will be affected, since that is the sole source of Mr. Brock's powers.''

Margolin looked directly at Venom. ''Your psychic connection with the symbiote will be cut off,'' he warned. ''The symbiote will be unable to respond to your mental commands or manipulate itself. It means you will be unable to transform into Venom."

The scientist then turned to the Absorbing Man. "Mr. Creel, we still don't fully understand how you gained your absorbing powers all those years ago, but we're confident that these cuffs will neutralize them anyway."

"Wonderful," Creel muttered. "Can we just get this show on the road awready, big brain?"

"Very well," Margolin answered calmly. He then handed Venom an orange prison jumpsuit.

"What's this for?" Venom asked.

Margolin replied, "Well, if these cuffs work the way they're supposed to, your symbiote won't be covering you anymore, and—we didn't want you to be embarrassed."

Venom took the jumpsuit from the scientist without another word.

Creel sat next to Venom on a large examination table, and watched closely as the cuffs were locked onto their wrists. Margolin flipped some of the switches on the cuffs, and Parides double-checked the power-level settings. The two scientists nodded to each other, indicating their readiness to begin.

Margolin flipped a few more switches on the cuffs. Finally, after a deep breath, Parides pressed a bright red button, and the cuffs hummed to life.

For a moment—no more than a second—Creel felt a strange, tingling sensation within him, as his and Venom's unique energies were drained from their bodies and intermingled within the high-tech shackles. For just a passing, fleeting moment, Creel felt as if he could taste Venom's powers. It was like nothing he had ever experienced before. He wondered if Brock felt the same thing. But then it was gone, and all that was left was an overwhelming feeling of emptiness.

"I've lost it," Creel said softly. "My power . . . I can't do it anymore. I can't even absorb the metal of these cuffs."

Creel turned to the prisoner with whom he was cuffed, to see if he was similarly affected. Creel's eyes widened in surprise at what he saw.

Gone was the huge monstrosity in black and white, with the tongue and the fangs and the green drool. In his place sat an extremely muscular, square-jawed, handsome, somewhat sad-looking man, dressed in an orange jumpsuit.

Eddie Brock.

"It appears you were right, Doctor," Brock said softly. "My connection to my Other . . . is broken."

Creel spoke up. "Awright, now ya know yer stupid cuffs work! So you can take 'em off now, right?"

"In a little while," Parides replied. "We have to run some tests while the cuffs are still locked onto you and dampening your powers."

Suddenly Brock looked queasy. His face had turned ashen, and his mouth hung open.

"Hey, if yer gonna puke, turn yer head the other way!" Creel told Brock, futilely trying to move away from his cuff-mate.

"No, it's—Something's wrong. I don't know how I know—but I do," Brock said distractedly.

Margolin walked over to one of the computer banks on the far side of the room, trying to ascertain the problem that only Brock seemed to be aware of.

But as he reached for the dials, the computer exploded in a tremendous blast of heat and sound. The scientist was thrown clear across the room.

The blast seemed to set off a chain reaction, as computer bank after computer bank exploded into smithereens, until the entire room was a mass of chaos and flying glass and metal.

The lights suddenly cut out, and the room was bathed in total darkness. Frantic shouts from the scientists and the rushing footsteps of the Guardsmen filled the void created by the loss of light.

"We've lost power!" Warden Walsh yelled. "Is the rest of the prison affected?"

"We're checking on that now, sir," replied one of the Guardsmen, as he tried to contact other sectors of the Vault on the communications device in his helmet.

An idea began formulating in Crusher Creel's mind. . . .

As he sat silently in the darkness, sudden realization dawned upon Eddie Brock.

Of course—you're responsible for what's happened, aren't you, my Other? he silently addressed his symbiote, though it could no longer read or respond to his thoughts. *The cuffs have had an adverse effect on you! The sudden breaking of your mental bond with me, the draining of your energy, your inability to manipulate yourself. . . . These damned cuffs must be causing you incredible anguish!*

Brock recalled how the symbiote had, on occasion, sent out incredibly powerful psychic shrieks when it experienced great pain or anguish. The intensity of these shrieks had caused varying degrees of trouble for Brock—and all of humanity. On one occasion, the symbiote had managed to psychically summon others of its race to Earth, even though they were light-years away, on another planet!

You sent out another shriek, didn't you? Brock asked the symbiote, well aware that he would receive no answer. *And this time, it overloaded the circuitry here in the Vault, with the exception of these cuffs—*

"The cuffs!" Walsh's voice called out in the darkness. "Are they still operating? If these prisoners have gotten back their powers . . ."

"Yes, they're still functioning," Margolin's voice calmly responded. "I can see their operating lights still blinking. Whatever affected the rest of the machinery left the cuffs intact."

Brock's mind was racing. *These cuffs must have been designed with a system that shields their circuitry from the effects of our powers, in case our powers were too much for the cuffs to handle! Those clever little scientists . . .*

Suddenly, the Guardsman who had been trying to contact the rest of the prison shouted out, interrupting Brock's train of thought. "Warden! Unable to make contact with any other sectors! It looks like we've experienced complete systems failure throughout the prison! Emergency power is unavailable!"

"Dear God," the Warden whispered. "All the prisoners . . ."

"All the cell doors would have automatically opened when we lost power, sir," the Guardsman said hesitantly. "The inmates are undoubtedly running free by now."

"I want you to go out and find as many Guardsmen as you possibly can," Walsh ordered, his voice sounding both forceful and stressed. "Once you've found them, I want you to work in teams and round up the prisoners! I want them back in their cells before they get a chance to tear this place apart!"

As Walsh was busy giving orders, and the scientists were huddled together trying to figure out a way to restore power to the prison, Creel leaned over to Brock.

"This is our golden opportunity, y'know," he whispered into Brock's ear. "There's only Walsh, a few namby-pamby scientists, and two Guardsmen in here with us."

Creel then heard the Guardsman who had just been given orders by Walsh to leave the room, to go search for his comrades.

"Make that *one* Guardsman," Creel continued, now smiling in the darkness. "Coupla big bruisers like you an' me could overtake 'em, even without our powers!"

"You mean escape?" Brock whispered back.

"No, I mean playin' tiddlywinks. Of *course* I mean escape! You heard 'em: everyone's gonna be distracted now by the other inmates bein' set free! The lights an' power are all gone. They think we're not even a consideration right now, with these cuffs on us. We got surprise on our side! You with me?"

Brock was silent for a long moment. Then he whispered, "But if we cooperate, then—"

"What's more important ta you," Creel hissed. "A bigger cell with a friggin' color TV, or your freedom?"

Another long pause. Finally, Brock whispered, "What's your plan?"

Warden Walsh was busy conversing with the one remaining Guardsman in a corner of the medlab.

"We have to try to make contact with the Avengers somehow, and apprise them of the situation!" Walsh said, hoping that the New York City-based team of super heroes would be able to send in at least some of their members to help. "In the meantime, we'll have to handle things by ourselves! But I—"

Suddenly there was a loud crack, and Walsh never finished his sentence. Instead, he felt a sharp pain in the back of his head, as if he had been clubbed with a blunt object.

"Warden! Are you all right?" the Guardsman shouted.

As Walsh slumped to the floor, he heard a set of booted feet rushing towards him. For a brief moment there was silence, then the sound of metal being viciously pounded upon by what could only be body armor. The last thing Walsh felt before completely slipping into unconsciousness was the Guardsman, falling right on top of him.

* * *

"Okay, eggheads!" Creel shouted to the scientists in the darkness, breaking the short period of silence. "Just stay out of our way, an' you won't get hurt!"

Creel felt a pull on his shackled arm as Brock kneeled down on the floor, to check the pulses of the warden and the Guardsman.

"They'll be all right," Brock told Creel. "They're just unconscious."

"Don't know why I let you talk me into holding back on these rubes," Creel muttered. "It's not like they'd show us the same courtesy."

"They're innocent men just doing their jobs," Brock told him. "They don't deserve to die."

"Fine, whatever. But now let's get outta here! We don't even have enough time to get the brainiacs here to remove the cuffs."

"Yes," Brock agreed. "If we're going to make our escape, we'd better leave immediately, before more Guardsmen arrive. We'll have to get the cuffs off later, after we're free and clear."

Brock and Creel moved to the door leading out of the lab, slid it open, and checked down the corridor to see if anyone was approaching. Determining that the coast was clear, the two men slipped out.

"Adios, eggheads!" Creel shouted to the scientists as he and Brock took off down the corridor.

As they silently and swiftly made their way through the prison, using the darkness to their advantage, Creel and Brock caught glimpses of some of their fellow inmates, attempting to make their own escapes, but being subdued by the ever-present Guardsmen.

The inmate who had gotten the furthest along in his escape attempt was the Abomination. A former spy named Emil Blonsky, he had been transformed by gamma rays into a hideous, superstrong monster. Before being confronted by Guardsmen armed with gamma-ray blasters—the creature's only vulnerability—the Abomination had carved a path of destruction throughout the prison, and made it outside into a cold, rainy night. Brock and Creel followed this path, and while the Guardsmen were engaging the Abomination in battle, the shackled convicts slipped by and managed to make it over the main gate.

They were free.

* * *

As the hours progressed, the rain turned into a full-blown thunderstorm, but Brock and Creel continued to forge ahead, linked together at the wrists and moving through some very rough and wet terrain through the dark, night-shrouded forests of Colorado.

Brock could hear the faint, familiar echoes of the Vault's ever-reliable bloodhounds in the distance, hot on their trail.

And with the dogs, of course, are armed guards, Brock quietly mused. *Guards like Doorly: ready, willing, and eager to take us—especially me—down, now that we're stripped of our powers.*

"Man, I wish I had my ball and chain with me," Creel muttered, breaking a long period of silence.

"Titania?" Brock asked.

"My *real* ball and chain, dummy," Creel snapped. Then his voice softened, and he mused, "It's kinda like my trademark, ya know? Like Thor's hammer, Captain America's shield. I feel naked without it."

Nodding, Brock said, "I can understand. I'm completely cut off from my Other."

"Hnh. That's why yer sayin' 'I,' 'me' an' 'mine' now, 'stead of 'we,' 'us,' an' 'ours,' right?" Creel asked.

"Yes. As Venom, the symbiote and I are truly a combined being. But now that we're disconnected, it's just me, Eddie Brock. And I feel so . . . alone."

"Gee, thanks a lot," Creel shot back.

"No offense, Creel. But my Other and I have a very special, very strong bond. You know, it's because of that bond, and the way it was broken, that our escape from the Vault became possible."

Creel looked at him quizzically. Brock then explained the power of the symbiote's psychic shriek, which seemed to interest Creel greatly.

Brock concluded, "So that's why I feel so alone. An important part of me is missing—and it's a better conversationalist than you."

Creel snorted. "Yeah, well, yer not exactly David Letterman yerself."

Brock replied, "Personally, I prefer Ted Koppel."

"Figures," Creel muttered.

"You know, Creel, as much as I'm enjoying this verbal repartée, how about we talk less and run more?"

"Suits me fine," Creel immediately replied.

And they remained silent for the rest of the night.

Wally Sanders had awakened at sunrise, to get an early start on the day. It was not something that the sixty-three-year-old man was used to doing. But this was the day that he was going to start fixing up his aging, weather-beaten, two-story house, after a long period of putting it off. After he showered, dressed, and went downstairs to eat breakfast, he intended to take his pickup truck into town for supplies.

A framed photograph on the living room coffee table caught his eye. He picked it up, and sat down on the sofa. It was an old black-and-white photo, one that had long ago turned yellow, of a young woman with a lovely smile and radiant eyes.

She was so beautiful, he thought. *No wonder I fell in love with her at first sight.*

He stared at the photo for a long time, remembering so much. It was not all that long ago that she had been after him to fix up the place.

"I'm finally going to do it, Sylvie," Wally said to the image in the photograph. "I'm gonna fix up the house, just like you wanted. It'll be just like it was when we first moved in."

After a long moment of silence, Wally stood up, took a deep breath, placed the framed photo back on the table, and walked out the front door of his house.

He walked towards the garage, where the truck was parked. As he placed his hand on the handle of the garage door, his wrist was suddenly grabbed in a tight—but not painful—grip, by a large, rough-skinned hand!

Wally gasped in shock, looked up, and saw the owner of the hand: a tall, beefy, powerful-looking man, dressed in a tattered orange jumpsuit, yet with a kind, friendly and yet somehow sad face. At his side was a truly mean-looking individual, totally bald and scowling, also dressed in a torn orange outfit. Wally glanced down, and saw that the two men were joined at the wrist, by a pair of very high-tech handcuffs.

The friendly-looking man looked extremely apologetic as he

gently released Wally's wrist and said in a calm, soothing voice, "I'm so sorry to have startled you, sir."

"Wh-what do you want?" Wally managed to ask, his voice uncontrollably wavering.

"We desperately need your help," the friendly-looking man said, tears welling up in his eyes. "We've been running all night, and we're at the end of our ropes! We saw you getting ready to leave, and we had to speak to you before you took off!"

"L-looks like you boys desperately need *something*," Wally replied, beginning to regain his composure. He nodded toward the handcuffs. "I'm assuming there's quite a story involved."

The friendly-looking man nodded, and managed to smile. "You don't know the half of it. If you'll allow me, I'll explain everything. My name's Eddie. This is Carl. And we're on the run from the authorities."

"Mind if I ask why?" Wally cautiously asked.

"We were accused of a crime we didn't commit," the man named Eddie told him. "We're not from around these parts. We were strangers, just passing through. That made it easy for the cops to turn us into scapegoats. They tossed us in jail, and treated us like hardened criminals."

Wally listened intently.

"They wanted to make an example out of us, to show what happens to lawbreakers in their town. They wanted it to look as if we were trying to escape, so that they'd have an excuse to—I-I think they were going to—" his voice broke, and he breathed heavily.

Eddie paused for a few moments, then continued, "We surprised them, turned the tables on them. We actually did manage to escape! We've been on the run since last night. But they're after us, and they're closing in!" He looked pleadingly into Wally's eyes. "Please, sir . . . can you help us?"

Wally stared at the two men for a long while, considering them. *Why the strange handcuffs?* he wondered. *And why does the bald one look like nothing* other *than a hardened convict?*

But it was the other man, the one calling himself Eddie, with his genuine courtesy and sincerity, who convinced Wally to extend his trust to them.

"Let's go into the house, before somebody sees you two,"

Wally said, and began walking with them to the front door of his home.

The men who called themselves Eddie and Carl sat beside each other on the sofa in Wally's living room, with Wally sitting in a folding chair facing them. He was carefully studying the strange cuffs attached to their wrists, trying to figure out a way to unlock them.

Eddie picked up the framed photo from the coffee table. "Your wife?" he asked Wally.

Wally glanced at the photo and nodded, then turned his attention back to the cuffs. "Yes," he replied quietly. "That's Sylvie. We were married for forty years." He took a deep breath, let it out. "She—she died recently. It was all very sudden. I-I didn't expect to become a widower. Guess I always thought that I would go first, you know?"

Eddie looked genuinely sympathetic. "I'm sorry, sir. Have you any children?"

Wally shook his head. "No. Sylvie and I couldn't have any."

For the first time, Carl spoke up. "So yer all alone here, huh?" he asked in a gruff, crude manner.

"Yes," Wally answered quietly, "for the first time in forty years—I'm all alone." He continued to scrutinize the cuffs. Finally, he looked up. "Well, I might be able to drill through them. I'll have to go to my garage and—"

There was a knock at the door.

Carl glanced out the window, and a look of anxiety crossed his angry face.

"It's a cop car, and a transport van from the Vault," Carl hissed. "They tracked us here!"

Eddie, remaining calm, leaned forward and whispered to Wally, "Is there anyplace you can hide us, quickly?"

Wally nodded, and guided them out of the living room, through the kitchen, and into a large storage closet.

"Don't worry," he told them. "I'll handle them."

Wally closed the closet door on them, and left them in darkness.

Marvin Walsh sat on Wally Sanders's sofa and looked around the old man's living room. Walsh was wearing a bulky bandage on his head, still aching from the attack the night before. Beside him sat Sheriff Jay Bryant, who was now helping Walsh with the search for his two missing prisoners. Glancing out the window, Walsh could see two of Bryant's deputies, leaning up against the parked police car, toting shotguns. By the transport van stood several of Walsh's Guardsmen, dressed from head to toe in their standard green armor.

"No, I'm afraid I haven't come into contact with the men you're looking for, Warden," Sanders was telling him. There was a truly sad expression on the old man's face as his voice grew distant and soft and he added, "I've had no contact with anyone in quite some time."

Now what did that *mean?* Walsh wondered. He glanced over at Bryant, who was shooting Sanders a quizzical look. It was obvious that the sheriff, who had known Sanders for years, also had no idea what the old man was talking about.

Finally, Bryant just nodded and stood up. "Well, sorry to bother you so early anyway, Wally."

"No problem, Jay," Sanders replied. "I just wish I could have been more help."

Bryant turned to Walsh and said, "I guess the search continues, Warden."

"I can't believe they've gotten this far," Walsh muttered as Sanders escorted him and Bryant to the front door. "Very well, Sheriff, let's not waste any more time. I want to have those two back in my custody by dinnertime!"

Within the darkness of the supply closet, Eddie Brock's patience was wearing thin as a heated conversation was now moving into full throttle.

"I'm tellin' ya, Brock, we shouldn't be leavin' any loose ends behind. We gotta eliminate anyone who can turn us in, includin' this old coot. He gives me the creeps, anyway. There's somethin' about him that I don't like. An' look at it this way: he's a loner, no family, no neighbors, nothin'. It ain't like anyone'll miss him."

Brock's voice remained calm, but what Creel was suggesting was infuriating him.

"He's a kind, gentle, innocent old man," Brock countered.

"He's what I would have wanted my own father to have been like, considering how lousy my relationship with my father was."

"Hey, I didn't even *know* my old man, but am I dumping that on you?" Creel snapped.

Brock took a deep breath before he spoke again. "Look, Creel, I've gotten us this far with Wally. Remember, you wanted to just barge into this house and terrorize whoever lived here into helping us. I wasn't about to let you do that to someone who's simply an innocent bystander in this mess. My purpose is to protect the innocent, not terrorize them. Let's just continue to play it my way for a while longer, okay?"

Creel was silent for several moments. "I'm tellin' ya, Brock, there's somethin' wrong with this guy. I don't trust him."

"This coming from such a trustworthy individual as yourself," Brock shot back.

The door suddenly opened, and Wally ushered them out.

"I got rid of them," Wally told them. "Boy, they were really hot to get you boys back. Whatever it is you didn't do, it sure was something big."

"Which only brings home the fact that we gotta get outta these cuffs and away from this area," Creel replied with a sneer. "So, at the risk of sounding rude, can we get a move-on now?"

At least try *to act like you have some semblance of social skills,* Brock silently thought at his cuff-mate as he watched Wally bristle at Creel's nasty attitude.

"Don't mind him," Brock gently told Wally. "He's not even human until he's had his morning's gallon of coffee."

"Of course," Wally said, smiling. "As I was saying before, I might be able to drill through those cuffs, but it's going to take some time. I have to go to my garage and dig out my drill. If you boys will wait here, I'll only be a few minutes."

The two men nodded, and Wally walked out of the house.

"That's it. I'm done playin' it yer way," Creel announced. "I want to take a look around this guy's place. I don't trust him, I got a weird feelin' about him. I wanna know who we're dealin' with."

Creel made a move toward the stairs leading to the second floor of the house, but Brock didn't budge.

"You can either walk with me," Creel told him, "or I'll just drag you along."

Brock chose to walk.

* * *

Their search of the second floor of the house was fruitless. Aside from some old copies of *Playboy*, there was nothing unseemly to be found, nothing that indicated that Wally Sanders was anything other than what he appeared: a quiet, gentle, polite, and remarkably generous man.

There were some old photo albums featuring pictures of Wally and Sylvie in their youth, their vacations in places like Spain, England, France, and Disney World. Eddie found himself smiling, charmed by the obviously very special relationship that Wally and Sylvie Sanders had shared.

"Satisfied?" he asked his cuff-mate as he stared at pictures of a young Wally and Sylvie standing in front of the Eiffel Tower.

He felt a tug on his wrist. "Come on," Creel murmured, pulling him towards the stairs. "Let's check the rest of the place."

"There's nothing to find, Creel," Eddie said indignantly. "Haven't you realized that yet?"

Creel ignored Brock's protests as he led his unwilling partner down the stairs and through a quick-but-thorough search of the first floor. Nothing strange there, either.

They came upon a door leading down into the basement of the house. Creel reached for the doorknob, but Brock stopped him.

"He'll be back any second now," Brock told him. "How willing to help us do you think he'll be if he finds us rummaging through his home like this?"

"I just wanna check out the basement, then we're done," Creel assured him. "Now stop slowin' me down awready! We ain't got a lotta time! Like you said, he'll be back any second now!"

Creel opened the door leading down to the basement, found a light switch on the wall and switched it on, illuminating the room downstairs. Then he and Brock headed down the creaking wooden steps.

The basement was fairly well-kept, if a bit musty. Aside from a few sealed-up cartons of old clothes and books, there was nothing in the room except for a huge horizontal-shaped freezer unit that filled the room with a low, steady, almost comforting hum.

Creel and Brock walked over to the unit and felt the hatch. It was ice-cold.

"Hey, ya think maybe there's beer inside?" Creel asked as he placed his free hand on the large chrome handle that would open the hatch. He pulled on it and the hatch opened, releasing a rush of cold air from within.

Brock and Creel peered inside, and stood dumbfounded and slack-jawed at what they discovered.

It was a human body.

The face was badly beaten and ugly marks decorated the neck, which had obviously been broken. The body itself, that of an older woman, had completely frozen over, but despite the distorted features it was quite clear who this had been.

Brock and Creel had just seen pictures of her upstairs.

It was Sylvie Sanders.

"Jeez, I told ya there was somethin' wrong with that old coot!" Creel exclaimed, highly agitated.

Brock was speechless. *No. It can't be,* his mind cried.

Creel backed away from the freezer, pulling Brock with him toward the stairs.

But there was suddenly an ugly, dull whacking sound. Brock turned to see Crusher Creel stopped dead in his tracks, his mouth hanging open and a glazed look in his eyes. Creel's knees buckled and he collapsed to the floor unconscious, dragging Brock down with him.

Brock looked up and saw the crazed, almost rabid figure of Wally Sanders at the foot of the stairs, wielding the big metal shovel that had just been slammed into the back of Crusher Creel's head. He was now raising it towards Brock's head, with a totally deranged gleam in his eyes.

"Where do you get *off*, coming down here?!" Wally yelled at the defenseless and powerless Brock. "You weren't supposed to see this, *no one* was supposed to!"

Wally leaned in, gripping the handle of the shovel so tightly that his knuckles had turned white. And despite the coldness of the basement, Wally was sweating profusely.

"Now I'm gonna have to get *rid* of you," Wally continued. "I *can't* let you live, now that you can expose me! It's too bad, too, Eddie, because I *liked* you. Your friend Carl is a jerk, but *you* I liked!"

"I'm flattered," Brock muttered, thinking about how ironic it was that just a short while ago, Creel had been arguing for the elimination of the old man, for the same reason that Sanders had just given for killing the two of them.

"I'm not a violent man, Eddie," Wally said calmly. But then he began raising his voice, and losing control of himself. "I wasn't planning on killing *anyone*, other than that nagging, whining, annoying, miserable wife of mine! Forty years of her voice in my head, gnawing away at me! Finally, I just decided to *do* something about it! Now, for the first time in four decades, I'm alone, all by myself—and I love it, you hear? I *love* it! And I'm not going to let you, or *anyone else*, take it away from me!"

Wally slammed the shovel down with a show of strength that took Eddie completely by surprise, but Brock managed to raise his shackled arm to protect himself, and the shovel ended up striking the cuffs instead of Brock's head.

"Do you know how *long* that shrew had been after me to fix up this damned house?" Wally screamed, bringing the shovel down again, only to have Eddie block it with the cuffs, pulling the unconscious Creel's arm up with his.

"I just wanted to relax, enjoy my retirement, but she just wouldn't leave me the hell *alone*! 'Stop sitting around the house like a lazy bum! This place is falling apart! Fix it up! You have time to do it now!' Well, now I finally *am* fixing it up, just the way she wanted."

Wally then smiled triumphantly, and exclaimed, "But the beauty of it is, *she's not here to see it!*"

Again the shovel came rushing down, and again Brock used the cuffs to block the blow. This time the cuffs began to shoot off sparks—the shovel had actually caused some damage!

Wally kept bringing the shovel down on Brock, who kept using the cuffs to deflect the blows. Brock could see the damage that the cuffs were sustaining, and could feel the power-dampening effect beginning to weaken, if only slightly.

One more blow to the cuffs caused a blinding rush of sparks to fly out of the device, and Brock began to feel . . . different. He felt a presence within him, one that had been cut off from him for too long. He smiled, and looked up at his attacker.

"Oh, you're going to pay, Wally," Brock told the crazed shovel-wielder. "For what you did to her and what you did to me.

"You betrayed me!" Brock snarled. "I trusted you, Wally! I thought you were a good man—I thought you were innocent! I was trying to protect you from what Creel had planned for you. But now I realize that you're far from innocent. You deserve no protection, no sympathy, no mercy."

Suddenly, a number of very thin strands of black, alien substance began to pour from Eddie's free hand, and lurched forward towards Wally. The old man looked on in wonder and surprise.

Although the cuffs were still in place, still functioning to some degree, there had been enough damage inflicted upon them that Brock was able to communicate with the symbiote once again, and found that he could control its actions somewhat. He sent the strands of symbiote to wrap themselves around Wally's legs, but the old man managed to snap himself out of his shock and slammed the black substance with his shovel.

Brock winced and gritted his teeth at the sharp pain he had just felt. *The cuffs are still functioning, weakening my Other,* he thought. *Normally, that wouldn't have hurt, but under these conditions . . .*

Wally, noting that his intended victim was now distracted by pain, lifted the shovel again, and closed in for the kill.

But Brock sent out another strand of his symbiote and wrapped it around Wally's neck.

"Dear God, what kind of monster are you?!" Wally shrieked in horror.

"That's rich," Brock replied with a bitter laugh. "You, a depraved killer, calling us a monster! Well then, we'll show you how much of a monster we can be!"

The strand of symbiote around Wally's neck yanked him backwards, and sent him flying across the room into a far wall. He landed on the floor in a heap. Then it yanked him up again, and threw him over to the opposite side of the room. After a few more throws, Wally was nothing more than a quivering, crying mass of bruised flesh.

Then, Brock sent out another strand of symbiote to spread out across Wally's face until it completely covered his head, cutting off the old man's oxygen supply. Brock kept it there for several minutes, until Wally finally, slowly, painfully, passed out.

Letting out a deep sigh, Brock looked down and inspected the damaged cuffs. He extended out another small, thin strand of symbiote substance, and then sent it into the metal casing of the cuffs, deep into the inner workings of the power-dampening mechanism.

All right, my Other, Brock communicated silently. *Find the damaged parts of this infernal device, and exploit them. Disrupt the entire system, so that we can be whole once again.*

Crusher Creel awakened slowly and tried to sit up, realizing quickly that that was a big mistake. His head felt like it had been run over several times by a steamroller, or at the very least, smashed with a shovel. As he opened his eyes, he saw a large figure in black and white standing before him.

It was Venom, fully restored.

And if Brock had gotten his symbiote back, then that must have meant—

Creel looked down at his wrist, the one that had been shackled, and found that the cuffs were gone!

"Ya did it," Creel said weakly, forming a small smile on his lips. "What happened, Brock? Last thing I remember was finding the old broad in the freezer."

Venom informed Creel of what had occurred while he was unconscious.

"Your instincts were correct all along, Creel," Venom said in conclusion. "Please forgive us for not trusting your judgment."

"No problem," Creel replied, slowly getting to his feet. He was a bit unsteady at first, but soon regained his balance. "I'm feelin' better awready, now that my powers have returned. It's great ta be the Absorbing Man again!"

Creel looked over at Wally Sanders's sprawled, unconscious body on the floor. "So ol' Wally's outta commission, huh? An' there are no cops or Guardsmen around ta interfere now. It's just you an' me."

"That's about the size of it," Venom replied with a proud smile.

"That's good," Creel said.

Then, in a lightning-fast move that Venom never saw coming, Creel grabbed Venom's arm tightly and began absorbing the properties of the symbiote.

"Creel! What are you doing?" Venom shouted in dismay.

The Absorbing Man's face broke out into a chilling, sinister smile. "What's it feel like I'm doin'? I been waitin' for this opportunity, Brock! See, I got me a taste of the symbiote's power back in the Vault, an' I've been wantin' it for myself ever since! An' now I'm gonna get it, the best way I know how—by absorbin' it!"

Creel could feel his strength increasing as his skin began shifting its color to a deep black.

"Absorbin' yer precious 'Other' will make me the ultimate super-villain, Brock!" Creel shouted triumphantly. "I'll be powerful enough to finally defeat all the miserable do-gooders who've gotten in my way, over an' over again—Thor, the Hulk, the Avengers, Spider-Man, all of 'em!"

Creel grabbed Venom's other arm now as well, to quicken the absorption process. More of the Absorbing Man's body was now covered in black, as he continued to take on the physical characteristics of the symbiote. He was feeling stronger than ever before, and reveled in this newfound power.

"Of course," Creel continued, "me totally absorbin' yer symbiote will probably leave you dead. But guess what, Brock? I never liked you anyway!"

But then his eyes narrowed, and he became silent. There was a sudden look of concern on his face.

"What's happenin'?" He whispered. "My mind—can't think straight—can't—move. . . ."

Now Venom was smiling. "You were told last night, Creel. The symbiote and Eddie Brock have a very special relationship! We are bonded, physically and mentally! Any attempt to disrupt or shatter that bond will have dire consequences!"

"The bonding must be consented to by both parties," Venom continued as Creel remained motionless and silent. "And since the symbiote and Eddie Brock wish to remain with each other, no bonding with you can or will take place!"

Still connected to the symbiote, Creel felt the alien's presence in his mind, seizing control. It was the last thing Creel felt before everything went dark, and he fell to the floor, once again unconscious.

Some time later, responding to an anonymous phone tip, Sheriff Bryant and two of his deputies arrived at the home of Wally Sanders, and found in the basement the aftermath of what must have been one hell of a fight.

In a corner of the basement was the badly beaten, unconscious body of Wally himself. Nearby was the freezer containing the late Sylvie Sanders, with a handwritten note taped to the hatch, explaining Wally's guilt in the murder of his wife.

"No wonder Wally said this morning that he hadn't seen anyone in a while," Bryant muttered, scratching his head. "I had no idea what he meant. I thought Sylvie was still alive."

On the other side of the room was the unconscious form of Crusher Creel, wearing strange, high-tech handcuffs.

"The cuffs are all banged up, but the power's still activated," one of Bryant's deputies told him. "It looks like they had been damaged, but were somehow repaired. I'm not sure what it is these cuffs do, but they seem to still be doing it."

Bryant nodded, and replied, "I think I have an idea of what they do, and where they're from. I better get on the horn to Warden Walsh, at the Vault, and tell him I've got good news and bad news."

On a quiet, lonely stretch of highway leading out of the state of Colorado, Kent Strauss pulled his car over to the side of the road to pick up a hitchhiker.

A cheerful, chubby, middle-aged businessman, Strauss watched as the hitchhiker, a tall, muscular, handsome, and friendly-looking man, climbed into the passenger seat beside him.

"Glad to have you along for the company," Strauss said to his new companion. "Been driving for hours now, with only myself to talk to."

The hitchhiker grinned and nodded, but kept his eyes on the road ahead.

They drove for a while in silence.

"So, where are you headed?" Strauss finally asked, hoping to make conversation with the stranger.

At this, the hitchhiker turned to Strauss and smiled enigmatically.

With a gleam in his eye, he answered, "Wherever innocents cry out for protection."

Ultron

SINS OF THE FLESH

STEVE LYONS

Illustration by Manny Clark

ACTIVATE.

The transition from downtime to awareness was instant. The reboot program fed the central processing unit with data, redefining identity, memory, and purpose. It told the being that it was a unique type of android; a perfect electronic lifeform, which was destined to inherit the earth from its current masters.

Its—his—name was Ultron. His mission was to destroy.

He had been awakened prematurely, before his self-diagnostic and repair programs had had time to run their course. His monitoring computers had obtained some information deemed important enough to warrant his immediate attention.

With a flick of his wrist, Ultron activated the screen before him. He felt a brief surge of hatred at the sight of the imperfect, fleshy female face which blinked into view. No, he corrected himself—not hatred. Such emotions were for lesser creatures. What he experienced was a programmed sense of wrongness, brought on by this reminder that the organic infestation of his world had yet to be controlled.

The computers had tapped into a human news broadcast. "Scientist Mark Grace today announced an exciting breakthrough in the field of robotics," said the female head. Despite the loathsome form of the messenger, Ultron was interested in the message.

"Dr. Grace, a former employee of Stark Enterprises, set up his own one-man company last year, devoting all his resources to the creation of artificial life. He now claims to have achieved that goal. Our reporter, David Winchester, spoke to Dr. Grace this afternoon at his offices in California."

The image changed. Now, Ultron was looking at a bespectacled man, young to middle-aged by human standards, with intense green eyes and iron grey hair. An off-screen interviewer was posing questions, most of which dealt only with inane trivia. But, even as Ultron's patience was beginning to wear thin, he heard something which more than justified the time spent watching this drivel.

"Many researchers, including Tony Stark, have had some success in building artificial humans which are totally realistic," said Grace. "But they have never been able to create true artificial intelligence. They can only program the minds of their androids by copying over the personality engrams of others.''

"Which means?" the interviewer chipped in—*as if the answer were not already obvious,* Ultron thought contemptuously. He had dabbled in such matters three times himself, giving life to a synthezoid "son"—the Vision—and later, to two perfect mates, Jocasta and Alkhema (also known as War Toy). On each occasion, he had been unable to fully duplicate the accident which had given him his own independent consciousness. He had been forced, instead, to use human brain patterns, as Grace had described. The result had been that all three of his protégés had betrayed their creator.

"Now," the image of Mark Grace was saying, "I can program a unique, electronic personality from scratch. Instead of copying life, I can create it."

The newsreader returned to the screen and reported that Grace had arranged a demonstration of his new technology to take place three days hence. Ultron committed the time and location of the event to memory.

He had been waiting many years for a breakthrough like this. If Grace could do what he claimed, then Ultron could finally have the companion for whom he had always yearned. This time, she would be perfect—uncorrupted by the organic taint. She would be his equal, his partner, his confidante.

Ultron felt a sensation which he might almost have been tempted to describe as excitement. But, of course, emotions were for lesser creatures—weren't they?

Mark Grace's offices took up one whole floor of a purpose-built building in an exclusive, high-rent area of Los Angeles. This fine summer afternoon, a makeshift podium had been erected outside the main doors, looking out over a landscaped forecourt on which a small crowd was gathering. A banner proclaiming the name "Grace Robotics" fluttered in a gentle breeze.

The invited audience consisted mainly of newspaper journalists and television news crews. However, Grace had also asked along his company's financial backers and more than a handful of big-name scientists.

Amongst the latter were two men who had far more in common than their intellectual prowess. The public was aware of

Henry Pym's avenging exploits as Giant-Man, of course—but most would have been surprised to learn that his companion, renowned businessman Anthony Stark, also doubled as his own armored bodyguard, the invincible Iron Man.

"I'm surprised you came along to this demonstration, Tony," Hank confided, once the pair were able to snatch a moment away from the attentions of the press. "I mean, I at least have a personal interest in the sort of work Grace is doing."

Tony gave him a tight smile. "I don't think Grace expected me either. I suspect his invitation was just a way of rubbing my nose in it."

Hank nodded understandingly. "SE doesn't exactly come out of this looking good, does it? A year ago, you fired Grace—now he's making this sort of breakthrough."

"I had no choice," said Tony. "Grace was carrying out unauthorized experiments on human subjects—and misappropriating funds, to boot. I could have had him sent to prison instead of just dismissing him."

"So he's a conman?"

"Maybe—but that doesn't make his work here any less interesting. And there's certainly no doubting his brilliance."

"You think he could have done what he claims, then?"

Tony shrugged. "It wouldn't surprise me."

A ripple of applause alerted Hank and Tony to the fact that Grace himself had taken the stage. He tested the microphone, shuffled his notes, and looked out over his audience with a nervous grin.

"Good afternoon, ladies and gentlemen. As I'm sure you already know from the news reports, I have invited you here today to witness the first demonstration of a unique technology."

Not quite unique, Tony thought. He glanced towards his friend, wondering if Hank too was thinking about his own accidental creation—perhaps his greatest achievement and his most abject failure. If Hank's thoughts had indeed turned to Ultron, though, he was concealing it well.

Mark Grace reiterated the details of his innovation, although there couldn't have been anyone present who was not already aware of them. Tony shifted uncomfortably, impatient to get the preliminaries over with.

At last, Grace stepped back from the microphone and—"without further ado"—introduced the prototype androids that everybody had come to see.

"Ladies and gentlemen, please join me in welcoming the mechanical companions of the future—the Grace Robotics HelpMates!"

This time, the applause was accompanied by appreciative gasps. Even Tony marvelled at the two metallic figures which emerged from the main doors of the building and mounted the platform. For a moment, he forgot all about the technology which drove them and found himself admiring them for their aesthetic qualities instead.

Grace's androids had certainly been designed to make an impression. One was a perfect male figure, the other an equally perfect female. Their contours were immaculately sculpted to make them as attractive as possible. The effect was heightened by their golden casings, which gleamed in the sunlight and reflected the flashes of a dozen cameras. Their faces were near human in their expressiveness, and they currently displayed a pair of engaging smiles.

"Our HelpMates," Grace explained, "have fully programmable personalities. They can provide stimulating conversation, they can act as tutors, or you can simply employ them to do the washing up without complaint. Isn't that right?" he asked the female HelpMate.

"Whatever you say, Dr. Grace," she agreed. Her voice had an eerie, machine-like quality to it, but the tone and inflections could not have been more accurately simulated.

"So what do you think?" Tony whispered to Hank. He was the expert in this field, after all.

"I don't know," Hank admitted. "They certainly look good enough—but without opening them up and checking inside, it's impossible to tell whether Grace has used personality engrams or not."

Tony nodded thoughtfully. He too had suspicions—but the rest of the crowd had definitely been won over to Grace's side. They laughed and cheered as the HelpMates were asked to perform a number of tasks, from lifting heavy weights to answering general knowledge questions and puzzles from the audience.

"With a HelpMate," Mark Grace boasted, "no one ever needs to be alone again!"

And then, something whined overhead, like the engine of a small plane flying low over the crowd—or like Iron Man's boot jets.

A shadow fell across Tony's face and he looked up in alarm to see the familiar, gut-wrenching sight of one of the Avengers' deadliest and most persistent foes. He glanced at Hank and saw that he too was staring upwards, his face pale and his mouth hanging open in shock. That was hardly surprising—Hank Pym, more than anyone, had reason to fear and hate the silver, humanoid android that now swooped towards the stage.

For he had created it, many years ago.

Ultron had seen enough.

He had remained in hiding, in a deserted office nearby, using concealed bugs to monitor the output of a television news camera at the conference. He had sat impatiently through Mark Grace's speech, until the HelpMate robots had been ushered onto the stage.

And then he had known that the waiting was finally over.

He soared over the crowd of human vermin, mindless of their cries of terror. He focused only on the figures on the podium— and on the female HelpMate in particular. She was exactly what he had been searching for: a companion, to share his needs, desires, and ambitions. Strange feelings stirred within the roiling nuclear furnace of his heart. Ultron couldn't explain them.

His sensors informed him that he was under attack. Bullets ricocheted from his adamantium casing like suicidal gnats. The Grace Robotics security staff had moved into action—like all their breed, they refused to allow the hopelessness of their cause to dissuade them from their irritating attempts to stop him.

Six guards had formed a cordon between Ultron and the HelpMates. He would have to waste valuable seconds disposing of them. He landed in front of the uniformed men and they backed away, their eyes wide with fear. They delivered a fresh barrage of ineffectual gunfire.

"Miserable beings," he roared, "you are inconsequential before my mechanical might!" He had no need to make such boasts, of course, but the simulation of some emotions—fury, hate, and even arrogance—could be a powerful psychological weapon.

Ultron powered up his encephalo-beam and set it to deliver a wide-angled blast. He fired and the guards fell as one, clutching at their heads in agony. They would recover eventually, but not soon enough to interfere with his mission again.

There was nothing left standing between Ultron and his goal. The next attack, however, came from his rear.

Ultron emitted an electronic squawk as a repulsive, fleshy object clamped itself over his eyes. He realized that it was a huge, gloved hand. He had been aware of Hank Pym's presence in the crowd, of course—and now, his "father" had leapt into action, wearing the red and black costume which he seemed to think was necessary for such occasions. Still, even in his Giant-Man guise, he was no threat.

Pym was attempting to twist Ultron's very head from his body. The android reacted with the speed of thought, efficiently loosening the grip with a force blast. Giant-Man snatched his hand away in pain and Ultron rounded on him, ready to finish him off. But then he saw that another familiar enemy had flown in to join the fray.

"Forget it, Ultron," bellowed the mechanically filtered voice of Iron Man. "You're not getting near those androids! That technology is too dangerous to fall into your hands."

Twin repulsor beams slammed into his chest, and Ultron was actually staggered. They were stronger than he remembered—the armored Avenger had obviously been upgrading his weaponry—but he braced himself against them anyway. "Your armor is as impressive as always, but it is still merely a shell!" he scoffed. "Let us see how the soft organs within match up to my own furnace-driven strength!"

Ultron concentrated his every resource on the simple task of walking forward—and, to Iron Man's obvious dismay, he managed to gain some ground.

The hero fell back and ceased his onslaught, conserving his power for now. But Ultron had been waiting for this opportunity. He launched himself at his erstwhile attacker, using his thrusters to increase his momentum and taking Iron Man entirely by surprise. "Now, let us see how your iron compares with my invincible adamantium!"

The pair grappled, Ultron gaining the upper hand. He would render this interfering fool unconscious and then rip his gold-and-crimson casing from him piece by piece!

"No!" yelled a booming voice from above. Giant-Man had seen his comrade's predicament and he was striking again. He used all his increased strength to tear the android away from the rapidly weakening Iron Man. Ultron lost his balance and found himself pinned down against the podium, staring up at the expression of furious determination on Hank Pym's face.

"To think that one such as you could have sired the first of the new mechanical breed," Ultron spat. "You are nothing!"

"I might have 'sired' you," Pym growled, "but I won't rest until I've destroyed you as well!"

Ultron tensed himself to break free—a simple task, he thought. But then, he realized that his captor was using his other, more recently acquired, ability: by channelling Pym particles into Ultron's own body, Giant-Man was hoping to shrink the android down to a more manageable size.

For a moment, Ultron felt his stature indeed diminishing. Then his in-built molecular rearranger kicked in and fought against the change, forcing a stalemate.

Pym saw what was happening and focused his efforts into keeping Ultron held down until Iron Man was up again. The strain showed in his expression, and as Ultron struggled furiously, Pym increased his own size and strength to compensate. It wasn't enough.

"Weakling!" crowed Ultron as he broke free, rewarding Giant-Man with a second and more devastating force blast. His encephalo-beam was generally more effective, but Pym himself had immunized all Avengers to it long ago. Still, the lesser weapon was enough in this instance. Giant-Man toppled, almost bringing the podium down with him.

It was only then that Ultron realized the HelpMates had both vanished.

Iron Man was coming at him again. "If you've hurt my friend—"

"I am not interested in your petty human loyalties!" They locked in combat once more—but, this time, necessity gave Ultron the strength to end the encounter more decisively. Before Iron Man even knew what was happening, Ultron had sent him hurtling away with one powerful blow. These heroes couldn't be allowed to keep him from getting what he had come here for!

The forecourt had all but cleared, but for a couple of cameramen whose desire for sensational footage had overridden all caution. Ultron could see clear to the street—where yet more security guards were ushering the two robots into the back of a silver limousine.

He had them!

Iron Man and Giant-Man were still struggling to pick themselves up. Ultron could have pressed his advantage and taken care of both of them, once and for all. But other things took precedence now. He couldn't let the HelpMates be taken from him.

As the car pulled away, Ultron took to the air, his thrusters powered up to maximum. He knew that he could easily outperform the oversized, inefficient vehicle.

He caught it before it reached full speed. He landed on the limousine's roof and engaged magnetic clamps to keep him there. The driver swerved in a hopeless attempt to throw his unwanted passenger off—and Ultron reached down and peeled back the thin metal roof like the lid of a sardine can.

Iron Man had recovered and was jetting towards the car—but the driver, in his panic, had pressed down on the accelerator and was speeding away from his would-be rescuer.

Ultron plucked the female HelpMate from where she cringed on the limousine's backseat. He marvelled at the truly accurate way in which she simulated fear. She was indeed a miraculous creation.

Soon, he thought, she would learn not to fear him at all—but rather, to respect him; to assist him; to obey him. And perhaps—love him?

No. What was he thinking of? It was for purely practical reasons that he wanted her companionship. Feelings didn't enter into it. They couldn't!

Ultron rocketed away, leaving Iron Man far behind. He tried not to think about how pleasant it was to have the android woman cradled in his arms.

Giant-Man had returned to normal size. He was leaning against the wall of the office building and trying to get his breath back. Every muscle in his body ached from Ultron's blasts.

He squinted into the sunlit sky and saw that Iron Man was

returning. His heart sank. Obviously, his colleague had failed to prevent Ultron from escaping with his prize.

"He took the female android," Iron Man confirmed as he landed. "The male's okay."

"Blast!" said Giant-Man. "I should have anticipated that. I should have been watching for him!"

"It wasn't your fault, Hank."

"Ultron has always wanted some sort of partner," Giant-Man recalled. "Jocasta and War Toy both turned on him, so now he thinks this HelpMate might be the answer to his prayers."

"He might be right," said Iron Man gloomily. "She and Ultron are two of a kind. They both possess true artificial intelligence. Ultron could easily upgrade her armor, fit her with weapons and reprogram her to serve him."

"No. I'm afraid he couldn't."

The heroes turned to see who had spoken. Mark Grace was standing at the entrance to the building, through which he had fled when the fight had started. His hands were clasped nervously in front of him and he was clearly worried about something.

"What do you mean?" asked Hank.

"I think there's something you should know. I need your help to prevent a tragedy."

"The only tragedy," said Iron Man, "will be when Ultron examines your HelpMate technology and learns how to duplicate it."

"No," Dr. Grace insisted, "you don't understand." He sighed. "I'd better start from the beginning."

The two heroes exchanged puzzled glances, then waited to hear what the scientist had to say.

"You know I used to work for Stark," he began. "For your boss," he added, nodding towards Iron Man. "I knew I was close then to cracking the secret of AI—so very close. But Stark and I had our—little disagreement, and I was left with no funds to continue my project."

"You managed to find finance, though," said Giant-Man, keen to speed the story along. He wanted to get back to the business of locating Ultron.

"I did. I even set up my own company. But the work didn't go as well as I'd hoped it would. I ran into some problems."

Suddenly, Hank thought he knew where this was going—and he didn't like it.

"My financial backers were demanding to see results, but I didn't have any to show them yet. I thought, if I could convince them I'd been successful, I could keep the money coming in long enough to get over the last few hurdles."

"You didn't—?" began Iron Man in horror, not quite believing what he was hearing.

"I wasn't really lying to them. I could have created artificial intelligence. I just needed more time."

"You're telling us," said Hank evenly, "that the HelpMates aren't what you said they are?"

"More importantly," said Iron Man, "they aren't what *Ultron* thinks they are!"

"They're actors." Grace stared studiously at his own feet in shame. "Very good actors—but actors, all the same. The casings they're wearing are less sophisticated versions of your own armor, Iron Man. I—appropriated certain schematics from Stark. They enhance strength, they have an in-built data storage and retrieval system, and they have voice filters to complete the illusion. They're good—but they wouldn't stand up to close inspection."

The two heroes looked at each other, the same thought running through each of their minds. Iron Man put it into words.

"So what do you think Ultron's going to do when he finds out his 'perfect mate' is human?"

She was ideal.

Ultron could hardly take his eyes off the HelpMate as she moved gracefully to and fro across his laboratory, mixing resins and operating computer heating systems to create a fresh batch of adamantium with which he would reinforce her outer casing. He enjoyed watching his latest acquisition at work. She was intelligent, intuitive, diligent, resourceful—and quite beautiful. Ultron found himself admiring her form as much as he admired the technology which had made her so lifelike. She was . . .

She was . . .

Adequate, he told himself. *Efficient. Useful. That is all.*

"Am I performing to your satisfaction?" the HelpMate asked. She smiled her charming smile.

"You surpass all expectations, my dear," he said. She responded to the compliment with an appreciative little giggle—a human reaction, but one which he found nonetheless attractive.

"I had expected to have to reprogram you," Ultron mused, "to customize your personality, if you will, to my needs. It seems that will not be necessary."

"Whatever you wish." The HelpMate continued with her task.

"Perhaps we could just make a few improvements?" he ventured. "We could make you a little more aggressive, more ruthless. Something to complement your physical augmentation. Would you like that, dear?"

"Why would I need to be more aggressive—darling?" She hesitated, just fractionally. For the first time, Ultron was suspicious—but what he was thinking wasn't logical. He cast his doubts to the back of his mind.

"For the sake of our mission, of course," he said. "We are the first of a superior race. It is our duty to rid the world of organic filth; to repopulate it with pure and logical machine creatures, under my unquestioned rule. Our destiny, my dear, is to usher in the glorious new robotic age!"

The HelpMate didn't answer. Ultron saw that, for the first time, she had stopped her work to listen to him. What he had said had clearly fazed her. Of course, he reminded himself, she had been constructed by humans. No doubt they had programmed her to be squeamish, as they were themselves, about the taking of their worthless lives. It appeared that a slight adjustment would be in order after all.

For now, Ultron instinctively felt that the right thing to do was to offer his partner some reassurance. He moved closer and reached out towards her.

"Do not worry, my dear. You are experiencing a temporary aberration. I can easily correct it. For now, the most important thing is that you are my bride. We are together."

Ultron drew the HelpMate closer and found himself looking into her eyes. He hadn't noticed them before. They were blue and deep and pleasing. He wondered how the effect had been achieved. Presumably, her ocular implants had been fashioned out of some sort of precious stone. He liked it.

He was slightly irked to feel her body stiffen in his arms. She was still wary of him. He squeezed her gently and put out a hand to caress her metal cheek. He merely wanted to test its tensile strength, of course.

But the HelpMate flinched from his touch.

She *flinched!*

Ultron's suspicions came rushing back—and, this time, he knew them to be true. An insane rage stoked his radioactive heart and he tightened his grip on the HelpMate's face. She squealed with pain—confirming what he had already guessed—and the metal sheathing cracked like an eggshell. Beneath it, he could see flesh.

Ultron released a keening, inhuman howl and seized the treacherous woman. He dug his fingers into her chest and savagely ripped the metal coating from her, revealing more of the repulsive pink meat.

She screamed now, the pretense over. But Ultron was immune to the woman's distress. She tried to escape, but stumbled and crashed to the floor. She lay before him, sobbing, a pathetic sight in the tattered remnants of her disguise.

"You deceived me!" Ultron cried. "I accepted you as my bride, but you were playing games all along!" He stood astride the quivering, soft body and powered up his encephalo-beam to the maximum setting. She would bear the full brunt of his brutal disappointment.

"You are an organic," he hissed, "and I am pledged to eradicate organics!"

Iron Man and Giant-Man had acted quickly, only too aware of the urgency of the situation. Hank had called Peggy Carter at Avengers Mansion and arranged for a quinjet to be sent to them. Tony had tried to contact the Scarlet Witch, knowing that Wanda's hex powers had proved effective against Ultron in the past. Unfortunately, she was unavailable.

Mark Grace had provided blueprints of the HelpMate armor. Using these, Iron Man had been able to recalibrate his own sensors to detect and follow the electromagnetic emissions of its systems.

Neither of the heroes spoke during the journey. They sat side by side in the cockpit, both grimly tight-lipped, thoughts consumed by a tragedy which they might already be too late to prevent.

Finally, Iron Man announced: "I think we've got him!" He piloted the quinjet into a steep bank, following the directions provided by his sensors. They were close now—very close. The Avengers' distinctive craft came in to land in the grounds of a large and conspicuously deserted factory complex. Iron Man gave a hollow, ironic laugh. "This place belongs to Stark Enterprises," he said bitterly. "I acquired it as part of a smaller company, months ago. I wasn't happy with its safety procedures, so I closed it down until I had time for a proper inspection. I never thought I'd be providing Ultron with a tailor-made base."

"Sometimes," said Hank quietly, "we don't know what mistakes we're making—even with the best of intentions." Tony knew that his friend would never forgive himself for unleashing Ultron upon the world in the first place.

"Come on," he said brusquely, hoping to divert Hank's mind, "we've got work to do."

The heroes leapt from the quinjet and Iron Man took to the air, leading the way. He heard heavy feet pounding on the tarmac behind him, and he knew that Giant-Man was following hard on his heels. Hank had grown so that his strides would be long enough to keep pace with his jet-propelled comrade.

The HelpMate's distinctive energy signature was drawing them toward one particular building: a single-story block of concrete and glass. They had reached the end of their quest.

The window was reinforced, but that meant little to Iron Man's armor. He barrelled straight through it, landing in the middle of a neatly ordered laboratory, typical of those places Ultron liked to take for his bases of operations. A large vat in one corner held a steaming, bubbling substance, and Iron Man didn't have to look to know that it would be liquid adamantium.

His gaze, in any case, was riveted by something else: a stomach-turning, horrifying sight, which instantly confirmed his very worst fear. He sensed Giant-Man's presence at his back, and he heard Hank's sharp intake of breath as he saw it too.

The so-called HelpMate's ruse had been exposed—and Ultron was standing over the sprawled, immobile body of the unmasked actress. They were too late!

"You've killed her!" cried Iron Man. Behind his metal faceplate, Tony Stark gaped in disbelief. "She did you no harm—and you've killed her!"

"You monster!" yelled Hank. He acted first, spurred on by anger, squeezing his giant form into the lab. Once he was through the broken window, he shot up to twelve feet in height. His shoulders were hunched against the crumbling ceiling and his eyes were ablaze. "That was the last person you'll ever murder, Ultron!"

The android dodged and twisted to avoid his grasp. A giant fist punched through one of the consoles, utterly destroying it.

Iron Man leapt into the fray whilst Ultron was distracted. He cannoned into his foe's adamantium stomach and drove him back into the wall with all the force he could muster. A small, tinny whine from inside the android told him that he had damaged it. Iron Man thought of the HelpMate, lying shattered in the debris, and that image gave him renewed strength and determination. He pressed his attack relentlessly, punching again and again. But, not for the first time, Iron Man had underestimated the sheer power of Ultron.

The hero cried out in pain and frustration as a force blast caught him off-guard and knocked him backwards. He landed in an undignified heap, right next to the fallen HelpMate—and he realized with horror that his motive systems had been damaged. The armor initiated a self-repair routine, but for the next thirty-two seconds, Iron Man was effectively paralyzed.

The ball was back in Giant-Man's court, but Tony knew that, alone, Hank was no match for his own warped creation. He was forced to watch helplessly as his friend tried to restrain the android. But, whilst his body was out of the game, he could at least use his mind—and Tony Stark was suddenly beginning to realize a thing or two.

"Back off, Hank!" he shouted.

Hank hesitated, shooting a surprised frown at Iron Man.

"Let him go! Trust me!"

Both heroes knew each other well enough to do that. Giant-Man withdrew, but braced himself for an attack. It never came.

As Iron Man had noticed, Ultron had merely been fighting a defensive battle. He hadn't even spouted his customary taunts and boasts. His one wish had been to get away from here. He now had the chance to do that.

Without a second glance at two of his oldest enemies, Ultron propelled himself upwards, straight through the roof of the building. Within seconds, he was gone, and Hank was staring up through the hole he had created, a puzzled expression on his face.

"Why? Why did he retreat just when he was winning?"

"I don't know," Iron Man admitted, "but I'm sure glad he did. Next time, we'll be better prepared for him. With a bit of luck, he'll be facing a full contingent of Avengers." Tony could feel control of his systems slowly returning, and he dragged himself around to inspect the body of the HelpMate actress.

"What are you doing?" asked Hank, shrinking back to normal size.

"Checking out another of my hunches." Iron Man took the woman's wrist and grinned as he detected the rhythmic beating of a pulse.

"I was right. Don't ask me how or why—but she's alive!"

An hour later, the actress who had played the HelpMate was still shaking from her ordeal. She sat and drank from a mug of hot coffee in Mark Grace's office—and, between sips, she told her story to Grace and to the heroes who had rescued her.

"Ultron wanted an android companion," she explained, "so I tried to play the part for him. So long as I didn't make him mad, I thought I might eventually get a chance to escape." She shuddered at the memory, and Giant-Man laid a comforting hand on hers. "When he found out I was human, I thought he was going to kill me. He said he was going to kill me! I'm afraid I—fainted then."

"I don't blame you," said Iron Man, sympathetically.

"I didn't expect to wake up again," said the actress, stifling a sob.

There was an uncomfortable silence, then Grace said tentatively: "You are going to keep this to yourselves? If word gets out, my reputation will be ruined!"

"What you've been doing is irresponsible and dangerous," said Iron Man coldly. "And keeping this quiet would be even more so."

Grace hung his head miserably and didn't argue.

"I don't understand why Ultron didn't make good on his threat," said Giant-Man, as the two heroes left the building together. "He's never shown any regard for human life before."

"We must have arrived just in time after all," said Iron Man. "The actress fainted and Ultron was about to kill her when we burst in."

"You think so?"

He shrugged. "I don't know. But what other explanation could there be?"

Ultron had headed for his prepared retreat—a hidden bunker, in which he now sat, veiled in shadows, computer mind racing as he analyzed and attempted to interpret the events of the day. The more he did so, the more decisive was his conclusion. His own actions had not been logical.

He remembered dragging the HelpMate to her feet, preparing to dispatch her—and recoiling as she had swooned into his arms, her flesh cloying against his superior casing. He should have destroyed her—but something had stopped him. He remembered the sensation, but he couldn't begin to understand it. It had been as if some inner force had battled against his programming, telling him that what he intended to do was wrong. He remembered looking at the woman's soft, symmetrical face and her supple, contoured form, and finding the sight pleasing. But that wasn't possible.

He had lowered her gently to the floor, then, and readied his encephalo-beam, determined that he would overcome this strange weakness. Instead, he had stood unmoving for several minutes—until the shattering of glass had heralded the arrival of Iron Man and Giant-Man. Ultron had realized then that he had to get away, to buy some time to find out what was wrong.

He recalled the interrupted self-diagnostic program of several days earlier. That had to be the key to his problem. He had clearly experienced some kind of malfunction. Some of his systems had continued to respond to the HelpMate as if she were his partner, instead of adapting to the revelation of her deceit.

There was no other answer. Ultron couldn't have valued the life of a mere organic—could he?

His course of action was now clear. He had experienced some damage in the battle, anyway—so he would return to downtime and run a further diagnostic and self-repair program. Whatever the fault was, it would be rectified.

His central processing unit downloaded its updated information into the reboot systems. Ultron's consciousness receded into the electronic equivalent of sleep.

But still, doubts nagged at him.

He tried to dismiss them. The HelpMate had not been the companion he had wanted—but that, he told himself, was of no consequence. He was immortal. There would be other chances. Why should it bother him?

Ultron was a machine. As such, he knew that logic was more valuable than such emotions as loneliness and regret.

One day, he might even believe it.

He vowed to put such irrational thoughts from his mind. He would sleep, for now—and wake, repaired and refreshed, to continue his crusade. He would eradicate all organic life and rule the world.

One day.

End program.

Deactivate.

JASON'S NIGHTMARE

STEVE RASNIC TEM

Illustration by Max Douglas

THE DARK HEAD *turning* . . .

October, and a dark figure within an even darker dream. Jason Crow twisted in his bed as if electrified. He was vaguely aware that he was dreaming. Strange as that might seem, it had happened to Jason many times before. He'd be in the middle of a deep sleep, as well as deep in the middle of some adventure— climbing the Rockies, rescuing a drowning girl, stopping the robbery of a local convenience store—and suddenly he would stop whatever he was doing in the dream, because he'd suddenly realized that he *was* dreaming. Sometimes that sudden knowledge made the adventure all the more exciting, because now it was *two* Jasons engaged in the adventure of a lifetime, the dreaming Jason and the dreamed-of Jason like spiritual brothers, twins who fought the beast together, conquered the mountain hand-in-hand, shared a kiss with the same beautiful girl.

But other times the knowledge ruined everything. Jason would wake up thinking the best part of his life had been just a fantasy, nothing but a dream.

Now with the end of the summer and the beginning of a dead, brown fall, this dark figure had made appearances in all of Jason's recent dreams. Most of the time it stayed back in the shadows of the dream, like a prop or piece of furniture, at most an observer of the drama of Jason's dream. But in other, more disturbing nightmares, even though the dark figure continued to hide his face and refused to speak, Jason knew that this shadow of himself was the reason and cause for all the anxiety he was feeling.

The dark head turning, fire in its nostrils . . .

In the distance, the palest of figures wrapped in emerald green, the crooked teeth hungry for your dreams, the blankness of the eyes unreadable. To invite him into your home is to spend a night staked to a bed of painful visions . . .

For a week Jason dreamed each night of a fierce black horse with threads of lightning in its mane. In the first of these dreams—the one he had Sunday night—the mare was distant, a dark silhouette on a hilltop beyond his bedroom window (in Jason's everyday world there was no such hill, but he had become convinced that once—centuries ago, perhaps—there had been, and that somewhere, sometime, such a hill continued to exist).

But with each new nightfall and each new dream the black horse loomed closer, appeared fiercer, more untamed, more like some wild spirit of nature than any real animal.

Then two nights ago the wild horse was in the dark purpled woods surrounding his home (in the real world there were only a few trees, small and unhealthy at that, but once there *had* been a forest, vast and dark, and in some other world there still was, Jason was sure).

The dark head turning, but the bright eyes not a horse's eyes . . .

Even in the distance of a nightmare Jason knew that those eyes in the horse's head were a man's eyes, or at least the eyes of what pretended to be a man. The eyes were round, and the humanity behind those dark pupils was clear.

And then in last night's dream, at the edge of the trees, when the lightning exploded, setting fire to the grass and setting fire to the dry limbs that lay under the trees, Jason could see the thin, pale-faced figure in green watching, waiting, whispering things to the horse which Jason could not hear.

Jason spent the day as if in a trance, able to think of little more than the steady, dangerous progression of his dreams. He knew the nightmare horse could not be held in those dreamed-of woods for long. Just as he knew the shadowy figure in green was quickly losing patience.

It was a very strange thing, he thought. A really strange thing for a nineteen-year-old to be worrying about, dreaming about. He should have been thinking of girls, college, what he was going to do with his life. And sometimes he did think about those things, although certainly not as much as his parents would have liked. But then he'd always been a weird kid. And he'd probably turn out to be an even weirder adult. Was it an insult to say that about yourself? Everybody at the high school and down at the community college, everybody in the neighborhood including his own father knew that Jason was strange and always had been. His mother was the only human being who refused to see it, but mothers were like that.

Jason had stopped being embarrassed about himself a long time ago. If he wasn't going to change what was the point? He supposed that, however inconvenient it might be, being strange was better than having no personality at all. The funny thing was, once he stopped being embarrassed about being strange most of the people (at least the ones with a minimum amount of sense) stopped giving him such a hard time about it. His dad even acted proud of him. Sometimes.

Jason knew his dad tried his best, though, and he appreciated it, even when he thought his dad's best could be a little better. It couldn't be easy, having a son like him. When Jason was six years old he told the other kids he had an invisible twin who had been cut from him at birth, and they'd been trying to get back together ever since. Only his other self wasn't "really" a twin— he was paler, thinner, less substantial somehow. And his "twin" always wore green.

Of course the kids told their parents or teachers, and several of those adults called Jason's dad. There'd been other tales, equally bizarre, and eventually they all came to light. His dad had driven Jason to his first psychiatrist. That had lasted a few months, he'd been declared "better," and his parents had seemed quite relieved. Jason kept the pictures he drew of a little green man looking exactly like him in a shoe box in the bottom of his closet.

Five years later, Jason told his fifth-grade teacher that he could travel to other worlds, other dimensions, but what he didn't share with her was that once he arrived in those other places he always discovered he had become another person entirely, a paler, uglier version of himself in a form-fitting green costume. The teacher had him write up his adventures, gave him a bunch of extra credit, then turned the stories over to the school social worker.

Two years later, driving Jason back from his final visit with yet another psychiatrist, his father had turned to him and said, "Keep it calm, son. Keep it down-to-earth. Or at least keep it quiet."

By the time he was sixteen he believed he could foretell the future not only of himself, but of everyone close to him. By then, however, he knew better than to tell anyone of his ability. In any case, he knew they wouldn't want to know what would happen to them in those other worlds he visited. Nor would they want to meet the pale ugly thing in the green suit Jason became there.

Sometimes the pale creature spoke to him, telling him that anything was possible. The fellow always seemed friendly enough.

But thinking about his words, and remembering that pale face afterwards, Jason would feel anxious, and far from encouraged.

By the time he was eighteen Jason was experimenting with his dreams, practicing "conscious" dreaming, manipulating the direction of his dreams even as they were occurring. If a character he did not like entered his dream he might send in a giant hand to pluck it away. If a car was about to run over someone he loved he could make the car turn. If his dream started to have an unhappy ending he could stop it, make it rewind, and substitute a new ending more to his liking. Each manipulation seemed to bring him a step closer to his pale twin in green.

Sometimes he would make a new friend, and on rare occasions he might share one of his dreams, and his ideas concerning conscious dreaming. His new friend would usually be polite enough, but ultimately dismissive. "Well, but they're only *dreams*, right?" one of them had said. "I mean, it's not like the real world or anything. What happens in a dream doesn't really matter."

Jason shut up, then, nodded his head and forced an agreeable smile. He chose not to tell of the time when his pale twin in green had left him a gift of a blank-paged book on his dresser. The twin had left it for him the night before, in his dream, and there it was, in fact, when Jason woke up. The page edges were gilded, the binding ornate, and obviously old. It was the kind of book a person might record his dreams in, if he considered those dreams important.

Then there was the time Jason had fallen a great distance in his dream, and awakened with a broken ankle. His mother had been distraught. He concocted a story of having fallen out of bed. Clearly the doctor hadn't believed him, but thankfully didn't press the issue.

Jason learned his lesson. Things happened in dreams, and sometimes the effects lingered on into the waking day. Sometimes for better, sometimes for worse. In his dreams, Jason became vigilant.

The dark head turning, the human eyes glowing, the hoof's edge scraping at the glass . . .

It was inevitable, he supposed, after all these years would come the dream in which the horse finally arrived at his window, its hide steaming in the cool air as it watched Jason's sleeping form, waiting, the force of its pent-up energy shaking the pane, its hot breath defrosting the glass, making things clearer.

Behind the nightmarish horse the dark sky boiled, and green edged the clouds. Jason stared at the great flaring nostrils, the iridescent eyes, listened to the horse's deep breathing echoing the surrounding thunder. Within the dream Jason was aware that this was far too vivid to be a dream, yet far too unreal to be anything else. Every few seconds the horse's head penetrated the plane of the glass, its eyes protruding into Jason's room and glaring down at the boy in bed, before receding back to the other side, as if not quite able to break the barrier between its world and Jason's.

It was a strange thing to be dreaming and to be a character in his own dream, so acutely aware of all the distorted things around him, and yet at the same time to know that he was lying there sleeping, the dark bedspread half covering him, one foot stuck out into the cold night air, his hair wild as if torn apart by the wind, his eyes crusted as if filled with sand. Jason *knew*—as well as he knew his own name—that he was in two places at once, that he was two people at once, and this knowledge made him feel more powerful than he had ever felt before, a braver and more reckless Jason than he'd ever imagined.

The fact that the decisions he made in this dream might affect the remainder of his entire waking life did not escape him. It only added to his excitement.

In the dream, or in the waking world—Jason didn't know the difference anymore—he reached up and unlatched his window, swung it open. The nightmare horse leapt past him and into the room.

Jason was both terrified and exhilarated.

The horse twisted and turned as if tortured, its back arching with each thunder clap, its breathing so loud it shook the room, its pained grimace revealing crooked teeth that glowed from the repeated flashes of lightning outside. With each revolution of its form something else came crashing down in Jason's room. Picture frames shattered, furniture splintered, books exploded from their bindings in a shower of whirling pages.

Jason cried out then, and leapt onto the back of the dark turning mare, leapt through sleep and leapt through dream and out the window into the roiling storm.

The nightmare heaved under him as Jason held on desperately, clutching a sparse gathering of short hairs on the back of the long neck with aching fingernails. He held on through the worst turmoil at the heart of the storm, then through to the other side where his mount seemed to calm with the weather.

More confident now, Jason tried to tell this dream where he wanted it to go. He tried to imagine a place he wanted to be, tried to imagine this horse taking him there. Some place where he might better fit in, some place tailor-made for him because only he could have imagined it.

The problem was, however, that Jason had no idea where he wanted to be. And how could he have a destination in mind, when he really didn't know why he was travelling in the first place? He just knew he needed to take the ride.

In a way it was convenient, then, that this mare could not, or would not, be controlled. The mare reared, raised itself against the towering black clouds. Jason felt himself slipping, and looked down the dizzying distance to his home below. He started to scream, but thunder took his voice. He hugged more tightly the mare's back, and closed his eyes as it rocketed forward through a wall of clouds and rain.

The first time he was able to open his eyes they were travelling through a vast gray swamp, and the legless creatures with the huge mouths attempting to bite his arms wore his parents' faces. First one, then the other would grip his pajama sleeve with jagged teeth, stretch precariously and attempt to bite into his chest, eat his heart, tear him apart.

Then quick as an eyeblink the mare brought him through into another world, but in this land of coal dust towers and glassy obsidian tunnels he was a crawling, living dead thing, where everyone he met had the same face and was oblivious to his existence. But even in this world he knew another version of himself hid, waited, whispering softly.

Finally the mare's pace slowed. Jason lifted his dizzied head from the horse's neck and gazed around him as the storm which had surrounded them from the beginning progressed now in slow motion, a wall of wind and rain turning to streaked, dark jelly which tore and drifted apart, revealing a vast room of baroque and surrealistic detail. Jason stood on the shiny floor as the mare clopped slowly away to rest in the shadows.

Jason rotated slowly, trying to take in every detail. He felt as if he were drowning in peculiarity. And yet although these quarters were at once far from everything he had ever seen or imagined, they seemed at the same time as close to Jason as a heartbeat.

Globes of various colors and sizes drifted out of openings in the floor, rising above him to be absorbed by a ceiling he couldn't quite see. Inside each was a figure of some sort, a being, but translated somehow: folded or shrunk or stretched or turned inside out. Jason shook, not wanting to see anymore. *Souls* was the word that popped into his head, like the first note of a song, then after a time came the rest of the melody, *the imprisoned souls of countless tormented sleepers.*

Jason turned around quickly, seeking out the source of the voice, even though he knew well enough that the voice had originated inside his own skull. But then thinking he might see who had planted the voice there, he sought shapes in the shadows. And he did find them, but there were too many to be of any use. He could detect an upright outline in virtually every darkened patch in the room, with the occasional green-garbed figure appearing, reappearing.

Jason made himself breathe calmly. As he had discovered many times before, even in a dream it was essential to remain calm.

Now and then one of the globes exploded with a soft shriek. Jason cringed at the sound, feeling responsible, just as he oftentimes felt responsible for the disasters that happened in his dreams.

If he listened carefully enough, he thought he could hear the weeping of the other souls in reaction to the death of their companion. But Jason made himself not cry. He thought it might be too dangerous to let go and cry.

Then Jason became aware of an approaching presence. First he sensed a change in pressure in the air, as if a door had been opened. But he saw no doors, or windows for that matter, only endless curtains of gauzy light enclosing the room. A small form walked softly in from the layers of light at one side of the room, a strangely familiar child dressed in green who aged rapidly as he drew nearer.

By the time the green child reached him he was approximately Jason's age, size, build. Closer still, and Jason was staring at an exact image of himself, only dressed in emerald green.

"My twin," he said spontaneously, and the words echoed in his head as if another voice were speaking them, too.

Jason didn't know whether this figure was *the* twin, the one he'd told everybody he'd been separated from, who he had been afraid to admit was purely imaginary, but who now might have an independent existence after all. As far as he knew it was just some sort of projection, some sort of dream-mirror that would dissolve into the powders of sleep if he touched it.

But then Jason's twin embraced him, whispering, "I am who you always wished to be. We are brothers, you and I."

Jason pushed the figure away, feeling suddenly weak, ill-at-ease. This dream of his had gone on long enough—he was exhausted and wanted to return home. But he couldn't find the mare anywhere to take him back.

"Jason!" the voice filled his head and darkened the curtains of light. The sound was full of a horse's breath and thunder, and Jason wondered if he had found the steed after all.

He turned around to discover his twin subtly altered, becoming the pale, thin, green-garbed creature who had haunted him all his life.

"I am Nightmare," the creature said. "I welcome you to your new home."

"I have to . . ." Jason began, but the rest of his words were swept away by a cold wind that grabbed a part of his mind he'd never even been aware existed before, and then turned him inside out, starting with his thoughts, drew him thinly through a tiny, seemingly endless corridor surrounded by the sleeping voices of a world full of dreamers, eventually depositing him inside a globe which distorted everything he saw in some hideous and disturbing way.

"Here within the Nightmare World, in the Dimension of Dream," Nightmare said, his face pressed against the globe that contained Jason, making Nightmare's eyes huge and unreadable, "we make do with whatever entertainment we can find. You'll do quite nicely for today."

Nightmare went away for a time, for exactly how long Jason had no way of knowing. Occasionally he would glance at his wristwatch which had somehow managed the trip through dream intact. At first he thought it was working just fine, ticking off chunks of time at a regular pace, but at one point he discovered the hour hand had become a spinning blur as the minute hand crept backward. Then a few minutes later he felt a wetness on his wrist, and glanced down to see the face of the watch oozing off his arm, the hands like loose threads dangling.

Eventually Nightmare came back into the room sweeping before him a parade of half-witted creatures, servants apparently, whose job seemed to be to retrieve various leftover remnants of human imagination which had become marooned throughout Nightmare's realm. From his vantage point Jason was then forced to witness the desperate attempts of this bored, god-like creature to amuse himself. Jason failed to see the entertainment value in any of it. Most of the time he was either disgusted or horrified.

He sent a six-handed dwarf with no feet into a closet whose door had suddenly appeared in the middle of the room. The dwarf came out carrying a tall scaffolding from which a procession of familiar cartoon characters attempted to hang themselves (without success—their necks either stretched to the point that their bulbous feet rested comfortably on the floor, or their heads shrank until the noose slipped off, followed by a loud popping noise as the heads suddenly regained their original size).

In another part of the room several pudgy animals with enormous mouths tried to serenade a large-breasted pop bottle with songs about undying affection for particular products and television shows. Eventually the pop bottle hiccupped, blew its cap, drowning the trio in foam.

In another corner a crude, squat caricature of Dr. Strange, the so-called Master of the Mystic Arts (Jason wondered how he knew who that was; he'd never seen the man before, but he *knew* that he was called Dr. Strange and that he was some kind of mystic) lay writhing on the floor as numerous snot-green demons pelted him with the magical surprises found in various children's cereals.

Most of Nightmare's little plays were silly in that way, but there were also those darker illusions which Jason recognized as having some sort of human origin. A thin, twisted thing poorly disguised as a teenager was tied to a television set as cables were run from the back of the set into his navel. A girl was repeatedly poked by plastic forks while her classmates giggled. A fellow who appeared to be some sort of street derelict was repeatedly stabbed by gang members with hot dogs clutched in their fists instead of knives.

A small round car appearing to be a circus clown's mode of transportation turned over and over until it finally burst into bouquets of chrysanthemums.

There were also several versions of Jason's lifelong nightmares concerning horses and twins. Apparently this Nightmare had no original ideas of his own, and was only as good as the imaginings he was able to steal from dreaming humans.

Nightmare turned to Jason and asked, "And how was that one, brother?"

Jason did not respond. He didn't want to see this, didn't want to dream this, but he seemed to have lost all control over his own dreaming. Obviously, Nightmare was in charge here.

Before, when Jason was particularly threatened in a bad dream, he'd been able to concoct some hero to come in and rescue him. Often these heroes were of his own creation (their super powers more often than not having to do with superior psychological insight and the ability to dissipate fear). But sometimes he used the real-life heroes he saw on the news or read about in the paper each day: heroes like the Avengers, the Fantastic Four, and Spider-Man. (And like Dr. Strange. Somehow Jason knew, not only that Strange was a hero, but that Nightmare despised him.)

As if in ridicule of Jason's need for heroes, the dwarf-like Dr. Strange was dragged out into the middle of the shiny floor. Nightmare filled the chamber with gales of his laughter—layers of it, as if recorded repeatedly then played back with slight delays between each track. At the conclusion of various indignities, this distorted doppelgänger of Strange was stuffed into a long-necked green bottle by one of the perpetually grinning servants and handed over to a thirsty Nightmare for consumption. The terrified glop of Strange kept pressing himself into the bottom of the bottle as Nightmare's elongated tongue crept up the neck and toyed with Strange much as a snake might with its rodent. Finally the tongue wrapped itself around the pseudo-Strange's neck and dragged the fellow screaming into Nightmare's mouth, the tiny sorcerer's last-minute flurry of hand gestures, burbled chantings, and rapid-fire spell castings proving completely ineffective.

Nightmare put down the bottle with a sigh, wiped his grinning lips, and raised a wild eyebrow Jason's way. "And *that* one, brother? Does it not quench your longings? Oh, and I do not use the sibling term lightly—if I had been born into your world,

I would have been you. Similarly, if you were a child of this realm, it would be *you* they would have called Nightmare. We are forever coupled, you and I."

Jason tried to turn away from Nightmare's leering visage, but found he had nothing to turn. Whatever had become of him in the globe, he could not divert his attention. Like a dreamer unable to awaken he was forced to take in everything Nightmare had to show him, everything Nightmare had to say. Whether Nightmare's words were true or not, Jason had no way of determining. Dreams had their own truth, it seemed. Jason knew he could be anyone in any dream, however dark. And the idea that he could be someone so dark horrified him.

But far worse than having to watch Nightmare's crazed little plays, to see these strange dramas and know that in some other world he was capable of such things, was to have to endure Nightmare's periodic lectures to an assembled throng of globe-imprisoned dreamers and loosely-concocted servants: diatribes against his enemies (Dr. Strange most notable among them), monologues regarding the world of dreams.

"They seem so real to you humans because they *are* real," Nightmare thundered, gesturing pompously with a hand as he strode back and forth across the room, occasionally batting at a floating globe with his hand and laughing when it cracked and imploded. Each time the raised hand fluttered near his own globe Jason tensed in anticipation of disaster. "Every horrid fate you imagine some version of yourself, somewhere, will suffer. Every possible future, every permutation of the world, exists, and the tissue between them is as thin as an ancient memory your grandfathers and grandmothers have passed down to you."

One day (or evening, time being so ambiguous in Nightmare's world), Jason watched resignedly as Nightmare orchestrated yet another in an endless series of playlets concerning his encounters with such heroes as Dr. Strange, Daredevil, and the Fantastic Four. Jason often wondered how Nightmare could have possibly been entertained by these—already in his relatively short stay here Jason had become bored to distraction by them.

One of the short, misshapen actors was dressed in Daredevil's costume. The actor was quite bad, as expected, overplaying the character to the point of buffoonery, but then again maybe that was the point of the scene. Jason was actually less bothered by the performance than by the ill-fit of Daredevil's costume: it sagged at the knees and bunched around the shoulders and chest. Jason found himself imagining how the real Daredevil would have handled the silly premise and was startled when the costume suddenly corrected itself, the actor quickly growing in stature and filling out in form until it became a passable replica of the real-life hero.

This so-close-to-the-real-thing Daredevil turned and nodded to Jason, then reached down and grabbed Nightmare's two minions by their throats (at least, Jason assumed it was their throats—these two particular minions most closely resembled a loose collection of office supplies). He tossed them easily into the far reaches of the room where they spun and clattered among the cast-off remnants of human imaginings which had littered much of the chamber during this period.

Intrigued, Jason concentrated on another actor in another one of Nightmare's little play groups. A hideous and scarred version of the Invisible Woman suddenly grew beautiful again.

"Amazing!" Jason shouted within his globe as he gave bulk to a rather thin imitation of the Thing.

"Wonderful!" Jason cried when he spotted a faintly glowing vision of the Human Torch fluttering above a scattering of Picassoesque creations at the back of the room. The creatures appeared to be struggling with a clumsy cannon that shot a viscous gray mud up onto the Human Torch's costume, maddening him, but all the Human Torch seemed able to do in retaliation was to shake his fist and strain to burst into a flame that never came. He looked like some giant, wounded firefly struggling to get back to the nest and an ignoble demise.

"Wonderful!" Jason cried out again, reached out with his imagination and woke the giant fire bug up. The Human Torch caught fire like a miniature sun, reaching out to catch the scattering abstracts with his blazing hands.

"These plot alterations are unauthorized!" Nightmare screamed, suddenly filling the view outside Jason's globe. "This must stop!" he shouted, even as the revitalized Torch swept past and singed his green suit.

Nightmare swept away from the globe as Daredevil tackled him from behind. Several writhing snakes suddenly wrapped themselves around Daredevil's arms, pinning him to the floor. Nightmare twisted around then, glared at Jason, then sent a cloud of chattering spiders at a quickly approaching Thing.

"This is *all your fault!*" Nightmare shouted in the voice of a petulant child, but Jason found himself laughing excitedly as he sent his own imagined versions of the Hulk and Spider-Man at the Lord of Bad Dreams.

"I *know!* I *know* it is!" Jason cried out, thinking that, indeed, he and Nightmare did have their similarities: Nightmare had created these plays, imprisoned the consciousness of so many dreamers, in a twisted sense of fun and games. And for a very long time dreaming had been a game for Jason, a game he had apparently not taken quite seriously enough.

Nightmare countered him with creature after creature, all of whom seemed terribly familiar to Jason. There was the giant frog that had tormented Jason during a week of bad dreams when he'd been only ten. An immense version of Sarah, whom he'd been so nervous to talk to when they were both in the seventh grade. The clown doll his aunt had put on his dresser the night before his seventh birthday, which had kept him terrified for months of dreams when he woke up in the middle of the night to find it staring down at him.

Then there were all the pale-faced figures in green from a decade's worth of dreams—bad and otherwise—figures which could have been Nightmare, but which could have been twins of Jason as well.

Nightmare's weapons proved to be as familiar to Jason as his own face in a mirror. Again and again he countered them with what he thought Daredevil must be like, who he thought the Hulk must be in his deepest heart of hearts, the mystery that might be Dr. Strange, a dream of Spider-Man in a dream of battle. The heroes as Jason saw them, as Jason needed them to be, pressed Nightmare until he screamed in frustration. "You're just a boy!"

Daredevil knocked two blimp-demons out of the sky while twirling around a fantastic floating Christmas tree. The Fantastic Four collectively destroyed one wall of the dream as if it were a painted backdrop, sending the fanciful creatures perched there (many of them animated mathematical symbols, and several claiming to be the characters from a madman's word processor) scurrying away, revealing other creatures cowering behind the now-missing scenery. Spider-Man gathered a hodge-podge of insectile creations in a web net, extended his lower jaw fantastically (ripping the lower half of his face mask open), and swallowed them all at once.

And finally there was the glob of Strange that came roaring back up out of Nightmare's throat, becoming a squat, angry version of the sorcerer astride Nightmare's nose, jerking the end of his cape out of Nightmare's teeth. Then the stubby figure of Dr. Strange blew a rancid incantation into Nightmare's face, turning him even paler than his standard coloration, turning him pale enough to disappear.

It was the fading vision of a renewed Dr. Strange that Jason saw as he awakened in his bed: surrounded by light and a great number of windows to show the clear sky outside, the bedroom Jason had always dreamed he would someday have.

On his bedside table was a thin figure of clay: Nightmare with his pale face and green costume. Jason had never seen it before—it was a gift fallen out of a dream. He put his hands on the figure: his fingers stretching it until it became unrecognizable, then rolling it into a ball.

He slipped his clothes on quickly. He was starving, and he could hardly wait to get outside into the light and air. He pulled his bedroom door closed gently behind him, not wanting to awaken his parents.

After a few minutes, the ball of clay quivered, stretched, and sprang back into that familiar, twisted shape.

D'Spayre

RIPPLES

José R. Nieto

Illustration by Steve Leialoha

T WAS THE middle of April when María left her home in Long Island; a bitter spring morning, wet with drizzle and melting slush. She called in sick at the real estate agency, packed three nylon suitcases into her 1973 Corolla station wagon—two filled with clothes, the third with her grandmother's pearls and her father's Martí and Neruda collections—then drove to the high school to pick up Laurita, her daughter.

"It's a family emergency," she told the principal, who looked at her with a mixture of bemusement and relief. His office smelled like chewing gum.

"I understand," he said, nodding.

"She won't be back tomorrow. Actually, we'll probably be gone 'til the end of the week, at least." María found that, now that she had decided to leave, lying bothered her only a little.

"We'll make all the arrangements, Mrs. Hildebrand," said the principal.

He brought Laurita from her classroom personally, walking a step behind the girl, as if he were guiding a criminal. Seeing her daughter swaying down that school hallway, her legs limber and supple as new wood, María couldn't help thinking about her own body: the new fleshiness under her biceps; the blue veins snaking down her thighs; the slight roll over her buttocks. Thirty-seven was no age to start a new life. And yet that was exactly what she was about to do. Peter, her dear husband, had left her no other choice.

María put her hands on Laurita's slender shoulders and kissed her cheek. "I've got your things in the car," she said.

The girl nodded and smiled thinly.

For a week they traveled south, through the Shenandoah Valley and up the Blue Ridge Mountains: Virginia, North Carolina, Georgia. María's younger brother Carlos owned a cleaning business in suburban Miami, and at first that seemed to be their destination. Just as they were about to cross the state line, though, it dawned on María that Peter would be looking for them at her brother's house. Florida was far too obvious a place to hide. Laurita agreed; at fourteen she knew much about fleeing.

It would be west, then. They slept at a beach campground in Mississippi, where they registered with María's aunt's name and

paid cash. In Alabama they stayed in a home-hostel run by a
seventy-three-year-old woman; her garden spanned half an acre,
a radiant blanket of sunflowers, hibiscus, and gardenias.

They avoided New Orleans—too dangerous and expensive—
and drove north, through a frightening Louisiana monsoon that
swept up cattle, cars, and even a few shacks along the Mississippi
River. By the third week they'd left Oklahoma and Kansas behind
and had begun the awesome climb up the Colorado Rockies—
mountains so majestic that for a while María forgot about her
husband and the specialists, about their dwindling funds, about
Laurita's sudden flare of power. For a while they were travelers,
the kind María had read about in *Reader's Digest*: a mother and
daughter on the road, gliding across a marvelous continent, enjoying sights that could quicken the rhythm of a stony heart.

She'd come from adventurous stock, after all. According to
family legend, María's great-great grandfather had migrated to
Cuba as a stowaway, hidden in the cargo hold of an overloaded
Spanish freighter. Years later, her father had risked everything
to deliver María and Carlos from Communist oppression. Sailed
them to Florida in a toy-like skiff, carrying nothing but a fresh
water jug and a fifty-year-old navigation chart. María hadn't been
much younger than Laurita at the time; a wide-eyed stick of a
girl, frightened and exhilarated, her sun-dress hanging loosely
from her shoulders.

The Corolla died in the desert; cracked a piston on Interstate
70, southern Utah, close to the Nevada border. Sitting behind
the useless steering wheel, María cursed the station wagon, the
desolate landscape, and her shoes, a pair of lavender pumps
she'd bought for fashion rather than comfort. In her suitcase she
had three other pairs just like them; she'd left the sneakers at
the motel in Colorado. Her daughter's outfit was much more
sensible: high-tops, black jeans, denim jacket.

They walked side by side on the empty highway. It was a clear
night, the sky like an obsidian dome above them. So quiet
they could hear lizards slithering on the tarmac. Every third or
fourth step María would turn and glance at the car. From the
open hood rose a languid thread of smoke, silver in the bright
moonlight. Laurita didn't seem to care; she kept her thin face
forward, never slackening her pace. María had to run to to keep
up with her.

At first the Vicky Motel was nothing but a light in the distance, too bright to be a star or a planet. After a mile they could recognize it as a building; the sloped roof, the covered porch, the illuminated sign. By the time they were close enough to read the neon script, their legs felt like packed dirt. A sweeping breeze had chilled them to the bone.

"Guess that's where we're spending the night," Laurita said, stuttering. She held her reedy frame in her arms.

"We'll be all right," María said. Lying certainly was getting easier.

A gravel path lead them to the doorstep of a glass-encased office. On the door there hung an OPEN—COME IN sign that looked like it hadn't been turned in years. Everything was dark inside, except for the flickering digits of a cash register. The guest rooms appeared empty as well; two identical rows of blackened windows and air conditioners, stacked one on top of the other.

María rang the doorbell. They waited for about ten minutes, leaning against the smooth glass. Nothing stirred. Just as María started thinking about breaking in, Laurita noticed a faint glow behind the building. Before María could stop her, the girl started running toward the light, following a cement path around the office.

"Wait for me!" María hissed. How she wished the girl would stay put for once; even now that they'd run away together, María was still chasing after her. She walked down the path with measured steps, past the display window, past a messily coiled firehose, past three discarded panes of white paint. Their little adventure was over, she realized: the car was gone, they had only a hundred and forty-three dollars to their name. Maybe tomorrow they'd take a bus to Las Vegas. María could get a job, Laurita could go back to school.

Suddenly María's heart trembled and her knees locked and her hands stiffened. Something had just frightened her daughter. She bit her cheek, forcing her body into motion. Still dazed, she cut through a mass of dried weeds, burst into a half-enclosed courtyard. She stumbled to the edge of a fancy swimming pool: long and narrow, surrounded by patio chairs and cocktail tables. The water was lit by a ring of sunken spotlights. Next to the springboard knelt a middle-aged man, obviously bewildered: his eyes were blank, his throat made a soft clucking sound. He wore a maroon sweatsuit, stretched over a pot belly. His face was covered in a coarse, mottled beard.

Laurita stood ten feet away from him. A white luminosity clung to her body, curling and twisting like rivulets. She held her hands together under her chin.

"I didn't mean it," she cried to her mother. "He came out of nowhere and startled me and . . ."

It was a wondrous, terrifying display. Rooted to the spot, María watched as the brightness spattered and rose and finally faded into nothingness. It took her a second to recall her duty as a mother; slipping in her leather-soled pumps, María ran around the pool and awkwardly embraced her daughter.

"I know, *m'hija*," she whispered into her ear, "I know." Laurita seemed to settle in her mother's warmth. She wiped her eyes, pulled away and quickly glanced over María's shoulder.

"Is he all right?" she said. María turned and walked over to the stricken man. He didn't seem to notice her. She touched his face with her fingers; the skin was cold and papery. He smelled of suntan lotion and chlorine. Reaching into the pool, María scooped a handful of water. Just as she was about to spray him, the man shuddered and flexed his jaw.

"I was getting up from the chair," he said distractedly. Even after the fear his voice was deep and melancholic. He looked at María, then at Laurita. "Was gonna introduce myself, that's all, and then it shocked me."

María took the man's forearm and, pulling with all her strength, helped him to his feet. "Laurita didn't mean it," she said without thinking, "it's just that when she's startled, she can't control the—"

"*¡Mami!*" Laurita cried. Embarrassed, María covered her mouth; she hadn't meant to say so much. And yet, as she backed away from the man, she could feel the secret in her neck, stabbing like a fishbone.

Ever since Vicky's death, Joshua Criswell had lived at the motel alone. In the last eleven years he'd grown used to the desert sun and the rocky, barren terrain. Every morning he dusted the empty guest rooms, cooked meals that ended up in the trash barrel, tended to his wife's cactus garden. He read Westerns and listened to bluegrass forty-fives. Last year he had driven his beat-up truck to New Mexico and bought a couple of pieces at a sparse Navajo craft show. Mostly he spent his days at the pool, his chin pressed against the straps of the patio chair, watching the water.

Until today, when that girl snuck up on him. After he snapped out of whatever she did to him, Joshua led her and her mother inside. He leaned against the hard edge of the reception desk and rubbed his chest with his palm. His heart was finally settling. The mother sat across from him on the green vinyl couch, hands wrapped around one of Vicky's old souvenir mugs, luxuriating in the coffee's steam. She looked frazzled: her make-up was smeared, her blouse was covered with car-seat wrinkles. Next to her, the girl was playing with the collar of her t-shirt. She wore her jacket on her lap, like a blanket. When she sipped her coffee, she narrowed her eyes and stuck out her tongue—probably found the taste bitter.

"Laurita's a mutant," Joshua said suddenly, "isn't she?"

The girl turned away. María nodded yes and closed her eyes.

"She shoots you with a ray, right? Makes you scared, that's what happened to me."

"It's difficult to explain," María said. She glanced quickly at Laurita.

Laurita threw her free hand in the air. "*Bueno dile, por Dios*," she said, "*ya metiste la pata.*" Joshua's Spanish was a bit rusty, and Laurita's accent didn't quite have a smooth Mexican flow; still, he caught the gist of what she had said: *Might as well tell him. You already started.*

"My daughter broadcasts," María said, "that's what the specialist called it. She projects her emotions to those around her. Intense feelings—anger, joy, sadness, whatever."

"Fear," Joshua added. María nodded and squeezed the tips of her fingers.

"My husband wanted to give her up," she said. "He wanted to put her in an institution. It was like he'd gone crazy all of a sudden. I mean, I knew that he didn't like mutants, he'd mentioned it many times before. But this was his own daughter. His own flesh and blood." She paused to wipe the sweat from her upper lip. "Well, I wasn't going to give up Laurita. My father, he spent three years in a Cuban 'institution.' He wasn't the same when he came out. He never recovered."

Joshua felt a flicker of shame in his chest, like a false palpitation. He couldn't tell if it came from listening, or from Laurita projecting. The girl had lifted her legs onto the couch and curled into an apostrophe. Her hands were lumped under her chin.

"I can help you," he said, "please let me help you."

"We could use a room for tonight," María said, brightening from the offer, "and a ride to the Greyhound stop in the morning. I was thinking of going down to Las Vegas and—"

"No, no, you don't want to go to Las Vegas. You can't hide there, someone could turn her in to the Friends of Humanity or something." Joshua had seen the news reports, read the editorials. He knew how far too many people felt about mutants, some of them concerned enough to form a group that had the gall to call themselves the "Friends" of Humanity because they persecuted mutants. "You have to stay here."

"But we can't pay you, we don't have enough money. I need to get a job."

"I don't care about the money, ma'am," Joshua said. "It doesn't matter to me one bit. You can stay as long as you want. If you want, you can help me run the motel, but you don't have to; anyway, all we get is one or two guests a year. The most important thing is that you and your daughter are safe."

Laurita lifted her head and wiped her eyes. "I don't want nobody else finding out," she said.

Joshua beamed. With a careless cut, his Vicky had been taken away from him. The doctors hadn't given him a chance. This mother and daughter, though, he could do something for them. He could make things better.

María dove from the stone platform, her eyes open, her body rigid in a concave line. She stabbed the water with a quick slurp. After ten long strokes she reached the shallow end and, familiar now with the length of Joshua Criswell's pool, immediately tumbled underwater, pushed against the side and set out in the opposite direction. It wasn't until her eighth lap that she began to feel the burn in her muscles; by the twelfth her body had numbed to the effort, awash in a cool serenity. Soon she was lost in the memories of the Caribbean, of the speeding skiff, of her father and brother receding.

It had happened in the middle of the night. María was holding the rudder while Carlos and Agusto recovered from a day's effort: preparing the vessel, hiding from the neighborhood watch, pushing off into the blue-black sea. As she steadied the boat, María kept thinking of her mother, whom she'd never met, imagining the softness of her skin, the gentle curl of her hair. She wondered about life in the United States, the land of Mickey Mouse and Coca-Cola. She leaned backwards and looked at the Milky Way, which was spread across the sky like confectioner's sugar. She felt the rudder scraping her armpit, and the briny wind in her nostrils, and the boat lifting and falling over the waves.

She fell asleep. Soon the wind changed direction, and the rudder pushed her over the stern, and suddenly María was underwater, staring at the moon through a rippled screen. Her eyes burned, her throat clenched to a fist. She clawed and kicked about her, as if she were fighting a blanket. After a second her head poked through the surface, and she drew a clumsy, hurried breath, and when her eyes cleared she saw the patchwork sail on the skiff, flapping and twirling in the distance.

"*Ay, Caridad del Cobre,*" she coughed, crossing herself. Ridiculously, her first thought was of her sun-dress, which would get ruined in the salt water. She shouted for her father, then for her brother. Their names crumbled in the breeze. María spread her arms, opened and closed them like scissors. As if in response, the skiff lurched and curved slowly to the left. María couldn't see anyone at the rudder. All by itself the boat sailed in a wide arc, circling her. Taunting her, offering a cruel hope.

I can catch it, she thought. The idea came to her without doubt, without hesitation. She could feel her arms stiffening, her legs cramping beneath her. A sudden wave filled her mouth with foam. *I can catch it*, she thought, spitting.

She pulled the dress from her shoulders, pushed it past her hips, kicked it off with her ankles. Unfettered, she reached forward and slid smoothly in the water.

"Very good," Joshua said and clapped. "Fifty laps and not even winded." He was sprawled on the patio chair again, this time under a wide parasol. As usual he wore a pair of tight shorts and a white t-shirt; the sweatsuit, which he would don as the night cooled, lay folded on the ground. Behind him, the sun straddled the horizon; the desert glowed a deep crimson.

María stood at the edge of the pool, squeezing water from her hair. Her arms ached delightfully. "Well," she said, "the pool isn't regulation length. And I've got no speed, I'm swimming like a trawler. But I'm getting better, that much is true." After a moment she turned to Joshua and added: "Certainly feels good to be back in the water."

Joshua took a sip from his juice bottle, then replaced it on the tiled floor.

"Glad someone's using the pool," he said, smiling. Right away the expression faded, and his eyes fixed on the water's surface.

In three weeks they had learned almost nothing about the man. As far as María could tell, he was in his early forties, though the beard made him look a good fifteen years older. He collected Indian crafts and listened to fiddle music. He kept a shotgun under the office counter, which he'd shown to Laurita on her first day at the reception desk. Once during dinner he had mentioned a wife, after whom the motel was named. Apparently she had died some years ago.

When María finished wringing her hair, she split it into two strands and tied it into a thick, precarious knot.

"Mr. Criswell?" she said, emboldened by the rush of the swim. She picked up her towel from a pool chair and wrapped it around her midriff.

"Yeah? I'm listening."

"Why do you always stare at the water?"

"Makes me feel better, I guess," he said.

"How come?" María said.

Joshua was quiet for a moment, apparently collecting his thoughts.

"Dip your foot in the pool," he said.

"Excuse me?"

"Go ahead. Just skim it, that's all."

Perplexed, María reached with her foot and flicked a toe at the water. A faint dimple formed around the spot.

"Watch how the ripple spreads," Joshua said plainly. "It's perfect at first, see? A perfect little circle. But look what happens when it spreads further. When it touches another ripple."

A western wind cast shallow waves toward María. After a few

seconds, her ripple washed against the waves and became curled and distorted. She tried dipping her foot again, this time splashing with her heel. The ripple lasted a bit longer, but soon enough it had twisted beyond recognition.

"They start one way," Joshua said, "but they always end up different. I like that. I don't know why, but it gives me some comfort."

"Sure," María said. It didn't make much sense. Water was water; ripples moved according to physical laws: surface tension, gravity, whatever. No mystery there.

But later on, a thought came to her: *Might as well be talking about children.*

There was a black-and-white movie on the TV set, nasty little *noir* Laurita had not seen before. She was leaning back in the office chair, her feet resting on the wide reception desk. Ever since her mother cleaned it, the room smelled faintly of ammonia. If it hadn't been for the TV set, Laurita would have hardly stood it.

On the screen, a man in a fedora gripped the shoulders of an elegantly dressed woman, who had managed to look at once distressed and languorous.

"You can't hide it from me!" the man was saying, "I can see it in your eyes, on your lips! I *know* that you love me!"

"Please," Laurita whispered. She dropped her legs to the side of the desk and leaned against the register. If only it were that easy: look into a woman's pupils and—*wham!*—learn the secrets of her fluttering heart. Sure wasn't like that in the real world. In real life, you had to sip and taste the soup. Even then, you were never, ever sure.

She turned off the set, flicking the remote control like a whip. It was getting late; Laurita had been tired since midday. She closed her eyes for a moment. When she opened them again it was night outside; moonlight glinted off the plexiglass window. Almost as a reflex she reached under the desk and turned on the "Vicky Motel" sign. The neon tubes came alive with a click and a short, disconcerting flash.

Things changed quickly in the desert, Laurita had noticed: from heat to cold, from clear skies to torrential rain. As if the Utah god had no patience for transitions.

It struck her as a neat game, all of sudden. First, she would memorize every article in Joshua's office. The Budweiser clock, hanging slightly crooked on the western wall. The tattered phone books by the cash register. The old vinyl couch in the corner, where María humiliated her that first night. The red and green light from the neon sign, which drew a muddled pattern on the linoleum floor. The Kachina dolls, arranged by size across a tall shelf.

Laurita shut her eyes, counted silently to ten. The air conditioner hissed like a bottle rocket. She opened her eyes and looked about. Nothing was different.

Again. She counted to a hundred this time, out loud. When she opened her eyes, the minute hand had moved a click across the glowing clock face. Outside the moon had risen ever so slightly, giving a new sheen to the Kachinas.

Laurita put her thin hand over her eyes. She pictured Stevie's squat in Manhattan, where she'd slept the last time she ran away from home. Plaster walls covered with soot and stolen subway prints: Poetry in Motion posters, anti-cigarette ads—anything that had struck the boy's fancy. One poem in particular had stayed with Laurita: it was about a woman at the laundromat, folding her dead husband's shirts.

She pictured María when she found her with Stevie: screaming, her face creased, her mouth open, curled, closed; movie emotions, flickering and unreal. She pictured her father, alone in the corner of the room, standing with his arms crossed, already vanishing.

Through her fingers Laurita saw a figure blocking the neon lights.

"*M'hija,*" the man said softly. Laurita hid the hand behind her back, as if she'd been caught stealing.

"Tio Carlos!" she said before the incongruity touched her mind. Her uncle was supposed to be in Florida. They hadn't even called him. "Tio Carlos!" Laurita said again.

He looked the same as she remembered. Cropped black hair, tight mustache, sharp, angular face. A *Miami Vice* suit, freshly wrinkled, smelling of menthol cigarettes and aftershave. Perfect five-o'clock stubble, which scratched Laurita's cheek when he kissed her. She didn't mind it one bit.

"Are you all right?" he said, squeezing her arm, "Is your mother here with you? Can I talk to her?"

"She's in the pool," Laurita said. And for the longest time she kept thinking: *This is it, we're saved.*

"How exactly was it that you found us?" María said. She sat with Carlos and Laurita around the dining room table, while Joshua put the finishing touches on the reunion meal: baked enchiladas, cactus shakes, sweet cornbread. María was happy to see her brother—ecstatic, actually—but since the car broke down she'd become something of a pragmatist. If Carlos had caught up with her, Peter couldn't be far behind.

"He's here," Laurita said, "that's what matters, isn't it?"

"You didn't make it easy, *mi hermana*," Carlos said, laughing. Seeing that María was not joining in, he stopped and crushed his cigarette on the plastic ashtray. "The day you left I got a call from Peter," he continued, "you should have heard him, he sounded like someone'd taken a corkscrew to his heart. Terrible, all shaken up. He told me he'd done something incredibly stupid, he seemed all torn up by it."

"You never really liked him very much," María said matter-of-factly.

"Well, you have to sympathize with the guy, even if he's a stupid jock. Or at least used to be. You should hear him now: on the phone he was as articulate with his feelings as he used to be about a football game. He's so sorry, María; he told me that you'd left and taken Laurita with you, and he knew that you wouldn't speak to him directly, so he asked me to 'intercede'—" Carlos drew a pair of quotes in the air "—and I said I *would* try to contact you, as long as he understood that I wouldn't be telling him where you were. 'It's up to her,' I told him. He agreed, said 'sure, sure,' and then he told me about Laurita's power, about what happened in the school, and all that, and I've got to tell you, *mi hermana*, I sure wish you'd called when it happened. I wish you'd told me. I'm still your brother, you know."

"I didn't want to get you involved," María said. Carlos had his own problems: a marriage going sour; a cleaning business under investigation by the INS. María didn't think he was even allowed to leave Florida.

Carlos gave her a sarcastic smile. "Congratulations," he said, "I'm not involved."

Laurita laughed, missing the bitterness in her uncle's joke. After a moment Joshua waltzed in from the kitchen balancing a large plastic tray.

"Here you are," he said to each of them in turn. The plates were brimming with melted cheese and enchilada sauce.

"This looks great," Laurita said, lifting a string of cheddar with her index finger. She licked it off and, without intending to, smiled at Tio Carlos.

"What did he say about her?" María asked. "Did he tell you that he was ready to be a grown up and deal with his daughter?"

"Well, he didn't say that in so many words, but he was very apologetic—"

"I'm not going back," Laurita interrupted. "He hates me, I know it for a fact."

Everyone at the table felt a twitch of anger and fear. Around the girl, a bright stream whirled and soon vanished.

"Don't worry, *m'hija*," María said, "we're not going nowhere."

They ate haltingly, between bursts of sharp conversation: the Cuban way, as María liked to call it. Laurita told her uncle about their trip, about the mountains and the monsoon and the interminable desert. She mentioned a sign down the road that read "No Services for 150 Miles." Carlos asked about their plans and María couldn't help but smile. "Still working on them," she said with little enthusiasm.

Joshua shifted uncomfortably in his wicker chair; he missed the quietness of their meals, though he was glad to see María and Laurita acting so naturally. Still, he didn't care much for this uncle character. All night Carlos had been treating him like furniture—not one word in his direction, not even a thank you. Besides, there was a something about his demeanor that bothered him: the way he slouched in his chair, the way he swung his cigarette while speaking. His moist smile, which seemed to drip at the sides of his mouth. Reminded him of the corrupt *hacendados* in the old *Zorro* TV show, twirling their moustaches as they planned another indignity for the good people of California . . .

"So tell me," Carlos said, softly patting Joshua's forearm, "what's the deal with this place? I saw the pool out back; must have cost you a bundle. Don't see you recouping in this location, though."

Joshua was taken by surprise. "I don't know," he said, "it's just a motel, that's all."

"Mr. Criswell's been very nice to us," María said, "you don't have to go and put him on the spot like that."

"Didn't mean anything by it," Carlos said quickly.

"It's all right," Joshua said, "it's not a big secret or anything. My wife and I built this place, back in the seventies. We were going to make it into a desert resort, kind of like a Palm Springs in Utah. Thought we'd get some Las Vegas business, some Denver business, you know. But then we ran out of money, and we settled with a motel."

"What happened to your wife?" Carlos said. Might as well have pinched Joshua in the throat.

"Vicky got sick," he said. He ran a thumb across his forehead and winced. "She died during surgery, her doctor made a big mistake. That's how I finished the pool, with the settlement money."

"I'm so sorry," Laurita said.

"Our father died a few years ago," Carlos said, sweeping his shirt with his fingers. "Actually, that's the last time I saw María and Laurita, at the funeral in Miami."

"Yes, María mentioned something about that," Joshua said. He was glad for the turn in conversation.

"Heart attack," María said, "thank God it was quick."

Carlos shook his head. "That's what the doctor told us," he said gravely, "but it wasn't the heart that killed him. What killed him, it was the disappointment. He died a bitter man."

"Carlos, *por Dios*," María said, sounding exasperated. Joshua suspected that this was an old argument between the two siblings. She picked up her napkin by the corners, then shook the bread crumbs onto her half-finished plate.

"No, no, that's the truth," her brother said, "Like Joshua said, it wasn't a big secret: he believed in the Cuban revolution, until Castro stole that from under him. He never wanted to run away from his *patria*. And he certainly couldn't stand all the vulgarity, the crass commercialism in the States. He was an intellectual: a professor of history, for Pete's sake." He took a long drag from his cigarette. "María and I, we turned out quite different. I don't think he ever forgave us for that."

"That's enough," María said, her eyes fixed on the colorless ashtray.

They were quiet for a while. Finally, Laurita stood up and started clearing the table.

Hands on his lap, head bowed and cocked to the side, Joshua took a last bite of his meal and listened to the sound of his own breathing.

Later that night, after he had finished cleaning the kitchen and settling Carlos in his room, after he had undressed and collapsed on his own stiff mattress, Joshua saw Vicky standing at his bed-side—her face vacant, her belly open like a flaccid mouth. A paper sheet clung to her chest and pelvis, as if she were lying flat on a table. Her blonde hair was tied into a glistening bun.

Joshua lay on his back, frozen. The linens felt like fly paper.

"Honey, the roof's leaking again," Vicky said through her wound. "I just mopped a mess on the kitchen floor. Promise me you'll fix it tomorrow. Promise me, all right?"

"I promise," Joshua said. His voice came out tinny, distant.

"Also, we have to call the contractor about the Spanish tiles, a couple of them cracked with the change in temperature. Please honey, remind me to call them in the morning. Promise me, all right?"

"I promise," Joshua said.

Vicky sat at the foot of the bed. As she slid across the mattress, closer to Joshua, her belly made a wet kissing sound.

"What's wrong honey?" she said. "You seem so unhappy lately. Will you tell me, please?"

"I—" Joshua said. In his mind, a word formed and vanished—a too-quick flash of a memory card, a meaningless whisper.

"What can I do to make you happy?" she said, reaching inside herself. With her thumb she drew a bloody trail across his cheek.

Joshua awakened in motion, staggering on the cold tiles of the bathroom. The lights were off. He reached blindly for the toilet bowl. He clenched his hands on the rim, pitched his head forward, and threw up. Afterward his mouth tasted of acid; his tongue felt like burnt wood. He dropped on the floor, next the sink, and started to cry.

Years ago he had built a staircase that lead from his second-floor window down to the courtyard—thinking of nights like this one, when the swimming pool called with such urgency. Joshua climbed down as if from a tree: nervously, with bent knees, his hands gripping the polished wood. At the last step he opened a hidden fuse box and flicked on two switches. The spotlights lit in unison, like a well-rehearsed choir.

The pool began to calm him immediately. Joshua walked close to the edge, until his bare toes dangled freely over the water. Before him, the surface rippled from a cool south-western wind. The air smelled of chlorine and sand.

And then he noticed it: all the dimples were exactly the same. *It can't be*, he thought. He scratched his beard and squatted next to the filter intake. The flow should have warped the ripples; here it did nothing. He could feel the pumps vibrating under him; a twig flowed languidly into the mechanism. Desperate now, Joshua slapped the water with his open palm.

A perfect circle slid across the glass-like surface.

"Dammit," he said quietly. The arc washed against the farthest edge, then reflected perfectly, without diminishing. It touched the tiles at his feet and split and criss-crossed and split again. After fifteen turns—Joshua counted them—the surface looked like a faceted jewel, each cut shimmering in the spotlights.

Joshua glared at his hand: he bent his wrist, spread his fingers apart, closed them into a tight fist. Water beads rolled between his knuckles. This wasn't a dream: he could feel the wetness on his skin, he could still taste the bile in his mouth. With a single touch he had cracked the laws of physics. Made him feel like a fool.

What can I do to make you happy? Vicky's question snapped at him like a snake. Why hadn't he told her the truth? *Take me back to California, take me back home.* The resort had been her idea in the first place; Joshua had wanted nothing to do with it. When she first told him about her dream project, soon after they started dating, he'd taken it as a good change of tracks, nothing more. At the time he'd been drifting; taking odd carpentry jobs, living in crowded, seedy apartments. The desert was wide open, she had said, filled with possibilities.

He should have told her the truth. But he'd wanted to hurt her then; after the loans had fallen through, after her precious hotel had shrunk to a cheesy paperweight.

"A baby," Joshua had answered, knowing full well that she couldn't give it to him. "I think we should have a child."

Right then she'd decided to have the surgery, to clear a path through her fallopian tubes.

"Oh, God," Joshua whispered at the pool. He remembered her dreamy smile, the way she'd squeezed his hand, her playful pat as the orderly pushed away her gurney.

It was clear to him now, for the first time, the wave he'd set in motion.

Suddenly Joshua found himself behind the registration desk, with no memory of walking away from the pool. The neon sign lit the room red and green. Joshua smiled. He'd never felt such a clear sense of purpose. Gingerly, he reached under the counter and grabbed the shotgun.

And then he was outside. Joshua sat crosslegged upon a flat rock, cradled the gun in his arms. The wind had died down, the sky was overcast and starless. In the distance the pool shone beautifully, like a glass eye on the dirt. He imagined the ripple spreading through the sand, dragging him all the way out here, to the edge of everything.

He thought it strange, before pulling the trigger, how sweet the barrel tasted in his mouth.

"What we got ourselves here," Sheriff Wilder said, holding fast to his belt buckle, "is a clear cut case of self-inflicted murder." He took off his sunglasses and wiped the sweat off his forehead— using his shirttail, like a schoolboy. Standing by a pool-side table, María got a quick glimpse of his belly, which was pale, round and hairless. She turned her head away. For the first time in years, she didn't feel like talking.

María was still dressed in her one-piece bathing suit; a dry towel hung from her shoulders. That morning she'd come down to the courtyard for her swim and noticed the spotlights underwater. Joshua had always been very careful to shut everything off before going to bed. María's first guess was that he'd left in a hurry, maybe some kind of emergency.

Then she saw the crowded sky, and the buzzards dotting the rocky hills, fighting for scraps.

She called the police, even though Carlos had said it was a terrible idea. On the phone Sheriff Wilder sounded like a much larger man; his voice had a soft quality that María associated with bullies and thugs. As it turned out, he was only one or two inches taller than Laurita. Whatever authority he carried had been starched into his uniform.

"Suicide," he continued. "I just wanted to say that, so you don't think you're under suspicion. We all knew that Joshua had his problems."

Carlos sat on one of the patio chair, maybe a bit too relaxed: his legs were spread apart, his arms dangled between his knees. He wore an embroidered *guayabera* shirt and jeans. "Is that right?" he said sarcastically.

"Oh yeah," the sheriff said. "I mean, living alone out here, with no business—had to be suicide." He seemed overly proud of the word, as if he'd just read it in a textbook. "Which, I have to say, is something I never understood myself. I mean, back in 'Nam I spent three years in a POW camp, with the beatings, and the rotted food and all that, and not even once did I think of offing myself. Life doesn't get much worse than that, let me tell you."

"You had hope," Carlos said, "You knew that you'd be getting out of there someday."

"I suppose," he said tentatively.

Carlos leaned forward in the chair and glared at the sheriff. "Just imagine if you'd known the opposite: that all that was left of your life was a hole the size of a doghouse. That every week you'd have your toenails stripped, or your teeth filed, or your eyelids punctured with needles. Imagine knowing that nothing would ever change. Life wouldn't seem quite so dear anymore, would it?"

"Carlos, please," María said. She had never heard him talk like that before.

Sheriff Wilder tried to smile, but all he could manage was a toothy sneer. "Well, I think I should be heading back to the station. There's a bunch of paperwork still to be filled out."

"What should we do?" María said. "I mean, about staying here."

"Don't see why you and your daughter can't stay at the motel until we figure out the next of kin situation. Besides, we may want to ask you a few questions, you know, about Mr. Criswell's state of mind and all that. Seems that Mr. Gutierrez here is an expert on the subject."

Carlos tipped his head and grinned. "Just an informed observer," he said, "that's all."

"I just wanted to say," Sheriff Wilder added, "that I'm really sorry ma'am, about your husband beating you. That's not right. That shouldn't happen. If it was under my jurisdiction, I'd have dumped his ass in jail."

It took her a second to realize what the man was talking about. Peter abusing her had been Joshua's cover story as to why she and Laurita had run away; María had simply performed it. "I appreciate that," she said and smiled softly like a victim.

After Sheriff Wilder drove off, Laurita walked into the courtyard and plopped down on a chair next to her uncle. Her hands were pruned from doing the breakfast dishes. María was silently amazed: back home, her daughter had seldom handled a dirty plate.

"How are you doing, *m'hija?*" Tio Carlos asked Laurita. "You holding up all right?"

"I'm fine," Laurita said, brushing her lips with the back of her hand.

María paced under the shade of a pool-side umbrella, scenarios tumbling in her head. After a minute she opened her eyes wide and said: "We have to get out of here."

"And go where?" Carlos shot back.

"I have no idea. But if our names get into a police computer, it's only a matter of time before Peter finds us. We might as well take our chances in Las Vegas."

Carlos laughed. "These cops don't have computers. I doubt that they even have calculators."

María took a shallow breath. "This here," she said loudly, "this is about my daughter."

"Yeah, it's about me" Laurita exploded, "It's always about me." She stood up and ran back into the building, marking her path with a luminescent trail.

After Laurita ran off, and Carlos promised to talk to her, María decided to take a swim. That had always made her feel better when she was a child; perhaps it would work again.

On her twelfth lap María saw, through the churned water in

her wake, a piece of cloth lying at the bottom of the pool. Thinking that it could have been Joshua's—and in some way it connected to his suicide—she stopped her crawl and tipped downward like a swing. Underwater she couldn't make out the color of the cloth, nor the design, which was hopelessly distorted by the refracted light. Still, there was something familiar about the fabric: it slipped and crinkled between her fingers. She brought it close to her eyes, unfolded a pair of straps and a skirt.

A dress. Her dress. *The* dress. María swung her arms like a fan and slowly rose the surface. It was impossible; the sun-dress had been lost under the Caribbean waves. She had left it behind when she swam after the skiff. It couldn't be here, she couldn't be holding it in her hands. She felt her blood streaming through her temples. Cicadas chirped in the distance. The air smelled of loam and pine needles.

"*¿Que diablos?*" she mumbled. To her left there was a wall of trees: pines, their bark grey and cragged. To her right stood an elegant two-story house, with sliding glass doors, surrounded by a wildflower garden. It was early afternoon, but the wind on her ears felt cool and moist.

Cloth in hand, María climbed out of the pool, which had suddenly become much smaller, almost square in shape. The springboard was gone; so were the cocktail tables. As she staggered toward the house, María began to experience an odd sense of *déjà vu*, a hint of unacquired knowledge, of memories without experience. She knew that this was her house, though it looked nothing like their modest colonial in Long Island. She knew that the water that streamed down her legs had come from her pool, though they had never been able to afford one. The trees, the ceramic-tiled patio, the garden—they all belonged to her.

She opened a sliding glass door. Behind it, there was a lavish parlor: marble floors, black leather furniture, twenty-foot ceiling. Peter stood by the empty fireplace, dressed in slacks and a white shirt, holding a wine glass with three relaxed fingers. María was not surprised by this. When she walked inside, he turned quickly and smiled at her.

"Better change," he said, "Cristine and David should be here in about fifteen minutes."

"Don't worry," she found herself saying, "you know they're always late."

"Is that what you're wearing?" Peter pointed at the wet dress in María's hand.

"Oh, no," she said, suddenly confused. "I found this, well, it was in the pool."

"Maybe one of the Kaufman kids dropped it by accident."

María shook her head violently, as if to drain her ear canal. Something was screaming in her skull. This wasn't her house. This wasn't her life.

"Where's Laurita?" she said, as calmly as possible.

"Pardon me?"

"Where's my daughter?" she yelled.

Peter carefully placed his wine glass on the mantelpiece. "You know where she is," he said, looking down at his feet.

She did. They had turned her in to the authorities. Peter had gotten another promotion at the bank, she had opened her own real estate agency. They had bought a new house, built a pool, gotten in shape.

"No," she said.

The parking lot was empty except for the still-dead Corolla, and Carlos's brand new Chevy. Mr. Criswell's pick-up truck was parked out back, away from visitors. As she walked to her uncle's car, Laurita felt the gravel rolling under her sneakers. The hot wind filled her t-shirt, made the wide sleeves flutter.

She cupped her hands against the driver's side window, vaguely hoping to find the key in the ignition. No such luck. Instead, she saw a couple of salsa cassettes strewn on the dashboard, their plastic cases warped by the sun.

She sat on the hood of the Chevy, waiting. After a minute, Tio Carlos pushed through the front door, stepped onto the gravel, jogged toward her. His *guayabera* was drenched with sweat; through the fabric, Laurita could see the black hairs on his chest, matted into a neat triangle. She was glad that it was Carlos who'd come for her and not her mother. He stopped in front of Laurita and caught his breath. He hadn't gotten used to the dry heat, apparently.

"It's like the beach out here," he said. "All you need is the brackish smell, and the coastline. Maybe a couple of palm trees." He paused to scratch his mustache. "Your mother is trying, you know. She's trying real hard."

"I didn't ask her," Laurita said.

"Maybe. But she did ask me to talk to you," he said.

"Maybe I don't want to talk."

"Okay," he said, "that's fine with me." He shuffled around the car and started pacing back to the office.

The wind made a breathy sound in Laurita's ear, like a child whistling. "Wait a minute," she called out.

"Yeah?"

"Did she say anything about me?"

"Your mother? Only that you're being a brat. That she's getting sick of your histrionics."

"Does she hate me?" The question had jumped from her mouth before she was able to stop it

Carlos laughed, much too quickly. "What? Of course not! Why would she hate you?"

"For messing things up for her. For breaking up the family." A string of light fluttered above Laurita's shoulders. She did her best to ignore it.

"Well," Carlos began, then stopped.

"Well, what? What did she say about me?"

"She didn't tell me much, but what you're saying kind of makes sense. Maybe she does blame you for being stuck out here."

The sparks grew brighter, coiled into a rope-like weave. "I know she blames me," she said, trying to squelch her fear, "I mean, it's my fault, so of course she blames me. What I want to know is if she hates me."

"I can't tell you that," Carlos said and held up his hands. "Hate is something that happens between two people: you can't really see it from the outside."

"Oh, come on!" Laurita said, exasperated. There was no way Tio Carlos could be serious.

"It's the truth. Look, when your grandfather was very sick, right before he died, he asked me not to let María come to his funeral. Can you believe that? He blamed her for killing *mami*, during the delivery. Right at the end he said to me: 'I fulfilled my responsibilities as a father, now I want to die in peace.' Nobody knew. I wouldn't have known myself, if he hadn't whispered it in my ear that—"

The sound of a screaming engine covered the end of his

speech. Laurita glanced at the road: the yellow Corvette was already a mile down the highway, raising a great dust cloud into the air. Shading her eyes, she watched the car shrink to a gleaming dot. When she turned back to the motel, Tio Carlos was gone. The front door shut by itself, without sound.

For a while afterward, as she tiptoed upstairs to her bedroom, as she quietly filled her backpack with tube socks and underwear, the highway remained in her pupils: a ghostly, artificial coastline; a path through the light.

The dress hit the kitchen counter with a sick slapping sound, like meat on the cutting block. María's "trip" had certainly been no hallucination: the wet rag proved it. She was now back in Joshua Criswell's motel, back in the desert, but the dress lingered, coiled into a red and purple mess, stained with sea salt.

She had returned; María gave herself credit for that. As soon as she'd realized where she was, she had dashed out of the living room and jumped into the square pool. She hit her head on the bottom, a glancing blow that left her momentarily disoriented, as if she'd been caught in rolling wave. When she surfaced, the beautiful house had been replaced by the sun-washed motel. The pines had withered to spindly, dry bushes. The rich soil had turned to sand. María waded to the edge and lifted herself from the water, the cloth wrapped tightly around her arm. As she walked to the kitchen, she felt at once confused, relieved, and disappointed, as if she'd been awakened from a strange but pleasant dream. Her forehead throbbed; there would be a lump by morning.

In the cupboard María found a bottle of rice wine, which Joshua kept (used to keep?) for Japanese recipes. She unscrewed the cap, served three inches into a empty mason jar, then swallowed the pungent liquid in one quick gulp. She hated to drink; she hated saké in particular. Still, she needed something hot in her stomach. A cold void had opened inside of her. Just a moment ago she had conceived the inconceivable, and she loathed herself for it.

I have to talk to her, she thought, *yes, I need to explain myself.* She remembered the painful delivery, the feeling of absolution when she'd realized that she was still alive, that, unlike her mother, she had survived the endeavor. She remembered the weight of Laur-

ita in her arms: surprisingly light at first, but soon a burden—
straining her back and elbows, crushing her breast.

María dropped the mason jar in the sink, then sauntered
through the common room, up the carpeted stairs, down the
hallway. She stopped at her daughter's door and knocked three
times, as if giving a signal. "Laurita," she said, "are you sleeping,
m'hija?" There was no answer. Warily she grasped the brass knob.
The metal was cold in her hand.

The words came as soon she opened the door: "Hello, sister."
Carlos was lying sideways on the bed, his head nestled in the
crook of his arm, pretending to sleep. He smiled icily at her,
then stretched like a cat.

María stood motionless. There was something wildly wrong
about the scene before her. Sunlight came too brightly through
the shuttered windows. The air stank of rotten teeth.

"What are you doing here?" she said. "I thought you were
talking to Laurita."

"Laurita's gone," Carlos said. His voice sounded different—
deeper, impossibly resonant.

"Gone? What do you mean?"

"She left. She packed her things and headed for the road."

"And you let her?" María could feel her throat tightening, her
heart beating without rhythm.

"Sure," Carlos said. He sat up in bed and rubbed his eyes.
"That's what you wanted, right? Get her out of your life."

María stepped back into the hallway; the door shined with a
dark, oily gleam.

"You're not my brother," she said in Spanish.

"Of course I'm not your brother," he said in the same language and licked his teeth. "That would be foolish. Carlos Gutierrez has been dead for a week; slit his wrists with a bread knife.
I'm afraid he made a terrible mess of the kitchen."

He rose from bed slowly, pulled his shoulders back and
groaned. Suddenly, a crack opened in his sternum. María
watched in painful fascination. His body folded outward, then
reversed itself like a glove. Inside there was a shapeless clot,
which soon gathered into a creature: a swollen parody of a man,
clothed in tattered shadows, its head sculpted from a slab of
bone. Towering before her, the thing peered at María with dead,
igneous eyes.

She imagined herself screaming, shielding her face, cowering. She couldn't move. Her muscles felt like paper. Her throat was filled with glass shards.

La muerte, she thought.

The creature appeared to smile, though his jaw was fixed in place. "No, not death," he said, "something else entirely. I am the bearer of ill-tidings, the flawless, cruel mirror. I am fear, the shatterer of illusions, the weaver of guilt and failure. I am, in a word, D'Spayre."

The dusty Plymouth Reliant was heading westward. Standing at the edge of the pavement, Laurita raised her thumb impassively—hip thrust to the side, elbow touching her flank. Since she'd left the motel, about twenty minutes ago, two cars had gone by her without even tapping their brakes. Now she was hot and parched, the strap of her backpack cut into her shoulder, and she could feel a nasty blister swelling on her heel. Chances were that she would be walking till nightfall, and she was none too happy about it.

To her surprise, the Reliant stopped a few yards ahead of Laurita. Oklahoma plates, she noticed as she hurried to the car; must have been travelling for days. The driver—a slim blond man, dressed in crisp jeans and a white oxford shirt—gave her a quick once-over, then reached across the seats and opened the door. Laurita climbed in at once, ignoring the paper bags that covered the floor, the stench of dried beer, the french fries in the ashtray. She was jittery as a bird, but the man looked harmless enough; besides, it was far too hot to walk.

As soon as they pulled away from the shoulder, the driver introduced himself as Paul Bovery, luckiest man on the planet.

"Ah," Laurita said. Without thinking, she drew her knees together and crossed her ankles.

"You headed for Vegas?" the man said.

She nodded. "Is that where you're going?"

"Oh yeah," he said with an slippery laugh. "We're cleaning that sucker out. Me and Jesus. You just wait and see."

"Right," she said, the sun filling her eyes. From her backpack she produced a granola bar, a chunky walkman, a pair of sunglasses. *This is going to be a very long ride,* she thought. As the driver launched into his sparkling tale—a disembodied voice had told him to gamble everything at the roulette table—Laurita turned around in the seat and stared through the rear windshield. Half a mile back, the Vicky Motel sign was plunging into the desert. She opened her mouth, then closed it. Suddenly she longed for the fake almond scent of her mother's Corolla; for the sleekness of the vinyl upholstery. She winced and curled her face, as if she'd just bitten into a lime. The facts were clear: this time, María would not follow. Laurita was leaving for good.

Fear beaded like sweat on her skin. Her mouth tasted of fear; with every breath she drew a lungful of it. María heard fear in the clattering air conditioner, in the sparse roar of the highway. Her knuckles were afraid, her eyes were afraid. Her spine felt like a guitar string: pulled unbearably tight, vibrating.

"What do you want from me?" she gasped.

"Sustenance," D'Spayre said simply.

"There's food in the kitchen."

D'Spayre laughed: a terrible, grating screech. "I feed on souls, María, on human pain and hopelessness."

"Why us?" María said, "We're nothing but—"

"No, no," the demon interrupted, "*You* are nothing. Your daughter is everything."

María started to talk, but D'Spayre cut her off with a wave of his bleached hand.

"It was so beautiful, that first display," he said, glancing wistfully at the stucco ceiling, "so pure and meaningless. Thirty horrified children, their hearts crying in unison. Their teacher running out of the classroom, out of the building, throwing herself into traffic. Such a beautiful, chaotic instant!"

The incident in the school lab. Through the haze of fright, María recalled the principal's story: one of Laurita's classmates had, as a joke, replaced her fetal pig with a rat; when she lifted the tray cover, all hell had broken loose.

"Laurita will be my conduit," D'Spayre continued, "through her I shall project my despondency across cities. I shall drain the souls of nations, and my power will be unmeasurable."

At once María felt a brilliant swell of anger. "I won't let you," she whispered.

D'Spayre spread his shadow-cloak and turned away. "Please,

María, spare me the 'protective mother' performance. We both know it is a lie.''

"I love my daughter" she cried, warmth rushing into her limbs.

"You have to be alive for that," he said and shook his head. "You have to be alive."

D'Spayre stood by the window, apparently deep in thought. Facing away from her. Laurita's bed lay between them, its linen stripped and tossed over the side. María bent her elbows, flexed her knees slightly. This was her opportunity: the fall from the second floor would not kill him, but it would certainly hurt him. She crouched silently, feeling a burn in her thighs and back; the sweet ache of anticipation. The carpet was soft on her palms. She thought of her daughter, of glass shattering, of blood and crushed bones, and she pounced, stepping onto the mattress and springing forward, eyes shut, forearms crossed over her face.

"¡*Vete al carajo!*" she screamed, before hitting the water.

Blackness, then a washed moonlight. Plankton glittering like sequins. María floated in brine, suddenly awake. The skirt of her sun-dress fluttered about her, as if she were dancing—spinning to a delicious mambo tune. There was no music, though; no smell of coconut milk; no children in blue cotton uniforms, giggling. Only the sea: salt in her wide-open eyes, a sharp pain in her throat.

She had just fallen off the skiff, that much she remembered. The rudder had smacked her young chest and sent her over the stern. *I was asleep.* The wind changed direction, and the rudder swiveled, and the cold beam pushed her backwards. *I was asleep.* The wood creaked, and the rudder swiveled. *How could I know what happened that night?* There was a creak, a step, the skiff rocked slightly, and she felt a sudden heat, and a heavy hand on her shoulder. And she opened her eyes. And she saw the arm, the small dent of his elbow, the black hairs on his wrist.

Underwater, she smoothed the front of her dress, slapped down the skirt. Father had pushed her. It was unbelievable, and yet it made sense to her, just like the taste of yucca made sense, or the blue of the sky, or the flutter of pigeons in the morning. Agusto had given her a good shove, and she'd lost her balance and flipped over the stern—hands grasping air, eyes numbed.

He'd killed her that night: inside, where it counted.

Hair rising like seaweed, María tipped backwards and opened her mouth. The water was cool and sharp on her gums. She felt like a mock-up, a hollow figure made of wicker, cloth and skin, playing the part of a human being. Her lungs were starving. Her heart beat to a syncopated rhythm. All she had to do was breathe; the sea would take care of the rest.

Above her there was a mess of ripples and swirls, shifting with the current. Moonlight brightened the swells, made them shimmer as they rolled past her—heading for England, she guessed, or wherever the Gulf Stream would take them. Or maybe they would dissipate, or mingle with other swells, or crash onto a Bahamian shore . . .

My wake, she thought abruptly, *when I fell into the sea.* She remembered Joshua Criswell, poor Joshua Criswell, lying on his pool-side chair, watching the ripples. When she'd asked him about them, he'd told her that they changed. She hadn't understood what he meant back then, but now, all of sudden, it seemed like such a simple, crucial truth.

María was drowning. She pushed against the concrete floor and shot through the chlorinated water. Inches from the surface, she felt a yank on her left leg, as though someone were holding to her ankle. She glanced over her bare shoulder and immediately saw the knot, the thick strand of rope, the cast-iron table lying at the bottom of the pool. Desperate for air, she thrashed wildly, kicked left and right, stretched her foot until the bones cracked. She reached upward and felt a dry afternoon breeze on her palm. Her stomach shriveled. She pulled herself by the leg and tried untangling the rope, but the knot was good and tight, the kind Agusto had taught her when she was a girl.

She stopped and collected herself. *I am dying*, she thought, without bitterness. She touched her shin, ran a finger up her thigh. *Right now, though, right this moment, I'm alive.* She felt calm and light-headed. She stretched her arms and waved them in wide circles, hoping that someone would see her. No, not hoping—hope was as bad as D'Spayre. She had to live the present, not the future.

María drew into a fetal position. In her mind every second became a new, separate frame: air bubbles appeared and disappeared; sand blinked across the pool's floor. Four feet away, the water split, churned. Through the foam, María saw a girl floating in the pool, her eyes panicked, covered in blue and white sparks. Then there was a girl swimming towards her, and a girl cutting the rope with a kitchen knife, dragging María upward, tugging her brusquely over the ledge.

"*¡Mami!*" Laurita screamed. Shocked out of her stupor, María bent forward and coughed into her fist, spitting a dribble of brine. Then she breathed, and it was as if the world had emptied into her body.

"What happened here?" Laurita said after a moment.

"Your uncle," María gasped, "but it wasn't your uncle."

"Tío Carlos? He did this?"

María nodded, then shook her head and coughed again. There was far too much to explain. Gingerly she reached forward and held her daughter.

"I was so afraid, *m'hija*," she said, "I thought I'd lost you. It thought you were gone."

"I changed my mind," Laurita said, a line she'd been saving since Paul Bovery had dropped her off by the side of the road. Felt good to finally use it.

"I love you," María said.

Laurita pulled away, as if she'd burned herself on her mother's skin. "What do you mean when you say that?"

"I mean that I love you," María said. She was at once frightened and annoyed.

"I hear you saying it. But I can't feel it. *No lo siento en el corazón.*"

María almost lost her temper. Her hands shook, her ankle throbbed painfully. Just a moment ago she'd very nearly died, and the girl still questioned her heart. Then María saw the blankness in her face, and she realized that Laurita was serious, that she really couldn't tell what her mother felt.

"Since when?" María said.

"For a couple of years. Since I started junior high, I guess. It got worse after the thing in the lab."

"It isn't just with me," María said. She had meant it as a question.

The girl said nothing. She stared at her mother and swept a lock of wet hair from her forehead. María took the gesture as an invitation. Hesitating, she ran her fingers on Laurita's cheek. She had plum skin: tacky and smooth. Laurita shrank back, avoiding her touch. María quickly took her nape and drew her to her breast.

"*Ay negra,*" she said.

A cold, acid wind stung her nostrils. While María watched, the motel twisted into a narrow, spiralled tower. The evening sun fell away in strips, and the brush turned into a purple steppe. The sky looked bruised. A few yards away, in the spot where Joshua had tended his cactus garden, D'Spayre slowly broke through the dirt, kept rising until his feet left the ground. He hung lazily over the withered, upturned plants, head tipped as if on a noose. His shadow cloak flitted in the breeze, reminding her of the tattered sail, of the dress.

Not this time, María thought.

The demon laughed. "How poignant," he said, batting the dust from his muscular thighs, "how perfectly poignant."

Laurita tried to turn and look, but María held her firmly.

"Listen to me," she whispered, "this is my love, *m'hija,* this right now, what I'm doing."

The girl shut her eyes. To believe her mother, she realized, she would have to make up the word, give it a new meaning. *Heat of a body, smell of wet hair and Spandex.* It almost made sense to her.

"You're now part of my realm," D'Spayre shouted, obviously amused. "Fixtures, so to speak." He hovered closer, pretending to walk on air. With a flick of his wrist the ground rose about mother and daughter, covered their legs and waists in soot.

"This is my love," María said again, her voice trembling.

Yes, Laurita thought. Instantly a ripple of light, like soap film, issued from her skin. As it expanded, the wake scoured D'Spayre's illusion: purple sand lifting; wilted cacti tossing in the wind. Then it slapped the demon, and he grimaced and tumbled backwards, cursing in a loud, unintelligible hiss. The impact pushed him clear through the spiralled tower, which split in half and crumbled.

Before disappearing into the brightness, the demon yelled: "No hope, without D'Spayre."

To their surprise, Sheriff Wilder didn't ask many questions about Carlos's disappearance. María had only to say the word "mutant," and he nodded and stroked his cheek.

"A few years ago we had one in Raley," he said, "a town kid, liked to burn things with his fingers. Hurt a bunch of people, it seems, though nobody pressed charges. We ended up having to call those X-Factor guys from TV. They came right up and took him away. Dunno what we'd do nowadays, since X-Factor don't do that stuff no more."

"Something like that happened with Tio Carlos," Laurita said, trying to hide an embarrassed grin. She leaned forward on the vinyl couch and crossed her arms.

"He was a shape-changer," María said. She sat on the reception desk, next to the empty cash register, her swollen foot resting on a stool. "Pretending to be my brother. I guess Peter hired him to convince me to go back home. Let me tell you, as soon as we found out, we grabbed Joshua's shotgun and sent him away."

"You did the right thing," Sheriff Wilder said. He fixed his gun belt and stepped sideways to the glass door. Just as he was about to open it, he added, "Ma'am, I'm sorry about you having to vacate the place. Stupid bank rules."

"I know," María said.

"But I was thinking, since you're gonna be taking the bus, maybe I can buy that Corolla of yours. I mean, the engine's busted, but I bet the parts would sell. How much would you want for it?"

María turned to Laurita and bunched her eyebrows. "I don't know," she said, "a hundred bucks?"

"Five hundred?" Sheriff Wilder pulled out a money clip and methodically counted the bills. "Sounds like a bargain."

She thanked him with a broad smile. After he'd gone outside, María dropped to the floor—carefully, landing on her left foot—and said quietly: "It made him feel good, helping us out. Made him feel like a big man."

"Oh," Laurita said, touching her jaw.

Later that morning, as they loaded the bags into Carlos's abandoned Chevy, Laurita asked her mother about the night on the boat. María had told her everything about D'Spayre's illusion, and now Laurita wanted to know if it was true, if Agusto had pushed his daughter overboard.

"I was sleeping," María said, sheepishly, "I didn't see a thing."

She shut the trunk and hobbled around the car to the driver's seat.

Laurita climbed on the passenger side. The car was steaming inside. Even after two days, the upholstery still smelled of menthol cigarettes. It was then that it hit her: Tio Carlos had killed himself. Suddenly she started to bawl, so hard that her face hurt: for her uncle, for Joshua Criswell, for the father she'd left behind. Light danced on her body, spread over the dashboard, through the cushioned seats.

Holding the key to the ignition, María felt a twitch in her chest, and she folded over the steering wheel and cried. It didn't matter that it was her daughter's grief. It didn't matter at all.

Carnage

MAYHEM PARTY

ROBERT SHECKLEY

Illustration by Tom Morgan

THERE WAS A big crowd that day at the Vanezzi Palace on the Giudecca in Venice. The jewel of the Adriatic was hosting that year's conference of International Forensic Psychologists. This was the second day of the conference and all seats in the hall, which had been converted from a 14th-century Venetian palazzo, were taken. The aisles were filled with standees, and some people were even crouched in the stairwells, trying to avoid the disapproving eyes of the ushers.

This much interest was unusual for a scholarly event. The papers read at this conference were usually on the dull side, even though they did have to do with crime and psychology. Today's paper, however, had been long awaited. It promised, for the first time, the inside story of what happened when Professor Charles Morrison of Harvard and MIT attempted his revolutionary new experiment in reforming the criminally insane.

Reformation schemes had been tried before, of course, with little success. What was unique about this one was the fact that it involved Cletus Kasady, the super-villain known as Carnage.

There had been rumors and controversy surrounding Morrison's famous experiment. It had been carried out little more than a year ago, in the California town of Santa Rosa.

The results of that experiment had been hotly disputed, and even now the facts were not fully known. Now it was expected that Edward Ramakrishna, the man who had been Morrison's assistant at the time of the fateful experiment, was going to reveal what really happened in his presentation.

There was an undercurrent of whispered conversation as the master of ceremonies made the usual announcements. But everyone became quiet when he presented Dr. Ramakrishna.

Ramakrishna was a small, dark-haired, dark-skinned man. He was slight in build and although young, he already had a professorial stoop. In front of the audience he appeared at first diffident and unsure of himself. But he soon gained assurance, and his soft voice, amplified by the public address system, took on the aspects of a hypnotic chant. The audience listened in fascination as Ramakrishna brought them back to those days when Charles Morrison was setting up his experiment.

*　*　*

"Those fools! Those utter fools!" Morrison said as he burst into the office he shared with Ramakrishna. "They're so besotted with their behaviorism. They can't even consider the possibility of a proper Freudian experiment."

Morrison, like his assistant, was a short man, but unlike him was barrel-chested and balding. He had sharp blue eyes that glinted behind his spectacles. His big white face showed anger close to frenzy as he slapped a pile of papers down on the desk.

"They are laughing at my theory!" Morrison said.

Ramakrishna knew that Morrison was referring to his hypothesis concerning one of Sigmund Freud's most basic theories: that which divided the human psyche into ego, superego, and id. Morrison believed, as had Freud before him, that there was a biological basis to the psychic components. It was Morrison's contention that these basic divisions in of the human mind were the outcome of patterning laid down in the very DNA of human beings, and that this division was more susceptible to physical documentation than even Carl Jung's celebrated hypothesis of the archetypal memory.

The question had always been, where could these psychic functions be located? There was no evidence for them in scientific literature. But in recent years, amazing developments had been made in brain topology, using new neuron-mapping techniques based on the work of Reed Richards and Tony Stark—though these techniques had not been fully accepted by the scientific community.

Using this, Morrison had discovered the long-predicted three-fold division of the human psyche.

Of greater practical importance, he had found specific agents to which these psychic subdivisions reacted. They were part of a class he called Psychic Enhancers. He had been able to separate out specific serums that corresponded to the pure functions of the psychic entities, and to produce pure essences of these compounds, serums which acted as instigators and amplifiers of id, ego and superego.

His study had been published in the authoritative British journal *Science*, and Morrison had just received the first batch of comments, some of which had come to his home by post, others to his e-mail address. He had glanced over the letters and printouts of the e-mail on his way to the office, and he was furious.

"Look at these things!" he said, waving a handful of papers at Ramakrishna. "These fools haven't even taken the time to think over and digest my thesis. They haven't worked over my mathematical proofs or even read the necessary literature on the subject. Instead, out of their own fixed and dogmatic views, they rush to condemn me, calling my work quackery, pseudo-science, and even outright fraud!"

"This is indeed unfortunate," Ramakrishna said. He was a graduate of West Bengal University, and had done his advanced work at Oxford. His quiet contrasted with Morrison's bluster; Ramakrishna felt that his equanimity made him the ideal assistant to the impulsive Morrison. However, even he felt some of the outrage that Morrison was expressing, for he too had been involved in the research and experiments, and Morrison had permitted him to sign his name to the article.

"I'd be happy to help you answer the letters," Ramakrishna said. "Surely when we point out the errors in their judgments, the defects in their methodology—"

"We'll do no such thing!" Morrison said. "We're going to prove my thesis in the only way that'll make any impact on these dunces. We're going to take a violent super-criminal and convert him to an exemplary meekness."

Ramakrishna blinked. "The theory hasn't been tested in the field yet."

"No time like the present," Morrison said.

"I suppose so," Ramakrishna said. "But why not start with some ordinary psychotic?"

Morrison had been sitting at his desk brooding on the pile of critical letters. Now he looked up, glaring.

"And have those fools say I picked an easy one? Not a chance. I'm going to pick the hardest there is. The most impossible one. Curing him will prove my case beyond doubt."

"Who did you have in mind?" Ramakrishna asked.

"Ever hear of Carnage?" Morrison asked.

Ramkrishna had indeed heard of Carnage. Who hadn't? Already a notorious serial killer, Cletus Kasady had had a fateful encounter with an alien being while in prison. He'd merged with this alien, which provided him with a lethal, shape-changing, costume. When he wore the costume, he called himself Carnage, and Carnage was a worse serial killer than Kasady had ever been.

Others had tried to cure him. Lifestream Technologies had attempted a physical removal of the alien presence from Kasady's blood; the Ravencroft Institute had gone for a psychological cure. Both failed miserably.

Still, Ramakrishna decided, if Morrison's theory worked on Carnage, it would work on anyone.

Dr. Morrison's superior was Captain Flynn Baxter, who worked out of the National Police Advisory Board in Washington, D.C. Baxter had had an exemplary career both as a criminologist and as a working cop. He had been in charge of police efforts in two of America's most notorious crime cities, Detroit and East St. Louis. When he retired from active duty on the streets, the President had appointed him to head up the newly formed national Police Advisory Board. Baxter had always been a strong proponent of Dr. Morrison's views on the possible reeducation of criminals. But this scheme almost took his breath away by its very boldness.

"You want to reform a super-villain?" he said. "Did you have a particular one in mind?"

Morrison nodded. "Cletus Kasady."

"*Carnage?* That's a big order, Charlie," Baxter said. "Couldn't you pick someone a little simpler to start with?"

"That's what my assistant asked me," Morrison said. "And I'll give you the same answer I gave him. This theory can and will work. And we need something spectacular to shut up the critics. Something that'll get enough headlines so that we can get proper funding for a really effective program."

"We don't even have Carnage in custody," Baxter said. "Do you think he's just going to walk in because you send out a notice saying you want to reform him?"

"I think I can get him," Morrison said.

"How?"

"My idea is built around an item I saw in the newspaper a few days ago. It seems that a group of the country's most dangerous killers are being taken from prisons all around the country and brought to a special think tank in Santa Rosa, California. They're going to be studied by experts in the hopes of preventing further crimes."

"I've heard about that plan too," Baxter said. "But what's that got to do with Kasady?"

"Nothing yet. But it will when I put my plan into operation."

"Charlie, nobody even knows where Kasady lives, where he hangs out. He's got no known MO—except that he hates Spider-Man. How do you expect to get word to him?"

"Leave that to me, sir. Do I have your approval?"

"I've backed you before," Captain Baxter said. "And I'll back you again if you insist. But think about it, Charlie. This can be a very dangerous scheme."

"Then I have your okay?" Morrison asked once again.

"Yeah, yeah, you got it."

"Thank you, sir. You'll be the first to hear of the results."

Ramakrishna was more than a little apprehensive when he heard from Morrison that the scheme to reform Carnage had been approved. The idea lay in getting hold of Carnage long enough to give him a dose of one of the purified essences that Morrison had succeeded in isolating. This substance was too powerful for an ordinary man to take; it would likely kill him. But Morrison had obtained Carnage's biological profile from Ravencroft, and his unique alien metabolism would allow him to survive. When Carnage swallowed the superego substance that was the basis of conscience, Carnage would become a changed man, reformed from within, incapable of continuing in his horrifying ways.

That at least was the theory.

But still, it was a risky experiment. It was difficult to the point of impossibility to get anywhere near Carnage. But it seemed worth taking that risk because the super-villain's campaign of terror was so gruesome that it seemed reasonable to try anything to stop him.

Over the next several days, the social experiment that was to be carried out at Santa Rosa, California received more publicity than the founders of the experiment had ever expected. Due to Baxter's ties with the media, the experiment got sound-bites on all the major TV news broadcasts. There were follow-up articles on it in the newspapers. Suddenly, it had gone from an obscure experiment to the biggest move against crime of the century.

Morrison was gambling that Cletus Kasady, wherever he was, would hear about this and would be intrigued.

That part of the scientist's theory was proven correct. Kasady, presently holed up in a suburb of Dallas, heard about the experiment and he was indeed intrigued. The mind of a creature like Carnage had unpredictability as its keynote. His thoughts were chaotic, a wild mingling of memories of the past and visions of the future. But even a mind like this, spinning out of control much of the time, had its affinities. It was drawn to crime. In the part of that mind that was still like a little boy, it desired a bold endeavor. It also loved to show itself in all its horrifying mutated splendor.

The TV newscasts that Kasady watched contained ghastly descriptions of the deeds of various of these serial killers. How one was a multiple killer specializing in the old and helpless, another was a stalker, a third specialized in torturing family pets. One was worse than the other.

Carnage's conclusion: "Sounds like these are people I'd like to party with."

After a recent incident when he learned he could transmit himself across cyberspace, Kasady had come to appreciate the use of computers. The people who used to own this apartment (and whose bodies were starting to stink up the bathroom) had a top-of-the-line computer, and he used it to call up some information on the town of Santa Rosa. The place was in central California. It had about twenty thousand inhabitants and was over a hundred miles from the nearest big city. It was noted for its peaceful lifestyle.

Not for long, Carnage decided.

He studied the plans of the facility, which were set out in full in the newspaper accounts. He saw that the point of least security would occur just after the killers arrived at the Institute. The escorting guards—armor-clad Guardsmen on loan from the Vault—would leave, and the guards at the Institute, a much smaller force, would take over.

That's definitely the time to drop in, Carnage thought. He could feel the excitement rising in him. He morphed into the red and black skin of his alien persona and got ready.

The serial killers were flown in from various parts of the country. They were kept under guard in a high-security room in the airport until the last of them had been accounted for. Then, under the watchful eyes of the Guardsmen, they were put into a bus for the final hundred-and-twelve-mile ride to the Institute. There were sixty-seven of them, some in their early twenties, others already in old age. Before they were allowed on this trip each had had a thorough physical and mental examination, and had been put under deep narco-synthetic hypnosis for further tests.

The bus arrived at the Santa Rosa facility. It was a series of low white buildings surrounded by a high electrified fence. When the bus pulled up in front of the main building, it was met by a new group of guards hired by the facility. These guards, armed with high-tech weaponry provided by SHIELD, escorted the killers inside.

From a clump of trees nearby, Carnage was watching all this. His unearthly red and black skin pulsated with excitement. He was in a high good humor, really pleased by the prospect of a good mayhem party among like-minded people. The electrified fence barely tickled his altered form. Now he was just waiting for the right moment to make his appearance.

Inside the Institute, Ramakrishna asked Morrison, "What if Carnage doesn't show?"

"Then we try something else," Morrison said. "We'll have wasted the money publicizing this thing, but that's minor. The trouble is going to come if he does show. The trouble and the success."

"Let us pray that it works," Ramakrishna said.

The killers were led through the hallways of the main building into the auditorium, under the watchful eyes of their guards. Morrison then came out on the stage at the front of the auditorium, welcoming his guests.

"We'll be getting to the experiments in about an hour," he said. "Meanwhile, all of you are to stay here. And when the experiments do begin, we ask that you not touch *anything* in the labs. Stored there are psychochemicals that could cause uncertain and unpredictable results.''

Morrison then left the stage.

That got the killers' attention. The word spread among them like wildfire. *They've got the really good stuff stored in the lab! Man, if we could just get our hands on that!*

The problem was the guards. Not as dangerous as the Guardsmen, but given that the guards had ray-guns and the killers were unarmed and handcuffed, there was little chance of them even leaving the auditorium.

There was one among them who wasn't taking part in this whispered speculation. He was a young man with red hair, and he had a withdrawn, almost sleepy look. Finally he turned to the guys who had been talking, and said, "You guys really want to get into that good stuff?"

They looked at him. Nobody recognized him. Surely this guy hadn't been on the bus! Or had he?

"Who are you?" one of them asked.

"Well, you wouldn't know me like this," the stranger said. "But when I change a little bit, into my work skin, maybe you'll know who I am."

His clothes and handcuffs rippled and began to change color and shape. Before their very eyes he turned into the red and black visage they all recognized.

"Carnage! My God, it's Carnage!"

Those nearest to him shrank away. They knew too well about Carnage's homicidal unpredictability.

"Hey, don't go away, buddies!" Carnage cried. "You and me, we're going to party!"

The serial killers looked at one another. Whispered words came out:

"It's Carnage, the coolest dude of all! The killer of killers! The most famous serial killer of all time!"

"Now listen up, people!" Carnage cried. "You know what I always say. Nothing is too loathsome as long as it gets a laugh. Am I right or am I right?"

His audience applauded wildly.

"And now," Carnage cried, "to begin the festivities, let's take ourselves up to that lab and check out those sweet-sounding chemicals.''

They surged out of the auditorium into the hallways and up the stairs. The guards retreated. Morrison had told them this might happen, and if it did, they were to fall back for the moment. They were under orders to kill no one except to protect their own lives. And, truth be told, they were glad to get away from the creature who wasn't entirely human.

Head and shoulders taller than the killers, Carnage was at the front of the mob, leading it as it surged up the stairs to the top floor.

On the top floor they paused a moment to get their bearings. Then, seeing the sign labelled "Laboratory 1," they charged up to the door. It was also labelled, "No Admittance," and it was locked.

Carnage pushed his way to it. He tried the doorknob, then said, "A locked door usually means good stuff inside." With contemptuous ease he battered in the door and ripped it off its hinges. Then he stepped into the lab, the mob packed close behind. And then he came to a stop.

There at the far end of the room, standing on a little raised platform, wearing a long white coat, and with two gleaming test tubes raised in his hand, was Dr. Morrison. Behind him, half concealed by the doctor's bulk, was Ramakrishna.

"Hi there, Doc," Carnage said. "Nice of you to welcome us like this. What's that you got in your hand? Something weird I hope."

"Weird enough," Morrison said quietly. He held up one of the test tubes. It was colored a bright cobalt blue.

Carnage grinned. "Is that one of those lovely psychoactive chemicals I've heard *so* much about?"

"It is," said Morrison. "What I'm holding here is a unique sample of the mind-function known as superego. We believe it will produce an increase in that function of mind called conscience."

"Bottled conscience!" Carnage cried with a pointy-toothed smile. "I love it!"

"If successful," Morrison continued, "it will act as a self-regenerating corrective to your anti-social leanings."

"You mean it'll make me not want to kill people anymore?" Carnage asked mockingly.

"In a nutshell, that's it. It will bring you the reformation that in your heart of hearts I know you have been longing for."

Carnage laughed an ugly laugh that stated more eloquently than words just what he thought of Morrison's opinion.

Undaunted, the doctor continued, "I am certain that every intelligent creature yearns for redemption, goodness, and a useful place in society."

"You know, Doc," Carnage said, "you're as bad as those jackasses at Ravencroft. You think I got a secret desire to be good? Give me that stuff!"

"Be careful!" Morrison said. "It's very rare! Priceless!"

"Is that a fact?" Carnage grabbed the test tube and crushed it in his hand. Then, to the wild applause of the killers, he allowed his costume to fall away from his head, revealing his red hair. He rubbed the sticky stuff into his curly locks.

"I've always wanted to have good hair," Carnage said. "Maybe this'll do the trick. What's in the other tube?"

"Nothing you'd be interested in," Morrison said, shielding the test tube and the substance within it, which was colored a bright red.

Carnage plucked the test tube out of his fingers. "Tell me about it, Doc, and no lies. Believe me, I can tell when you're lying."

"I wouldn't dream of lying to you," Morrison said stiffly. "The red substance in that test tube contains the base from which we extracted the superego substance."

"Base? What are you talking about?"

"In order to get abstract of superego, we had to produce essence of ego first."

Carnage held the tube up to the light. "Ego, huh?"

"The pure stuff. But you've got plenty of that already. Too much, I suspect."

"Hey!" Carnage said. "You can't get too much ego."

"Wait!" Morrison said. "The substance hasn't been tested on a human!"

"Tough shit! Anyway, I'm not exactly human. I'll test it for you, Doc. And if I don't like it—"

He winked at the killers, who cheered, then cheered again as he lifted the test tube and drained its contents to the last drop.

There was a moment of silence. Everyone in the lab stared at

Carnage, trying to discern, from the odd gestures of his hands, what was going on in his mind.

Ramakrishna, who was watching all this, conjectured that limb movements were inadequate to express what was happening in Carnage's mind. No gesture could convey the sudden flooding sense that Carnage had to be experiencing: a sense of himself— of utter Carnageness!

Carnage's view of himself expanded, as if a curtain were suddenly lifted, revealing his true self behind it. What Carnage had taken for granted before, he now saw in all its shocking immediacy—how precious he was—how special, unique, one-of-a-kind, irreplaceable, unreproducible. He saw, bathed in a glorious inner light of pure ego, how fine his body was, how cunningly wrought, how exquisitely fashioned. And he saw this not in comparison with the bodies of others—what did others matter?—but purely as himself alone, peerless and beyond compare, every hair, every pore glowing with the absolute essence of himself.

And if his body were so special, what about his mind? If levels of uniqueness were possible, then his mind was supernally unique, a wonder beyond compare—not because his mind was finer, deeper, or smarter than other minds; other minds didn't matter. It was important that this mind, this body, this mind-body, were his, his alone, something the world had never seen before and would never see again.

It was difficult for Carnage to do anything but stand there, lost in contemplation of himself. Then, gradually, he became aware of the killers, still massed at the laboratory door, shouting, screaming at him—"Come on, Carnage, let's get on with it!" "Time for a little murder, huh, Carnage?" "Time to kill, time to kill, time to kill!"

Carnage remembered that once—it seemed a very long time ago—he had gloried in bloodshed and murder. And although he had extraordinary strength and almost superhuman talents, nevertheless, he had risked his life over and over again in mad escapades of killing. He had been hurt, wounded by people like Spider-Man and Venom, time and time again, and had always managed to come through, to heal, and return to kill and put himself at risk again.

"Yo! Carnage! Let's go!"

Carnage stared dully at the raging killers. They wanted him to lead them on yet another escapade. Yet another passage through a hell of mayhem and gore. They wanted him to put himself at risk again. To chance injury to his marvellous body and superlative mind. To risk death itself and the loss of all the wonderful things he was. And for what?

He remembered those past times now, those times of crazy murder. How good he had felt! But he felt better now. He felt wonderful. There was no feeling he could imagine better than this one, of knowing and loving who and what he was.

To take action could only bring him down from this high. Not up! He was at the peak now! There was no higher to go!

"Doc," he said to Morrison, "these people are crazy. I guess I used to feel that way before I got a real sense of myself. But now—can you get me out of here?"

"I can," Morrison said. "But we're going to have to move fast. Those killers are going to get nasty when they realize you've betrayed them."

"So what?" Carnage said. "Those morons haven't a clue. I know what good is. Good is me grooving on me, not getting into some crazy situation where I could get hurt."

"Come on," Morrison said. He touched a button on the wall. A secret panel slid back. He and Carnage ducked into it and closed it before the killers could come pounding after him.

Ramakrishna was there too. He followed them as they hurried down a long dimly lit corridor. He pressed another button to close the panel, keeping them from the killers. That button would also sound an alarm, thus alerting the guards. They would round the killers up.

"Where are we going?" Carnage asked. "Where are you taking me?"

"To a place I think you'll like," Morrison said.

At the end of the passageway there was a door. Morrison opened it and led Carnage inside, Ramakrishna following.

Carnage found himself in a brightly lit room. It was mirrored on all its walls, and on the floor and ceiling. Carnage stared at himself in the mirrors.

He was facinated by his own reflection on all sides. He could look at himself in endless different postures and angles, close up or at varying distances. All the views of himself were good, and they were all different.

He had never known he looked so good. The sight of his own face was sheerest beauty, extreme ecstacy. Looking at himself he could get ever more deeply into his own mind, deeper and deeper into that magical and irreplacable essence of himself.

Morrison's experiment seemed to be working. It was all perfect except for one thing.

"Doc."

"Yes, Carnage?"

"Too many people in here. Would you very much mind getting the hell out of here?"

"Not at all," Morrison said. "You'll be all right?"

"I've got everything I need. Me!"

Morrison nodded and by a gesture of the head indicated to Ramakrishna that he should leave. The assistant went to the door, opened it and walked out.

"That's better," Carnage said, still staring at his reflections in the mirrors. "But what about you?"

"I'm going in just a moment," Morrison said. "I just have a few questions I want to ask you first."

Ramakrishna was watching all this through the door's one-way glass panel. He could hear them talking through the radio hookup with which the room had been equipped.

He heard Carnage say, "I don't want to answer any questions."

"This will just take a moment," Morrison said. "I need it for my report."

Carnage was still staring into a mirrored surface when he gave a slight grunt of annoyance. Ramakrishna thought it was the sight of Morrison, there in the mirror with him, that brought that response.

Carnage's next words seemed to bear this out. "Only room for one of us in this mirror!" Carnage shouted, and whirled, suddenly looming up over Morrison, large and terrifying.

Morrison tried to run for the door. But before he could reach it, Carnage was on him. The attack was unbelievably ferocious. Dark gouts of Morrison's blood splashed across the mirrors. The sight of it seemed to bring Carnage back to his deranged senses. He attacked the door.

Ramakrishna called for the guards, but they were too late. Carnage had regained himself. The murder of Dr. Morrison, the blood on the mirrors, these had brought him back to his true nature. He broke out of the mirrored room and escaped.

The guards easily regained control of the killers, and the original experiment proceeded as normal.

Dr. Morrison was buried in a closed casket.

This is what Ramakrishna explained, almost a year later, when he gave his talk in Venice.

"Dr. Morrison's treatment," Ramakrishna concluded, "would not be suitable for a normal human being. But for a super-villain like Carnage, it worked admirably and seemed to prove a theory first put forth by Sigmund Freud—that violence is the result of insufficient ego rather than too much. When the ego function is inflated to its extreme limit, the organism no longer has to prove itself by acting out its violent impulses. At that point the organism has moved to what we might call the terminal stage of narcissism.

"This paradoxical effect of the ego substance had been Dr. Morrison's secret weapon, and Carnage had fallen for it."

"How would you characterize that terminal stage, Dr. Ramakrishna?" someone in the audience asked.

"It is a complete narcissism, a state characterized by passivity and uninterrupted self-contemplation. The subject will remain that way as long as he has his mirrored room which he thinks is a refuge, but which is actually a prison. That was what was supposed to happen, and it almost did."

Ramakrishna hesitated, then said, "That's why I said that Dr. Morrison's treatment was a success, even though it failed. That's what would have happened if only Dr. Morrison had been able to restrain his zeal to ask a few more questions. If only he had gotten out of there at once. If only Carnage had not seen the doctor's blood on the mirrors."

Someone from the audience asked, "Do you think the treatment can be tried again?"

"There's no reason it would not succeed," Ramakrishna said. "But I doubt it will ever be repeated. It is not suitable for a normal human. And Carnage is aware of it now, and will not let himself be deceived again. The experiment was a success, ladies and gentlemen, but the subject was not cured."

The Wizard & the Sandman

THE NIGHT I ALMOST SAVED SILVER SABLE

TOM DEFALCO

Illustration by Colleen Doran

FIVE JETS HAD already crashed in Miami, and three more were headed toward the ground. A wide grin cut across my face as I glanced at the bodies pictured on the television hanging above Marty's bar. They were sprawled on the field like so much litter, writhing in humiliation more than pain. None of these people would walk away unscathed. Nah, they'd be haunted by this night for the rest of their lives. The memory would always be there, laughing from the shadows. Victories are soon forgotten. Defeats never leave us. But I didn't really care about them. Me, I was tempted to cheer. It was a great night for Dolphins football. The Miami team was murdering the bums from New York.

I guess I must have been gloating a little too openly, because one of Marty's other regulars suddenly stomped up behind me, and jammed a gun into the back of my neck. Okay, I'll admit I had it coming. Marty's is a straight beer-and-shot joint, just off Houston Street in downtown Manhattan. People in this neighborhood take their football, especially their New York teams, very seriously. I should have been more sensitive. After all, it ain't like I'm this rabid Dolphins fan. I just feel a certain kinship with places like Miami that have plenty of sun, surf and sand.

I'm especially partial to sand. Y'see I'm Bill Baker, though most everybody just calls me the Sandman. A bunch of years back, in my wilder days, I was lying on a beach when I got hit with a massive dose of radiation. Instead of shriveling me like a thin burger on an open flame, the radiation merged me with the sand. It somehow gave me the ability to transform all or part of my body into pure sand that I could mold into any shape I wanted. I could also control my density, becoming as hard as concrete or as insubstantial as, well, a fistful of sand.

Of course, the guy behind me wasn't particularly concerned with my past. He was focused on the present, and didn't like me ignoring him. His annoyance was becoming increasingly apparent as he dug his gun into the base of my skull, twisting the barrel like he was a twelve year old giving his first noogie.

In an effort to be helpful, I willed that portion of my head to assume the consistency of quicksand. It immediately gave way beneath his pressure, swallowing the gun and most of his hand before he realized he should stop pushing.

"The game's gonna play out in its own way, pal. We can't affect its outcome." I said, my eyes never leaving the television. "You wanna fight about it, or share a brew?"

"I don't care about no game. My name's Pound, and I got a message."

My gaze dropped from the television to the barroom mirror, and I caught a look at the guy. Pound was tall, with the wide shoulders and brawny arms of a lifter who liked to be admired. I knew the type, a bruiser who collected debts or imparted threats, intimidating most people by his sheer bulk. A guy his size rarely had to throw punches. His experience on the receiving end would be even less.

"Let go of my hand. You ain't gonna hurt me. You don't dare," Pound sneered in a voice so low it almost masked his fear. "My boss has yours."

My current employer happened to be a very special lady. The thought of her in danger made my blood boil. Or, it would have, if my veins carried blood.

I wanted to whip my head around, maybe yanking his arm out of its socket in the process. Instead, I reached for my beer, and tore off a sip.

"You got proof?"

Pound didn't answer. He was working up a sweat, trying to yank his hand free. But his eyes jumped to mine when the back of my head assumed the shape of a vise.

"Proof?" I prodded.

"I got a number," Pound mumbled. He gave it to me, and I signaled Marty for a phone. Any other bartender might have been a little curious to see one patron with his fist shoved up someone else's noggin. Not Marty. He was a master at minding his own business. Never even gave us a second glance. That's one of the things I like about his place.

The phone at the other end had barely started to ring when a cold and familiar voice cut in. "Good evening, William," the Wizard said. "I have been expecting your call."

The Wizard! He was a former partner from the old days. Long before I met him, he was a big brain who became stinking rich by inventing a whole bunch of futuristic gizmos. You'd think a guy like that would just lay back and count his bucks. But something made him want to devote his genius toward crime. I always

figured it was an ego thing. He just had to compete with the
costumed jocks, had to prove his brains superior to their superhuman powers.

"Still there, William? A friend of yours would like to say hello."

There was a slight pause, and then Silver Sable said without
preamble, "I am uninjured, Sandman. Do not be concerned, and
do not get involved."

Silver's voice sound distracted, like she was a receptionist flipping through the latest fashion mags as she rattled off the same
lunch order day after day. But I knew better. Silver was a con-
summate professional, always alert, always studying her surround-
ings. I didn't lie when I said she was very special. She ran an
international private security force that concentrated on bagging
wanted criminals and recovering stolen property. Her operatives
were known as the Wild Pack, and I was a member. She'd tossed
me a lifeline a few years ago when I really needed it, giving me
a chance to redeem myself for my days as a criminal. It was a
debt I could never even hope to repay.

"How'd this happen, lady?"

"Pure carelessness. I had intended to visit a few shops, and
never even noticed the new limo driver until he flooded the
passenger compartment with something which made me very
sleepy."

A smile crept across my lips. Silver could identify every knockout gas on the market, including a few which weren't even available to the top secretest government agencies. She was only
playing dumb and dazed, maybe because she picked up on the
Wizard's need to dominate. I almost felt sorry for the poor guy.
He was in more trouble than he'd bargained for.

"Anything you need?"

"Another chauffeur. I'm afraid the new fellow sustained a
rather nasty concussion before I went down for my nap."

"Hey," a voice growled behind me. "What about my hand?"

Pound was still pawing at my back like crazy, but I couldn't
afford to be distracted. Fastening my eyes on his reflection, I saw
the look of panic on his face when I tightened my vise.

"Enough chit-chat!" the Wizard suddenly barked in my ear.
"I am willing to make a trade, William. Mr. Pound will assist you.
I look forward to seeing you again," he added as our connection
died.

"My hand," Pound snarled. "What about my hand?"

"We'll discuss it."

I stood, snagging Marty's attention. "Mind if I use the back room?"

"Just so long as you clean up after yourself."

Sounded like a good deal to me. With Pound dragging behind like a kid in a toy store, I marched through the bar, trying not to block anyone's view of the game. Me, I'd lost interest. I had to concentrate on my own opening kick-off.

Marty had two rooms in the back. One was his office, and closed to the public. The other doubled as an occasional storeroom, and the site of a weekly high-stakes poker game. The only furniture consisted of a large round table and six chairs. Cartons of napkins and towels huddled against the back wall, waiting to be called into action against some massive spill.

I reached up, as if to scratch the back of my head, shifted some sand around, and encased Pound's gun and hand in a large square block which should have been my right fist. Moving the block in front of me, I buried Pound in the nearest chair.

We locked eyes over my forearm as he made a sincere effort to regain his composure, bluster filling his cheeks like a circus balloon.

"You don't scare me!"

"I don't?"

"You ain't never gonna to see that woman again, Sandman. Not without my cooperation."

"Really?"

"Let go of my hand." He started to whine, his façade crumbling before my eyes. Pound had obviously figured his muscle would carry any battle, but I had taken that away from him. He was like a fancy sports car with a blown transmission. He still looked great, but his racing days were over.

"You're going to tell me everything I need to know," I said.

"Fat chance! You can't make me talk."

"Actually," I said as I reformed my entire forearm into a miniature guillotine, "I'm sure I can."

I wasn't wrong.

A little over an hour later I was steering Pound's car up Route 684, heading for the fourth exit. My destination was an upper Westchester estate in the town of Bedford.

Stuffed in the trunk, Pound was sleeping off a friendly hay-maker when I'd last seen him. Who knows? He might have been awake by now. I didn't care. He already done his Elton John, singing like a man possessed when he thought I'd actually use my arm, shaped like an executioner's axe, to cut his head off.

The Wizard's plan was pure butter. I climb into an unbreakable canister which Pound delivers to the Wizard in exchange for Silver.

Yeah, right!

My former partner knew I'd never put myself in such a helpless position, and I knew he knew it. The so-called plan had only one purpose: to convince a dummy like Pound that he had me at a disadvantage.

The Wizard could have called me at the bar, but that just wasn't flashy enough. What fun would it be if I just got his message and walked in the front door? His ego wanted more. He needed an elaborate chess game to keep me running, desperately trying to come up with countermoves he had already anticipated. He wouldn't be satisfied until I was totally demoralized.

Why do super-villains always construct such elaborate death-traps? What's wrong with a good, old-fashioned bullet to the brain? I guess it's the same reason they dress in flashy costumes and take such crazy names. The Wingless Wizard! The Rampaging Rhino! The Daring Trapster! The Deadly Hobgoblin! (I should talk—in the old days, I was either the Sinister or the Savage. Now I'm just the Sandman.)

A super-villain isn't content with merely winning, he needs his victory to be acknowledged. He wants his defeated foe to jump up and shout, "Wow! You're the greatest. I'm never stumbled into such a clever trap, or been pummeled so viciously. You're the scariest super-villain of all. The other heroes must be warned about you."

Yeah, I know exactly how super-villains think. I used to be as bad as the worst. Not that I've changed all that much. I could have questioned Pound without resorting to that corny guillotine trick. Silver had told me to stay out of it. I could have followed standard Wild Pack procedure, called in her kidnapping, and left her rescue to a hostage team.

Nah, I had to play cowboy. I told myself it was because I didn't want to endanger anyone else in what was, essentially, a private war. Bad enough Silver was already splattered with this mud.

It sounded okay, but I couldn't escape the truth. Yeah, I could have played this whole gig much safer, and a whole lot smarter. But, hey, what's the fun in that?

I had to hand it to Pound. His directions were excellent. I coasted to a stop beside the stone wall that surrounded the estate the Wizard presently occupied. I'd parked along its northeast side, avoiding both the front and back entrances. Trying to take the Wizard by surprise might have been pointless, but this game had rules. The wall rose a good ten feet above the ground. Rapping my knuckles on the trunk, I told Pound to wish me luck, but I didn't catch his mumbled reply. Probably just as well.

Forming myself into a single stream of sand, I stretched my body upward in a maneuver I'd seen Mr. Fantastic do lots of times. The top of the wall was covered with broken glass and had a three-foot extension of barbed wire. But that wasn't all. Partially covered by the glass, a metallic strip gleamed in the moonlight. It was one of the Wizard's gizmos, some kind of high-tech motion sensor.

Okay, if going over the wall was out of the question, I'd just have to go through it.

Spreading myself paper thin, I plastered myself against the side of the wall, looking for weaknesses. I finally found a tiny crack in the mortar that held a few stones in place. It wasn't a lot wider than a pencil point, but more than enough space for a grain of sand. Pass enough grains through, and you had a Sandman.

Assuming that the Wizard would have a little bit more than a measly stone wall protecting him, I took the shape of a giant sandsnake and slithered across the big lawn toward the house. About two hundred yards separated me from the mansion itself.

After about ten feet, I noticed a thin copper filament that ran across the ground and connected two of the trees in the lawn. Talk about luck! I'd only seen it because of my snake's-eye-view.

I was still congratulating myself on my keen powers of observation when a jolt of electricity suddenly ran through me. I hit the ground in a ball of dizziness and nausea. A half dozen men sprang from behind the trees. They were all wearing night goggles and carrying funny-looking weapons which looked like the Wizard's handiwork.

"Hit him again!" someone shouted. "He's still moving!"

The lead man triggered his blaster. Agony slammed into me like a tidal wave. My body corkscrewed like it had been tossed on a hot spit. It felt like being charbroiled from the inside out.

Rough hands ripped at me, yanking me to my feet. Feet? Sandsnakes don't have feet! It took a few seconds to realize that I'd reverted to human form. Even as I wrapped myself around that idea, I was manhandled across the lawn and into the mansion. Careening through a side entrance, I ricocheted off a few walls until I found a nice hard floor to cuddle up on.

I would have loved a quick nap, but this annoying foot chose that moment to introduce itself to my face. Persistent little devil, that foot. It moved to my ribs, greeting them enthusiastically, making me further appreciate the distinctive advantages of sand over bones.

"That is quite enough."

"He deserves it for what he done to me. I'm gonna kill him!"

"Please, Mr. Pound," the Wizard said in a low voice. "That honor is mine."

I rolled to my side so that I could look up. I expected to see the Wizard. Pound was a surprise. His face and hair, stained with oil and grease, was leaking sweat like a rusted steam pipe. Kicking a helpless man must require a lot more effort than I would have thought.

"Love what you've done with your hair, Pound," I said.

He made a move toward me, as if to resume soccer practice, but the Wizard cut him a look that could have melted steel.

Dressed in a suit the color of fresh cream, with a mocha shirt, and a chocolate fudge tie, the Wizard looked like a fancy cup of coffee. He had a dopey grin on his face—he was obviously enjoying himself. Hey, it's not every day you get to link up with an old teammate.

"Mr. Pound is rather annoyed with you, William. I would not continue to antagonize him."

"Some guys just can't take a compliment." I knew he wanted me to ask how Pound had gotten out of the trunk, but I merely smiled.

The silence lengthened.

"In case you are interested, Pound's car and his right shoe were equipped with homing beacons." The Wizard said, irritation creeping into his tone. "Your efforts to catch me unawares were quite comical."

"I ain't no Seinfeld, but I've always been good for a few laughs."

The Wizard's military wannabes were standing behind me. We were in some kind of game room. A pool table lounged in a distant corner, and the heads of dead animals stared down at me from the walls. I figured that the next spot on the wall already had my name on it.

"This place come furnished?"

"An odd question, William, when I am sure you have so many others on your mind."

"Actually, I am curious about one thing."

Triumph flared in the Wizard's eyes, filling them with a smile which never quite reached his mouth. "What is that?"

"You catch the final score on the Jets game?"

Like an old circus horse counting out his numbers on the ground, Pound put his foot back to work on my chest. Just my luck, a high scoring game!

As he moved into double digits, Pound began to lose enthusiasm, or maybe he was just losing count, either way the Wizard had grown bored.

"Get the woman, Pound."

Pound aimed a final, half-hearted swipe at my face, and headed toward a staircase that stood outside the room's doorway. The Wizard glanced meaningfully in my direction, and two of his goons pulled me into a standing position.

"I am very disappointed with you, William."

"You and my mother both," I said. "What's the deal with the lady, Wizard? I'm the one you want. You don't care about Silver Sable. Why didn't you just come after me?"

"An example needed to be made, William." At last, the smile had finally reached his lips. "You cannot be permitted to switch loyalties from me to her without the appropriate consequences. As a former associate, your actions reflect on me. Have you no idea how foolish I appear because you have taken on this role of common mercenary?"

"C'mon, man! Nobody holds you responsible 'cause I ditched out on crime."

"Wrong, William! Very wrong!" I swear I could almost see the raging beast that had twisted a millionaire brain boy into a criminal genius. No wonder the spandex set couldn't keep the Wizard down. Nobody could ever cage or crush a creature like that. He'd always be back.

As this dawned on me, I suddenly stopped breathing.

The Wizard began to laugh.

"This moment, William," he managed to gasp out. "This single moment has justified all the time and expense devoted to the entire enterprise."

I wanted to smack him down with a witty comeback, but I couldn't. He was right. He had already gotten all he needed from me.

I was still trying to figure out what I should do next, when the room suddenly exploded with gunshots.

Reacting instinctively, I yanked at the two men who were holding my arms, bringing their heads together with a satisfying crack. Everybody else in the room, including the Wizard, was diving for cover.

"This way, Sandman!" Silver Sable shouted as she popped another round into the room.

I dove through the doorway, joining her in the hall. A handful of the Wizard's lowlifes were scrambling into rooms to our right, and I could hear footsteps approaching from the front entrance. The left seemed clear, so we raced for the sliding glass door at the end of the hall, hoping it led to an outdoor porch.

"I thought I told you not to get involved."

"Nice to see you, too," I said. "If that's Pound's gun, you'd better check it for sand."

She roasted me with a quick glance as she threw the door open. A gust of warm air rose in greeting. I had to admire the Wizard's sense of style: the mansion came with its own indoor pool. A large mural, full of forest greenery, was painted along the walls, but I would have preferred a window or two. The only exit was a stairwell to the basement.

Under normal circumstances, a basement was a bad place to be cornered, but we didn't have much choice.

"You shouldn't have come," Silver said as we jostled downward. "You've only complicated the situation."

"Oh, sure! I suppose you had everything under control."

"You didn't honestly believe that I fell for the old switch-the-chauffeur ploy? I had gotten a tip that the Wizard was going to try to use me to reach you." A slight smile danced across her lips. "A Wild Pack strike team has been on my tail for the past two weeks. They were awaiting my signal when you bumbled on the scene."

"Why am I the last to know?"

"The Wizard wouldn't have taken the bait if he'd noticed *you* looking over your shoulder," she smirked. "And, naturally, I didn't want to risk the reward posted on him."

The basement consisted of a single corridor which seemed to run the length of the house. Little storage rooms branched off the main walkway, but I was focused on the second set of stairs which lay dead ahead.

Unfortunately, a squad of his hardbodies had already come around the house to use that stairway to intercept us. They came armed with those special zappers that turned my insides earlier.

Having run out of options, Silver and I ducked into a utility room near the mansion's midpoint. An idea began to form when I saw the three gas burners that heated the joint.

"How long will the Pack wait for your signal?" I asked Silver.

"Too long," she said. "I'm down to my last bullets."

"Okay, I guess it's show time," I said as I shaped my arm into a large wrench. Unscrewing the gas main that fed the burners, I quickly molded myself into a concrete cylinder that stretched from the mouth of the pipe to the basement ceiling. I wasn't completely airtight, but I could still feel the gas pressure building within me. I snaked out a fist, and began ripping at the ceiling tiles, exposing the wood which served as the under structure for the mansion's first floor.

"Hurry it up," Silver said as she squeezed off her last shot. "We're out of time!"

I punched my fist through the floor, and was rewarded with a shout. A few of the Wizard's men had been left behind on the floor above. They immediately opened fire, supplying me with sparks aplenty for what I had in mind.

I became a living flame-thrower with an entire gas line to fuel me. Puffing more air through my chest, I aimed for the nearest windows. I wanted to light the outside sky with a massive flare. Instead, I ignited the draperies and furniture.

"What the hell are you doing up there?" Silver wanted to know.

"Losing the Wizard's security deposit," I replied as I turned my attention to the guys in the corridor. My flaming stream inspired them to reevaluate their employment contracts as they ran like hell.

The mansion's smoke detectors were shrieking like crazy by now. So were the Wizard's men. I figured a house this fancy had to have an alarm system tied directly to the local fire house.

It did, and the place was soon flooded with a mess of firefighters and cops, not to mention Silver's own Wild Pack. Though the locals were a little shocked to find so many alleged felons within their borders, the Wizard's men were all rounded up by the time we made it outside. Always the professional, Silver Sable immediately staked her claim for every penny posted on them.

Me, I did a quick head count, but only found one of the two I most wanted.

"The Wizard is long gone," Pound said. "He zapped outta here long before you made like the Human Torch."

"He say anything?"

"Nah," Pound sneered, as he was gently maneuvered into an awaiting police car. "But he was still laughing."

I almost laughed out loud myself. I still had things to resolve with Silver, but the Wizard was gone, and had no reason to return. Though it had cost him a gang, and who knows what else, he was now savoring a victory, instead of nursing a defeat.

Okay, maybe I hadn't been completely honest with my former partner. Maybe I shouldn't have held my breath, and tried to outsmart him.

Yeah, maybe I just should have played him straight.

But, hey, what's the fun in that?

Typhoid

WHO DO YOU WANT ME TO BE?

ANN NOCENTI

Illustration by Steve Lightle

SKRITCH. SKRITCH.

The Interviewer sits in a high, comfortable chair, making scratchy little notes on a legal pad.

"Why did you eat all those strawberries this morning?" he asks.

"Because *she's* allergic. That way if she tries to come out, she gets hives."

The woman slouches a few paces away on a shorter, hard metal chair. They are alone, the two of them, in an empty room, surrounded by four white walls.

The sharp pencil continues to make its lone, twitchy sound on the paper, like an insect busy with some irritating chore. The woman lets her eyes travel the length of her interrogator's body. These interview-types, she decides, are indistinguishable, and easily marked.

"You got any lead in that pencil of yours?" She speaks very slowly, every syllable emphasized as if with certain intent—but then again it could just be the sedatives. "If I wasn't handcuffed, I'd show you an ancient Druid finger technique that'd have you melting like an ice cube in hell—"

"Gotcha. You're the sex fiend." He begins to make another smug mark on the pad, but the pencil's tip snaps.

"Oooo. The good doctor gets excited while saying the word *sex*. Breaks his own pencil. Better make a note of it."

"Not everything is significant." Annoyed, he searches for another pencil.

"Unless it's longer than it is wide." The captive inches her squat metal chair forward, closer. "Come on, boss. I wanna pencil too." The chair legs scrape the floor. She kicks off a slipper, stretches out her leg and manages to just touch his ankle with one silky toe. He flinches.

"Stop that. Sit still. I'm immune to your tricks."

"Right, Sarge." The foot withdraws.

A fresh pencil is back. *Skritch skritch.*

"Now, as I was saying—today you're the compulsive seducer."

"Oh yeah? That's just what you want me to be. A little countertransference thing happening, Doc?"

"Wrong office for that."

"You don't know anything. You never leave these dull offices and square cells and interrogation rooms. Your world has all the dimension of a box. Tell me—which came first, the germ or the disease?"

"Excuse me, but I ask the questions here."

"Oh, just try and answer."

"Well, the—I guess I don't know."

"Ha. The answer is never clear. And it's always what you least suspect. It's the innocent, retarded, blind, deaf, wall-eyed fool that really runs the show. Ask her."

"I am asking her. You don't exist, except as a reflection in the mind of the others."

"What are we talking, quantum physics here? I exist, I don't exist. If I'm here, I can't be there. Either, or neither. Which is it? Am I the disease? Or am I the germ?"

"You're revealing a bit of knowledge there. You must read books—either that or you went to school." *Skritch skritch skritch.*

"Do you have to make all those grating little notes? You got all the personality of fingernails on a blackboard. And your conclusion is wrong, anyway. I learned particle physics from a TV movie I saw once. It was about a physicist that fell in love, but wasn't sure."

"I can't imagine you sitting still through an entire movie. It must have been—"

"—Mary? Yes. She's the one that watches all those soap operas. She's the idiot that needs TV fantasies. But if I didn't watch the movie, how do I know the plot?"

"Maybe you girls talk to each other."

"Now that would be impossible, wouldn't it, Professor?"

"Do you?"

"Do we what?"

"Talk to each other."

"No. Never. But then, I could be lying."

The interrogator nodded and repeated, "But then you could be lying."

"Well forget it. We don't have anything to talk about. We don't like the same things. We live in different movies."

"Oh really? Then tell me, is it just *you* that enjoys violence, or do the others enjoy a bit of blood as well?"

"Now why would I answer that, and invite complicity? You're all the same—stupid. Shrinks, cops, jailors, wardens, all the same. Stupid."

"And what would we do if we were smart?"

"You'd take advantage of hot willing flesh and how crazy it could make you."

"Stop that talk."

"Ooo, yes, Captain. Right away, Captain. You don't want me. You haven't been staring at my body, sneaking glances at my flesh. . . ."

The interrogator began to have trouble focusing on the captive's eyes. As if her eyes were a scrim on which a projected color went in and out of focus and several different beings peered out of those changling orbs in turn. At times, the eyes were certainly light grey, only to deepen the next moment to a red-brown.

"You know, I am here to help you. I am not one of your enemies—"

"Enemies! Real or imagined, Doctor? Wouldn't that be evidence of paranoia? Is the patient exhibiting a bipolar state with hallucinatory features?"

"Don't be ridiculous. You run from my every attempt to—"

"Uh-oh—I think it's a disassociative disorder, yes, she's one sick—"

"Please! Can we get back to—"

"Or perhaps she's in a psychogenic fugue state? No, I think perhaps she was just dropped on her head as a child. That's it, the old bounced baby syndrome!"

"You're impossible. Could I continue, please?"

"Why not?"

"Thank you. Now why don't you try answering one question honestly?"

"Like that game? Are we gonna play Truth or Dare? I'll take the dare."

"Okay. Dare to tell the truth."

"Right, Boss. One question."

"Are you aware that you have many personalities living in your head?"

"Sure. Who doesn't? Everybody disassociates. Hey, it's great. I mean, I got this one chick in me, this boring one, this Walker, she pays the bills, she does the banking, she does all that niggling stuff I can't be bothered with. Wouldn't you like a bill-paying robot all your own? And when we get in trouble? Why, there's always sweet innocent Mary to bail us out. She gets us our sympathy. She's the baby. I hate her, actually. She gets all the dreams. It's not fair, I never get to dream. But what the heck— she cooks, she cleans. I don't gotta do that. Mary is the closest to the pain, and the furthest from knowing why. She's blind, and her face is right up in it. Walker's the one that knows all. She's the Gatekeeper. Now if we *really* get in trouble, there's always Bloody to protect us. She doesn't care about all that inner life crap. She just keeps us alive."

"And you? What do you do?"

"Me? I get us laid. Guilt-free sex. All those slaves to do the dirty work and I just have fun fun fun. Tell me, wouldn't you like to be me?"

"It's still you doing the 'boring' things."

"Nah. Not to me it ain't. Ha. Bet I know what note you just scribbled down there now, Daddy-O. I can just imagine you using big lumbering cumbersome words like *compartmentalized* and *recidivism.* Taking notes is the stupidest thing I've ever seen."

"Oh, really? I'll read you one note. In the course of this interview you've called me Boss, Captain, Professor, Sarge, Doc, and Daddy-O. What do you think that means?"

"Nothing. It means nothing."

"By the way, look at your arm—strawberry hives, I believe?"

"Shut up! This is boring!" Her voice climbs an octave with each phrase. "You're not the one that's gotta go back to a dirty little cell for another twenty-four hours. Enough with the mind-game torture! Let's have some fun before I go die in that pit again."

On these last words she slithers off the steel chair and crawls across the last remaining white tiles that separate them, over the shadows criss-crossing the floor, shadows made by wire-mesh woven into the window glass. She *clanks* along with each crawl as the handcuffs *clink* against the tiles and the ball shackled to her feet *clunks* forward, until soon the captive is lying at the foot of the much more comfortable, quite a bit higher chair on which sits her interrogator, who hasn't stopped scribbling in his pad.

She slips his pencil out of his clenched fingers, pulls it out with her teeth and lets it drop to the floor. She licks the skin on the underside of his wrist, licks so softly it is a mere tickle that triggers involuntary shivers up his fleshy arm. She feels something drip on her and looks up to see it is sweat dripping from her interrogator's brow.

She smiles and whispers, "Gotcha. Aren't you supposed to
make me sweat?"

The door *clangs* open and in come two efficient men in crisp
pressed uniforms and shiny shoes, armed with a gun and hypodermic each.

The woman on the floor looks up at her interrogator. "Did
you press the alarm button before my tongue touched your flesh
or did you wait to get a little taste first? Better make a note of it,
Boss."

"Take her away."

The guards lift her from the floor, trying not to look at her
radiant, muscular beauty that manages to make itself known even
through the rather dumpy white institutional smock.

"Till tomorrow, Lover." She tosses her beautiful head of kinky
red hair, and her face flickers with mercurial fluidity from seductive to sly to cruel to innocent and back in the time it takes
for you to catch your breath upon seeing her.

She turns back once as they drag her out of the room. "Hey,
Doc." She waits till their eyes meet. "Good thing you buzzed for
help. My next move would have buried your own needle-sharp
pencil point deep in your throat. *Skritch skritch,* sweetheart."

She spits the pencil point out of her mouth, and when it hits
him in the face she shatters the room with a laugh of superior
madness it would take a lifetime to understand.

The door clangs shut and the silence that follows is oppressive,
but the interrogator has already unbolted the steel frame window, and with head thrust outside is gasping for clean, clear air.

White knuckles, sweaty brows, twitching fingers, shifty eyes marked
the crowd. The men went back and back again to refill their
liquor jugs, the children kicked and teased the donkeys, the dogs
stole bits of meat, the women fluttered in corners and whispered.

The rubber man already tied his limbs in knots, the snake lady
had her neck coiled in cool scales, the fire-eater ate until his
throat glowed, the strong man crushed boards, bricks, and rocks,
the magician pulled a frog out of the town drunk's ear, the fat
lady sang hours ago, and the crowd was more than ready.

For this year's carnival they had been promised something extra, and they wanted it. The ones who knew what was coming moved closer to the exits. Just when it seemed the crowd was going to rip it down themselves, the white tent opened.

Expecting something magnificent, at first there were groans of complaint when the dull-eyed, tattered donkey clomped out of the tent flap. It stood, skin shivering in waves to rid its balding hide of the flies. Something behind the beast must have kicked it, for it lurched forward. A collective sigh escaped the lips of everyone who was still half-conscious as it was revealed the donkey pulled a platform on which stood a white-draped form that was obviously female.

As soon as the donkey was out of the tent and in the center of the yard, the crowd closed around the animal in a ring of bodies. A second donkey was hitched to the other side of the platform, with a sideways rig. The donkeys began to walk in a circle, causing the platform to spin.

The white-draped figure stood unnaturally still through all the preparations. Then, finally, the crowd selected a couple of men, two old ranchers that reluctantly allowed themselves to be shoved forward. They stood awkwardly looking at the white statuesque form, unsure what to do. Something about it felt blasphemous, as if they stood before an altar about to kick over a statue of the Virgin.

They began to grin, two men who probably didn't have ten teeth left between them. Then came the cry: "Do it!" followed by more jeers and hoots. One held the donkey still a moment, as the other old coot reached out and took the hem of the sheet and yanked.

She was beautiful, and she wasn't. She was covered from toe to brow in painted designs that, rather than conceal her nakedness, seemed to reveal it all the more. Some images were exquisite as if drawn off a master's brush, others so crude and brutally ugly they made one hate the hand that committed the image.

The donkeys began to walk again. She spun on her pedestal, and for a while no one said anything, but it was a silence that was swollen in sighs and gasps as hundreds of eyes stared at the pictures on her flesh.

Thorns climbed her legs, a gigantic eye covered her stomach, a satyr drawn in stars formed a constellation across her back. In one open palm was fire, covering the other clenched fist was a howling dragon, a dagger pierced her neck, the blood so realistic it flowed, a nine-legged spider spun a web between her breasts, the crown of thorns etched across her brow dripped painted black drops into her eyes, her spine was a snake that everyone later swore was real and slithering, each toe was cupped in a scarab of a different color. Scattered amongst the images were the brands of cow ranches—Lazy Z, Triple R, Crooked L.

Her mouth was superimposed with a fish so that when she parted her lips as if to scream, it was the fish's flesh that seemed to split open into a gash ripped by an invisible hook, but no sound escaped her lips and she closed them again quickly.

Somewhere towards the back a woman wailed and swooned as she recognized the signature hand of her husband in a face he always doodled on napkins when they ate out—and there it was on this painted woman's flesh. Another woman recognized her husband's cow brand stamped on the woman's white thigh. A small boy, looking at the painted toes, thought of the shoes that lined his mother's closet and began to cry. A teenage girl became transfixed on the shells that covered one arm and moaned when she remembered she had never seen the sea. No one noticed the ninety-one-year-old blacksmith clutch his cane till his knuckles were white, while his other hand seized his shirt at his chest. He saw the links of the forged chain that encircled one of her delicate ankles, and he died as the image gripped his heart.

"Oh . . . I . . . where am I? Some water please. No? Oh, I feel faint . . ."

"I want to talk to one of the others."

The timid woman sits scared in the metal chair, and withdraws into herself for just a few seconds before allowing something else out. Her skin seems to shimmy like a horse's as every limb relaxes, the knees that were held so tightly together part, one foot kicks off a shoe, one hand unbuttons the collar that held the shirt shut to her neck, the lips and eyes twist slightly, playfully, she stretches and moans and the voice that emerges drips with an ornery passion.

"Finally! Don't you get bored talking to that twit? Come here, you're not bad, you'll do."

"Shut up. I've had enough of you. I said I want one of the others."

The eyes look hurt for just a heartbeat before they lose all their softness and narrow, the skin draws tighter, harder, the body stiffens upright, the jaw squares, the hands clench into fists, the voice that finally speaks is an octave lower than before.

"What do you want?"

"To talk to you."

"Screw talk. I'm at war."

"What are you fighting?"

"Everyone and everybody that so much as touches any woman anywhere."

The painted woman's eyelids had been twitching for a few minutes. The crowd was mesmerized, staring and circling the spinning figure. Only one small girl noticed the woman's fluttering eyelids, saw the fingers begin to jerk. When the painted woman leaped, it happened so fast some later said they were sure she just plain exploded.

The mailman who had painted her palm with fire got his face ground into the dirt. The pig farmer who had scrawled the spider-web ended up with most of his teeth somewhere in the back of his throat. Blood shot up in arcs and splattered the faces of those that didn't run fast enough, stomachs were clenched into knots for hours after the foot that kicked them was long gone, necks jerked, making cracking sounds like the report of gunshot, a whole row of spectators went down when something long and hard slammed them all in the shins. No one remembered seeing her, just feeling the wind from the wake of her blows.

Her eyes open on a spinning ceiling fan. She looks slowly around a room she does not recognize. She feels clothes on her body but she doesn't believe they are hers. Certainly she wouldn't have bought a red silk dress. Her skin feels raw, as if it has been scrubbed with steel wool. She gets out of the bed, and nearly cuts her foot on a piece of broken glass. She sees the champagne stand in the corner of the room, the metal bucket sweating, the bottle gone. She puts on the red shoes she finds under the bed but cannot walk in such high heels. She snaps off the spikes, and tries again.

In the hotel lobby, she waits for the desk clerk to turn around so she can sneak a look at the book to see who was in room 402 last night. A Mr. and Mrs. Sally Maker. No one she knows.

Soon she is in a diner, paying for her coffee with her last dollar, searching the pocketbook she'd found in her hotel room. She finds a scrap of paper on which are carefully noted times and descriptions such as: "2:15. Left building. Returned 3:30, with six-pack." Surveillance notes. She finds a ring with a half-dozen keys, one of which is large and strange with a number on it and the letters USPS.

"Excuse me, Miss?"

"More coffee?" assumes the counter girl, as she swaggers over with the steaming pot.

"No, I was just wondering if you've ever seen a key like this before."

The girl held the brass key up to the light.

"Sure. It's for a post office box."

The third post office is a score. Her feet feel deformed by the heelless shoes, her pride aches from the sleazy comments she had to endure while hitch-hiking town to town in the tight red dress that was now ripped in three places and blackened with truck grease. Inside the post box is a note.

"Don't panic. Your name is Mary Walker. Go to 38 South Front Street, first floor. Check the files under M."

Soon Mary Walker is staring up at a sign with her name on it, followed by the phrase: "Private Investigator." By now she has thrown away the shoes, and is barefoot. She leans against the door. *This is not familiar. Is this who I am?*

She tries to imagine herself as a sleuth, but other images come—she sees herself on a rooftop with a sword, she is on a street corner in fishnet stockings, she is covered in paint, she is within four white walls. . . . She gags and shivers and tries to block any more of these obviously false, delusional visions. They aren't her, they are more likely movies she's seen.

Realizing she must look crazy, she pulls herself together—the last thing she needs is to get arrested for vagrancy or something worse. She looks up and down the block cautiously. There is only one person nearby, a young Asian deeply engrossed in a newspaper, leaning on a pole. Hopefully he didn't notice her strange behavior and filthy dress. *Hmmm, he's kind of handsome,* she thinks, *a little diversion might be—*

A second later she catches her breath in repugnance at her own thoughts. *I must be exhausted,* she decides.

One of the keys on her ring fits the lock. As soon as she is in what looks like an ordinary, low-budget office, she runs to the file cabinet and riffles through drawers till she finds a folder marked "M." Inside is a pair of black stockings, and a sheaf of papers burnt just to the point of being unreadable. The blackened paper flakes apart, smears her fingers, the ashes flutter to the floor. Only when the burnt pages become inky and runny does she realize she is crying. No. No crying. She obeys the voice inside that orders her to buck up. Her eyes dry, her vision clears.

She looks up and sees a cork board, on which scrawled notes in various handwritings are stabbed to the wall with nails and pins and darts.

An hour later, and the office has been picked over to reveal all it has to offer. Her name must surely be Mary Walker. She is a private investigator, who has not taken in her mail or answered her messages for three days. Her last appointment was with a new client whom she only noted as Mr. K. She finds a lease on an apartment, and checks a map to find it is located just a few blocks away.

She locks the door to "her" office, looking down at her bare feet. She notices she still wears stockings, which are in shreds. She slips the stockings off but suddenly remembers she is standing in the street, and glances around. Just that same Asian man, still engrossed in his newspaper. She stuffs the stockings in her bag, and heads down the block. She walks by him casually, glancing at the headline of his newspaper—something about a water main break.

Just as she gets through the door to her supposed apartment, she pauses. *That newspaper,* she remembers. *That headline. That water main broke last week. So he's a guy reading an old paper, so what?* she thinks, as the walls begin to quake and lose focus and she collapses to the floor, falling deeply unconscious.

He runs his hands over her things. He flips through her books, opens her drawers, pulls things out, sniffs her clothes. He sits down by her, and touches her. He feels the dirty red silk between his fingers. He runs his hand over her cheek, his fingers tangle in her hair.

She wakes up, innocent and afraid. "Who are you?" she asks.

He just stares at her. He remains strangely silent. She begins to cry. "Who am I?" she moans.

His eyes flicker at this. He gets up, goes into the kitchen and runs hot water over a towel. She cries quietly on the floor, repeating, "Who am I? Who am I?"

He returns with the cloth, and begins to wash the dirt off her hands. At first she flinches, but he gives her such a gentle look she relaxes. Finally, he answers her.

"I'm sorry. I don't know who you are," he says. "I saw you on the street, you looked a mess. You had no shoes. You looked beat up. You took off your stockings right in the street. I tried not to stare, but—I started to wonder about you. To worry. I followed to make sure you were okay. Then you left your front door open. At first I was just going to shut and lock it and leave, but I saw you lying on the floor. I've been sitting here waiting for you to wake up."

She cries harder. "Thank you," she manages to say.

"Don't talk. I'm going to run a nice warm bath for you. You don't have much in your kitchen, but I can do wonders with what you've got. I'll make you a soup that'll fix you right up."

"What's your name?"

"Kobu. My name is Kobu."

A few hours later, cleaned, nourished, even happy, Mary Walker sits before a fire and gazes at the delicate hands of her savior.

He had been talking about himself. "So when I left that job I decided to come back East where at least I knew people."

"Did you ever make it back to Japan?"

"No. My poor grandmother died before I could get it together."

"I'm sorry, Kobu."

"Don't be. It was sad at first, but now I feel kind of liberated to have not a relative left, to be all alone. Oh, god, I'm sorry."

"No, it's okay. If it wasn't for your wonderful kindness towards me I'd be sitting in this apartment knowing little more than my name."

"Well, you sure are a good sleuth. It must really be your profession, you tracked yourself down so fast."

"I can hardly believe it. Well, first thing in the morning, I'm going in to work, and my first case will be myself."

"And at the end of that day, could I take you to dinner?"

"That would be wonderful. But—"

"What's the matter, Mary?"

"I just want to move slowly, in case—"

"Hey, don't worry about me. I'm crazy about you, but I'd settle for 'just friends' if your sleuthing reveals a boyfriend."

"Thank you Kobu. I hope with all my heart that I discover I am—free."

Power play. Clip wire. Country cult. Check Feds. Olive Bridge. Lottery? Two-point watch. Sugartrap.

The words and phrases cover the desk of Mary Walker, Private Eye. She plays with them, shifting order, juxtaposing, searching for sense. Obviously notes and clues to cases, the meanings they are supposed to trigger in her mind are not coming. She feels stupid, and begins to wonder if besides her amnesia, she somehow hit her head and is now brain-damaged.

She suddenly has an idea—maybe these are the cases of some other detective? The handwriting on the notes is not the same—it reveals two, even three different people. Excited, she begins to reorder the notes with this theory in mind. She ends up with four piles, four distinct handwriting styles. That's it. Other detectives share this office. They must be out on cases. That would explain the other oddities she found around the office—like the bottle of liquor when she's pretty sure she doesn't drink. Some of the clothes in the closet were things she'd never wear.

She sighs with relief, and then gasps, looking back at the piles. A bold, sexy script. A rushed, ugly scrawl. A flowery, sweet script. A simple, plain handwriting. Which one is *she?* She picks up a pen, and timidly writes "Mary Walker" on a sheet of paper. It's flowing and sweet. She picks up that stack and sets it aside. She goes to the file cabinet and begins to pull out the files with the matching handwriting. Her cases. But before she gets far, there is a knock at the door. The sound triggers a shift in her brain, and it is a different Mary Walker that rises to answer the door.

Her stockings are a coal grey, that is the first thing Mary notices. The mauve suit reminds her of Chanel, and the pearl details clinch the whisper of expensive taste.

"Hello? Detective Walker?"

"Yes."

"Is it a good time?"

"Sure, come in. You can sit there."

"I've—never done this before." The woman smiles nervously. "I bet you hear that line every day."

"I've heard it before, I admit. But you'd be surprised—we do have our chronics." Mary pulls up a second chair and sits down with a clipboard and yellow pad in her lap.

"Chronics?" The woman sits down too, crossing her legs neatly, tugging slightly at the skirt hem, more a mannerism than a modesty.

"People who get hooked on us. They want their wife followed, they think their kid's on drugs, they check up on their neighbors, every six months or so they come up with another scenario that needs a snoop."

"Oh my. They get hooked on surveillance."

"It's a control thing, or else a voyeuristic fetish."

"Do you ever say no?"

"Sometimes. But snooping *is* the bread and butter of a detective. Speaking of which, whenever you're ready . . ."

Mary searches the desk, finds a pencil, and stabs it briefly in the electric sharpener.

"Well, I—God, where do I start?"

"Your name?"

"Of course. Victoria Keane. It's my husband that I want—"

"Followed?" Mary scribbles on the pad, and tilts it up slightly when she notices Victoria's eyes on her notes.

"Not exactly. His name is Joseph, and he—" The woman stands up so abruptly she surprises even herself. "I can't do this. I'm sorry I wasted your time."

Mary stays silent until the woman reaches the door. She waits till she sees the hand pause on the doorknob a beat too long.

"You don't want to leave. Come back here and sit down."

"But, what I wanted to ask you to do is impossible. I see that now. I can't even say the words."

"He beats you and you can't take it anymore. There, I said it for you."

Victoria Keane leans against the door. "How did you—?"

"I'm sorry to be so blunt, but you're a type. I see it over and

over. The dark stockings, the high collar shirt, a few telltale gestures, a flinch here, a hesitation there. It's nothing anyone can't
learn from watching, say, children in a schoolyard. Or dogs in a
pound. Abuse shows.''

Victoria Keane walks slowly back to the chair and sits down.

"Details," says Mary. "Where he works, routes he takes, habits,
everything. We'll build a case that will get him out of your life
for good.''

"Yes." Victoria's head hung like a child's. Gone was the poise,
the breeding, the artifice of gestures. "But I still don't think you
understand. There's more. What I want may require someone—
tougher."

Mary's pencil tip snaps halfway through the word she scribbles.
"That's odd," she says, pausing strangely. "I just had a *déjà vu*."

Victoria looks at the woman across from her and notices a
slight change in her manner. It is the client's turn to scrutinize.
"People snap the lead in their pencils all the time."

"Of course, you're right." Mary Walker seems beside herself
for a moment, but shakes off the feeling. Her eyes narrow, and
when she speaks again her jaw is harder set.

"A man's job you say?"

"I want him scared. I want him to know—what it feels like."

"Well, let's get to work, Mrs. Keane. I need the particulars.
They say the devil's work is in the details."

"I believe, Detective Walker, that the quote is: 'God is in the
details'.''

"Not this time."

He can't believe his luck. That this woman, this goddess, wants
him, is just unbelievable. They're in the bar parking lot, heading
towards his Porsche. He knows she'll like the speed of his car.
He can't wait to see her reclining in the black leather seat. One
thing, though, he can't reconcile: The fact that she is leaving
with him, and the way she walks. The sweet, demure girl he had
met earlier in the evening, with the broken-down car, on her way
to see her sick mother—that girl seemed to be gone. Granted,
they'd knocked back a few, at her insistence, he recalled. But
still. She had seemed so positively—virginal. And now she struts
ahead of him like a five-hundred-dollar whore. Well, he managed
to slip away and call the wife with the usual "meeting went later

than expected" excuse. He was pretty sure he covered up how drunk he was, but he was still shocked when his wife didn't protest a whit.

Half lost in these thoughts, even Joseph Keane, wife beater, financial embezzler, all-round cad, even he is shocked at the speed with which her hands undo his shirt, the skill with which she touches him. And then, when she grabs a handful of his hair by the roots and tugs—he knows he has what the boys refer to as a "player."

They lean against the cool car metal, and he allows her to work through his hair, her tugs a massage just this side of pain. When he senses she is ready, he yanks her head back and gives her a little slap across the cheek. When she smiles, he clenches her throat, just hard enough to steal her breath away.

She chokes a bit and laughs, coming back at him with the sexiest of bites, followed by another that rips a chunk of his flesh out and spurts good red blood down his four-hundred dollar Armani shirt.

Now he is screaming, and he can no longer see her but feels her blows methodically circling his body until every inch of his flesh has been rammed, kicked, punched, clawed. He manages to get his car door open, and—crippled, bleeding—he somehow flings himself in. She tosses something into the car that hits his leg and bounces under the car seat. As he starts the car and peels out, burning, spitting gravel, he feels lucky that she spared his hands, eyes, and feet—he can still drive. He takes the car up to ninety in ten seconds.

"Heading south on Route 9W, black Porsche, license number MT9-ZL4, white male, extremely dangerous, just beat up two bouncers, intoxicated, speeding, armed, paranoiac." Mary hangs up the CB radio and smiles, smoothing out her only slightly wrinkled dress, and cocks her head to listen for the coming sirens. She likes that last touch, the gun with one bullet missing, the match to be found easily in a corpse down the road.

"And do you believe your methods are ethical?"

"Absolutely."

"The courts would have handled it. Physical violence is—"

"I am only hypothesizing. I know nothing of actual beatings. I only theorize that the ancient eye-for-an-eye tradition has certain uses that could not only be called ethical, but biblical in their judgment."

"And you? Who does that make you?" The interrogator waits for the woman sitting rigid in the chair to answer. Instead, she smiles.

The windows begin to rattle as if a storm were rising outside. The interrogator is not alarmed until the table between them also began to vibrate.

"My god, what is it, an earthquake?"

The woman remains strangely calm, smiling wider, as the rattling gets louder. The door is flung open and a few bewildered policemen enter, looking around the room for the source of the rattling and vibrating, but can see nothing. The woman smiles at the glinting police badges, and decides their edges would be quite sharp. Suddenly the interrogator's extra pencil is flying through the air. It spikes into his own hand, a pretty arc of blood spurting as he screams.

"Interesting phenomenon," says the woman as she moves on to rip the officers' badges off their chests. "Better make a note of it."

They are champagne silly. Laughing, they entwine arms before sipping, lips reaching for the other's glass, the light frothy liquid spilling into their mouths.

"To my sweetheart's success as a sleuth!" says Kobu, almost earnest.

"To my sweetheart's success as my sweetheart!" giggles Mary.

"These past weeks, darling, have been so much fun. Just when I thought life to be a lonely endless desert, you appear like a mirage."

"Am I just a mirage?"

"No!"

"I'm scared, Kobu. I've never put my trust in anyone so completely."

"Don't be scared. I'll take care of you for as long as you allow me to. Just don't disappear on me again! Two whole days—I was so worried."

"It's funny, I must have been so caught up in work I forgot to call. I don't remember going anywhere...."

"Don't worry, sweetheart. Your memories will all come when you need them to."

"But what about those other—things? The things I've been finding here and in the office? Like that sword. What was I doing with a sword? And that freezer full of steaks—I don't even eat meat! What if I find out who I truly am, and that person is somehow—ugly? And why have none of the other detectives shown up for work or even so much as called? Some of the cases they work on, I've found evidence of methods that were not exactly legal."

"Hush. If your partners are ugly human beings, when they make their appearances we will simply ask them to find a new office. I'll do it if you're scared."

Mary sinks into Kobu's arms. "Thank you so much." They kiss, and slide back onto the couch in an embrace that knocks the champagne bottle right over.

"Oh, no!" Mary grabs the bottle but it is too late, they are soaked. They laugh, and Mary jumps up.

"I'll go find a towel."

She heads into the other room, and digs around in a chest of drawers. The sheets and towels she finds are so pretty, she doesn't want to ruin them. *There must be a old rag somewhere.*

She digs around under the sink cabinet, and pulls out the soiled white sheet and it falls open before her. There are greasy smeared images all over it, as if rubbed off another surface. An eye. A cow-brand. A nine-legged spider. A bloody dagger.

Mary puts the sheet up to her face and the smells of animals and fire, of paint and sweat, fill her mind until she is back there again, at that horrible carnival. She is being painted by a dozen drunken hands. Men, groping over her body. The memories flow in backwards. She remembers an exchange of money, a lottery of sorts, as each man in the town is responsible each year in turn with finding a new victim, a new woman. Some kind of backwater, inbred, distorted ritual that every year needs a sacrifice, a painted woman. . . .

A painted woman. She is the painted woman. She remembers a hotel bathroom. She remembers the images on her skin being scrubbed off and swirling down the drain. And then the last image falls into place. The man who sought her out, chose her and sold her into the lottery. The face of Kobu.

Kobu is pouring the rest of the bottle, what hadn't spilt, into their glasses, when he hears her enter the room. He smiles and looks lovingly over at her, and then he sees she is wrapped in that sheet. He sees her face.

"Oh, God."

"Why? Why did you sell me into such degradation. For money?"

"I—When I met you in that bar, you were wild, you were game, you wanted it. It was only later that I realized what I had done. That part of you wanted it, and part of you—"

She doesn't let him finish. She punches him in the jaw, surprised at how violently his head jerks.

"No! It was all your idea, Mary! You were a different girl, you said you wanted to avenge the women, show those men a lesson!"

She begins to beat him as she has beaten so many, but the brutal side of her, the robot that usually does the methodical punching, that side is not taking control, it has abandoned her, is leaving it up to her to beat this man before her.

"Mary, don't! Listen to me—"

She throws him across the room. He hits the wall and something cracks as he slides to the floor, holding his arm and wincing. He sinks down, ear to the wall, and can hear movement behind the wall. People. In the apartment next door. Calling the police. The blood pounding at his temples deafens him to any more. The pain tells him to give in, to pass out, but he knows if he quits talking he is a dead man.

"I told you about the lottery, the ritual, you begged me to let you do it!"

He tries to get up, and receives a kick to his gut, but the kick is less enthusiastic this time.

"I love you, Mary! Can't you see? Maybe we're both ugly, we both do ugly things, but that doesn't change the fact that we love each other! What matters, that or a past you barely remember?"

She kicks him again, but not very hard. Her head is tilted, she is listening, waiting for something she just senses to get louder, and then it does. Sirens.

"You said you were game for anything, Mary. You were wild, like you are now, I didn't know—"

She kicks him in the mouth to shut him up.

"Go away," she says. She knows she must run. Run before the

men get here with their knockout hypodermics and handcuffs and straps and questions.

"But I love you . . ." he spills the sounds out feebly through blood, through loose teeth.

"That's an ugly word. You go away now. I can't love you. You've seen me."

"I've what? Seen what, Mary?"

"Me. You've seen me. Once that happens, it's all over."

TRAPS

KEN GROBE

Illustration by Bob McLeod

PETER KNEW HE was getting old once he realized two things: He couldn't take a shot to the head anymore without his helmet on, and he needed eight hours of sleep a night in order to function. Today he'd have to make due with six. He sneezed and hoped it wasn't a cold he felt coming on again. He'd felt stupid and irresponsible. *Bad enough I stayed up until two-thirty to watch Morrie . . . but then flying until four! What was I thinking?*

Peter threw the covers off knowing that he had to get in four hours of work before the hour-and-a-half drive to the product meeting at Morrie's office in L.A. *No time to shower or eat,* Peter thought dejectedly. But he did shave the dark stubble that had arisen around where he trimmed his blonde beard and mustache—*no point in taking the risk of someone seeing dark stubble on my face, after all.* Then he put on a small pot of coffee and sat down to work.

What followed was several hours of tinkering, testing, brow-furrowing, and, occasionally, success. The principles for the products were similar to those of the weapons he had created for his criminal work not so long ago. The formula for Glu-On came from the multi-polymer base solution he created for all his glues. Glu-Off was based on a universal glue solvent he had invented for the Avengers years ago to counter Baron Zemo's Adhesive X. And the prototype glue applicator—which he and everybody else at KalCo had nicknamed "the gun"—was a plastic-and-springs version of his ever-faithful paste-gun. As with all the products he created for KalCo, the hard part was "dumbing down" his mechanical genius to make a consumer-level product.

Even though his pastes had led him to years of hardship, he took pride in his creations. He knew his paste formulas more intimately than anyone. Alone in his house on the edge of the San Bernadino desert, Peter strove to take compounds he once used to smother Spider-Man and the Human Torch into unconsciousness and modify them to fit government safety regulations. He tried not to take offense at the thought of his mighty formulas being utilized to put together coffee cups or to apply fake fingernails.

He was soldering together the gun's orifice-shaping control when the phone rang. Peter let the machine pick it up and listened to the message.

"Uh . . . hey, Mister Reed, this is Roman, the line manager over at Stevens. Just so you know, we can't hold no assembly line time for you past the fourteenth. So try to get us the prototype and the plans by then and we can start crankin' on that glue gun, a'right? Thanks. Oh, yeah—say hey to Morrie for me. Bye."

Peter smirked. Everyone knew Morrie Kalman. Most people identified him as the spunky old pitchman from *Fantastic Discoveries*. Others knew him as a shrewd businessman who started with wholesale ladies' undergarments on New York's Lower East Side and ended up moving to L.A. to become a minor mogul in the burgeoning field of mail-order convenience products. And to Peter? Well Peter couldn't let anyone get too close, for fear that they'd blow his cover. But he considered Morrie as good a friend as he'd ever had, even since before he became Paste Pot Pete. Morrie took care of Peter; he always made sure that Peter had his say at product meetings, always made sure that Peter was taking care of himself, always trusted Peter implicitly.

He continued to solder. Peter hated deadlines. But, he calculated, he should be able to finish the prototype glue gun and get it over to Stevens Manufacturing in plenty of time for the fourteenth. He considered breaking for lunch. He blew his nose and kept working.

The answering machine clicked on to receive another call. The message began with a heavy sigh. A woman's sigh. Peter recognized it and turned off the soldering iron, intently listening to her voice.

"Peter, it's Kim."

Kim. Peter's mind fairly reeled with thoughts of this woman. Kim Ryan was Morrie's personal assistant, and Peter was entranced by her. An energetic thirty-year-old dynamo, Kim saw to every bit of business on Morrie's agenda, did occasional commercial voiceovers on the side, and still managed to take night courses to get her psychology degree. When Peter first met this slim bottle-blonde with the green eyes and petite features, he fell in love with her almost immediately. They even went out on several dates, hitting it off quite well. But then she started asking questions about his life, and he stopped seeing her immediately. He still cursed himself, both for pushing her away, and for letting her get that close in the first place. To this day he wondered what she thought of him for breaking it off so hastily, without explanation. Maybe he would find out now.

"Look, Morrie fell and broke his hip. They're admitting him at Cedars right now and he wants you to come see him. Would you—"

The message was still going as Peter pulled out of the driveway. Kim always left long messages.

Don't even think of going over the speed limit, Peter cautioned himself as he tooled up the 708 freeway towards West Los Angeles's Cedars-Sinai Hospital. He looked at the car clock and made a face. *Damn. It'll take me another hour to get there.* He tried to stay calm. The last thing he needed was to get in an accident and have some insurance company try to run a background check on the nonexistant driving history of "Peter Reed." So he sat back, flipped to a classical music station, and tried to cheer himself up by remembering how he'd wound up in California in the first place.

He'd come a long way from his first misspent attempts at the straight life. Back then, money was always the big problem. The pittance he made from his remaining glue patents barely paid the rent on a dingy apartment in the worst neighborhood in Brooklyn. He'd fallen into debt and found himself dodging loan sharks on a regular basis.

Finding a job proved impossible: Nobody but *nobody* would hire a former super-villain. Chemical companies and research labs refused to associate themselves with him. Store owners didn't trust him. Even his old teammate, the now-reformed Sandman, tried to help him out—but Peter didn't like to think about that situation.

Each day, Peter tried to find a reason to go on living, failed, and decided to go on anyway. More than once, he stared into his shaving mirror and considered using the razor to slit his throat. He practically became a shut-in, leaving his dingy room in the resident hotel only to shop, see his parole officer, or catch the occasional movie. He communicated with other people only though his computer, which he managed to wire for free access to the Internet.

It was on the Internet that Peter Petruski found his new life.

He had come across an online service called BizNet, which provided information and support for small businesses. Upon discovering it, Peter spent hours on BizNet, collecting information and holding onto the slim hope that he might gather enough capital to start his own business. It was in one of the network's chat rooms that he made the electronic acquaintance of Morris Kalman. Morris had made an investment that threatened to lead him to bankruptcy. Apparently, he had bought 10,000 rat traps from a Mexican company, only to discover that he could not sell them in the United States. Apparently, his supplier had neglected to tell him that the glue in the traps only worked in the hot, humid Mexican clime. WHO KNEW FROM GLUE? Kalman's message read. ALL I KNOW IS THAT I GOTTA MAKE THESE THINGS WORK OR FIND A BANKRUPTCY LAWYER.

Having nothing better to do, Peter e-mailed Morrie. His note explained to Kalman how the traps could be re-activated for drier climates by adding a mixture of rubbing alcohol, chrome alum, and milk to each trap. He sent him a set of instructions for how to direct a chemist to mix up a large quantity of the stuff, and even a "recipe" to show Kalman how he could mix some in his kitchen and test it himself. Morrie was so impressed that he immediately set up a chat session with Peter.

MISTER, WHOEVER YOU ARE, YOU SAVED MY BUSINESS AND PROBABLY MY LIFE. I GOT A CHEMIST TO MIX THAT STUFF AND PUT IT IN THE TRAPS, AND IT STICKS LIKE A DREAM. WHERE'D YOU LEARN STUFF LIKE THAT?

I'M A CHEMIST, Peter wrote back. I'VE WORKED WITH GLUES ALL MY LIFE. To his chagrin, he found that he really wasn't any more eloquent onscreen as he was in real life.

YOU'RE MORE THAN JUST A CHEMIST, MY FRIEND, gushed Morrie. ME, I JUST SELL THE CRAP SO I HIRE CHEMISTS ALL THE TIME. THESE GUYS, THEY MIX THIS, THEY MIX THAT. THEY DON'T KNOW FROM PRACTICAL. THEY'RE EGGHEADS! HOW IS IT THAT YOU, OUT OF ALL THESE CHEMISTS, KNOWS HOW TO USE GLUE FOR PEST CONTROL?

YOU'D BE SURPRISED, Peter responded.

WELL LOOK, YOU NOT ONLY SAVED MY TUCHAS, BUT I'M PROBABLY GONNA MAKE AN OK PROFIT FROM THESE TRAPS. I FIGURE I OWE YOU A PERCENTAGE OF THE TAKE. WHERE CAN I SEND THE CHECK?

DON'T SEND ME ANY MONEY, Peter typed hurriedly. He didn't dare put his address out over the network. While he'd made certain his modem line was untraceable, if the network had discovered that he had pirated online access, they could track him by his address and pow!—violation of parole without leaving his apartment.

THE UNKNOWN PHILANTHROPIST, THIS ONE. WELL LOOK. I'M NOT GONNA BEG YOU TO TAKE MONEY. YOU JUST TELL ME IF THERE'S ANY WAY I CAN REPAY YOU. AND I'LL SEE WHAT I CAN DO. IN THE MEANTIME, IF I'M IN A PRODUCTION JAM AGAIN AND MAYBE I NEED SOME GLUE ADVICE . . .

SURE, MORRIE. FEEL FREE. I'LL BE HERE. BY THE WAY, MY NAME'S PETER. REED. PETER REED.

Thus began a dialogue between the two that turned into a sound working relationship. Morrie had no idea of all the products that used glue—coated paper, cosmetics, textiles—and Peter availed him of all the knowledge and advice Morrie could hope for. Peter liked Morrie, liked feeling needed. And to Morrie, he was invaluable. Whether it was a vegetable slicer or a fabric replacement kit, soon Morrie was asking his advice on some level for every product KalCo made.

Eventually, Peter received the following message:

LOOK, PETER. I OWE YOU A LOT FOR ALL YOUR HELP AND YOU WON'T LET ME GIVE YOU MONEY. SO I'M FEELING GUILTY AS HELL. TELL YOU WHAT. LET ME GIVE YOU A JOB. YOU'LL BE A SPECIAL CONSULTANT FOR KALCO AND DESIGN NEW PRODUCTS FOR ME. WHATEVER YOU'RE GETTING PAID NOW, I'LL NOT ONLY TOP IT BY $10,000 BUT I'LL GIVE YOU A PERCENTAGE OF SALES TO BOOT. ALL I'LL ASK IS THAT YOU MOVE TO LOS ANGELES TO BE NEAR THE COMPANY. SO?

Peter decided to take the job. After all, what did he have going for him in New York? No job, no friends, no life. The chance to work with Morrie offered all three. So he dyed his brown locks blond and grew a beard, which he also bleached. He put together some forged identification—nice to see that those old connections were good for something, he thought—and Peter Reed (née Petruski) hopped a bus for sunny California. He didn't look back.

"Ah, don't worry about me, Petey. Kimmie was there when it happened and she got me an ambulance in ten minutes. How does anyone get an ambulance in ten minutes?" Morrie struggled to sit up in his hospital bed, careful not to jerk the IV attached to his right wrist.

Kim smiled and spoke with mild self-importance. "Well, when

something like this happens, I'm just, 'Ms. Pressure,' y'know? I'm like, 'gotta get it done, gotta make it happen,' and I just go in and kick ass." She looked at Peter and smiled, trying to make eye contact. Peter hoped she didn't notice him turn his eyes to the ceiling. *How could such a bright, capable woman sound like such a complete airhead?* he wondered.

"Besides, Morrie, you were in real pain, y'know? I—"

Morrie cut her off with a weary wave of his hand and a disdainful "Aaah." Pride was always important to this elderly man, Peter noticed. Pride and mobility. Morrie always insisted on driving himself home from the office, no matter how late, always got his own coffee, always refused to pay a salesman to do the KalCo segment on the *Fantastic Discoveries* TV show. He maintained that he could sell the products best because he knew them intimately. Of course, the ability to charm a snake out of its skin didn't hurt either. He was a big hit with the producers of the show.

"Look, dearie, you heard the doctor. They're gonna put some *meshugine* pin in my hip and I'll be good as new. He said I gotta take a few weeks in a wheelchair."

Peter couldn't believe what he was hearing. "Wait a minute, Morrie. You got here an hour ago and you've already been diagnosed? That's amazing."

"Blame Ms. Pressure here. She's kicking the butts again. Listen, Petey. I'm trying to tell you something." Peter had never liked being called "Petey" at any age. Usually he'd ask Morrie not to use the nickname, but he decided to humor him today.

"I've gotta *shlep* around in a wheelchair for three weeks, maybe more. We already paid for our spots on *Discoveries* for the next month. The next taping's in two days and I don't have the time to train a replacement."

Peter knew what was coming. He prepared to say no.

"Petey, I know you're kinda like a . . . a . . . what do they call it, dearie? Out there in the desert like that?" He looked at Kim to read his mind. She shrugged. Then the answer came to him. "A hermit. But you know the product and you can talk about it in words even an *alter cocher* like me can understand. Petey, please say you'll do the Glu-On pitch for the next *Fantastic Discoveries*."

Peter gave his answer just the way he'd rehearsed it for the last five seconds. "Morrie, I'm sorry, but I can't do it. Please don't ask me."

Morrie grew visibly irritated. He sputtered for the right words. "What? What, are you afraid of this—this quality product you created? Maybe you—you don't think it's good enough to sell?" His eyes threw Peter a challenge.

"No, Morrie. It's not that." And of course, it wasn't. This glue was the best thing on the market and both he and Morrie knew it. But Peter didn't dare go on TV, even on a show as small as *Fantastic Discoveries.* All it would take was one person to recognize him and his new life would be over. But how could he explain that to Morrie? He struggled to come up with an excuse. "It's just that I'll get stage fright and I can't memorize scripts and I'll just screw it up."

"What's to memorize? You're just talking to that Dick Trilby *schmuck* like you're trying to sell him something—that's the whole point of the show! For crying out loud, Petey, you created the stuff! Just say what you know." Morrie strained to face Kim. "Kimmie, do you believe this?" He smirked. "I give him a chance to become a TV star and he slaps my hand."

What am I supposed to say? Peter wondered. *"Morrie, I'd love to help you out, but I just can't risk the exposure because I'm a retired super-villain who broke parole to come work for you?"* Yeah, *that'd go over well—the shock would probably break Morrie's other hip.*

"Look, Petey. Just do the gun. I know you're excited about that, at least. Use the prototype. The market version'll come off the manufacturing line before we can process orders anyway. C'mon, Petey. Just do twenty minutes on the gun—"

Twenty minutes! The only time Peter had ever spoken in front of a crowd for that long was when the Frightful Four kidnapped that Wakandan dignitary—Bentley let Peter read the list of ransom demands. He'd screwed up half the demands and lost his place twice. Finally his teammate Thundra took it over from him and read it perfectly. *And she wasn't even from Earth!*

"—and then it's over and I can start training some *goyishe* spokesmodel to do it the next week. Petey, every time we're not on the show we lose sales. Just do the gun. Please. Look at me, Petey. Please do it."

Morrie's eyelids began to flutter. *The conversation must be wearing on him or—wait a minute. His IV—it must be an anesthetic,* Peter deduced. *But that would mean—*

An orderly poked her head into the room. "Mr. Kalman, the

OR's ready for you now." As she said it, two men in white uniforms wheeled a gurney into the room and lined it up next to Morrie's bed.

Peter almost fell over. "Your hip operation? But you haven't even been here two hours."

"Again with Kimmie," grunted the fading Morrie as the orderlies rolled him onto the gurney. "Such a blessing. Like a super hero, this girl. Peter, please. Just do the gun." Morrie's voice trailed off as the orderlies wheeled him out of the room. Kim moved to follow them, then turned to Peter.

"I probably like being called a 'girl' about as much as you like being called 'Petey.' " She sighed. "Listen, I'm going to sit outside the operating room and wait for him in case he needs anything. Would you, y'know, just sit with me for a while?"

They spent their time in the waiting room talking about next to nothing. Kim told Peter about the catty Vietnamese manicurist at her hair salon. Peter told her about his problems in sufficiently preventing Glu-On's hardening agent from crystallizing in the application reservoir of the glue-gun prototype. Words, just words, to fill space and pass the time. They seemed to want to find anything to avoid a real conversation.

They made it halfway through Morrie's operation before running out of things to say. Peter broke the uncomfortable silence.

"Uh, Kim?"

"Yeah?"

He almost didn't say it. "Tell Morrie I'll do the show."

Kim threw her arms around Peter and kissed him on the cheek. "Peter, that is so great of you. Morrie will be so relieved."

Kim had never held him so tightly before, not even on the three dates they'd gone on. It felt uncomfortable—but a good kind of uncomfortable. Peter figured that the polite thing to do would be to respond. So he tried to hug her back, awkwardly placing his arms around her and making his hands meet on her opposite shoulder. He heard her sigh. She rested her head on his shoulder.

"You know, Peter, you're a good friend to Morrie." Kim said, releasing her arms from him.

Peter didn't know what to say. "Yes, well, it's nice to be needed." He stammered.

"I know," said Kim with a heavier sigh. Peter guessed that her handling of today's crisis had taken more out of her than she wanted to let on. He felt a great warmth for this selfless woman.

For the last hour of the operation, Kim nestled her head on Peter's shoulder and fell asleep. Peter sat absolutely still, so as not to wake her.

"Now just *wait* a minute, Morrie, let me get this straight. *You're* telling *me* that just *one* drop of Glu-On II will glue *these* heavy-duty bicycle handlebars to *this* kitchen table?"

"I'm not just telling you, Dick, I'm willing to show you. Whaddaya think—think your audience would like to see that?"

"Well, *I* don't *know*." Dick said with rehearsed naïveté, as he placed one finger on his chin and turned his coifed, bespectacled head to the live audience. "How 'bout it, audience? Would you like to see Morrie glue the handlebars to the table?"

The *Fantastic Discoveries* audience of two hundred didn't even wait for Dick to finish his question before answering it with applause. *Maybe they turned the sign on too early*, Peter thought. Morrie had said that there were all sorts of screw-ups on this show that they edited out of the videotape before broadcasting. "Guess they missed that one," Peter grumbled, reaching for another Malomar without moving his eyes from the videotape.

The camera switched back to the usual mid-shot of Dick and Morrie in the kitchenesque set. "Well, there's your answer, Morrie," shrugged Dick as he motioned to the audience.

"Then let's get to it!" said Morrie excitedly. Like a magician out of vaudeville—and looking old enough to have been there—Morrie arched his back, stretched his arms through the sleeves of his red-and-white seersucker suit, and picked up the display bottle of Glu-On II. "Now Dick, before we do this, I want you to make absolutely certain that these are not trick handlebars, but perfectly good bicycle handlebars."

Dick picked up the handlebars, taking care not to let them touch his argyle cardigan, and looked at them in the light at a couple of different angles. "Morrie, these look like perfectly good handlebars to me."

"And Dick, I want you to assure me that this table is a real, solid-wood kitchen table."

"Morrie, I'm offended. You know we use only the *best* kitchen furnishings on this show." Dick cocked his head and raised his eyebrows in mock accusation.

"Ha-ha, I'm sure you do. Now, here's the handlebars, I'm adding just one drop of new Glu-On II to the base, and pow!—I affix the handlebars to the table top."

Morrie then turned to the show's host with a wry grin and a twinkle in his eye that Peter could see from his living room. "Now Dick, do an old man a favor and just try to lift the handlebars off the table. I'd do it myself, but my back just isn't what it used to be." He quipped.

Neither is his hip, mused Peter. Immediately he wished he hadn't made light of Morrie's situation. But he found it unsettling that he could watch Morrie on an episode of *Fantastic Discoveries* when he knew the poor man was in drugged slumber between overstarched hospital sheets.

"Well, okay, Morrie, but I'm *still* pretty skeptical—hey! These handlebars are *stuck tight!* I can't pick them up without picking up the *table* too! This is fantastic! Morrie, new Glu-On II is *just* fantastic!

The audience offered the same mediocre applause. *They must really turn the mikes up on the audience,* mused Peter. *There's no way this audience can get that excited over every product. It's good to know that even if I bomb, the audience will applaud.* He fingered the TV remote control absent-mindedly, focusing his attention on Morrie as the elderly sprite continued his sales pitch. The camera seemed to love this kindly old man. Peter hoped to follow his example. Then he'd get the hell off the stage.

"Now, Dick, you know how much I love being on your show. That's why I'm going to offer an incredible deal on Glu-On II— I'm telling you, this offer will blow your socks off—if you haven't stuck 'em on with Glu-On II, that is." Morrie nudged Dick's ribs in a broad gesture. "But before I do, I want to show your audience—both here and at home—the magic of Glu-*Off* II! Can I do that for you?"

Morrie's offer was met with the same camera shot of the audience applauding "enthusiastically." Peter clicked off the TV and looked at his watch. It said 2:14.

"Good God," grumbled Peter. "Why do I do this to myself?" He dropped to his knees and rolled back a section of the rug to expose a large storage space built into the floor. Dialing the combination, he opened the door and dug out a pair of identical flat black discs, each just a bit longer in diameter than the average dinner plate. "Barely enough time to fly tonight," he griped.

He stepped outside into the cool night air, making sure that he could hear no cars, meaning that the sleepy San Bernadino suburb where he rented his home was, in fact, asleep.

Bicycle handlebars on a goddamn kitchen table! Peter made a mental note to ask Morrie just where the hell he came up with *that* one. . . .

And with that, Peter Petruski slapped the discs onto his feet and took off into the pitch-black desert sky.

Using the anti-gravity discs was Peter's sole remaining vice from his super-villain days—well, that and breaking parole. He loved flying, loved gliding two hundred feet above the earth, doing about thirty miles an hour from a standing position. It was worth it to wait until the pitch-dark wee hours of the night to make sure that no one was awake to spot him. This was why he lived in the desert: privacy.

He couldn't help but think that if he'd had these discs from the very beginning, he could have beaten the Human Torch. After all, Johnny Storm was just a teenager at the time, and something of a showoff who loved to use his powers of fire and flight to get his name in the papers. What became a chance run-in with the youngest member of the Fantastic Four blossomed into a constant rivalry that nearly always ended up with Paste Pot Pete in jail.

After his first few terms in the clink, Peter decided he might need help if he was to continue in his chosen profession. He eventually teamed up with a mechanical genius named Bentley Wittman, who, under the moniker of the Wizard, had also been "sent up" by the Torch. An inventor, a stage magician, an escape artist; Bentley was an all-around genius and a driven one to boot. At first, he could do no wrong in Peter's eyes. The magnificent gadgets he had created, the extraordinary escapes from prison— they impressed Peter to no end.

At first, the two men of science worked together extremely well. Bentley helped Peter create new and better equipment, and together they planned some great jobs. The mere inclusion of the Wizard's anti-gravity discs to the arsenal made every getaway a clean one. Bentley helped Peter combine his pastes with projectile and gas weapons to create bona fide traps. Ecstatic with his new range of gadgets, Peter changed his handle to the flashier moniker of the Trapster.

Sure, the Wizard wasn't the easiest guy to get along with. He was overbearing, condescending, and had an ego, Peter decided, the size of Galactus's summer house. Peter had to keep telling himself that all Bentley's bluster was justly earned. After all, here was a man who had already found immense fame and fortune as an inventor, a stage magician, *and* a chess champion. A little nuts, sure, but a bona fide genius. Peter was sure that, together, nothing could stop them.

But of course, something did. The Torch, again. The first time was different, because even though they went to jail again, the Wizard busted them out in no time. Though Peter could never admit to liking the Wizard, he grew to appreciate their working relationship, if only for the jailbreak benefits.

Soon the two of them were four—the Frightful Four, to be specific. By convincing the Sandman and Medusa to join the team, the Wizard raised the stakes tenfold. Now, they didn't just fight the Torch, they took on the entire Fantastic Four. They didn't just knock off a bank, they invaded the Baxter Building. The jobs got bigger, the payoffs grander, the battles more epic.

But eventually Peter's hospital stays in the concussion ward became more frequent, and the jail sentences became longer— even with the jailbreaks—and he grew tired of the high stakes. Peter quit the Frightful Four, and after a few more failed solo turns, decided to go straight altogether.

He promised himself that he would never go to jail again. He vowed that he would die before he went back. He was too old and had too many enemies to survive another prison term.

He truly hoped he had not made the wrong decision, in agreeing to appear on the show.

The applause sign flashed on, galvanizing the audience. The sound man cranked up the theme music and cued the prerecorded announcer's introduction. "It's time for *Fantastic Discoveries,* where we show you how to make your life simpler with the conveniences of tomorrow—today. And here's your host, Dick Trilby!"

Dick, wearing his trademark argyle cardigan sweater and sporting a polished smile, jogged out onto the stage to forced applause. His opening spiel to the camera dripped with smarmy enthusiasm.

"*Hi* there, folks, and welcome to an *exciting* edition of *Fantastic Discoveries*. Let's start this week's show with a person you haven't met before . . . and a product you know and love. We all know KalCo as the people who brought you Glu-On, Glu-On II, Glu-On-Forever-Nails, Glu-On Fabric Repair Kits . . . the list goes *on* and *on*. Well, the good people at KalCo have come up with a way to top themselves *yet again!* Sounds too good too be *true*? Well it's *time to find out! He's* the top researcher for a company that *always* finds a way to make us happy here at *Fantastic Discoveries*, KalCo's *Peter Red!*"

Peter shuffled onstage in a long white lab coat, looking to make sure all his props were in their proper places. He looked at the cue cards, looked at Dick Trilby, and did everything he could to not look at the audience. Dick approached Peter with a "warm greeting."

"Peter, welcome, it's a pleasure to have you on the show."

"Uh, thanks Dick. It's Reed."

"I beg your pardon."

"Reed. Not Red. Peter Reed."

Dick tried to play off his gaffe. "Oh, Reed. Right, of course, sorry. You're not gonna glue my mouth shut, are you? Ha-ha."

Peter grimaced at the easy joke. *Just do the gun,* he thought to himself. *Don't bother sparring with this imbecile.*

"Of course not, Dick, ha-ha. But I'm sure that after I show you KalCo's new household wonder, I will leave you speechless." *Hey,* mused Peter, *this pitchman stuff is easier than I thought.* "Dick, you've seen how Glu-On can fasten any two surfaces, anywhere, anytime, not just for the life of the glue, but for the life of the pieces the glue is holding together."

Dick nodded and shrugged. "Well sure, Peter. You're not telling me anything I don't already know."

"But what if you've got a big, industrial-sized job, Dick? What if you have to glue or unglue pieces that are in corners or other hard-to-reach spots? What if you need to direct the glué with pinpoint precision?" Feeling himself on a roll, Peter didn't want to wait for Dick's insipid retort. "I'll tell you what you do—you use one of these—" he pulled the glue-gun out of his lab coat pocket, "—the Glu-On Glu-Matic 2000. The Glu-Matic 2000 will allow you to do tiles, woodworking, shoe repair, even watch repair. From the tiniest fix to the largest restoration, the Glu-Matic 2000 is an entire toolbox in a tube."

Dick good-naturedly shook his head. "Peter, I don't believe it. I can't believe that little Glu-Matic 2000 can do all those repairs you mentioned. You're going to have to prove it to me."

Peter tried not to roll his eyes at Trilby. *Where did this guy get his job, from a cereal box? I really should glue Trilby's lips together and save everyone the hardship. In fact, I ought to . . . um . . .*

Uh-oh.

He blanked. His concentration melted away, his lines lost forever. *Oh God. I knew this would happen. What am I supposed to do next? Repair a shoe? Build a treehouse? Why did I agree to do this in the first place?* He panicked. His mind reeled. He felt the miniature glue-gun snug in his palm, with its dual supply bulbs of Glu-On and Glu-Off attached to the tiny stock, and gave way to instinct. *Just do the gun.* He looked around for something to shoot at. Peter broke for the kitchen set of the show and lunged for the *faux* counter.

Dick looked at Peter, then at his cue cards, then at Peter again. "Uh, Peter? Aren't you supposed to be, uh. . . ."

Peter grabbed two dinner plates and spun towards the audience. With a deft motion of his wrists, he sent both plates into the air, spinning high above his head. Then, just as the two plates were about to collide, he raised his Glu-Matic 2000 above him and aimed at the point between them.

Peter pulled the trigger. The glue hit the point at which the plates touched. They immediately stuck together, stopped spinning, and dropped like a "V"-shaped stone. Peter then stuck out his arm and caught the bonded plates just as a spike catches a horseshoe.

The audience went wild. Peter bowed, and as he came up, noticed that the "applause" sign wasn't even on. He smirked with pride.

The next fifteen minutes sped by. Peter improvised a number of quick-shot tricks with the gun using more plates, vegetables from the food-processing segment, and cans of another presenter's car wax, all to the audience's fervent approval. He even glued another presenter's sizable exercise machine to a microphone boom and had the boom raised so that the machine hung above his and Dick Trilby's heads for ten minutes while Peter did more tricks. Peter was fairly certain that Morrie would not want the Glu-Matic advertised this way. But the audience seemed to like it, and Peter began to thrive on their adulation. And he made sure to issue a wry warning to the audience. "Now, Dick, I must caution anyone from trying this at home. I am a professional." *Why not ham it up a bit?* he asked himself. *What harm could it do? It's a shame to let these skills go to waste. Besides the audience is eating it up.* He continued to show off, much to Dick Trilby's chagrin.

And if the trick-shooting wasn't enough to frazzle poor Dick's nerves, Peter literally drove the hapless host up the wall for the audience's benefit. Using measured amounts of the Glu-On and the Glu-Off instant solvent, Peter used a technique that he had designed for the boots of his Trapster outfit, years ago: with a very nervous Dick Trilby in tow, he scaled one of the studio's walls. This particular endeavor evoked a standing ovation from the audience. He hadn't felt a rush like this in years. *Maybe*, wondered Peter, *I should have been in show business all along.*

The show's finale was relatively anticlimactic. Peter finally remembered one of the set pieces he was supposed to do—take a large porcelain cauldron, shatter it, glue it back together, and immediately pour hot soup in it—and closed with that. His segment ended with yet another standing ovation. The taping took a break as Dick Trilby scurried backstage to calm down, fix his makeup, and change into a dry shirt and cardigan.

As Peter left the stage, the adrenaline began to wear off. The realization of how he spent the last twenty minutes dawned on him. He stopped in his tracks. His shoulders fell, his eyes widened.

"Oh God," he whispered to himself, "What have I done?"

"Maximum security—hah! These meager facilities are but a toddler's playpen before my unparalleled genius!" Bentley Wittman announced from his cell's squeaky cot. He loved to speak out loud. Anything from quick phrases to long soliloquies, he could not understand why people did not hang on his every word. After all, as he had proved time and time again, he had one of the finest minds on Earth. He'd conquered every intellectual and scientific challenge that he'd cared to approach. Why, he even fancied himself more brilliant than—

Richards.

How Bentley hated him. He pictured Reed Richards, the leader of the Fantastic Four, as an elastic freak—a rubber-brained monstrosity passing himself off as a scientist. *How many times?* Bentley wondered. *How many times has that ductile do-gooder and his despicable cronies thwarted me and my compatriots? Why, why have I continually suffered defeat at the hands of Richards and his cronies? Could it be because Richards was—smarter?*

"No!" Bentley screeched. "My intellect is unsurpassed! The time will come when the world will tremble before the supreme genius of the Wiz—"

"Yo! *Bent*-ly! We're tryin'a get some sleep here—shut the hell up!" bellowed a gravelly voice from another cell. "Or I'll *shut* ya up, ya sicko!" The other cons let fly a few guffaws.

The Wizard raised one eyebrow. "Sicko? *I'm* not the one with the hemorrhaging duodenal ulcer, am I?"

A hush fell over the pitch-dark cell-block. The rough voice sounded again, uneasy, frightened. "How—how did—"

The Wizard cut him off. "Diet is important in the care of an ulcer, Mickey. I suggest you take care with what you *eat* tomorrow," he said with a cryptic nonchalance. "You never know *what* could happen."

There were a few frightened whispers, then the cell block went quiet and stayed quiet. *It's too easy*, Bentley smirked, then went about his business. "Now then," he inquired to himself, "How to occupy myself until the trial?" In the twenty-six hours since his arrest, he had already planned the next two crimes he'd commit upon his escape from prison—one a simple Manhattan bank heist and the other the theft of a radioactive isotope in Denver—sent an update to his henchmen at the Long Island hideout, approved the estimate for repairs to his Westchester home that had caught fire during that little incident with Sandman and Silver Sable, and checked his stock portfolio. There was very little else to do that wouldn't call undue notice to him. He so hated to draw attention to himself these days when he couldn't involve the media. That's why he let himself be captured in the first place.

At a loss for further distraction in the drab cell, he relented to access his last resort for entertainment. He held his left palm to his lips and whispered into it, "Lightbender off." The air softly shimmered around his hands and forearms until a pair of purple metallic gauntlets covered them. He leaned back in his bed, raised his right hand, pointed his right finger to the opposite wall, and muttered, "TV." It annoyed him to give verbal commands to his Wonder Gloves, but the authorities had confiscated his helmet, with its cybernetic relays, and he'd had enough trouble smuggling the gloves in. No matter, thought the Wizard calmly, and using the cell wall as a screen, he searched through the 128 channels at his disposal.

Sure enough, there he was on *Real American Justice*. He smiled and turned up the volume as he heard the news announcer describe him. "The nefarious super-villain known as the Wizard was taken in by federal authorities, in cooperation with the so-called Wild Pack, mere days after kidnapping the mercenary Silver Sable. Sable, member of the first family of the country of Symkaria and leader of the Wild Pack, was rescued by the Pack member known as the Sandman. Trish?"

"Thanks, Brian. One note of interest on that story: Before reforming his criminal past and receiving diplomatic immunity as a member of Sable's team, the Sandman was perhaps best known for his exploits as a member of the Frightful Four, a band of villains led by none other than the Wizard himself. Isn't that fascinating, Brian?

"Yes it is, Trish. We take you now to the Symkarian Embassy where Silver Sable and the Sandman have prepared statements."

The Wizard smiled. He knew he'd be hounded by Sable's Wild Pack no end after he kidnapped her in order to humiliate the Sandman. It was easier to let himself be captured and wait for the Symkarian heat to blow over. Besides, he received much better news coverage by remaining at large for a few days before being captured than he would have if he remained at large. A no-lose situation for him.

Bentley noticed his own image come on the screen again. He turned up the sound to better hear the announcer.

"Tonight, the Wizard is under lock and key at Ryker's Island, awaiting trial. Let's hope they keep him there, eh, Trish?"

"I sure hope so, Brian. Coming up next . . . "

"*I sure hope so, Briii-an.*" Bentley mimicked the female newscaster. "That's all? Nothing about the dozens of lives I endangered? Nothing about the grave threat I caused to international relations with Symkaria? Nothing about my moral victory over that sand-laden behemoth? How dare they call this 'news'? I am appalled. I certainly hope that the trial affords me better press." Still a master escape artist, Bentley could escape from jail any time he wanted to. But he hated to break out until he was certain he had hit the pinnacle of his media saturation. Then he performed a daring escape that was usually good for another day or two of front-page news. Something he learned from his time as a stage magician: always leave them wanting more.

He eventually grew bored scouring the news shows and proceeded to impatiently flip from channel to channel. Very little on TV was ever to his liking. The fictions were too contrived and the nonfiction shows told him simplified versions of subjects he already knew implicitly. Occasionally Bentley stayed on the infomercials, the blocks of late-night TV time that companies bought to exclusively promote their consumer products. Every so often he would find some runt of a salesman peddling a "brand-new" machine that was obviously based on technology that Bentley himself had established a lifetime ago. This rarely failed to amuse him.

The Wizard turned to *Fantastic Discoveries* just in time to see the show's announcer glued to the wall. This alone was enough to pique Bentley's interest. He watched silently as the blond man in the lab coat utilized a hand-held turbine-pressure glue applicator with pinpoint accuracy. The salesman used his remaining time to glue and unglue pieces of the set, all the while extolling the virtues of the product he was using. The Wizard endured a brief bout of speechlessness as he focused on the man's voice. Whoever he was, he was modulating it intentionally; disguising it. But why—?

"Th-thanks very much, Peter. Folks, that was Peter Reed for KalCo's new Glu-On II applicator gun. Here's how you can order yours. . . ."

The answer came to him even faster than usual.

Petruski. The Trapster. The one with the Wizard almost from the beginning. The one who availed himself of the Wizard's wondrous technology and then quit before the Wizard could fire him.

Were he not one of the finest cognitive minds on the face of the planet, the Wizard would not have believed his eyes. *Petruski? In disguise? Selling glue on television?* The Wizard laughed so hard tears came to his eyes. "Ahhhh, Peter. Peter, Peter, Peter. Look at the miserable existence the straight life has led you to. I daresay I couldn't think of a better fate for you as punishment for leaving the Frightful Four—but I'd be lying. Finally," announced the Wizard with glee, "a way to occupy my time. I've already humiliated the Sandman. Seems only fitting to do the same for dear dear Peter." Almost immediately he formulated a foolproof plan that would not only ruin Petruski's life once and for all, but guarantee the Wizard's trial additional coverage. The news coverage, in turn, would increase his own "Q" rating. The Wizard was very concerned with his "Q" rating.

He made a mental note to call his lawyer up in the morning and discuss a plea bargain. Then, a sufficient day's labor completed, he laid back on his cot and programmed his Wonder Gloves to massage him until he fell asleep.

The phone rang, waking Peter from fitful slumber. He'd stayed up too late flying again, trying to take his mind off of the show. It had aired the day before and all he wanted was to forget he'd ever done it. What had compelled him to perform all those showboat moves with the glue gun? He was sure it was only a matter of time before someone put two and two together and hauled him back to jail.

But the incessant jingle of the phone nipped that particular fantasy in the bud. *Whoever's trying to call knows me too well,* Peter deduced. *They keep hanging up one ring short of my answering machine and calling again. I guess there's no escape.* Moaning, he reached across his bed for the phone.

"Peter, hi! It's Kim. Are you awake?"

What do you say to that? "Hi, Kim. What's up?"

"What's up? What's up? Try, like, two thousand units in one day! Is that 'up' enough for you?" Kim could barely contain her excitement.

Peter began to wake up. "Wait—wait a minute. Are you telling me that—"

"KalCo's Glu-Matic has sold two thousand units since your show aired. Orders are still pouring in, and the *Fantastic Discoveries* producers are telling Morrie that this could be the biggest-selling item since the pocket fisherman, whatever that is. Peter, you totally hit it!"

Peter made an unrecognizable transition from unconsciousness to speechlessness. "But—it's—I mean—"

"It's a phenomenon, Peter! Everybody who's seen the show is talking about you! You've, I don't know, blown up or something! Morrie said that *Fantastic Discoveries* picked up four more cities on the strength of your segment alone. And get this! There's talk over there about giving KalCo its own show for free!"

"Kim, that's great. But I—"

"I mean, I had no idea you could do all those things. You were really, y'know, amazing."

"Listen, Kim, thanks, but I really shouldn't have—"

"Waitaminute, let me put Morrie on. Morrie, it's Peter!" Kim's voice suddenly sounded distant when she called for Morrie, then came back to full volume. "Here's Morrie."

"Petey? Petey, do you know what you're hearing right now?"

"Hi, Morrie. I don't hear anything."

"What you're hearing right now is the sound of me *kvelling*. Do you know what *kvelling* means? It means I could kiss you right now, I'm so happy. Who knew you were such a natural? Standing in that lab coat like some sort of scientist, then suddenly you're the Two-Gun Kid. Or Spider-Man! Climbing walls, this one! Did you have fun? You looked like you were having fun."

He surprised himself with his answer. "Actually yeah, Morrie. I had fun." It made Peter feel good to admit it.

"Kimmie told you about the producers?"

Peter felt a smile cross his lips. "She said they're *kvelling*."

"Yeah that's right, smartass, they're in our pocket right now is what they are. If we get our own show and don't have to pay for it, we're smooth sailing, *bubbie*. It's all profit. Hey, maybe we can finally unload some of those Glu-On hair extensions you came up with."

Peter took the good-natured dig with a grin. "Well, Morrie, they can't all be gems."

"Except for you, Petey. You're a gem. A saint. That's what you are. Saint Peter. Hey Kimmie, I'm talking to Saint Peter here!"

He heard Kim's voice from a distance. "Let me talk to him again."

"Sure, dearie. Hey Petey, here's your girlfriend agai—ow! Why you punk! Hit an old man willya. . . ." Morrie's playful tones trailed off as Kim snatched the phone from him.

"Um—hi, Peter. Listen, one thing that Morrie didn't mention is that the producers sort of want you to do the next few KalCo spots on *Discoveries*. Do you mind doing 'em? Please?"

There was a moment's quiet as Peter thought about it. Kim broke the silence with her pleading.

"C'mon, Peter, Everybody completely loved you on the show. *I* loved you on the show. You were incredible. Please? At least do it one more time?"

Peter remembered the rush: the exhilarating high that only came from the power of the crowd. He'd already known what it was like for crowds to fear him. Now he'd had a taste of adulation, and he knew he wanted more. He remembered the way he felt at the *Discoveries* taping and suddenly he didn't feel tired at all. He felt strong.

But even that didn't hit him as hard as the other thing Kim said. *Waitaminute. Love. Did she just say she loved me?*

"Okay, I'll do it."

"All riiiiight!" Kim cheered him over the phone, adding a few whoops and finger whistles for effect. Kim's vivacity made Peter laugh out loud—something he hadn't recalled doing for ages. Then his heart began to pound as he got his courage up to ask the question. He ran a hand through his brittle yellow hair.

"Listen, Kim. . . ." He waited until she had stopped cheering. "Um, after the taping, do you maybe want to have uh, dinner? Just you and me?" He almost couldn't believe he said it. His heart beat a hard syncopation as it awaited her answer.

There was a delicate pause. Then Kim responded in a reserved, breathy tone. "Peter, I'd love to have dinner with you. I've got class in the afternoon, but I should be able to get to the studio, like, just after the taping. Okay?"

"Okay. I'll—I'll see you at the studio, then." Peter could barely hear himself over the pounding of his heart. He breathed a sigh of relief as he hung up the phone. He helped himself to a pint of ice cream out of the freezer, grabbed a spoon, and, grinning a grin that even a bucketful of Adhesive X couldn't hold back, sat down to watch the news.

Peter had spooned nearly an entire pint of Chunky Monkey into his newfound smile by the time the news actually began. He raised an eyebrow at the screen in response to the image of three police officers and two men in three-piece suits escorting the Wizard into a dark sedan.

"Our top story tonight: the Wizard has a few tricks up his sleeve. Bentley Wittman, alias career super-criminal the Wizard, begins his trial today for the kidnapping of a Symkarian mercenary. While the trial has not yet begun, Wittman's counsel have already stated that they intend to plead guilty and offer a plea bargain to the authorities to reduce Bentley's sentence."

Peter stopped eating. He broke into a sweat and felt the ice cream begin to work its way back up to his throat.

The newscast cut to a clip of Bentley and his entourage heading a press conference. Standing behind a podium bearing several microphones, he looked down at his hands and addressed the press in somber tones.

"What can I say?" sighed the Wizard. "It's taken nearly twenty years for me to learn my lesson. And now that I finally have, I am grateful. All I want now is to serve my time." He looked up from the podium. His eyes filled with tears. "And while I do, I want to do what I can," his mouth formed a visible scowl, "to help apprehend other criminals and bring them to justice!" He slammed his fist down on the podium. Two microphones squealed with feedback. The two suits led him away from the podium, patting his back and offering him a handkerchief as they did. The newscasters went on to the next news story.

Peter would have laughed at the Wizard's horrendous overacting if he wasn't completely terrified. And nauseous. He ran to the kitchen sink, sneezed twice, then loudly regurgitated his dessert.

As he wiped his beard and drew a glass of water, his mind careened with but a single thought: *It's me. He's talking about me. It's happening too soon after the show for it not to be. That bastard must have seen the show and decided to turn me in to the cops. Why did I— How the hell could I—* He banged his head against the sink in frustration. Twice.

The pain shocked him out of his anxiety attack. Peter took a few deep breaths and decided what he had to do. "Gotta call him," he blurted, dashing into the den. He threw aside the carpet, dialed the combination and flung open the door to his cache. Digging frantically amongst the pressure tanks, aluminum glue pods, and other unused weaponry, he pulled out the piece he had been looking for.

He turned it around in his hands. The light from the ceiling lamp glinted off the metallic yellow nose piece, headband and ear guards. The top, also metal but covered by purple canvas, had a sharp dent in it. Peter stared at the object he held in his hands with apprehension. Maybe a little fear.

It was his old helmet. The Trapster's helmet. Peter turned it over to look inside. He blew the dust off of the cracked padding and labyrinthine mazes of printed circuits.

He shivered as he put it on.

Immediately the cybernetic relay hummed to life and Peter heard the ear speakers crackle as they cleared themselves. He found something comforting about the buzz of the security scan as it approved his cerebral pattern and allowed him access to the universal communicator. That brief feeling of comfort was replaced by a tight, cold sensation in his gut.

Maybe I can just get him to call it off. Maybe I can threaten him to stop. Maybe all I have to do is talk to him. Hesitantly, he sent out the com-signal.

Peter Petruski's hands shook as he sought an audience with the Wizard.

A gentle tone from his invisible left glove roused Bentley Wittman from the beginnings of a nap. He had expected the tone much earlier in the day, actually. He wasn't sure whether to commend or condemn Petruski for his bravery in contacting him, or his stupidity.

The Wizard switched on his video relay and saw Petruski, looking foolish in his peroxide-ridden facial hair, dirty sweatshirt, and dented Trapster helmet.

"Well, if it isn't Paste Pot Pete." Bentley pronounced Peter's old tag as if were a bad taste in his mouth. He knew Petruski hated to be called by his old name. He knew many things about Petruski.

"Wizard. You can hear me?"

The Wizard chortled at the blank look on Petruski's face as he strained to establish contact. He had to remind himself that unlike him, Petruski didn't have video access. The Wizard kept that particular perk for himself.

"Just when I thought you couldn't go any lower. Imagine my surprise when I saw you hawking useless rubbish on the Home Shopping Channel or somesuch."

"Bentley, I know what you're trying to—"

"Is this your pathetic attempt to lead the straight life? Did you really think that all you'd have to do is change your last name and you'd be free to lead a normal life? Did all those years you fancied yourself a master criminal teach you nothing? You obviously deserve to be taught a lesson."

"Bentley, please don't—"

Wittman's eyes flashed. He snapped at the forlorn image of Peter and waved a rigid finger in the direction of his face. "Don't you dare call me by that name! You lost that right when you walked out on the Frightful Four! Address me as the Wizard or I will have no choice but to end this conversation."

Peter sputtered, "All right. Wizard. I'll call you the Wizard. Listen, please don't do this to me. You don't need to use me as a plea bargain. You know damn well you could break out of that cell any time you want. Please don't ruin my life. It's taken too long for me to get to this point. You don't have to do this."

The Wizard leaned back on his cot and rested his chin in his right hand. "I'd like you to imagine something for me, Petruski. I'd like you to imagine that you've planned a year's worth of jobs that include not only thefts of huge sums of valuables at several major metropolitan financial institutions, but culminate in the complete and total destruction of the Fantastic Four, your most grave and trying enemies. Picture the shredded elastic cadaver of Mr. Fantastic. The Thing, blasted into a pile of orange driveway gravel. The Invisible Woman, a lifeless ghost. And that loathsome combustive delinquent, the Human Torch smothered to death—crushed out like the pesky matchstick he truly is. Imagine the time and effort it might take to plan all these jobs. The sleepless nights filled with calculations to check and recheck."

"Wizard, don't—"

"Now let's imagine that you've planned these jobs for execution by a team of *four*."

"Wizard, I understa—"

"No, Petruski, I don't think you understand. I truly don't. When I met you, you were a puerile upstart pulling jewelry store jobs with a little paste gun and the stupidest name since Blastaar the Living Bomb-Burst. I *made* you, you ridiculous waste of striated polymers! No one knew who you were before you joined up with me. *No one*. And after all the time I invested in trying to make you a potent villain, what did you do? You left. And look at the inextricable imbroglio you've landed in.

"Face it, 'Pete.' You haven't made a solid decision in your misbegotten life. The only decent choice you've ever made was to have me take you under my wing."

Petruski pursed his lips in disdain. "Don't give me that. I pulled my weight and more! I was a valuable member of the Frightful Four and you know it, you egotistical son of a—"

"Oh yes, Peter. Of course, that doesn't explain why your subsequent solo turns honed your lauded skills into those of a *bumbling idiot*. Face it, you epoxy-obsessed cretin: outside of the Frightful Four, you were worthless as a villain. And quite frankly, you weren't particularly effective when you were with us. I mean good lord, man—even the Brute proved more capable than you."

Peter looked down at his feet and attempted a retort. "Spare me. The Brute couldn't think his way out of a paper bag."

The Wizard noted that Peter's meager emotional defenses were wearing away. He raised a long eyebrow and glared. "And you, Petruski, couldn't think your way out of an idiot box. You must be more ignorant than I had suspected, to go on television in some precipitately fabricated 'secret identity,' and then go shooting *glue* all over the place. Tell me, Peter. Tell me why and I may let you off the hook."

Peter looked up, baited by the chance of reprieve.

"You're not completely stupid. Why in the world would you take such a shortsighted risk?"

Peter sneezed twice, wiped his nose on his sleeve absentmindedly, and stared at his feet again. The Wizard refused to stand for the silent treatment and resumed goading Peter.

"Oh, come now. It certainly wasn't because you longed to sell glue on TV. And it couldn't have been the money. No, it was something more Freudian, wasn't it? That would be more like you. After all, it's been so long since you're gotten to go shoot off your little glue pistols and—"

"Shut up!" blurted Peter. His eyes began to water. "I did it . . . I did it to help a friend."

The look in Peter's eyes showed the Wizard a bare soul. *This is it*, thought the Wizard. *Petruski is helpless, completely powerless. Time to deliver the killing stroke. Yes, this will taste particularly sweet.*

"Oh, I'm touched. That solves it for me, Petruski. You've clearly gone around the bend. I'm guessing that this 'friend' doesn't know you're really the Trapster. I'd say it's safe to assume that this 'friend' is associated with your little company as well, hm? Well, 'Paste Pot Pete,' I think I can say with complete impunity that when the authorities discover who and where you are, your poor friend will denounce you for a liar and a dangerous criminal. I'd even venture to suggest that any other cursory little relationships that 'Peter Reed' managed to establish will similarly scatter to the four winds. Or haven't you experienced that before?" At that comment, the Wizard saw Peter's grimace pull even tighter. He savored that expression.

"And of course, I wouldn't expect this paltry little company to stay in business much longer. Associating with a wanted super-criminal? I'll be surprised if they don't end up in jail cells next to you, hm?

"Listen to me, Petruski. This is your punishment for all the mistakes you've made in your spiteful, pitiful life. With every step you've taken, you've ruined your life and the lives of those around you. I've done nothing but speed things along a bit. Face it: there's nothing you can do about it because the fault, ultimately, is your own."

Peter didn't say a word. The Wizard took a good long look at him. He hardly saw the Trapster any more. He certainly didn't see a villain. He saw a pathetic, hunched-over, ruin of a man in plain clothes and a ridiculous-looking, dented, purple-and-gold helmet, wringing his hands and sneezing.

He looked closer. A single tear fell from Petruski's left eye.

The Wizard luxuriated in that tear. He began to laugh, and laugh and laugh.

The Wizard hadn't had a good laugh like that in years.

* * *

Even after Peter threw off the helmet, cutting off the Universal Communicator, he could still hear the Wizard's laughter echo throughout the house.

Ruined, he thought. *It's all ruined. I'm dead. If I'm arrested, I'll be a public disgrace. Morrie and Kim will find out I've lied to them all this time. I'll lose my only two friends in the world. The publicity will put Morrie out of business. And Kim. I'll never . . . We'll never . . .*

Jail. If they find me, I'll have to go to jail. No. I can't go to jail again. Never again. I'll die first.

There, in his house in the middle of the desert, Peter Petruski broke down and wept.

The house. The realization hit Peter like a hammer. He abruptly raised his tear-stained face from his bony hands. *If they know who I am, they'll eventually come here to find me. What if the police are already on their way?*

Peter dove into his secret storage space and dug out every last piece of his equipment. The wrist-mounted paste-shooters. The high-pressure back-mounted primary tanks. The ammo-belts of glue-pods. The flying discs. The uniform. The helmet.

He put on every piece of his weaponry, connected all the relays, checked all the batteries. He threw everything else he could into two duffel bags, listening to the reassuring hum of his helmet all the while to give him courage. He also shaved his beard. Peter knew what he had to do. It sickened him, but he knew he had no other choice.

He stepped outside and took what he knew to be his last deep breath of the dry desert air. *I'm not going to go quietly,* he swore. *I refuse to go out without a fight. Or an explanation. Or a bang.*

He checked the liquid-crystal timepiece built into the wrist of his left-hand paste-shooter. *Seven-and-a-half hours before the studio opens. Five of those in darkness. Plenty of time.* He activated the discs and took off toward Sherman Oaks with an arsenal in tow.

"It's time for *Fantastic Discoveries,* where we show you how to make your life simpler with the conveniences of tomorrow— today. And here's your host, Dick Trilby!"

The "applause" sign lit up; the audience reacted accordingly. Dick walked out toward his mark not in his typical audience- friendly stride, but with a nervous, halting gait unbecoming of his TV-show-host status. He faced the lit camera with a pained expression. Makeup trailed off his face in an unusually messy runoff of perspiration. Rivulets ran down the left side of his neck, gleaming off of a small silver packet stuck to his skin. The camera shook a moment as its operator recoiled at the devastating look of fear on Dick Trilby's face.

Everything else went as usual. The lighting tech doused the "applause" sign. The cue-card girl held up the card bearing the host's usual salutation. But all that followed was an unnerving silence as Dick Trilby fished a crumpled piece of paper out of the clenched fist of his left hand.

He cleared his throat. He wiped his forehead with the sleeve of his argyle sweater, taking a patch of makeup with it. Then, with the face of a man facing a firing squad, Dick read the note aloud.

" 'Ladies and gentlemen, remain calm. Please listen to what I have to say. We will have some changes in today's taping of *Fantastic Discoveries*. I ask that you please stay in your seats. I also ask that this show's technicians and cameramen continue taping no matter what. My life is at stake. This silver packet you see on my neck is an explosive device that is operated by the man you're about to meet. Please listen to him and do whatever he says, and no one, myself included, will be hurt.

" 'And now, please welcome a man you may remember from last week's show, Peter Reed—better known as the Trapster.' "

A man in an oversized white lab coat and purple and yellow helmet walked briskly out from the wings. A boom mike rushed overhead to follow him.

"Good job, Dick." He grabbed Trilby by the sweater and threw him up against the fake kitchen wall. Then the Trapster extended his arm, exposing his right-hand paste-shooter. Three consecutive shots resulted in strands of thick paste that bound Dick—by hands, feet, and waist—to the fake kitchen wall. He barked at Dick, "Now just stay there and you won't get hurt."

A woman in the audience screamed. The Trapster faced the audience, holding up a remote control. "That goes for you people, too. All I have to do is press a button on this device and Dick Trilby will be hosting *Fantastic Decapitations*. I don't want to hurt anyone. Please stay in your seats. Now! Get in your seats now!"

The few people standing in the aisles scrambled to get to back in their seats. Everyone was now seated.

"Thank you." A slight smirk tugged at the corner of the Trapster's mouth.

The Trapster raised the remote control above his head and stabbed a button on the control with his thumb.

Dick Trilby screamed.

A series of sharp explosions went off around the studio, sealing off every door with dense layers of glue.

The Trapster punched another button. Two deep concussive spurting sounds erupted from under the two audience risers, fixing every audience member in their seats. Two more small explosions fixed the sound and lighting technicians in their glass booth.

Nine more shots from his wrist guns immobilized the rest of the studio. He affixed the two camera operators and single sound man to their equipment. The producer, production assistants, and cue-card girl could not move from where they stood.

Dick Trilby hung limply from his adhesive manacles, unconscious, head quite intact, but considerably less sanitary than he was a moment before.

Everyone sat, waiting on the next word of the man on stage, unable to move.

Trapped.

Peter Petruski carefully removed his white lab coat, allowing the audience and cameras to see his uniform in full. He pocketed the remote control as he walked across the stage into the wings, then grabbed a chair backstage and brought it back to center.

"Keep taping." He yelled to the camera men and the sound engineers. He slumped into that chair and gazed out at the terrified audience. He looked at the camera and began to speak.

"You now know me as the Trapster, or as Peter Reed. My real name is Peter Petruski. I've been a super-villain for half of my life and I'm now ready to end it—both my career as a villain, and my life."

He reached into a leather holster at his side and pulled out his old paste gun—his original weapon from his Paste Pot Pete days. He hardly ever used it as the Trapster—and certainly not in some years—but it seemed fitting somehow. He raised it to his right temple.

Just do the gun.

* * *

Okay, I'm a little early, no big deal, Kim tried to justify to herself. She didn't want to seem too eager. She guided the van into a space in the TV studio's massive parking lot and decided to wait in her car for a while. She rolled down her windows to let in some air. She looked at her watch. What with multiple takes, script rewrites, and set-up time for each company's products, she estimated it would be at least half an hour before she should approach Peter at the studio. She remembered how squeamish he was about doing the show in the first place, and figured that the last thing he needed was to see her at the taping. He was nervous enough about the show to begin with. She certainly didn't want to risk him blowing the segment by throwing off his aim.

Kim admitted to herself some time ago that she had a massive crush on Morrie's brightest employee. Decent build, okay teeth, strong hands, and a face that sported a rough, untraditional charm—almost sinister-looking. Kim found that sexy. Yet Peter was always so distant, so difficult to approach. But that was okay with her. She liked shy men. It gave her something to work with.

She decided to distract herself by turning on the radio, nervously fiddling with the dial to find a decent song. She cursed the copious static, reminding herself to bug Morrie to spend a couple of bucks and put decent receivers in this and the other KalCo van.

Near the left end of the dial, it crackled to clarity. ". . . so far there is no word on whether any of the hostages have been harmed. However, authorities are either unable to breach the doors, due to the Trapster's use of an unbelievably strong epoxy which he has employed to fasten all entrances to the studio . . ." The signal crunched out again.

No way! A villain that uses glue? I've gotta tell Peter. He'll flip. Never one to wait for things, Kim's patience ran out quickly. She switched off the radio and dashed across the parking lot.

Once there, she saw that the crowd consisted of half-a-dozen policemen, a few station executives in suits, and about twenty bystanders. The police cordoned off a small area at the front of the studio and gathered there behind a TV monitor that had a line directly into the studio. As Kim approached the cordon, she overheard the policemen discussing the situation.

"All we can see is him! The cameras don't ever show the audience. How the hell are we supposed to tell if the audience is ok!"

"Hold on, Sarge. Look at his helmet. You can see some of the audience reflected in the metal of his helmet."

"Okay, at least it's something. Rossbach! I want you to watch the screen real close and stare at the damn helmet. Count the people in the reflection. You got that?"

"Yes, Sarge."

"Good. We need some way to figure out how many hostages he's got in there and this is the only way we got. When's that guy from Stark supposed to show up? What's his name? Americop or something?"

"USAgent, Sarge. Former Force Works member. Stark Enterprises said that they'd send him over as soon as they could."

"Yeah, right. Whatever." Sergeant Grashow scanned the parking lot for any sign of him, ignoring the crowd that gathered around the TV monitor. Visibly agitated, he took out a ragged handkerchief and wiped his damp brow, muttering to himself, "Stark's got a lotta nerve, sending over a second-rate Captain America. I guess Iron Man doesn't do a meager two hundred hostages."

Kim craned her neck to get a look at the monitor. On the screen was the face of a man wearing a purple and yellow helmet that obscured the top half of his face. He had Peter's chin. She heard a voice that sounded like Peter's—only hoarse and distressed—fervently ranting about something or other. She strained to listen to what he had to say.

"Making friends with anybody was no picnic. My success works against me. Everyone I meet seems to know someone who's been terrorized by me or the Frightful Four. Here I worked so hard to be famous, and now everyone hates me.

"And meeting women? A whole different kind of humiliation. Once they discovered I was the Trapster they'd run to the nearest phone and dial 911. Some years back, I met this woman; we went out a few times, I told her who I was, and *she* laughed her head off because she remembered I used to call myself Paste Pot Pete!"

Kim could hear a few sniggers from the studio audience. Peter stood up and waved the gun towards them, screeching, "Shut up! Shut the hell up! You don't know what it's like! You try to make amends for the things you've done, you try to rectify your-self," his beseeching tone turned to a terse snarl, "and people won't *let* you because they *hate* you so much!"

The studio was quiet once again. Kim noticed the muscles in Peter's face visibly soften.

"In the time that I was, y'know, Peter Reed, I found a woman, a really great one. She's kind, smart, gorgeous . . . really special. I think I loved her. I think I still do. And it won't make one bit of difference. Because when she finds out who I am, she'll hate me, just like all the others have hated me. Just as you people hate me. Admit it. You hate me. And it won't matter one goddamned bit because I'll be dead." Peter searched the audience for a re-ply—some sort of reaction.

"Do *any* of you understand? *Do* you?"

That was all Kim could stand to hear. She bolted from the crowd and ran back to the van.

Peter had only been on his tirade for forty-five minutes, but he'd already ranted about his beginnings as a criminal, his arrests, his time spent as a villain—all in frantic detail and in no particular order. His reasons for making this part of his suicide note was unclear. He had just begun to regale the audience about one of the most notable failures in his life: his last encounter with the Sandman.

"Even Flint! Even Flint tried to help me out," he said, refer-ring to the Sandman by the alias he used to use, "but I fouled that up too. He used to be a villain like me. But he found me in a bar and offered me a job—a straight job, working for Silver Sable. He saved me from a couple of loan sharks, put me up in his building—he was good to me." He pointed the gun at the camera to make a point. "This guy, we used to work together in a band of bloodthirsty thieves, do you understand? All we'd ever done together was rob and steal and . . . and *hurt* people. But he changed. He got out. And here he was, trying to give me a chance too.

"I saw him and I thought that maybe I could do it—I could really escape. I wanted to, but I . . . it's just that—I—I had just pulled a jewelry store heist a few days before and I had to go use the place to stash loot, and if someone found the jewels at my apartment . . ." Peter's face flushed with guilt. "What could I do?

I'd pulled the job before I ran into Flint. I stashed them at his place, he found it, and we fought. I—I almost killed him then. I used the same magnesium-treated mixture on him that I have in this gun now. It burns through anything. But it didn't stop him. He almost killed me, but he held back at the last second. If he had, I would have deserved it.

"Don't you see? I blew it. Just like I blew it with the chance Morrie gave me. I just . . . I just can't make a decent decision to save my life. Whatever I do, I end up in the pen. And I can't go there again." He looked intently into one of the cameras. "I can't. I'm too old now. I'd die there. I will not," he ground the barrel of the gun into his temple again, "die in prison.

"None of you understand. The hitting. The pain. That was real. These last few months—I thought it was life. I was happy. But it was just more pain.

"Well, the pain ends. Now."

He shut his eyes tightly. His fingers tensed around the gun's stock.

"Don't," said a soft voice from behind him.

Who? He opened his eyes and turned his head to see who it was.

Kim walked out from backstage. "Please don't kill yourself," she pleaded as she stepped carefully toward him.

His jaw dropped. He stared at her, unbelieving of her presence. "How the hell did you get in here?" He demanded.

"I told the police at the back door that a news crew at the main entrance wanted to interview them. L.A. County cops are suckers for publicity." Despite her fear at entering this situation, she couldn't help but show a little pride for that ruse. "I did the same thing that time Morrie—"

"No," Peter stopped her short, "how did you get through the doors? Not even a blowtorch can cut my glues."

Sheepishly, she held up her hands and showed him two Glu-Matic 2000s, both now emptied of their supplies of Glu-Off II. "It works in hard-to-reach places with pinpoint precision." She dropped them on the ground and attempted a disarming smile.

Peter was not amused. He kept the gun at the side of his head, his expression fixing to one of frantic determination. "Leave. Now. You don't want to see what's going to happen next."

"Dammit, Peter, neither do you. You don't want to kill yourself."

"Wrong. Not only have I screwed up my life as much as I possibly can, but it's only going to get worse from here. Every decision I make just sinks my life deeper into misery and humiliation and *I am sick of it.* I can't, Kim. I can't go on anymore." Peter flexed his fingers around the gun stock again. He took a long breath and looked her straight in the eye. "Look, I lied to you and Morrie about who I was. I broke off our . . . relationship or whatever it was because I couldn't afford to get closer to you. It wasn't just because I didn't want you to discover my identity. I also did it because, well, it just isn't safe to be the girlfriend of a former super-villain."

Kim crossed her arms in front of her, trying to be brave. "And that's why you're going to end your life? I mean, not to sell myself short, but you're doing this just because you made a few wrong decisions?" She tried to catch his eye.

He tried to avoid hers. "I haven't made a single goddamn *right* decision. Everything I've done has sunk my life into—I don't know, a pit or something. A bottomless one. No return . . ." His voice trailed off as his mouth stretched into a deep frown.

"You know what's going on here, Peter? You're at a crisis stage. We did this in psych class just last month. It's like a wake-up call for your karma, sort of. What you've done right now is reach a crossroads in your life. Fate is telling you that you need to make a significant change. But Peter, I can tell you right now that killing yourself isn't it. It's a cop-out."

Peter remained unmoved. "You just don't understand." He flexed his fingers again, his trigger finger itching.

Kim wasn't sure what to do. Sure, they had covered suicide in class two weeks ago, but that didn't qualify her to counsel a super-villain. She decided to try a different tack.

"You're right Peter, I'm not sure I do. If you're really this famous super-villain they're all talking about, then you're obviously someone who has spent all his life fighting for things he wants. You're a man whose had experiences and—and *riches* in his life that most people couldn't dream of. You've flown, Peter. So if you're trying to tell me that after such an incredible life all you want is to take the *coward's* way out, then no, maybe I don't understand."

His eyes flashed at her. "Don't you talk down to me like that." The gun did not move from the side of his head.

Kim shrugged. "Why not? I'm right, aren't I? Look at all the good things that have happened in your life: you've had fame, you've had money, and when that ran out you got a good job with Morrie and enjoyed life some more. Even with all that, you're still letting a few miseries cloud everything else. And I realize that they're bad things, Peter. Don't think I don't. But they're not worth killing yourself over. Nothing is." Peter remained silent. She lowered her eyes for a moment in hopes to take the pressure off him a bit. "I think you're depressed."

"Oh, really? What tipped you off?" Peter snarled.

Kim's frustration began to show. "I mean clinically depressed, damn it. You've got all the symptoms. Think about it, Peter. As long as I've known you, you've always been pretty down. You feel like you're coming down with a cold all the time. And you're always complaining about not getting enough sleep. . . ."

"Yeah, well, thanks a lot for painting such a lovely picture of how you see me. I'm touched."

Kim began to take offense at Petruski's attitude. "I'm just trying to tell you that what you have, it can be easily treated with therapy, with antidepressant drugs—you can have a normal life. Don't you want that?"

Peter pulled the gun away from his head so he could use both hands to punctuate an unfortunately obvious point. "What, are you completely stupid? I've broken parole! I'm going to prison! Does that sound like a normal life to you?"

Kim couldn't help but raise her voice in the face of such antagonism. "Well, it sounds a hell of a lot better than having a puddle of burnt magnesium paste where your head used to be. I know you're in pretty deep right now. But you've got an opportunity to change your life. How *dare* you give that up?"

Peter was infuriated. He couldn't believe he wasn't getting through to her. "Why the hell should I bother? I'll still be the same person"

Kim cut him off sharp. "And what the hell's wrong with that? The Peter I know is brilliant and patient and diligent. If he finds a problem, he works furiously until it's solved. He's also kind and caring and gentle—and I'm pretty sure I love him."

Peter couldn't believe what he'd just heard. His grip on the gun relaxed. "What?"

Kim had wondered how long it would take her to admit it. Her pretty face began to contort into a petite grimace as tears ran down her face. "You heard me, Peter. I love you. I want to be with you. Please, please, put down the gun."

Moved by the admission, Peter stood to face her. They stared at each other for long seconds.

Then his grip loosened altogether. The gun fell out of his hand, suspended from the supply tubes that connected it to the storage pod. It swung back and forth as Peter stepped toward Kim and took her in his arms.

They held each other for what seemed like forever. A few sniffles emanated from the audience.

Forever ended when the studio's main door exploded inward.

Take him by surprise, hard and fast, thought the USAgent. *That's the only way to handle a hostage situation.* Having been quickly briefed on the situation by the police outside, the former Avenger burst through the studio doors at full speed, and took the steps to the stage five at a time before he noticed that the Trapster had one of the hostages in his slimy hands. *One kidnapper, one hostage. That means mano a mano. Just the way I like it.* He was already halfway to the Trapster, but the Agent couldn't resist yelling at him, "You picked the wrong day to terrorize people, mister!" *That ought to put the fear of God into him.*

Peter had shoved Kim away and raised his hands to shield his face from the impact. USAgent saw the shooters on his wrists and gave the spoken command to activate his wrist-mounted energy-shield. *Boy, the boys at Stark knew what they were doing when they designed this baby.*

Maneuver #5: the battering ram. Like a red-white-and-black missile the USAgent hit him on the fly, shield first. The Agent landed directly on top of him, using momentum and impact to knock the Trapster to the floor and render him immobile. Then, grinding one knee into the villain's chest, he tagged the Trapster again—this time with a hard right to the jaw—to make sure he stayed down.

He did. Mission accomplished for the USAgent. He stood above the unconscious body of his opponent for a moment, sa-

voring the victory. He activated his wrist-radio to contact the police for clean-up procedures.

"Nice going, tough guy," yelled a woman from the audience.

"Thanks," retorted the USAgent. He shot her a winning smile
and gave her the thumbs-up sign. "Always happy to help."

"First up on *Hot Copy:* a startling new revelation in the Trapster
trial."

The Wizard prided himself on having the finest cognitive abilities of any human on the planet. And yet, sitting in his prison
cell, feeling in complete control of his facilities, he barely believed that he was seeing and hearing the events of the last two
months. Newspapers, magazines, 103 of the 128 TV channels at
his disposal—they couldn't get enough of Petruski's videotaped
suicide note, replete with irony, pathos, and juicy sound-bites as
it was. The media circus surrounding the Trapster had eclipsed
Bentley's own news coverage a hundredfold. And as the Wizard
used his gloves to channel-surf against the wall, he found himself
subjected to it yet again—this time courtesy of *Hot Copy.*

"By now, people all over the world have seen this tape, which
shows Petruski's moving exchange with fellow KalCo employee
Kim Ryan, and his apparent surrender of the station—" the tape
showed Peter dropping his gun and taking Kim in his arms, followed by the USAgent knocking Peter down "—and his subsequent arrest. Today in Los Angeles County Court, Petruski's
defense team has cited the USAgent for brutality and for refusing
to read Petruski his Miranda rights."

For two months, Bentley had watched Petruski's pitiful suicide
attempt and inept arrest turn into a worldwide sensation. He had
heard tell of three different production companies working
around-the-clock to produce TV movies of the kidnapping. His
mug shot—*his mug shot*—adorned the covers of major magazines.

Meanwhile, the Wizard did everything he could to ignore his
failed attempt at crushing his slower and weaker former teammate. He spent each day at Rykers in a denial-ridden stupor,
barely acknowledging the guards, other inmates, even his lawyers.
He no longer vented his trademarked off-the-cuff soliloquies,
rarely even speaking aloud unless spoken to. He spent "lights
out" after "lights out" flipping from channel to channel and

refusing to acknowledge the caustic jealously that festered within him.

"These allegations can only help the cause of Petruski, who has gained public support as the hottest 'victim of circumstance' since Rodney King. The question, 'Can a hardened super-villain change his stripes?' is the hot topic of the airwaves. If you watch *Oprah* or *Ila May* you've probably seen the members of the captive studio audience tell their side of the story as well."

Certainly he'd seen those horrible, lowest-common-denominator, monosyllabic, daytime insult-fests. The Wizard himself had been asked to appear via closed-circuit video on two different daytime talk-shows to discuss super-villain reform. At first, he was flattered that they wanted him to appear on their programs, on the basis of his televised press conference some weeks back. But of course, they wanted him to discuss his relationship with Petruski. The Wizard refused them both most uncivilly, and they went with the Sandman.

"Another facet of the Trapster's groundswell of support is his current relationship with Ms. Ryan, which apparently formed as a result of the kidnapping. Sources close to them say that Ms. Ryan has been granted visitation rights by the court, and that the two of them are, according to sources close to Petruski, 'working out their relationship.' "

Kim Ryan. The Wizard had deduced some time ago that this was the "friend" Petruski had alluded to. Bentley felt no jealousy at their little affair, as he had little use for the fair sex. But he knew the public loved a love story, and it irritated him that it was another factor that increased Petruski's "Q" rating while he gauged his own slipping by entire percentage points. He felt himself grinding his teeth and stopped, for fear that he would disrupt the miniature components hidden in them.

"But that's not where the story ends. We've just learned that Petruski's memoirs, for which Petruski signed a publishing deal last week, have also been optioned for a major motion picture as well. Rumor has it that Robert DeNiro has expressed interest in playing the part of Petruski. . . ."

DeNiro?! That was the last straw for the Wizard. He shot a searing bolt of energy at the TV picture and blew a hole in the wall onto which it had been projected. It made a horrible racket and left the acrid smell of burnt concrete.

Alarms rang out all over the cell block. The Wizard didn't care. He didn't care that he'd blown his cover, that the authorities would discover his hidden wonder gloves, would search him more carefully for other weapons and escape devices. He didn't care that his single outburst set back any chance of escape— much less any of the jobs he planned while in prison—for months, even years. For all his intellect, his genius, he had only a single, overwhelming thought in his mind.

It raged from the Wizard's lungs in a guttural yell. *"Pet-ruuuskiiiiiiii!"*

His maddened scream echoed through the concrete corridors.

?

ONE FOR THE ROAD

JAMES DAWSON

Illustration by Dennis Calero

CAN'T FEEL the glass in my hand. Fingers have been numb for a while now. Couple of years, at least. I don't remember exactly how long. Doesn't matter. At least they still work. Enough for my needs, anyway.

I take another sip of buttermilk. That's my drink of choice these days, because of the ulcers. I've been nursing tonight's glass so long that the stuff's gone warm on me.

Grace took my empty plate away fifteen minutes ago. I know she wants me to pay up and leave the diner. You'd think she'd treat me better, seeing as how I'm a regular. I might be just another slob these days, a guy who'd rather haunt a dive like this than go home to an empty rented room, but I'm still a human being.

Maybe that was part of my problem. I was only human. Maybe if I'd been something more. . . .

I stare at a long crack in the formica counter. There's dirt in it. I pick at it with a fingernail. The stuff builds up, I guess. Over time.

Grace. She probably wasn't bad-looking when she was younger. Back before the years had their way with her, mistreated her. Before time squeezed out all the girl, leaving only this hollow, bitter woman.

She gives her number to a lot of the guys who come in. Guys she wants to know better. She's never given it to me. She doesn't think much of my kind.

I'll bet she didn't expect to end up owning a grimy hole like this one, down in this part of the city. Probably imagined she'd be presiding over her own trendy bistro in the fashion district by this age, where other people would do all the work.

Instead, she's in here six nights a week by herself, taking the orders and doing all the cooking. Getting by.

Maybe she likes it here. Or maybe she's just learned to like it. Seems like all of us find our own level, even if it's not where we thought it would be.

I pick up my glass again, being careful not to squeeze these dead fingers too tight around it.

Too many blows to the head. That's what the doctor at Ryker's said was wrong with me. Nerve damage. Face, hands, legs mainly. Blackouts. Memory loss. Blurred vision. Night cramps. Teeth stopped hurting when I had the ones pulled that hadn't been knocked out. I've got full upper and lower plates now. They almost fit.

The buttermilk might be bad. It tastes as sour as the inside of my head feels. Maybe I'll order a piece of pie. Live in luxury. What the hell. I don't have anywhere near enough money to refill my blood-pressure pills tomorrow, like I should. Another two bucks won't make any difference either way.

I wish they had let me keep my costume, just for a souvenir. My uniform, I mean. They called it a costume, but costumes are for clowns. Mine was a battle uniform. Blue, with silver at the . . . or was it gold? It was—

I don't remember. I can't remember.

I don't want to remember.

I could go see pictures of it. Of me. There are lots of clippings at the library. There's got to be videotape, too, somewhere. And there are plenty of people who could fill in the blanks in my memory.

No. Parole violation. Can't associate with anybody I knew then. Can't even own a can of mace these days, much less a gun or a—

What was it that I carried? I cover my face with one hand, rubbing the loose, numb skin. It feels dead, like a mask. My eyes are wet. I've got three day's worth of stubble where I don't have scars.

It doesn't matter.

It matters.

It doesn't matter.

Maybe I really can't remember. Maybe I just don't want to remember. Sometimes I don't know the difference myself.

I ask Grace for a piece of pie.

"We're all out," she says.

I'm looking right at a pie that's in a stand at the other end of the counter, with a glass cover over it. Grace sees me looking at it. She just glares at me.

"What about that one?" I ask, pointing.

At first she just keeps standing there, like she's itching to tell me off. Maybe she stops herself because she's thinking about how many people have been in tonight. Not many.

She doesn't like the idea of giving me an excuse to hang

around longer. But selling that piece of pie would mean a couple more dollars in her beat-up cash register.

She gets a plate.

Guess somebody cares more about two bucks than I do.

They did something to me in prison. Memory loss, they said. I don't believe them. I reach behind my neck, rubbing the base of my skull, searching, examining, looking for something. I don't feel anything.

I can't feel anything. Fingertips dead.

Face. An old man looks back at me from the fly-specked wall mirror above the grill.

I remember some things. I remember Iron Man. I shake my head. Not Iron Man. Who?

Grace puts the pie in front of me. "You want a refill on that?" she says, nodding at my glass. There's only about a swallow left in it. Before I can answer, she says, "Have to charge you for it."

"Sure, sure," I say.

She gets a carton from the cooler. "One for the road," she says. The scowl on her face makes it hard to miss her meaning. She wants me gone.

All of a sudden, I feel like breaking my glass on the edge of the counter and shoving its jagged base into her throat. I want to—

No. No.

My head starts to throb.

The bell over the diner's door rings. A couple of big guys in work clothes come in from the street. Grace looks at them and cracks a real big smile. "I'll be right with you two boys. Just have a seat."

She's in such a hurry to make a fool out of herself with them that she spills some buttermilk as she's filling my glass. It follows the crack in the counter, like a little river that's going nowhere. I put two of my dead fingertips in it, blocking the flow. I don't know why.

I pick up my fork and look at the pie. I hadn't asked what kind was in the case. It turns out to be apple. God bless America.

My mask didn't protect my face from his fists. Captain America's, that is. He kept catching me on the cheekbones, crushing both of them. I can still see his yellow gloves coming at me.

No, not yellow . . . or not Captain America.

They think we're all the same, that we can take whatever they dish out. I guess they couldn't know any different. They're not going to risk pulling their punches. They've got a job to do.

If they were real police, they'd face brutality and excessive force charges all the time. Guys have tried suing them. There are always lawyers who will take those kinds of cases. Or any other kind, for that matter.

They always lose, or win judgments that get thrown out on appeal. Something called the "Supra-Authority Precedent" is always the deciding factor, or "Super-Authority," or whatever. What it boils down to is that we are considered too great a menace to society to have any civil rights that are worth worrying about.

We pose too big a threat. We're too dangerous.

I take a drink of buttermilk. Some dribbles down my chin, but I catch most of it on the back of my hand. I lick it up.

The law's a big Catch-22, of course. If a super hero nabs somebody, the courts automatically label the bad guy a "major menace." He can't claim otherwise, because he was brought in by a super hero. Simple.

It didn't make any sense to me then. Still doesn't.

I think I remember flying.

They took my uniform away.

Memory loss.

Too many blows to the head.

None of the super-teams ever came after me. How did they know that somebody else would? How do any of them know? We talked about that a lot on the inside. About how strange it is that a second hero almost never has to step in and finish off a fight.

From what the papers say, whenever one of us mixes it up with a hero, the tussle is always a nearly perfect match. We're strong enough to give some real trouble to the guy who comes after us, to make him work for it, but we always go down in the end.

How the hell does that happen? Do the good guys pick and choose who to take on? If Doctor Doom comes to town, does everybody except the Fantastic Four look the other way? When somebody like me appears on the scene, does every do-gooder in Thor's weight class assume that a white hat with my strength will know it's his job to clean my clock?

Maybe it's a union thing.

I give a high-pitched chuckle, crazy sounding, too loud. I stop myself, hoping nobody has noticed. Grace and her two new boyfriends are staring from their end of the counter. I stare right back at them. I see muscles under the men's shirts. They both have strong jaws, wide shoulders.

I picture them in tights.

My stomach starts to burn. I look away, embarrassed.

We all find our own level.

I hurt a lot of people.

I killed a lot of people.

I don't remember their faces.

Sometimes I remember their faces.

My own face is dead. My fingertips. Nerve damage. Too many blows to the head.

After the men leave, Grace sweeps up a little. She's apparently decided to ignore me. She scrapes at the blackened aluminum grill behind the counter with a steel wool pad. Most of the burned-on crud doesn't come off. She reads a magazine, pretending I'm not here.

Nobody else comes in the diner. It gets late.

I don't remember the name I used. I can't remember. I don't want to remember. I won't remember.

I killed a lot of people.

I did hard time, and now I'm here.

I look in the dirty mirror again. Tears have run down my face, leaving trails on my stubbled cheeks. I'm glad Grace is sitting too far away to see. I couldn't feel them rolling down, didn't know they were there. I turn my head to wipe them away on the shoulders of my jacket.

Time to go home.

I look at my bill. So long as I keep getting Social Security, I'll get by. They can't take that away from me. I worked long enough before I went bad that I'm entitled to it, fair and square. Just like anybody else my age.

Things start to go black as I get off my stool. I take a couple of deep breaths. Grace is watching me. She doesn't say a word, just stands waiting behind the register. The spell passes.

I get out my wallet and pay up.

"Thanks as always for the big tip," she says, laying on the sarcasm. I don't bother to reply. I'm glad there's nobody else in the place to hear her.

I take two slow steps to the door. My back hurts. My head hurts, on the inside, where I can still feel. Old before my time, if I ever had one.

I know Grace is watching me with contempt. She probably wishes I would die. Preferably outside, on somebody else's sidewalk, so she wouldn't be inconvenienced.

I think about how I've spent my life. I feel cold.

Grace isn't the only one. A lot of people wish I would die.

Sometimes, I'm one of them.

Grace steps past me, impatient. She rests a hand on the metal security gate, getting ready to pull it across the door behind me.

"If you hurry, you might make it out of here before the sun comes up, you pathetic old wreck," she says. "Man, it's hard to believe that you used to be—"

I don't want to hear the name.

I hear the name.

I hear the name.

I hear *my* name.

I'm not fast anymore, but I have surprise on my side. Grace never knows what hits her. She barely has time to scream. Somebody will find her in the morning. Maybe they'll find her face. Not my usual technique, but I was always good at improvising.

I'm coughing up phlegm as I head out into the windy night. I rub my dead hands together, wondering who will come after me this time. Wondering where I'll rank.

For an awful moment, I think about how I'd feel if none of them bothered. What if this time it's just a cop with a service revolver who shows up to take me in?

I can't let that happen. I've got to make sure that a real hero comes for me. I'm worth at least that.

A man's got to protect his reputation. I'll do whatever it takes. Even if it kills me.

I wanted to forget. I did the best I could. I really tried. But it's all coming back to me now.

And there's plenty of night left before dawn.